BREA GRAVITY

THE FALL BACK SERIES
BOOK TWO

AUTUMN GREY

We're all broken, that's how the light gets in.
—Ernest Hemingway

DEDICATION

To Elon.
One of the bravest people I know.
Keep breaking gravity, my friend.

PROLOGUE

Nate

Two years ago. . .

IF I HAD KNOWN THE NIGHT WOULD BE ENDING THIS WAY, I'D HAVE done everything in my power to stop it before it even began.

"Don't leave me," I beg, my gaze fixed on hers, watching as life floats in and out of her blue eyes.

She blinks and blankly stares at the starless dark sky. For just a second, I think I've lost her and my heart stops beating. And I can't *breathe*.

I can't imagine living without *her*.

Then she smiles. Air rushes into my lungs, and a sob bursts through my lips. Even looking like this, she's just as stunning as the first time I laid eyes on her.

"Don't you fucking leave me," I plead again in a hoarse voice.

"Never," she vows in a fading whisper. "I'll always be with you."

"God. Please don't take her away from me," I pray under my breath, muttering the words over and over, hoping someone will hear me. Hoping for some sign that everything will be okay.

I glance down at her neck.

Christ, the blood.

So much *blood*, and there's more still trickling from the gaping neck wound.

I need to get to her.

I climb on my hands and knees and crawl to her but fail and fall flat on my face on the dirty snow, crippled by the pain slicing through my shoulder.

"Keep your eyes on me, OK?"

"So cold—," she says. Her teeth chattering, then she coughs.

Through my blurred vision, I see her face has gone extremely pale, her breathing shallow.

"Baby, stay with me," I plead. More hacking coughs and my desperation drives me forward. "Come on, fucking stay with me!" My voice is weak and hoarse from all the screaming I've done.

Sirens wail through the silent, chilly air. Snowflakes continue to fall like ashes after a volcano eruption.

Her chest rises once and then falls. I'm watching her now, waiting for her next breath to assure me that she's still here with me.

Her eyes remain unfocused as life fades from their depths.

"No!" I scramble up but my feet are too weak, causing my body to slump back down. Darkness swirls in my vision, threatening to pull me under.

I can't black out now, damn it. She needs me.

"*You'll always be my hero,*" she once told me.

The last thought that fills my head before my world turns dark is that heroes are supposed to do everything to save lives.

I've let her down. All it took was three seconds to bring my world crashing down around me.

I'm no one's hero.

CHAPTER ONE

Nate

Six months later

I STEP THROUGH THE DOORS OF THE PLACE WHERE I SPENT MONTH after month of therapy to get my right shoulder and arm working properly again.

Just as my foot hits the sidewalk, my phone starts to ring. I shove my hand in my pants pocket to retrieve it, but the abrupt movement sends pain skittering from my right shoulder down my right arm. Holding still and feeling sweat form on my forehead, I grit my teeth waiting for the pain to pass. And just like that, the flashes of memories dance in my vision, taunting me with images of blood on white snow, blue eyes filled with trust.

The ringing stops, before it starts back up again. I retrieve it from the left pocket of my pants and answer the call without checking the screen for the caller.

"Rowe," I grunt into the phone.

An intoxicating giggle reaches my ear, followed by, "Hello, Grumpy."

My lips twitch, forming a smile at the voice that belongs to my sister and best friend. "Hello, Izzy."

"Wow. I love your enthusiasm. Can't you sound a bit friendlier when you answer your phone?" she asks, her voice amused.

I pull my car keys from my pants pocket and open the driver's door. "That *is* my friendly voice," I say, tossing the bag in the passenger seat.

"Do you sweet-talk girls with that voice? I can't even imagine what your *less-friendly* voice sounds like."

I chuckle. "Let's hope you never find out."

She snorts, and I know she rolled her eyes. "When will you be here?"

I still have a few things left to pack before moving from Chicago to Florida. I needed time to think about what I was going to do with my life, and being in this city only brought more pain, the memories too hard to handle sometimes. The first time I told Izzy about what I planned to do, she accused me of running into hiding. She challenged me to face my problems head-on.

I tried, but I didn't like what I saw. Confronting my inabilities, knowing I'd never be able to play cello again day in, day out was like living in the fucking Seventh Circle of Hell.

I clear my throat. "I'll be home on Saturday afternoon."

Silence fills the space between us. Unspoken words heavy in the air.

"Are you okay?" she asks—no—whispers, as if she's terrified of speaking those three words out loud. Guilt cuts through my chest. I put that uncertainty there two years ago when shit went to hell and I couldn't handle the pain, disappointment, unfulfilled dreams. I couldn't handle the kind of person I'd become.

I swallow, the bile rising in my throat. My mind flashes back over the past year. Months and days filled with pain, struggle and eventually acceptance. I'd spent years chasing my dream and finally, when I was living it, one single event destroyed everything, changing the entire course of my life.

"Nate?" Her soft voice interrupts the flash of painful memories.

"I'm fine," I say much more curtly than I intended.

"Nate—"

"I said I'm fine," I bite out. I sigh, rubbing a hand down my face. "Sorry. Can we not talk about this?"

"Sure. You know I'm always here if you need to talk."

"I do." She has always been there, even when I was being a dick. "Thank you."

"So when—" she stops abruptly when a howl pierces the air through the phone. Izzy mumbles a curse and yells, "Matthew Thomas Reed. Stop pulling your sister's hair."

"But, Mama, Kaylie started it."

Something clatters loudly on the other side of the phone, followed by a loud screech.

"Makayla! Leave your brother alone."

She returns to the phone. "Sorry. I have to go. See you at Sunday brunch?"

The thought of being surrounded by my family warms me, but the thought of seeing pity in their eyes kills me.

"No, Izzy—"

"Sunday brunch, Nate," she says in a sweet yet firm voice that tells me she won't take no for an answer. I'm older than her by two years, but she's had me wrapped around her little finger from the second my mom brought her home from the hospital. I've been such an ass lately; the least I can do is go for brunch. Besides, it's been a while since I spent time with my niece and nephew, and I miss that.

I sigh. "Fine. But if you and Mom start with your coddling—"

"I promise no coddling," she says hurriedly to the sound of yelling and screaming in the background. "I need to sort out these little monkeys. Love you."

She ends the call before I can respond.

I toss the phone on the dashboard, turn the ignition, then twist around to look over my shoulder for traffic. A sharp pain shoots through my shoulder, searing down my spine.

"Dammit!" I grit out, facing forward again.

Clenching my jaw, I reach for the yellow plastic bottle inside the glove compartment and pop a pill into my mouth, downing it with the bottle of water in the center console. Then I sit back and wait for the pain to recede.

The bliss that follows is fucking addictive.

Feeling the nerves and muscles in my shoulder and right arm relax, I clench the bottle in my left fist.

My salvation.

CHAPTER TWO

Nate

Six Months Later

MY ENTIRE BODY JERKS FORWARD AS A SILVER TOYOTA ON MY RIGHT swerves sharply, veering into my lane. The sound of metal scraping with metal fills the air. I grip the wheel tighter and twist it to avoid getting hit again. I glance at the rearview mirror, and my heart almost ceases beating in my chest.

Shit, *fuck*. shit. A truck is bearing down on me from behind. I quickly turn the wheel again and switch back to my lane, missing rear-ending the fucking Toyota by mere inches. Tires squeal on the tarmac as I slam my foot on the brake fast, my knuckles pale from clutching the wheel tightly.

I'm breathing hard, staring out the window where the car has stopped about ten feet away. The driver's door flies open, and a tall man wearing a baseball cap with the bill facing backwards steps out, looking less bothered about what just happened. He leans on the hood of his car, speaking into his phone. I glare at the asshole, my anger thrashing inside my chest like a wild beast, fighting to break

free and devour him. It's my first day of work at Rushmore School of
Music, and I'm running late because this idiot couldn't stop talking
on his phone long enough to concentrate on where he was going and
almost totaled my BMW.

Unable to contain my rage, I climb out of my car and stalk forward just as he sweeps a finger across the screen of his phone to end
the conversation and turns to face me. He swaggers toward me smiling wide and looking unperturbed as he digs his wallet from his pants
pocket and pulls out a card. He hands it over to me without preamble.

"I'm sorry, man." When I don't make any attempt to take the
card, he pushes it into my chest.

Clenching my jaw, I scowl at the paper, then eye the line forming
behind his haphazardly parked car, forcing other vehicles to inch past
it. Someone yells obscenities while repeatedly and impatiently pressing the horn. I pinch the bridge of my nose, trying to breathe through
my rising temper. There are two ways this could go: do as he says or
wipe the smug grin from his face with my fist. Or both.

The little prick jerks his chin to the card while staring at me down
his crooked nose. I curl my hand into a fist, but the burning sensation
from the scar on my right upper arm forces me to flex my fingers.

Goddamn it.

Ignoring the crippling pain, I step forward and grip the front of
his shirt. Whatever he sees on my face wipes off the smile on his. His
eyes widen in terror.

Good.

He tries to wiggle out of my hand, and my fingers tighten. "Let
go of me, asshole!" He squirms a little and huffs. "Get your hands off
me or—"

I tighten my hold and get in his space, then arch a brow. "Or
what?" I snarl.

"I'm—" he coughs and sputters, waving his phone in the air. I tilt
my head, fleetingly noticing the screen saver photo: a blurred image
of what looks like auburn hair and stunning, big eyes staring into the
camera. He coughs again, mumbling, "Dude, I'm sorry."

I turn my focus on him. "You're sorry," I state in a low voice, anger licking those two words. "You realize you could have hurt someone with your reckless driving, you little piece of shit?"

He nods quickly. "I said I'm fucking sorry!" He squeaks with some hint of stubbornness in his voice. "Call the number on the card, and the bill will be taken care of."

My right hand spasms, sending throbbing pain up my shoulder and spine, forcing me to uncurl my fist from the fabric. Frustration soars through me, fueling my anger to fury.

Stupid useless limb. It hasn't been working right since the accident.

Gritting my teeth, I snatch the card from his hand and scan the details.

Mr. R. Williams, Trading Analyst. New York.

I shove it inside my shirt pocket and aim a narrowed stare at him.

His chin wobbles as he continues to stare at me as if I'm crazy.

"You might want to remember you're in Jacksonville and not in New York, Mr. Williams," I warn, referencing the details on the card he gave me.

"Fuck you," he mutters under his breath as he turns and quickly shuffles toward his car while he tugs his khaki pants up.

I glare at his retreating back, then stalk back to my car.

Fuck.

It's going to take a few days for Antonio to fix the dent on the passenger's side car door. I really don't have time to wait for a taxi, so I climb inside my car, belatedly realizing that the airbags didn't deploy. I add that on the list of things to be checked, then back out of the spot, leave the chaos behind me and drive toward Rushmore School of Music. Ten minutes later, I park the car in the designated parking spot in the teachers' parking area. Given how my morning started, the fiery ache in my shoulder and the incident with the Toyota, I'm ready to murder someone. On a scale of one to five, the pain is a ten-alarm, but taking my usual dose of medication would render me stupid the next few hours. So I toss a tablet into my mouth to taper off the pain, swallowing it dry.

I make it to class five minutes before the bell goes off. As I'm watching students file in, laughing and heckling, my eyes land on a desk in the middle of the room where loud snores seem to be coming from. Biting down my temper, I stride toward the woman snoring on the desk, my gaze fixed on the mass of red hair sprawled across the top. I stop and glare, taking in the delicate features partially hidden by the hair: pert nose sprinkled with freckles, long lashes casting shadows on olive skin, a mouth—Jesus, that mouth—that's all kinds of innocence and trouble, top lip slightly fuller than the bottom one giving it a natural pout.

Something strange happens, some kind of stirring in my gut that I haven't felt in a long time. I shift on my feet, uncomfortable and feeling a little lost in all that red hair. Before I can allow my mind to sort out that emotion, I slam my left palm flat on the desk with a *boom*, then slowly straighten and wait. The woman bolts upright with a squeal and blinks rapidly, before darting a squinted glance around the class. I clear my throat and fold my arms on my chest, then wait. Snickers and giggles erupt around the classroom, but my entire focus is on her as she yawns widely, before wielding a pair of stunning, big, hazel eyes full of sleep in my direction. Different emotions roll in them. Shock, confusion, sadness. *Fear.*

Fuck! Those eyes slay me, rocking me to the core, and I know I'm in a shit ton of trouble.

Her *eyes*. I've seen them before, precisely thirty minutes ago on Mr. New York's phone.

I can't wrap my mind around what I'm feeling right now, and the loss of control sends irritation flaring through me.

I glower harder down at her while scrambling to gain ground back over this absurd situation.

CHAPTER THREE

Elon

Boom!

My head jerks up from my arms folded on top of the desk—my heart racing and head pounding. I squint around the class, letting my eyes adjust to the lighting.

Shit!

I slept in class.

Again.

I got in late last night from Willow Hill. Things haven't been easy for the past couple of weeks between driving home to help my older sister, Nor, with the kids while she took care of her husband, Josh, in the hospital and driving back to Jacksonville on days when I have classes early in the morning. Josh was diagnosed with pancreatic cancer six years ago, and since then, he has been in and out of the hospital. The thing is, Nor would break her back, working herself to the ground before she willingly asked me or my other sister, Elise, for help. It's not that she's too proud to ask.

No. Not at all.

She has been carrying our family's burden all on her tiny shoulders for as long as I can remember.

Someone clears their throat, ripping me out of my thoughts.

I bolt upright and glance around, belatedly noticing the large shadow that has fallen on my desk.

Slowly, I lift my eyes and meet thighs encased in a pair of black slacks, slightly parted in what looks like a relaxed pose. I inhale a breath and hold it as I continue the journey above a black belt and upward over a crisp, white, button-down shirt. A pair of equally well-toned arms with a dusting of fine dark hair are crossed on an impressive chest—

Holyyyy shit!

Is that chest real? Seriously, I can see the rows and columns of his abs outlined on the material. The sleeves of his shirt are rolled up to the elbows, revealing amazing forearms like you wouldn't believe, with veins running down to his wrists. On his wrist rests a watch. I stare at it, mesmerized as the second hand crosses over the word *Bremont* inside the watch. Next to that is a cute, braided, purple bracelet with a little pink heart, which looks completely out of place on that masculine wrist. His index finger is tapping on his bicep in what looks like an impatient gesture.

Finally tearing my eyes from that finger, I look past the thick neck column and scruffy jaw that's all angles and shadows.

Bracing myself, I lift my eyes to take in the rest of his face and immediately regret my decision.

Eyes the color of flint meet mine in a piercing glare, flanked by thick lashes and eyebrows which are dipped low in a scowl. Rich, dark brown hair is meticulously styled back. His lips are pressed together in a tight line. The man in front of me looks like an avenging angel, sent to Earth to punish sinners. At least that's what I imagine an avenging angel to look like, which kind of makes me wonder if I've sinned badly since my last confession.

Wait a minute.

I know *that* jaw. The manliest jaw in the history of jaws.

The man standing before me has been an inspiration to the music community. I've spent most of my life following his career. Looked up to him and measured my standards to his.

Nathaniel Rowe. God's gift to the music world—and Rushmore. Best freaking cellist ever and a member of the Chicago Symphony, that is until he retired three years ago.

The first time I saw him play, I was sixteen years old. He had flown in from Chicago and was playing in an open-air concert in the school orchestra at Rushmore's twenty-fifth anniversary. At that age, I already knew Rushmore was my college of choice after finishing high school. Knowing he had gone to school there sealed the deal.

He held a seminar last summer here in Rushmore, but I spent my summer holidays helping Nor with the kids and at the flower shop, so I didn't attend it. According to the rumors flying around, he no longer plays for the symphony. People's speculation suggests that he retired his position after an injury and vanished from the face of the earth until six months ago, when he turned up in Jacksonville.

Color me intrigued.

And now he is standing in front of me. I must be dreaming.

Seriously.

I have to be still dozing on my desk and dreaming about this guy. It's been a while since I saw anything as magnificent as this scowling creature—given the last couple of disastrous dates my sister Elise set me up on.

What the hell is he doing in my class?

"Name?" His voice is low, a rich baritone that reminds me of evening bonfires, honey and Nutella, touching me everywhere, sinking into my bones. It definitely doesn't go with that look on his face. The command leaves his mouth like a bullet, and my spine snaps straight despite the richness of his voice. Fear cuts through my chest, and I have to remind myself that I'm not a scared little nine-year-old girl and that he is not my father. I have to remind myself that my poor excuse for a father left us years ago.

I take a deep breath and sit up taller in my chair and raise my chin up a notch.

"Um. . ." Crap! My voice is stuck somewhere inside my throat, completely cowering away from Mr. Scowl-A-Lot in front of me.

One brow shoots up, a vein ticking furiously in his jaw. Heat floods my cheeks.

If this is a dream, I really want to wake up now. It's spoiling my fantasy of the real Nathaniel Rowe.

"I asked you a question."

"Elon Blake." I stumble on the letters, eager to part with them so that he can go away, leave my desk and go loom and glower elsewhere.

He shifts on his feet and the muscles on his thighs tense. I swear the scowl on his face deepens even further.

"Wipe your chin, Miss Blake." His gaze drops below my mouth.

Quickly, my hand darts up and swipes away the drool there. I groan inwardly when I feel the traces of dry slobber that have also escaped to my cheek.

Earth, swallow me now.

Please. Just open up and gobble me whole.

Feeling the weight of his stare on me, my cheeks burn as I lick my thumb and rub off the dried trail of drool. When I'm done, I sneak a look up to this mysterious man. Gone is the scowl, replaced by a frown. Those grey eyes studying me with intense concentration are a physical burn on my skin.

He blinks once, and the scowl returns with a vengeance.

Unfolding his arms, he leans forward, the tips of his fingers braced on my desk, forcing me to lean back in my chair. But there's no more room to flee from his imposing figure. His scent, woodsy and intoxicating, slams into me, making me feel dizzy.

"I don't take it lightly when people come to my class to waste my time."

His class?

Am I being punked? Did I wake up in an alternate universe?

"Your class?" The words slip out of my mouth before I can stop them.

He leans further, invading my personal space. My heart thrashes inside my chest as I try not to cower under his stern gaze.

"Yes."

I shiver at his tone, and all I want is for him to move back. Leave me alone. So I nod, drop my gaze and wet my dry lips.

This guy has just morphed from the avenging angel into Satan. I blink, feeling confused. What is he doing in my Music Theory class?

From the corner of my eye, I see him pull back, straightening to his full height—over six feet of intimidating, lean muscle. He turns and strides away in confident, purposeful steps and halts at the podium in front of the class.

Wiping my hands on my skirt, I blow out a breath through my mouth.

"Way to make a great first impression, Freckles," a male voice whispers. I look up to find Alex—my rival and friend—scooting into the seat on my right.

"Right? I'm a genius." I groan, rubbing my hands down my face to wake myself up. "Why didn't you wake me?"

"What? And miss seeing the look on your face you're wearing right now?" I glare at him and he chuckles, raising his hands up in surrender. "Sheesh, I just got in class at the same time he did. Where's Amber?"

"Doctor's appointment."

His face pales a bit, and he asks, "Is she sick?"

I roll my eyes. "You two should really learn to talk to each other. This on-and-off thing you have going on is giving me whiplash."

He grins wolfishly at me. "Have you had wild, crazy make-up sex?" It sounds like a rhetorical question, so I don't even bother to answer him. "Benefits of breaking up and making up, Freckles. Crazy, wild, off-the-roof hot—"

"UGH. Shut *up*," I say, trying not to think about the last time I even had decent sex. "Not interested in your sex life with my best friend."

I turn my gaze back to Professor Rowe, who is now standing with his butt propped on the desk.

"Poor guy," Alex murmurs under his breath.

"Huh?" I don't turn to look at him, my eyes still taking in Nathaniel Rowe, still unable to believe he is here in my class.

"Shame he quit playing for the Orchestra."

I nod, distracted. Three years ago, he and his girlfriend were involved in an accident.

I can't imagine ever giving up on my dream. I live and breathe playing the cello.

Mr. Rowe eyes everyone. "My name is Nathaniel Rowe. I'm stepping in for Professor Harris," he states, introducing himself in that voice that rumbles across the room, demanding attention.

Demanding to be heard.

Folding his hands behind his back, he looks around the amphitheatre lecture hall making sure to make eye contact with everyone, lingering too long when he reaches me.

After a few seconds of silence—which I think is intentional on his part to make us nervous or something—someone asks, "So Professor Harris won't be teaching us anymore?"

Satan shakes his head curtly. "I'll be teaching her class for now," he says definitively. "I have to warn you, I am demanding and I don't like people who slack off in class. I expect two hundred percent participation and hard work from each and every one of you."

The class erupts into a cacophony of murmurs, a mix of excitement and disappointment. Professor Rowe's gaze sweeps across the class and, as if on cue, the noise dies down immediately.

Could Professor Harris's illness have gotten worse over winter break? Before we closed for Christmas holidays a few weeks ago, she had been diagnosed with rheumatoid arthritis. She taught our Music Theory class when school opened last week on Monday, but she didn't show up to work the rest of the week and another professor had to teach her class on Wednesday and Friday. Maybe she got worse over the holidays?

My thoughts burst into chaos and my breath saws in and out of my chest.

Shit, shit, *shit.*

We're just a week into the second quarter of winter semester. My new professor and I didn't exactly get off on the right foot.

As if he can hear my turmoil, his sharp gaze cuts back to me, and I sink even lower in my seat.

God, I wish he'd just forget I exist. I was so happy, living in my quiet little bubble where I went unnoticed every day. Looks like I'll have to work harder now.

He turns around without elaborating and switches on the projector on his desk. The words *Tonal harmony-counterpoint-analysis* appear on the screen in front of the class.

My attention wavers, drawn to the way his black pants shift across his ass and the muscles on his back flex as he writes.

"Open your textbooks to page thirty-five."

Everyone, including me, scrambles to look up the page. He begins his lecture, and I grab my pen and notebook, ready to begin scribbling notes, the sound of his voice travelling across the room, capturing our attention. Little by little, the fatigue I was feeling before fades, enthralled by the words pouring out of his mouth. He's really good, I have to give him that. From what I've heard, his seminars across the country and in Europe have always been quite successful.

Glancing around the room, I realize I'm not the only one mesmerized by this striking man pacing confidently in front of the class. The entire female population in this room is literally swooning, jaws on their desks.

"God, that ass," a female voice whispers behind me.

"Have you seen the way those pants hug his thighs?" Another whisper, this one from a male voice, followed by snickering.

Ah, those perfectly strong thighs. They're thoroughly imprinted in my brain for life. Professor Rowe's stern gaze flickers above my head, and the hushed tones and giggles cease immediately.

"We're going to learn about composing a three-voice fugue." With the remote control gripped in his left hand, he clicks a button and the screen changes, displaying his email addresses, before turning around to face the class. "If you have any questions, you can either come and see me in my office anytime before five o'clock or email me."

Right before I jot down the email address, I notice his right hand shake. He clenches his fingers into a tight fist, his jaw clenched. A grimace appears on his face as he subtly lifts his left hand and massages a spot on his right bicep, moving up to his shoulder. His brows snap together as pain carves a path across his features. As if sensing me, his eyes fly open and find mine, and for just a second, I see something in their depths that has my heart stalling. It's gone before I can figure it out. Storm chases the pain and his cheeks flush. Obviously, the thought of being found experiencing a human emotion annoys him, given that look on his face. He narrows his eyes at me, and my heartbeat accelerates.

Look away before that look turns you to ice, Elon.

I scan the room and realize everyone else is caught up in writing the instructions from the screen, while I am staring at my professor.

The bell rings, and the room erupts into action. Books are slammed and bags are snatched from the floor. I quickly gather my pencils and drop them inside my bag without arranging them in their appropriate sections inside the pencil case and then shove my textbook inside the bag. Leaning down, I grab the cello case at my feet, stand up and strap it on my back.

"Miss Blake?"

My head swings in the direction of that voice.

"May I have a word?"

The students freeze in their movements at his words. Suddenly, their attention is redirected to him and me. The urge to duck under the desk to avoid the scrutiny strikes.

"What does he want with that cold bitch?" a voice that sounds suspiciously like Lara's says. Lara is your typical Barbie doll kind of girl. She's always a bitch to everyone who doesn't look at her with adoration, so our dislike is mutual.

"Quit being a dick, Lara," Alex comes to my rescue. I smile at him in gratitude, even though he really didn't need to defend me.

I'm already immune to people like Lara, so I brush it off and hold my head high.

Before starting my degree in Music here in Rushmore, I thought that growing up in a household where being yelled at and insulted by my own father had thickened my skin. Then I met Lara during my first day of school. She was mean to everyone, and I was an easy target. I toughened up, and when she realized her words couldn't punch holes in my armor, she went in search of another target.

Just because I'm quiet and I don't rise to her baiting doesn't mean I'm afraid of her. I just don't feel like wasting my energy on her, and I won't satisfy her thirst to hurt me with her words, so I glance over my shoulder and toss her a *'Yes, he wants to talk to this cold bitch'* smile and stand taller before turning to face the professor who's staring at me impatiently. He cocks an eyebrow in question, and I remember what he asked me before.

Like I have a choice. "Sure."

In my life, I've known three types of men. Men like my father and my ex-boyfriend, for whom abuse was second nature. Men like my sister's husband, Josh Holloway; his brother Cole; and my best friend, Nick, who are protective, loving and generous. And now I've met Nathaniel Rowe. He's difficult to read and I don't want to make things between us more tense than they already are, so I remain seated until the last person leaves and then focus on the brooding figure at the front of the room, trepidation sliding down my spine.

Is he going to give me shit for sleeping in class? *Before* it even started?

He sits on the edge of the desk, crossing his feet at the ankles and folding his hands across his chest.

"It would be easier for us to speak if you'd join me down here." He cocks his head to the side and stares at me.

Correction. His eyes blatantly rove between my neck and mouth, the grey darkening to charcoal. I bite my top lip between my teeth and shift on my feet. Being the sole focus of his attention is like being surrounded by warmth.

He slants his head in question.

Hmm, yeah. I don't think so. He still intimidates me, even from this distance. And if he's going to lecture me on the triviality of sleeping in class, I would rather hear it from back here.

I stand up, sling the strap of my bag over my shoulder and climb down two steps, making sure the distance between us is still enough so I can escape if things go south fast, fold my hands in front of me and lift my chin. If there is anything I learned earlier on in life, it's to always be ready for the unexpected.

A muscle ticks in his jaw as he scowls up at me, probably not used to people disobeying his orders.

"I'd like to apologize for sleeping in class earlier," I say, quickly beating him to whatever scolding he has in mind.

"You worked for Professor Harris," he says, effectively ignoring my apology.

Jackass.

"Yes, I do. Did."

My heart races, and I have to look away to prevent him from seeing what's going on behind my eyes.

It'd slipped my mind that my new professor would be replacing Professor Harris at the office, as well. I started working as her teacher's assistant to earn credit toward my bachelor's degree at the beginning of the fall semester last year. Before we left for the Christmas break, I was helping her with research and compiling notes on the History of Opera, as well as assisting her with the ensemble for first year class.

Does it mean Professor Rowe will be taking over her work? The thought excites and scares me simultaneously.

Shit. I feel as if the temperature in the room shot up a thousand degrees.

I wipe my clammy hands on my shirt, silently commanding my body to calm down.

"Miss Blake." His voice now carries a softness that wasn't there before, probably sensing my freak-out. I look up and shift on my feet.

"I will need help in familiarizing myself with a few things in the office."

I swallow hard and nod. "Okay."

With a curt nod, he says, "I will see you at one o'clock."

Professor Harris must have informed him that one o'clock is the time when I usually start working. It's also lunchtime on campus. But the thought of eating in the cafeteria with all the noise blaring around me makes me shudder. Plus, the cafeteria is just a place for gossiping, and I would rather eat alone than be a part of that. Why should I talk behind someone else's back when my own life is far from perfect? Besides, I find my own company to be pretty awesome and I enjoy going unnoticed, preferring to watch people instead.

I push the strap of my bag higher over my shoulder and clutch my cello tighter, then turn to leave but stop when I get to the door. I sneak a peek back and find him tracking me with those intense eyes.

He glares through narrowed eyes. "No more sleeping in class either."

Fire spreads across my cheeks, feeling embarrassed. I nod and turn to leave.

As long as you keep it entertaining. . .

"Miss Blake?"

I whirl around, frowning because what the hell does he want now?

He arches one dark eyebrow. And did his lips twitch? I can't be sure because he's been so aloof since I woke up earlier and found him scowling down at me. He says—drawls actually, "I'll make it my life's mission to entertain you."

My eyes go so wide, they almost bulge out of my eye sockets. *Way to go, Elon. Try to keep your thoughts to yourself next time.*

Before I can make an even bigger fool out of myself than I have already, I rush out of the room to the sound of a dark chuckle from behind me.

Outside the hall and away from Professor Rowe's overpowering presence, I slow down and take a deep breath while glancing around me. People continue with their business, laughing, talking, high-fiving each other. No one bothers to talk to me, which is normal, I guess.

Normal life.

Normal everything.

Yet, here I am, a bundle of nerves.

Mentally, I kick myself for making this larger than life. It's just a new professor and my boss. My *crush*. No big deal, right?

I wish my best friend, Amber, was here today. At least she'd give me a pep talk, and I'd calm the hell down and quit being a Nervous Nelly.

I have a free period for the next hour, so I march down the hallway to one of the practice rooms, my mind wandering back to the moment Professor Rowe caught me staring at him.

Darkness.

His eyes were full of darkness, the kind where monsters live, greedily waiting to devour you when you let your guard down. I'd know it anywhere. It has been my constant companion for as long as I can remember.

My childhood is scattered with painful memories of my father's emotional and physical abuse, his mere presence terrorizing us. His family. He never laid a hand on me, but he made sure we never escaped his demeaning ways and abuse. Every time I looked into Nor and Mom's eyes, I could see the darkness. Sometimes when I let my guard down, I see it staring back at me too.

We all have our own monsters, some more vicious than others. Some choose to play nice, while others simply don't care at all and play dirty if you let them.

I wonder what kind of monsters live in Nathaniel Rowe's darkness.

And why am I even interested?

Shaking my head to disperse those thoughts, I walk inside the practice room, unlock my cello case and pull one of the chairs that are scattered around the room and sit down. I dig out the music sheets of the classical music pieces we will be playing at the charity fundraising ball in the last week of February. It's organized by WAV—Women

Against Violence, a non-profit organization—and my cello tutor, Professor Masters. One month ago, she approached Alex and me, and we jumped at the opportunity to play with other well-known professionals. Adjusting my weight on the seat, I position the cello between my legs and then spend the next sixty minutes practicing the songs. I mess up the notes and have to restart seven times when my thoughts stagger back to my new professor.

By the end of the hour, I want to punch something. Tension has taken up residence in my muscles. The mere thought of seeing Professor Rowe again has my heart racing and my stupid hands shaking with nerves and reluctant excitement.

Shiiit.

CHAPTER FOUR

Elon

One o'clock finds me dashing from Brown Hall, where most of the classes take place. With my cello case bouncing against my butt, I sprint across the quad, past the bubbling water fountain, as fast as my legs can carry me. I'm heading to the Constantine Building, where the administrative offices are housed, while trying to pull my jacket together to defend myself from the January chill nipping at my flesh.

My English Lit class went longer than usual, and I kept squirming in my seat the entire time, the image of a scowling Professor Rowe flashing through my head.

I burst through the door, breathless, panting, sweating, and rush to my desk. The door to Professor Harris's—now Professor Rowe's—office is slightly open. I toss my bag on the floor, prop my cello case against the corner next to the desk and power up my laptop, before shrugging my jacket off. I hang it on the back of my seat, pat down the creases, then sit down. A pungent smell wafts up from the area around my armpits. I lift my arms and sniff. And choke.

Shit. I was such a mess this morning, I forgot to put on deodorant.

All this nervousness and sweating isn't doing me any favors.

Ugh.

I freeze when I hear a low murmur coming from Nate's office. His voice travels through the small, open space at the door. If my guess is correct, he's talking to someone on the phone.

"You mentioned there was another option?" he asks, sounding annoyed. There is a small pause, then, "So, you're not even sure if this is going to work? I'm not ready to undergo the whole process again if there is no guarantee that it will work." More silence. "Call me if you come up with a more definite solution."

What was that all about?

"*Fuck*!" The word is whispered in a sharp tone of voice, followed by a loud thud.

I leave my desk, cautiously approach the open door, and duck my head inside his office.

"Professor—"

He swings his head up and directs a fiery glare at me, and I stumble back to escape the force of that look.

He drops the hand massaging his shoulder and snaps, "It's about time you showed up, Miss Blake."

"My class ran a bit late, so I couldn't get here on time."

The glare deepens to a scowl, *that* muscle ticking furiously in his jaw. "Let's get this over with."

Anger begins to simmer in my veins, and for just a moment, the thought of lifting my arms and letting him choke on my deodorant-less armpits fleetingly crosses my mind. I roll my eyes at my childish thoughts.

Is he mad at me for being a few minutes late? It wasn't even my fault. What the hell is wrong with this guy?

I'm about to open my mouth to say something when I see him flex his right hand, wincing. Veins line his forearms and hands, and I can't look away. Who knew vein lines could be so distracting?

He reaches forward and pulls the laptop toward him with his left hand.

"Have you had lunch yet?"

That question catches me off guard, and I snap my gaze to his face.

"Um. . . not yet."

He lifts those flint-colored eyes from his laptop screen and looks at me. "Go ahead and eat first. We can do this once you've had some food."

Okay. Now I'm confused about this sudden change of course. And worse, my body feels as confused as my thoughts. Every time he looks at me, I feel warmth trickle down my spine. His expression tells me he's really looking at me and not through me like everyone else seems to do. When he centers his gaze on me, I *feel* it down to my bones.

It's very distracting.

When I don't make a point of moving, he nods his head toward the door, his features softening. I stop breathing, taking in the stress-free look on his face.

"Go ahead, Miss Blake."

I exhale and nod, still confused by this man's mercurial mood. "Okay." I leave the room, feeling his eyes on me.

After grabbing the files along with a few urgent documents that Professor Harris was supposed to read through, I dig my Nutella sandwich and a bottle of water out of my bag, then return to Professor Rowe's office and take a seat right across from him.

I hand him the first document. "This is the list of students that have applied for the one-week course in the spring."

Picking up a pair of glasses from the desk, he slips them on. My jaw drops as I gawk shamelessly.

Whoa!

He looks nerdy, hot and brooding, completely oblivious to the effect he has on me.

He takes the document from me, and for just a second, I wonder how that piece of paper must feel in his large, capable hands.

Biting back a sigh, I grab my lunch from the table, carefully unwrap the Saran Wrap from it and take a bite. Unable to help my curiosity, I steal a glance at Professor Rowe, feeling my fascination for this man creeping up again. His brow is furrowed in concentration, and his index finger is rubbing his bottom lip. Such an innocent act, and yet, I can't rip my eyes away from it.

Or maybe I'm just allowing the enthrallment I felt for him, *before* I actually met his moody ass, to blind me.

He drops the document on his desk and catches me staring at him. He leans forward, his eyes on my hand in a questioning stare.

"I need the sugar rush," I say, taking a huge bite from my sandwich.

His lips twitch like they did before, the only sign that shows he's at least slightly amused.

He clears his throat, staring at me intently, making me squirm under his scrutiny.

"I want to apologize for being a total ass today."

I blink in surprise, caught off guard by his words. "Okay."

"I was having a rough morning. It wasn't right of me to take it out on you like that. I'm in no way excusing myself for behaving the way I did."

I take him in, the way his body is angled forward toward me, his expression sincere, and I nod, offering him a quick smile. "Apology accepted."

He sits back in his chair, his shoulders loosening a bit like a weight has been lifted off him. I notice his fingers spasm on the desk, and he winces, readjusting his right arm and finally sighs in relief.

"Are you okay?" I ask.

His face shuts down, his expression reverting to inscrutable. He nods at the rest of the documents in front of me, and I have a feeling that little moment we shared is over.

I'm still surprised he apologized, and that alone makes me realize he's not the ogre he'd appeared to be earlier on today.

Over the next forty-five minutes, I continue catching him up on everything Professor Harris had been working on while I finish my sandwich, and he proceeds to send me terse glances from across his desk. His questions are direct, his answers are mono-syllabled. But by the end of my office hour, as I sling my bag over my shoulder and make my way to my next class, I think to myself, *that could have gone much worse.* I can't help but wonder how tomorrow will be.

CHAPTER FIVE

Nate

Right after work, I drop my car off at Antonio's Garage for repairs, then catch a cab to Reed's Restaurant & Lounge. As soon as I walk inside the VIP lounge on the second floor my brother-in-law, Bennett Reed, flashes me his trademark smile, bright against his brown skin.

"How was your first day, Teach?" Bennett asks.

I walk over to an empty seat, sink into it, lean back and look out the window. The Jacksonville skyline is reflected on the St. John's River a few feet away, the orange, gold and yellow of the setting sun splashed across the sky.

After arriving back in Florida last year, I was lucky enough that Bennett informed me there was a vacant apartment for sale in a nearby building on the fifteenth floor.

I relax into the seat, turning to face him. "Good."

"Yeah? We should celebrate then."

"Fuck, yeah. A shot of Macallan 18."

His brows shoot up. "Think you can tone down that order, bro?"

I smirk. "So, no lottery win yet?"

"Fuck you." He laughs. "Cheap Scotch?"

"Water's fine."

He gives me a disgusted look. "Really? You disappoint me."

Grumbling inaudibly under his breath, he pulls a phone from the front pocket of his white button-down shirt and punches in a few digits before pressing it to his ear.

Ordering water instead of Scotch is beyond lame. But my shoulder is killing me, and I'm not about to mix pain medication with alcohol. That would be careless and stupid. I might be dependent on my medication, but it doesn't mean I have a death wish.

After shooting off an order for drinks, Bennett tucks the phone back in his pocket and settles back in his seat. I catch him up on my day, including that prick who was driving the Toyota.

"Are you going to take the job at Rushmore?" he asks.

"Not sure yet. I'll see how this week goes."

Rushmore's Head of School, President Sara Bowman, called me last week before school re-opened and informed me that Professor Harris resigned from her post and her position was available. She went ahead and offered me the job as associate professor. I declined the offer. I wasn't in the mood to be reminded of my shortcomings every single day. I hadn't played cello for three years, and my damn shoulder didn't seem to be healing the way it should. Even after explaining my case to Mrs. Bowman, she changed tactics and convinced me the Department of Music Theory was in dire need of professors. Eventually she wore me down, and I accepted to step in to teach Professor Harris's class on a temporary basis. What I didn't count on was how much teaching seemed to pull my head out of my own problems, reminding me how rewarding it was teaching eager minds willing to learn. After feeling like I've been living in stasis for a long time, I felt useful. At least my family would back off and hopefully stop worrying about me most of the time.

The conversation with Bennett shifts to his plans to open another restaurant in Miami after the baby comes. He and Izzy seem to be on a mission to fill the earth, which is fine by me. At least it will keep my mother off my back about finding a girl and settling down. Since I moved back home, her efforts have doubled, dropping hints every now and then.

The door opens and a blonde waitress carrying a tray of drinks walks in. She sets down a bottle of water in front of me and a tumbler of Scotch in front of Bennett, then turns to leave, tossing a coy look at me over her shoulder. I give her a fleeting stare before turning to face my brother-in-law who's smirking at me.

"She likes you."

"Who?"

He rolls his eyes and shakes his head. "You know who."

"Not interested."

"When was the last time you got laid?"

Sending him a scathing glare, I ignore him, picking up my bottle of water and bringing it to my lips to take a long pull.

"She's hot," he says, bringing the tumbler to his lips and tipping it up.

"Are you a fucking matchmaker now?" I snarl.

"If the shoe fits." He grins, unperturbed by my tone, and puts the glass on the table, then slouches back in his seat, holding my challenging gaze. "Just looking out for you, Nate." Despite the nonchalant attitude, I see concern in his eyes and I fucking hate it. And he knows it.

"Well, stop it." Shoving my hands in my pockets, I pull out a bottle of pain pills from my jacket and pop off the lid. I toss one in my mouth and chase it down with water. I've been holding off on taking my normal dose of medication during the day because my concentration would be shot.

Bennett's grin disappears as he assesses me silently, his eyes lingering on my shoulder. "Don't tell me you held off until now. Christ, Nate. Are you made of stone?"

I close my eyes and ignore his words as I let the medication do its job.

"Any news from the doctor?"

I subtly shake my head.

We fall quiet for a short while. When I open my eyes, Bennett is staring at me with a worried look.

"She'd want you to move on. Cam—"

"Don't."

"You still blame yourself, but—"

"Fuck, *stop.*"

"Nate—"

"Shut up, Bennett. Just because you're my sister's husband doesn't mean you can go around poking your nose in my business."

"Don't forget, I'm also your best friend."

I glare at him, inwardly begging him to press on, then I'd have a reason to plant a fist in his face for reminding me how much of a failure I am. For three years, I've lived with the fact that I couldn't protect her and ended up breaking my promise.

As if sensing I'm spoiling for a fight, Bennett just sighs and reaches for his Scotch.

Tightening my jaw, I curl my right hand into a fist until I feel a burning pain in my shoulder, giving me a short reprieve from the guilt which has made a home in my chest.

Remembering I was supposed to call Izzy after my classes, I flex my fingers and pull out my phone from my pants pocket and power it on. I forgot to switch it back on after my class was over. A series of beeps echo around the enclosed space. Tiny envelopes pop up on the screen. I click the top one and bite back a groan as I read Izzy's message. I have a feeling all the other unopened messages are from her as well. I know this because the number of people who have my number is limited to only five: my mother, Izzy, Bennett, my friend, Wade Brass, and Dr. Rosenburg, my doctor in Chicago.

Izzy: **Done with school, brother dearest?**

Izzy: **You must still be in class. Call me as soon as you get this.**

Izzy: **Are you there yet?**

I scroll through the messages, shaking my head.

Jesus. I love that girl, but she can be a pain sometimes.

I look up from the phone only to find Bennett staring at me, one side of his mouth curled in a teasing smile.

"Your wife is a huge pain in the ass, you know that?" I mutter, quickly typing back a reply and failing miserably.

Shit. I hate this. The keypad is too tiny for my fingers, and even when I use the tip of my fingers, I still fumble onto the wrong keys. Jabbing at the keypad with my index, I am frustrated beyond words. The end result resembles that of a three-year-old attempting to draft a text message. I finally give up, close the text box, and call her instead.

"Hey, big brother!" she singsongs on the phone, her voice brimming with mischief. Somehow, she knows that I just spent five minutes struggling to text her back. She is fucking enjoying this.

"I think you love to torture me."

She bursts into laughter. "I've never met anyone who has such a strong aversion to texting like you do. So how was your day? Were the students good to you?"

My thoughts wander back to the moment I saw one student in particular—Miss Blake—sleeping in class. Snoring like a fire truck. In the middle of the day. "It was interesting."

A gasp sounds on the other side of the phone. "Is that a smile I hear in your voice?"

Surprise, surprise. Sure enough, my lips are slightly pulled up in a small facial grimace. Maybe one that would resemble a smile. "No."

She chortles gleefully. I swear she sounds just like she did when she was twelve. Carefree and very Izzy.

"I can't wait to hear all about it at Sunday brunch."

I groan. "There's nothing to tell. It was an ordinary class with ordinary students."

The big hazel eyes, freckled nose and pouty mouth that belong to Miss Blake fill my vision. I squirm on my seat, annoyed that I was able to memorize those details about my student. Or her graceful, long neck. Or the way her hair shone when the weak sunlight filtering through the windows hit it just right.

I cough quietly to get rid of the tightness in my throat, glance across the table from me and meet Bennett's curious stare.

Shit.

"What should I bring for brunch?" I ask, hoping to change the subject.

If she noticed my tactic, she doesn't mention it. "Pickles and jalapeño pizza from Jonah's."

"Got it. Anything for Matthew and Makayla?"

"A trip to the zoo?"

"Done." My lips pull up just thinking about my nephew and niece and spending more time with them. "Next week on Saturday?"

She sighs happily. "Perfect. Bennett and I haven't had a date night in forever, so that's awesome!"

"Good."

After wrapping up the conversation, we say goodbye and I stand up to leave.

"See you tomorrow?" Bennett asks in a low, concerned voice. "You going to be okay?"

I nod and leave the VIP lounge, heading downstairs. I walk out of Reed's Lounge and turn right, toward the main entrance of the building.

"Mr. Rowe," the doorman welcomes me, slightly lifting his hat in greeting as he hurries to the elevators to punch the arrow pointing upward.

"Good evening, Geoffrey." I return the greeting with a slight nod while striding inside the elevator as soon as the doors open.

His smile is the last thing I see before the doors slide shut. I lean my back on the mirror behind me and close my eyes. Dread settles in my bones at the thought of stepping inside my lonely apartment. Before I moved here to Jacksonville from Chicago, I *lived* and *consumed* that feeling like it was part of my diet, hating everyone and everything. I locked myself away in my condo for days, drinking to numb the pain, to forget my loss. I wanted to *die*.

Then I returned home and being with my family eased the hurt, eased the ache, but the scars on my body are a brutal reminder I may never be able to use my right arm again.

The pinging sounds jolt me away from my thoughts as the elevator reaches the fifteenth floor. I step out and head to my front door, exhausted. The gleaming 200-year-old Montagnana propped in its stand in the living room greets me as soon as I walk in, an inheritance from my father after he passed away years ago. Momentarily halting next to the cello, I gently pluck the strings with the fingers on my left hand, shutting my eyes as the sweet sound thrums through my veins.

God. I miss playing it so much.

Reality kicks in, forcing me to face the fact that I may never be able to play the instrument again, and the crashing pain settles in. Turning around, I storm toward the small bar on the other side of the room near the kitchen and grab the bottle of Macallan 18 my friend Wade sent me a few weeks ago from Chicago. I pour two fingers of the light mahogany liquid into a tumbler and toss it into my mouth, savoring the satisfying burn down my throat, numbing the ache of my loss. Then I head to my room and strip down to my boxers. I'm out as soon as my head hits the pillow.

I jolt awake, my heart racing, and a soundless scream is lodged in my throat. My hand shoots out, fumbling around for the side lamp in the dark. Seconds later, the room is illuminated in a soft light, and I have to squint my eyes to shield them from the sudden brightness. I turn to my side and my gaze connects with the framed photo on my nightstand. Smiling blue eyes stare back at me, and I take my time, taking in the elegant features on that face that once was, but no longer is. Guilt is like a sharp knife, slicing through me, replaying that nightmare over and over until I feel I can't get air in my lungs quick enough.

Swinging my legs over the edge of the bed, I brace my elbows on my knees and drop my head in my hands. I close my eyes as the last flash of blue eyes dissipate in my mind's eye.

Dragging my fingers through my hair, I stand up and head to the bathroom and splash cold water on my face. I return to my room, grab a pair of lounge pants and a T-shirt from the dresser and pull them on, then stride to the kitchen. Once I grab a bottle of water from the refrigerator and a small, black leather case from the cabinet above the sink in the bathroom, I walk toward the windows overlooking the river. Sliding the balcony door open, I step out into the cool night air. I set the bottle of water on the table, sit down and unzip the black case. My fingers bypass the black vape pen and snatch a joint instead, along with a lighter. Sitting back in the chair, I light it up and take a few hits. I feel the tension slowly leave my body, and my muscles begin to relax.

Another fucking sleepless night.

I close my eyes and let the drug sweep me into its welcoming arms, erasing the haunting memories.

For once in a long time, I let myself forget.

Forget the constant guilt.

Forget life screwed me over and ripped my dreams out from under me.

Forget everything and welcome the feeling of weightlessness taking over my body right now.

CHAPTER SIX

Elon

THE DOOR TO MY ROOM SLAMS OPEN, CRUELLY RIPPING ME OUT OF the hot make-out scene I was immersed in in the novel I'm currently reading. I glance up and see my roommate and best friend, Amber, stroll in with a huge grin on her face. She snatches the half-eaten Snickers bar from my hand and shoves the entire thing inside her mouth before throwing her petite body on top of my bed and moaning scandalously.

"God, I think I'm about to have an orgasm," she says, rolling her eyes back while writhing on the bed.

"I was about to have one myself, but you interrupted me," I say, shifting a little on the chair to alleviate the pressure on my clit. "Damn, that Holt guy knows how to put his mouth to proper use. He was about to slide his quivering member into her moist channel. . ." I deadpan.

Amber stops squirming and covers her ears. "Ugh. *Stop.* Jesus, E. Now that image will be stuck inside my head for a month. Thanks for ruining my sex life."

I laugh, knowing she'll be rolling between the sheets with Alex before the day is over. They break up as often as they make up. But at least she has regular sex.

Me? I get my fill from book boyfriends, the shower head and my vibrator—when I'm lucky enough to snag that elusive O.

"Spill everything," Amber orders with a little too much enthusiasm and a shimmy of her shoulders.

Sighing, I grab the bookmark on the bed and place it between the pages, so I can pick up later. Then I set the book next to the neat row of pens on my desk.

When Amber gets like this, there's no way I'll be able to get any reading done. Besides, I haven't seen her the whole day. I need an update on how her appointment went with the doctor.

I pull my legs up on the chair and sit cross-legged to face her. "Spill what?"

"The new professor, silly." Amber rolls her eyes. "Everyone is talking about him. Rushmore hasn't buzzed with so much excitement since—" Blood drains from her face, the rest of that sentence freezing on her tongue as she stares at me with wide, sympathetic eyes.

"Since Rick," I finish the sentence for her.

Rick is my ex-boyfriend. He and I dated for a year and a half before things went south. The last time I saw him was when he was being escorted by the police from the campus grounds after violating the restraining order I had against him.

"Shit! I didn't mean to bring that up—"

"It's fine."

She sits up and scoots over to the edge of the bed. "It's not. I shouldn't be allowed to open my mouth."

"Stop, Amber. It's fine, really."

She drops her gaze to her hands and bites her bottom lip between her teeth. Her eyebrows pinch in a frown.

I wait, wondering if she's going to tell me what's on her mind. Something else is going on; I can feel it.

Leaning forward, I capture her fidgeting fingers with my hand to still them. "What is it?"

Her head jerks up, and she stares at me nervously.

"What?" I ask in a panicked voice. The only reason I can think of for behaving the way she is is that maybe her doctor's appointment didn't go well. I whisper, "Tell me. What did the doc say?"

She smiles, looking relieved. I notice color flooding back to her face. "He prescribed a different medication. I have another appointment scheduled in a week to monitor the insulin resistance."

I nod, exhaling in relief. She's a type 1 diabetic. She'd been sick the past few weeks until she went to her doctor, who referred her to a specialist to get a full checkup.

I sense this is not what she wanted to tell me, but I don't press on. Instead, I squeeze her hands and say, "Promise me you'll take care of yourself."

She nods, tears brimming in her eyes, even though she's smiling. I prefer to keep my emotions in check, but with Amber, it's different.

We met the first day of school two years ago when I walked into my dorm room and found her curled up on her bed, sobbing her heart out. It was then that she told me she was scared of being alone. Her parents had sheltered her her whole life. And when she told them that she wanted to attend college in Florida, they had been heartbroken since it was far away from her home in North Carolina. Feeling confused, I had asked her why she was crying when she was the one who wanted to attend school here. She had told me that she wanted to be independent from her parents. She wasn't sure if she was crying because she felt relieved or because she missed her doting parents. Then Amber pulled me on the bed and demanded to be hugged. The only people I was close enough with to hug were my mother and sisters. Imagine my awkwardness when she grabbed me and wrapped her skinny arms around me, holding on for dear life. When she eventually let me go, I made her tea and we sat down and talked for hours.

I had never opened up to anyone about my family. It had been such a relief to talk about it, my family's history: my abusive father, my mom who spent most of my childhood trapped in her own mind,

Nor's self-harming. About Cole and my dad's obsession with Cole's mother, which eventually led to Cole being locked up for two years. I remember that horrible night years ago when I woke up to the sound of screaming and crying. I rushed out of my room and toward the stairs with Elise and froze in the middle of the steps. There stood Nor, crying as my drunk father loomed above her. I'd never seen him so angry before. Then everything seemed to move quickly. My mother trying to stop my father, Cole rushing through the door, fists flying. Then the police cars arrived, blue and red lights flashing, responding to the intruder in their fellow policeman's house. Minutes later, the police car drove off with Cole in it. After a little tryst which should never have happened during a visit organized by the warden, who was a friend of my grandmother, Joce and Cora, my nieces, were conceived. Upon my dad confronting Nor to ask if she was pregnant and who was responsible, Josh stepped up and declared the baby was his to avoid my father from sending his goons to rough up Cole in jail. After Cole's time was up, my father drove him out of town on the same day Cole was being released. Little did he know Josh had confessed, and my darling father had orchestrated his revenge perfectly. Nor and Josh walking down the aisle on the day of Cole's release from prison.

Every single thought bottled up inside me poured out in a torrent of words. I had expected her to run. But she didn't.

Amber grabs one of the numerous lilac pillows scattered on the bed and throws it at me. "Your turn. Is he hot?"

Hot doesn't do Professor Rowe justice. I nod and say, "Very hot." I blow out a breath and then drop my face in my hands. "He found me dozing on my desk when he walked in. I prefer to forget it ever happened."

"Oh my gosh! What did he say?" she asks excitedly, and I lift my face.

Straight-faced, I announce, "He patted me on the head and kissed my cheek." She gasps, her eyes wide with anticipation. If she was a cartoon, she'd have hearts for eyes right now. Amber believes in happily ever afters, which makes me a little envious sometimes. I wish

I was wired that way like her.

I laugh and say, "God, he was so annoyed, and I was so embarrassed."

She swats my arm and chuckles. "What happened to Professor Harris?"

"Early retirement." I reach for the white envelope on my desk and give it to her. "I found this on my desk in the office."

She takes and reads it, then slips it back in the envelope. "So the new professor is here to stay?"

My stomach flutters at those words. "Maybe." Shit. I hate my breathy voice right now. She frowns, not missing my reaction, so I say, "Nathaniel Rowe."

"What?"

"The new professor. It's Nathaniel Rowe."

The confusion fades, and comprehension fills her brown eyes. "No way. *Your* Nathaniel Rowe? The guy you've been crushing on since forever?" Her voice is full of disbelief and awe.

"The one and only," I groan. "Why did it have to be *him*?"

She snorts. "So it's like your fantasy came to life. Talk about fate, you lucky bitch." She does this pretend-shiver thing with her entire body. "Music Theory just got a lot more interesting. Don't get me wrong. I enjoyed Professor Harris's class. But a thirty-year-old cellist who looks like a GQ model? Sign me up for that shit."

I roll my eyes, snatch the envelope from her hand and toss it on the table.

"Holy shit! So if he's replacing Professor Harris, it also means you two will be working together!"

I sigh and nod.

Feeling edgy, I begin arranging the pens on my desk by color order, making sure the distance between them is the same.

"It bothers you."

"I hate change."

She grins wide and bounces a little on the bed. "This is a good change, E. You'll be working with someone you look up to. Not very many people get a chance like this."

I know she's right, so why do I feel anxious every time Professor Rowe wields his stare on me?

"Let's order dinner, yeah?" I grab the menu of the local Turkish restaurant we usually order from and pretend to read it. "What do you want?"

I feel her curious gaze on me, but she doesn't press me for answers. Instead, she hops down from the bed and says, "I'm heading out to get some tampons at the store. I'll pick dinner up on the way back."

"Sure. Just the usual for me." The usual being rice with *baba ghanoush*, extra spicy.

She nods and smiles, but it doesn't reach her eyes. She walks toward the door but stops suddenly and turns around to look at me, chewing her bottom lip nervously.

"What is it?"

She sighs and shuffles back to stand beside me. "I need to tell you something. I've really struggled with this the past week, but I can't keep it to myself any longer."

"Keep what to yourself?"

She looks like she's about to cry. "You're finally happy after *he* left."

He, meaning Rick.

My stomach bottoms out. My heart skips several beats before thudding painfully in my chest, and I can hardly hear a sound through the pounding in my ears.

No. Shit, *no.*

"Elon?" Amber's touch on my arm stills the raging thoughts inside my head. "Rick. . . he contacted me last week."

Just hearing his name out loud. . . God. I run my hands up and down my arms to soothe the goosebumps on my skin. My breathing hitches and my throat starts to constrict.

Amber drops to her knees and begins rubbing circles on my back.

"Shit. I'm sorry," she murmurs. "This is the why I didn't want to tell you," she says in a worried voice. "Come on, breathe, E."

The name *Rick* ricochets inside my head over and over as fear spikes like a potent drug through my veins.

I need to breathe. I can't let him win. Not again. I promised myself I would banish all memories of that jerk from my head.

Breathe in.

Breathe out.

I do this repeatedly until the lightheadedness begins to fade.

"I'm okay," I murmur, taking one big lungful of air, then sitting up straight. "I'm okay," I repeat, more to convince myself than to reassure Amber.

Her hand stills on my back, and she squats in front of me. "I'm really sorry."

I smile, trying to assure her that I'm okay, but my bottom lip quivers, destroying my attempt. I clear my throat to get rid of the tightness there and ask, "What did he want?"

She starts to chew her bottom lip again.

"I need to know, Amber. What did he want?"

"He tried to call you on your old phone number, but when he didn't get through, he called me. He said to tell you he wants to see you. To apologize."

God, no.

She must see the panicked look on my face because she continues, "But he can't do that. You still have the restraining order in place. He can't come within three hundred feet of you."

I shake my head, shutting my eyes and taking a deep breath. "It ran out six months ago."

This can't be happening. Not when my life is back on track and I'm doing so well.

"Shit," Amber mutters under her breath. "What do we do now?"

My eyes flutter open and I meet her worried gaze. "We wait."

"I hate this so much. Will you be okay?" Amber asks, rising to her feet.

"Yes," I say with false bravery.

She hugs me and turns to leave.

"Amber?" She stops and looks over her shoulder. "Add a bottle of wine for me, please."

"Got it."

Once I'm alone in my room, my shoulders fall, and I allow the fear I've been holding back to flood through my body.

There's no way I'll be able to work on the work I took home with me from the office after that news. I shoot up from my chair and head to the kitchen, my body buzzing with anxiety and nervous energy. My brain is on autopilot and my thoughts are a chaotic mess as I turn on the oven to preheat it, then pace around the kitchen, randomly collecting various ingredients and placing them on the L-shaped counter.

In most cases, baking helps me to de-stress, and right now, I need to get ahold of my emotions and not allow them to consume me.

I begin mixing the ingredients in a white plastic bowl, not sure what I'm working on. When the batter is ready, I pour it in a baking pan, slide it inside the oven and set the timer.

I don't want Amber worrying about me when she comes back, so I grab my cello and return to my room to work on reining in my panic. Setting the instrument between my legs, I let myself go, playing random pieces I've long since memorized.

Nor was right. Fear cripples us, makes us weak. If you allow it to take over your life, it can easily incapacitate you. But if you stare it in the eye, chances are you've already defeated that feeling. It's only through fear that we discover how strong we are.

CHAPTER SEVEN

Elon

THE NEXT FEW DAYS PASS IN A BLUR, AND BY THURSDAY OF THE following week, I'm desperate for the week to come to an end.

In between school work, my job, Professor Rowe and rehearsing for the fundraising ball, the news about Rick being in town is pushed to the back of my head.

Well, not as far as I'd like it to stay. My mind subconsciously plays the conversation I had with Amber last week, and I'm wearing paranoia like a second skin. Like the other day right after my cello practice when I was walking to the spot I'd parked my car in, I had this feeling that someone was watching me. Upon scanning the area and failing to see anything suspicious, I chastised myself for letting that asshole reduce me to the kind of person I'd fought so hard to forget. Always afraid of my own shadow.

Right after our Music Theory lecture, Amber and I walk out of class. She slings one arm across my shoulder, gently bumps her hip against mine and asks, "Want to grab a super early lunch before our next class?"

I shake my head and pat my bag. "I packed my sandwich this morning. Plus, I want to finish some work before—" *he gets there*, I finish the sentence in my head. Speaking out those words feels absurd. I've tried hard to avoid crossing paths with my new professor. Other than looking his usual surly self, Professor Rowe keeps mostly to himself. We hardly ever see each other outside of Music Theory class, and most of our communication is done through email, which is fine with me.

"You still avoiding him?" Amber asks, squinting at me.

I stare straight ahead. "Avoiding him? Don't be ridiculous."

She raises an eyebrow at me. "Your nose wiggled."

My hand flies to my face and duck my head. Stupid nose, giving me away.

She snickers and says, "Girl, I can't remember the last time I saw you this ruffled by a guy."

I roll my eyes to cover the fact that her words hit home hard. Honestly, I'm not sure if I've been avoiding him or opting to reduce the stress currently weighing down my life.

"Speak of the devil. . ." she murmurs, snapping me out of my thoughts. Then she drops her arm from my shoulder and steps back the way we came from and says in a loud voice, "Professor Rowe, I have a few questions about the assignment."

I groan inwardly. I swear I'm going to punch her in the boob. Since when did she have any questions?

Professor Rowe lifts his head, pulling his focus from his masculine watch on his wrist, his eyebrows bunched up slightly. The little frown clears as he halts a few feet away from us. He gives me a cursory glance before shifting those flinty eyes to Amber. "Come and see me after your classes. I'll be in the office until four o'clock."

Amber grins wide and nods. "Thank you, Professor Rowe." I send her a glare, trying to convey that she'd better watch out because I'm planning to throttle her.

Professor Rowe strides confidently down the hallway and disappears through the main door that leads to the quad, and I literally have to tear my gaze from the door.

"Drooling much?" She snickers. I pick up my jaw from the floor and clear my throat.

Her eyes grow big, literally bugging out of her heart-shaped face. "Oh my God, you're blushing!" she whispers loudly, making me cringe.

"I am not!" I whisper heatedly, glancing around and noticing a few students have paused whatever they are doing and are gawking in our direction.

Amber doesn't seem to realize she has unwittingly gained us an audience. She breaks away from me, shimmies her shoulders and starts singing the lyrics to "Crush" by Jennifer Paige, teasing me about my crush.

I swat her shoulder and laugh. "You're crazy. I'll see you at Sebastian Hall at two o'clock."

"Gotta love that Jennifer Paige chick, though!" she yells as I practically run down the hallway, stumbling out the same door Professor Rowe went through.

The sunrays splash across the campus grounds as I traipse past the fountain, heading to the admin building. I stop at the door, change directions, and walk off the campus grounds. The weather is great today. Maybe a little walk to the second-hand bookstore across campus will kick my mood up a notch. Books tend to do that for me. Besides, I need to replenish my to-be-read paperbacks pile so I can have something to read over the weekend.

Fifty minutes later, I walk into the office and drop my purse and the bag with my books on the floor, then lower myself into the chair. I grab the documents I printed out yesterday and begin to proofread them.

My phone pings with an incoming text message. I lean down and dig it out of my bag, swiping the screen.

Are we still on for tonight? :)

My heart slams into my chest, my eyes glued to the strange number the text came from. In light of Rick contacting Amber, my brain is in hyperdrive and I want to puke.

Could this be Rick? But how did he get my number?

Before I completely drive myself crazy with speculation, I wipe my clammy hands on my shirt and type, **Who is this?**

A message immediately pops up on my screen. **Sean.**

Seconds later, my phone pings again.

Your sister hooked us up?

I groan under my breath. Shit. I had completely forgotten about the date Elise had set me up on a week ago. A while back, she encouraged me to start dating again. She had played a big part in integrating me back into the dating pool by setting me up with men, since she seems to horde them.

Sean: **You're killing me here ;)**

Shit.

My fingers fly through the keyboard as I type, **Of course. Sorry. What time?** and then I press send.

It takes a while for Sean to reply, the message coming through after a few minutes.

Jet's Place on Jet Boulevard and 7th Street. 7 p.m. good?

Me: **Make it 7:30. I'll meet you there.**

Sean: **Can I pick you up? Let me at least do that. ;)**

Aw, gosh. He sounds so sweet.

Me: **It's fine, really. I have my tutoring class. It ends at 7.**

Sean: **Cool. See you later.**

I smile, dropping my phone back inside my bag. Elise and I have always had an easy relationship, and I wish I had had that with Nor growing up.

The hairs on the back of my neck rise, and my skin tingles in awareness. My head jerks up toward the door, and I see the tall shadow gracing the threshold, stealing the smile from my lips.

Professor Rowe.

My fingers shake a little, and I curl them into a tight fist to hide the nerves. I thought I'd be used to him by now, given that a week has already passed since he started teaching my Music Theory class, not to mention him being my boss.

I was wrong.

He's devastatingly hot and unforgettable, and the second he enters the room, his presence takes up the whole space. The air stills, tension in my body skyrockets and I find myself fighting to breathe.

Right now, he's leaning one hip on the doorframe, his hands tucked in his pants pockets. The look on his face is indecipherable as always, those lips stern as if he's ready to reprimand me.

Ah geez. Does he ever smile? Or maybe he has a hidden button that needs pushing before a smile appears on his face.

I clear my throat and say, "Professor Rowe." Heat rises to my cheeks, responding to his open perusal.

"Miss Blake." He curtly nods in greeting.

That voice startles the butterflies in my stomach, sending them flying all over the place, as if his mere presence isn't enough to leave my toes curling. As if his intense eyes don't make my heart skip a few beats.

Ack! I want to smack myself in the face for letting those lingering pieces from the crush I've had for this man since my teen years slip through my armor. The armor I built over the past few days.

I glance down at my laptop and let my fingers fly over the keyboard. From the corner of my eye, I watch him walk past me to his office. I exhale the air trapped in my lungs, and I bury my face in my hands.

Sheesh, control yourself, Elon.

My feelings are all over the place this week. First, the man I've looked up to—not to mention had a crush on—becomes my professor. Then Rick contacts Amber, asking about me. Yesterday, I spoke to Nor, who told me Josh's health has been declining every day. The only thing keeping him alive is his last wish to see his estranged brother

Cole, who he hasn't seen for nine years. I'm worried about what will happen if he. . . oh God. If he *dies.*

I'm an emotional wreck, and those feelings are looking for something to latch on to. So when Professor Rowe looks at me the way he does, my already weakened walls begin to crumble.

Time to put them back up and focus on other things. Like the mountain of second-hand romance novels on the floor next to my feet waiting to be devoured.

Inhaling deeply, I lift my head from my hands just as my phone beeps. Before I can dig it out of my bag, I hear Professor Rowe's terse, "Miss Blake".

My tummy flutters in apprehension as I make my way to his office, ignoring the beeping phone.

His head is bowed, his entire focus is on whatever he's working on on his laptop when I step inside his office. My fingers itch to sift through that chestnut-colored hair. I bet it's as soft as silk. His strong fingers reach forward and slide the pile of papers on his desk toward me.

I clear my throat to get his attention. "Sir?"

"I need twenty copies of Evolution of Music printed out." He looks up at me through his glasses. My knees quiver when his gaze meets mine, his eyes full of things I cannot fathom.

I nod and shift on my feet. "When do you need them by?"

"Tomorrow, three o'clock in the afternoon."

I nod again. "I transferred most of the files to your drive. Could you please check the ones on the D-drive, as well? I can delete or save whatever you don't need."

At first, I think he probably didn't hear me. He's staring at the screen in front of him, his brows deeply furrowed. But then he lifts those intriguing flint-colored eyes, and the second they collide with mine, the urge to shrink into my chair overcomes me. But I don't. He's like every other man, so why should I let him bother me so much?

He nods once. "Thank you." He's quiet for the next several seconds, just watching me, searching for something. But *what*? Why the hell does he look at me the way he is right now?

Feeling slightly perturbed and mildly hot, I smile at him briefly, hoping that the warm gesture will thaw that look on his face that's doing all kinds of things to me. The smile seems to work for like one point five seconds, and I see something else in those depths. Something that flashes across his face quickly, then vanishes before I can figure out what I just saw.

I clear my throat to get rid of the tightness that's there. "I was about to head out. Do you need me to do anything else?"

He sits back in his seat with his elbows propped on the armchair in a relaxed pose, which does wonderful things to his forearms. He tents his index fingers in front of his mouth.

"Running away from me again, Miss Blake?"

"What? No!" I answer quickly, caught off-guard by his voice, then follow those hastily-spoken words with an awkward laugh. No, a snort-laugh. My cheeks burn with embarrassment, but I don't look away from his gaze.

His eyebrows shoot up, amusement fleetingly washing across his face.

We hardly ever talk outside Music Theory class and usually communicate through emails in our small office. I didn't think he'd notice I've been sort of making sure our paths don't cross.

The curious, challenging look on his face sends a thrill through my veins, making me want to talk back.

And so I do.

"Why would you think that, Professor Rowe?" I ask softly, slanting my head to the side.

His eyes widen slightly, and I swear his lips twitch. But I might be seeing things. Dude never smiles.

"She talks back."

"I only speak when I have something to say."

He's looking at me again, staring at me as if he can really see me, the girl who wants to be more than her past. The girl who wants to hold on to who she is, while at the same time wants to break away from the invisible rope that tethers her to the earth. It's unnerving, and yet, having someone focus that kind of attention on me makes me feel *visible*.

He blinks and the look is gone. "Have you been avoiding me?" he asks, mirroring my pose.

Huh. Why would he care if I've been avoiding him? Maybe he senses I'm crushing on him and he's just toying around with me. Or maybe. . . maybe he feels *something*.

I laugh at that silly notion, but the noise that shoots out of my mouth is the most unattractive sound ever made in the history of this world. Professor Rowe's eyebrow arches up at the sound.

Oh my God. This is so embarrassing.

"Something funny, Miss Blake?"

"No." I spit out the lie swiftly. Way too quickly. "Why would you think that?"

"Think what?" he asks.

"That I've been avoiding you?"

"Because you won't look me in the eye, even in class."

Becauseyouhavethemostamazingeyesl'veeverseenandlookinginto-them—

"Miss Blake?"

". . . is like looking into a blazing fire." I finish my thought out loud.

He looks at me in confusion. "What?"

Shit. *Shit.* I can't believe I just spewed my thoughts out loud.

"Sorry." I inhale through my nose and exhale the words, "You're quite overwhelming."

Damn it. Why can't I just be normal around this man?

He blinks several times before he says, "Oh." He looks so cute right now as he grapples around trying to find his footing in this conversation. A ghost of a smile flits across his face before he taps his bottom lip twice and asks, "Who is your instructor for your private cello lessons?"

The abrupt change of topic gives me whiplash. Geez. Give a girl a warning, boss. "Professor Masters."

His lips slightly tighten as if mentioning that name irritates him. He nods and shifts his focus to the laptop. He starts typing and clicking his mouse, and if I could guess, I'd say he has completely forgotten I'm still in the room.

"May I ask you something?"

Leaning back in his chair, he props one elbow on the desk and waves his hand at me, so I assume this is a green light for me to go ahead and ask. The way he's watching me, though. . . *shit*. How am I even standing right now? I should be mush at his feet, melted by that smoldering look in his eyes. This man is a walking contradiction; his moods interchange between surly to smoldering. There's no middle ground, at least not what I've seen of him so far.

"You're looking at me—" I clear my throat "—again."

One dark eyebrow rises, amusement joining the wicked heat in his eyes. "Am I?"

Is he flirting with me? "Are you flirting with me?" I ask.

Those lips pull into a little half-smile smirk, like he knows something I don't. Something *naughty*. My brain and body scramble to adjust to this man's mood.

Holy sweet Mother Mary.

"That's what you wanted to ask me?" His tone of voice is light, playful even, but I can't be sure. It's just weird to see him like this

"Um. . .you are such an inspiration to me. I'm sorry about the accident." I say breathlessly, and I cringe inwardly.

Definitely not sexy. Not when I sound like I spat out the words in a hurry.

I clear my throat and plow on. "Do you think you'll go back to playing at the Symphony?"

I blame the nervousness gnawing at my stomach, just having all that intensity in his eyes on me. I can't even remember the last time anyone stared at me like I was interesting to look at. I can literally hear my skin humming with confused pleasure, and blood thrums in my veins. This feeling, this intangible emotion running through me, is addictive and freaking scary. It feeds that large part of me that craves attention. I can feel it sucking greedily, giving me a high like no other. I could easily get used to this feeling.

It's dangerous, and our situation is beyond complicated. It's highly inappropriate to have these feelings for my professor.

This has to stop. Nip the crush I've had for this man in the bud and concentrate on my studies.

His eyes leave my face and move to the laptop in front of him, taking the warmth with them.

I should be ashamed that not having him look at me bothers me.

I should be ashamed that I starve for his attention, even though I've lived the past twenty-one years without his eyes on me.

I should be ashamed because not long ago—exactly two seconds ago—I thoroughly chastised myself for allowing him to affect me the way he does.

But I'm not, and it's probably sad. I just want him to look at me one more time, which is why I find myself opening my mouth and saying, "I mean, your career was on the rise, and one article mentioned that you were being considered to take the position of the head cellist—" The rest of that sentence dies on my tongue the second he lifts his head and meets my gaze.

What I see in his eyes stops me short.

Pain.

So much pain it's a force all on its own, splitting the air around us into shreds.

I step forward without thinking, the need to console him is strong, but I stop mid-stride when his expression turns guarded.

"See you tomorrow, Miss Blake."

I shift on my feet before saying, "I didn't mean to pry—"

His eyes narrow, a muscle ticking furiously in his jaw. "Stop talking." My mouth snaps shut. "Don't you have a class starting in ten minutes?"

Right. "See you tomorrow in class, Professor."

I whirl around and literally fly out of the room, feeling the heat of his stare on my back the entire way. My eyes and nose burn. I'm not sure if the tears threatening to spill are because I'm embarrassed or because of my stupid feelings.

This is stupid. I reach my desk and shut down my laptop, then collect my things, unable to get the look on his face out of my head. I know that look, because it's the same one I see in my own eyes whenever I look in the mirror. A look born from loss, hurt and life fucking you over.

CHAPTER EIGHT

Nate

HOLY *SHIT*.

I'm not even sure what I'm feeling right now.

I want to punch the wall for showing weakness.

I want to split my head open and rip out the awful memories chopping greedily at my heart, then shove them in a dark pit.

I force myself to look away from the door Miss Blake disappeared through and run both hands down my hair.

When I walked into the office after the meeting with Bowman—after finally accepting the associate professor position—I found Miss Blake smiling, her fingers flying across the phone screen. My gaze swept across her meticulously clean desk with pens and pencils arranged in the usual way: according to color and size.

I stood at the door, taking in her relaxed features. The tight bun on top of her head—not even a single hair out of place—the way her eyes crinkled at the corners when she smiled too hard. The snort that burst out of her mouth as she read the text, the cute blush spreading across her freckled nose and cheeks.

Seeing her like that improved my already good mood and low-ered my guard. Plus, there's just something about the way she looks at me when I catch her staring unaware. Awe? At least it's different from the pity I'm used to seeing on most people's faces. I may sound like a vain prick. Fact is, I haven't felt like this in a long time, and damn if I won't chase the high wherever I find it.

Miss Blake accused me of flirting with her. Honestly? I may have been subconsciously doing it, wanting her to keep smiling.

God. She's fucking beautiful with those larger-than-life eyes that seem to say what her mouth doesn't. And those freckles on her face? They enhance her attractiveness instead of diminishing it. I fleetingly remember the screensaver photo on that fucker's phone a few weeks ago. Could he be her boyfriend? And why do I care?

I shouldn't, yet my mind keeps wandering to her even when she's not in the room with me.

She asked me if I would ever go back to playing at the Symphony, catching me off-guard. My mood went south from there. The pain—the memories—slammed into me like a tornado, ripping off the scabs from barely-healed wounds.

She probably thinks I'm an emotionally unstable asshole, when all I wanted was for her to see that I'm not a toad. Well, not on most days anyway.

Fuck if I know why I wanted her to see me in a different light than she's used to seeing me in.

I try to shake off the unsettling feeling that always accompanies her whenever we're in the same room. I can't exactly put a finger on what it is about her, which annoys me to no end. Her quiet demeanor soothes me. She's unlike most women who talk endlessly, trying to fill in the silence with idle chatter, when all you want is for them to keep their mouths shut.

Which makes Miss Blake dangerous. A woman like that has the power to get under my skin and stay there.

Eager to drown out those thoughts, I reach across the desk for my iPod. After scrolling through the playlists, I select a list and press

PLAY. "Wayward Son" by Kansas starts to play as I pick a file from the pile in front of me and flip through the documents, impressed by Miss Blake's meticulous filing skills. The names have been arranged alphabetically, and they correspond to the Excel Worksheet that she forwarded to my laptop. Little colored stickers are pinned on top of the files to indicate how many years each applicant has been practicing music. Most students who are admitted to Rushmore have been immersed in music for more than ten years.

The next few hours go by quickly as I go through the names and qualifications, making sure the applicants are qualified and up to par with Rushmore's standards. I don't like wasting time, especially during auditions, which is why I comb through the student's documents. I sit back and eye the growing pile of applications. I weeded out mostly students who haven't shown enough dedication to music to convince me they are really serious about pursuing a career in this field.

Pushing back my chair to stand up and stretch my body, I grip the edge of the table as a sharp pain pierces through my shoulder and down my spine. I'd been so caught up with work that I completely forgot to take my medication. Sweat beads on my forehead and I inhale deeply, waiting until the pain passes before sitting back down and pulling out a plastic bottle from my bag by the desk. After tossing one into my mouth, I swallow it dry and lean back, waiting for the burning sensation to recede and the feeling of weightlessness to set it.

"The prodigal son returns," a female voice says in a mocking tone, jarring me out of the peace that's cloaking me.

My head jerks up and my gaze zooms in on the woman leaning on the doorframe with her arms crossed. Her facial features—so similar to the woman from my past—twist with anger. The lightness settling in my body evaporates, replaced by a heavy throbbing inside my chest.

God, *no.* "Hello, Elizabeth." I force the words out of my mouth.

She studies me silently, a storm already brewing in her eyes. Then she steps inside the office and comes to stand in front of me. Her fists are clenched tight, causing her knuckles to whiten.

"When did you come back?" she asks casually, as if we're discussing the weather, but the hard look on her face says she'd rather I was dead.

"Last summer," I reply, feeling my body lock, readying for the shit-storm that's about to hit the roof.

"Have you started playing the cello again?"

I shake my head and wait.

"Good," she bites out with a snarl. "You took my daughter away from me, so it's only fair you got a taste of your own medicine. You poisoned Camille against me."

"Don't do this, Elizabeth," I warn in a tight voice.

"Do what exactly?" she asks, narrowing her eyes. "The truth hurts, doesn't it? You'd always been a selfish son of a bitch—"

"*Elizabeth.*"

"You took her away from *me!*" She pounds her chest, her eyes wild with resentment. She has managed to convince herself that I turned her daughter against her all these years.

"Are you serious right now?" I can feel my temper rising, no matter how much I swore I'd keep my cool if I ever saw this woman again. "*You* threw your daughter out after she told you your *husband* was making passes at her. *You* accused her of being jealous. *You* told her that you never wanted to see her again after that. *You* refused to attend her funeral. What kind of parent does that to her daughter?"

Her mouth gapes, obviously stunned by my outburst. She quickly recovers and jabs a finger in my direction. "You turned her against me! You convinced her to go with you to Chicago—"

Abruptly I'm on my feet, sending my chair crashing back into the wall behind me, forgetting where I am. "She was a fucking grown up, Elizabeth. When will you ever accept that?"

"It's your fault she's dead!" Sobs wrack her body as her hands cover her face. "She'd still be alive if you had stayed in Jacksonville and not dragged her with you to Chicago."

I'm trying hard to breathe past the pain in my chest, to hear anything other than my pulse pounding relentlessly in my ears. My hands curl into fists. I press them on the desk and drop my head forward.

Of course it's my fault. I made peace with that fact a long time ago. I don't fucking need anyone telling me the obvious, especially the woman who felt threatened by her own daughter and threw her out.

"Is that all you came here to tell me?" My jaw is clenched painfully tight. "To blame me for Camille's death?"

She clears her throat and says with a shaky voice, "The money she inherited from her grandfather. . . it belongs to me now."

I laugh bitterly and shake my head. "This can't be happening," I mutter under my breath, then say, "So that's it then. Her inheritance." The tension in my body escalates, and I feel like it is about to break into pieces. "Fucking *unbelievable*."

"But it's mine now that she's gone!" Her voice is full of indignation.

"Sorry to disappoint you. The money was donated to Lend a Helping Hand Organization in Chicago."

"You're lying."

I don't even dignify or justify that statement with an answer.

I remember the look on Camille's face when she came home one night and informed me that she wanted to use the inheritance to help other people who were in need of housing and education. The organization also fostered children who had a talent in music but had no money to further their career. I will not let Elizabeth destroy that memory.

Lifting my head, I dismiss her with a wave of my hand and say in a cold voice, "Next time you feel the urge to talk to me, call my assistant to book a fucking appointment. Have a good day, Elizabeth."

Her bottom lip trembles as she glares at me, then she turns and storms out the door.

Running trembling fingers through my hair, my eyes close tight. I take deep breaths to calm myself.

Fucking hell!

I had a feeling that woman would eventually show up in my office. I had assumed she'd pay me a visit when I was teaching the course here in Rushmore during summer break. Not that I could avoid her forever. Elizabeth teaches cello here at Rushmore. What I didn't expect was her waltzing inside my office and picking a fight with me over some stupid inheritance.

Christ.

Turning around and grabbing my chair with a lot more force than necessary, I sit down and drop my head in my hands and try to control my rapid breathing. Then I grab my phone from my desk and dial Izzy's number.

"Hey, Nate," she answers, her usual perky self.

"Meet me at Reed's at five o'clock."

"Hello to you, Mr. Manners."

"Sorry." I sigh, rubbing the nape of my neck with my hand.

"You okay?"

"Shitty day. Want to hang out tonight?"

She snorts. "Yeah, because I'm at your beck and call. Did you forget I'm a mom of two hyperactive little monkeys? And my stomach is the size of Texas and my feet. . . shit. They won't fit inside any of my shoes."

I sit back in my chair and smile. "Stop being so melodramatic, little sis."

"Melodramatic? Have you met me? I look like a whale." Her voice is high now, the latter spoken in a sob.

"You're hijacking my job," I declare in fake annoyance.

She stops sniffling long enough to ask, "What the hell are you talking about?"

"You're not allowed to make fun of yourself. That's what I'm here for."

"Jackass," she laughs, and I finally smile, delighted to hear that sound.

"Ask Mom if she can babysit the kids. We need to celebrate."

"Celebrate?" She sounds more animated now. "Celebrate what?"

I exhale, running my fingers through my hair. "I finally signed the contract. You are now speaking to Associate Professor Rowe at Rushmore School of Music."

She squeals and giggles. "Oh gosh! That is amazing! Congratulations! This is good. Very good." She finishes the sentence with a sob. "I'm so happy for you."

"I know," I say softly, knowing that if I mention the fact that she's tearing up, I'll be in trouble. Her hormones have taken over her life for the past few months, and they practically rule her mouth. She rarely goes out, instead she prefers to stay home with the kids, worried that something will happen if they are not in her direct line of sight. "Will you come?"

"You don't mind me showing up barefoot, do you?"

"Dress however you like. I just want you there with me so we can celebrate. I'll pick you up at your house."

"Shit. I need to look pretty," she mumbles anxiously. "I can't remember the last time I put on makeup. Oh my God! I need a dress that won't make me look like a hippo!"

"Hey, hey, Izzy. Stop it," I say firmly, cutting through her hysterics. "You're beautiful. You do not need makeup to look beautiful, all right? Why do you think Bennett never lets you leave his side when you're together?"

"Because I dazzle him with my smile?"

I laugh. "Yes. And because he loves you just the way you are. You had him so whipped by the time you were nineteen, he couldn't stop talking about how beautiful you were. He used to look at you like you were his lost star. Still does. Makes me gag sometimes."

She bursts out laughing. "You didn't speak to him for almost two months after you found out that he and I were secretly seeing each other."

I groan. "Don't remind me."

She laughs again, and this time I feel the lightness return to her voice. "You've got yourself a date, mister. I'll check with Mom and see if she can babysit. By the way, we'll have to celebrate again at brunch on Sunday or you'll never hear the end of it from Mom."

"Deal. Be ready at four thirty."

"Love you," she says, and she ends the call before I can say the words back.

Feeling a little relief after the phone call, I shut down my laptop and shove some files inside my bag. Between the five classes I taught today and the visit from Elizabeth, sitting in the office and pretending everything is all right is the last thing I feel like doing.

Once I'm seated inside my car, I pull the Jeep I've been using since last week after the incident out of the parking lot and drive toward Antonio's garage to pick up my BMW. After paying whatever I owe him for the repairs, I switch the cars and leave the Jeep at the garage since it's due for its annual service and drive home.

CHAPTER NINE

Elon

THE RINGING OF MY PHONE PIERCES THE SILENCE IN MY CAR JUST AS I'm pulling into one of the parking spots across from the restaurant where Sean and I are supposed to meet. I dig it out of my bag and answer without checking the screen.

"Elon, dear," my mom greets. For just a second, irritation rushes through me.

See, my mother and I have this weird relationship where I silently resent her for checking out on my sisters and me when we were young and letting us deal with our abusive father. Sure, I love and respect her. She's my mother, after all. I just don't understand why she couldn't stand up to Dad or leave his ass. I'd never show my bitterness in front of my sisters. We've already gone through so much to let trivial things like my silly feelings get in the way. And if I'm being honest with myself, I am mostly terrified of turning out to be like her. Rick is a good case in point. It took me a lot of courage to leave Rick, that bastard.

"Hey, Mom. Everything okay?"

She sighs wearily. "Can't I call you without you concluding something is wrong?"

Shit. "I'm sorry, Mom. I just—"

"You still despise me, I know. I miss you and your sisters, and sometimes. . . sometimes—" She stops talking abruptly, and I hear her boyfriend, Pete, say something in a low voice on the other side of the line.

My eyes search the front of the restaurant for my date. My jaw drops, my eyes trailing Sean as he paces up and down the pedestrian walk, dressed in a kilt and calf-length boots. He completes the look with a white T-shirt with Iron Man printed on the front and a leather vest. His long, dark hair is pulled away from his pretty face and flows down to mid-shoulder.

Were we supposed to attend a Game of Thrones-Iron Man-Braveheart convention?

My gaze wanders down to my knee-length, plum dress that hugs my curves in all the right places, black heels and a clutch to match. I don't go out on dates often, but when I do, I like to put a lot of effort into dressing up. This dress is one of my prized possessions. A sigh of disappointment passes through my lips when my gaze travels back to the boy-man across the street, but I'm trying hard not to judge him based on his attire.

"Elon?"

The sound of my name being called in my ear pulls me away from my stunned state.

"Um . . . sorry, Mom. I'm in the middle of something right now. Can I call you back tomorrow?"

Silence falls between us, causing guilt to stab my chest. Then she mutters, "Sure." A pause, then, "I love you, Elon."

"Um . . . I love you, Mom," the words stumble awkwardly from my lips. Crap. Why is it so hard to say those words to her, and yet, I find it easy to tell my sisters and Amber I love them?

Shaking my head, I shove the phone back in my purse and step out of the car.

Poor Sean is now nibbling his thumb and stopping every few seconds to look around, shaking his arms as if to throw off the nerves. He's probably just as nervous as I am. It wouldn't hurt to sit through dinner and try, for once, to enjoy someone else's company, other than a Judith McNaught novel.

I cross the street while murmuring a Hail Mary under my breath, begging her for patience and guidance and strength. As soon as Sean sees me, he stops pacing and flashes a bright smile in my direction.

"Elon, right?" he says with enthusiasm. I feel a little guilty for bitching about this date.

"Yeah." My hand shoots out in greeting, but he surprises me instead when he steps forward and pulls me into a hug, squishing me against his body. He pulls back and holds me at arm's length.

"I'm Sean. Oh man, the photo your sister sent me doesn't do you justice. You are hot."

I chuckle. "Thank you. You look um. . . interesting."

That smile grows even brighter, and he straightens to his full height. "You like? It's medieval night over at our frat house. Thought I'd just dress up for our date and the party over there later."

He's still grinning hard when he offers me his arm and I hook mine around his, then let him guide me into the restaurant. Despite my previous worries, I have to admit that it feels great to be treated nice by a guy as cute as Sean. After the headwaiter eyes us up and down, straying a bit too long on Sean, he shows us to our table. Sean pulls the chair out for me, and as soon as I sit down, he rounds the table and settles into his seat, scooting it a bit too close to mine. Our shoulders are almost touching. I catch a glimpse of his hand dipping down to adjust his junk.

Hell, *no*. He didn't just fiddle around with his crotch, did he? In the restaurant. Twice, as if to make sure everything is in place.

Another waiter appears at our table, pulling me from my thoughts.

"Good evening, I'll be your waiter for tonight." He hands us both a menu and tells us he'll give us time to look it over, turns and strides back to the bar.

Sean flicks his hair back and grins at me before his hand finds its way to his crotch. *Again.*

"Sorry. New underwear. Shit is getting real down there."

Oh, Jesus. I shaved my legs and dressed to the nines for this?

I swear this is the last time I let Elise set me up. There was this one time she set me up with a guy who couldn't stop talking about Jesus. We parted ways when he said he couldn't kiss me or touch me because I was the devil's temptation. Prior to that, he'd been urging me to dye my hair a different color because, according to him, women with red hair are Satan's little disciples. When I refused, he told me I desperately needed salvation. The little shit put the fear of God in me, and by the end of the week, I was a complete wreck. I ended up attending confession for the first time in my life for three weeks consecutively, fearing for my soul.

Even when I say no to the dates, Elise somehow ends up convincing me that I need to put myself out there for me to meet Mr. Right. What can I say? I'm a sucker for a happily ever after, even though all I've done is kiss frogs so far.

By the time my date with Sean is over—I cut it short with an excuse, telling Sean I have some homework to finish—my cheeks are permanently on fire due to the constant blushing I've done the past hour or so. The conversation ranged between hilarious and cringe-worthy.

All I want to do right now is go home, drink wine and watch cat videos on YouTube.

Inside my car, I kick off my heels and fish my phone from my bag. I quickly type a message to Elise.

Me: **You and I need to have some words.**
The phone chimes immediately.
Elise: **How was the date with Sean?**
Me: **One of a kind. I <3 you but I'm done. No more blind dates for me, sis.**

Elise: **Shit. Sorry it was a bust.**

Me: **I'm serious. I can't do this anymore.**

Elise: **Okay. No more blind dates. Please don't hate me?**

A laugh pours out of my mouth.

Me: **I couldn't hate you even if I tried.**

I toss the phone on the console and concentrate on pulling out of the parking spot.

The silence inside my beat-up Ford Fiesta is shattered by the ringing of my phone. I grab it and answer, pressing the speaker button. Amber's voice fills the space.

"Remember that swanky place I've been telling you about? Reed's Lounge?"

I squint at the traffic lights at the intersection through the windshield. "Yeah?"

"Meet me there in ten minutes. I booked us a spot."

"A spot for what?"

"Talent Thursday," she says excitedly. "An open mic of sorts."

"It's a weekday," I state firmly.

"Oh, come on, E. It's only 8 p.m. and we don't have class until 10 a.m. tomorrow."

"Amber—"

"Just two hours tops. Alex is—" Her words fade and Alex's voice replaces Ambers.

"Never thought you'd ever back down from a challenge, Freckles."

"I'm not in the mood, Alex—"

"Let's make a bet. If your performance receives more applause than mine, you'll receive an Amazon gift card worth twenty-five dollars," he announces in a confident voice, making me straighten in my seat.

"What if you win?"

He laughs. "Somehow I have a feeling you won't let that happen. But let me humor you. If *I* win, then you'll announce in class that I'm the best fucking cellist to ever walk the earth."

I laugh and say, "Too bad. That position has already been filled—"
by Nathaniel freaking Rowe.

"Feeling overconfident, are we?" he drawls with a chuckle "So, are we doing this or what?"

"Why are you doing this, Alex? Did Amber put you up to this?"

"Does it matter?" he asks. "Look, the past few weeks have been hard on you, dealing with news about that wanker Rick contacting Amber and your brother-in-law being sick. We might be competitors but outside of that, we're friends."

He's right. Thinking about Josh and how sick he has been and also the news about my ex . . . everything seems to be closing in on me. Cello is the one thing that has the power to make me relax. Make me forget about the things happening in my life.

"Fine. I'll just grab my cello from my place, then head over there."

"No need to do that. Amber brought it with her," he says quickly.

I sigh, turn the car around and drive back downtown. "I hope you have that gift card ready, Alex, because I'm planning to kick your ass."

He laughs and says, "You wish. Just hold on a sec. Amber wants to talk to you."

I hear them whisper for a few seconds, then Amber giggles before her voice fills the line. "How far are you from here?"

"Five, six blocks maybe. See you in a few minutes."

I disconnect the call and concentrate on getting to the Lounge.

As soon as I walk into Reed's Lounge, warmth engulfs me and I breathe out, feeling relieved to be out of the cold evening air. The large room is lit up in subtle lighting with the raised stage in the middle of the room illuminated with stage lights. On the second story, I notice what looks like glass booths made of black glass and steel. Very sleek.

Amber suddenly appears and pounces on me. She drags me to a booth in the back of the room where Alex sits cradling his cello like it's a baby. After a round of hugs, I shrug off my jacket. Amber and I sit down while Alex props his cello next to the table and heads to the bar to get us drinks after we give him our orders.

Amber shifts around in her seat to look at me. "You're up next—" she points at the stage, "then Alex and lastly me. So how was your date?" she yells, in an attempt to be heard above the woman shrieking "Someone Like You" by Adele on the raised stage in the middle of the large room.

"One of the most interesting dates I've ever been on," I say with a laugh, then proceed to tell her about my date with Mr. Grabbing-the-Crotch, while we wait for Alex to return with our drinks.

CHAPTER TEN

Nate

THE MEDICATION I TOOK A FEW HOURS AGO IS WEARING OFF. SWEAT beads on my forehead as my body attempts to fight off the ache slithering across my collarbone, down my shoulder and throughout my spine. The spasms in my right hand are more frequent now. I clench my fingers on my thigh to stop the tremors while shoving my free hand inside my blazer pocket, yanking out an orange plastic bottle.

Discreetly, I toss a white pill inside my mouth and swallow it dry, then cap the bottle and shove it inside my navy blue blazer before Izzy or Bennett notice my movements. Over the past few years, I've learned the art of discreetly taking pain medication. It's the only way I'd ever be able to function in society without curling into the fetal position and praying for death. A year after the surgery, my doctor at the pain clinic had thought it best to wean me off the medication. A week into the new pain regimen, I wanted to die. That and the urge to flatten everything in my path with my fist had the doctor reinstating my old dosage after I stalked into his office and threatened to tear his arm from his body.

Feeling the ache wane from my shoulder, my fingers loosen around my thigh and I sink back into the leather seat.

"Have you picked a name for the baby yet?" I ask, watching Bennett rub Izzy's feet in his lap. We made it to the restaurant an hour and a half later than planned. I couldn't get Izzy to calm down. She was utterly nervous when I went to pick her up. My sister always has the hardest time leaving the kids, even if it's just to steal away to grab a bite to eat.

"Yeah. Harper if it's a girl and Henry, after your dad, for a boy," Bennett says, a big grin on his face. He is so in love with my sister he can't see straight, which is fine with me. I would kick his ass several times over if he wasn't.

Izzy grabs his face and pulls him in for a kiss, then rubs her nose against his in an Eskimo kiss.

I look away, not because I'm embarrassed.

God, no.

Seeing them like this reminds me how amazing it feels to be held by someone that adores you and vice versa. Sometimes I miss sharing the kind of love Izzy and Bennett have so much that it causes a physical pain inside my chest. A desperate longing and unquenched thirst for someone to look at me like I'm more than my dead career.

My fingers wander to the scar on my shoulder, subconsciously tracing a path down my upper arm.

"Nate?" Izzy's soft voice calling out my name jolts me from my thoughts. "Are you okay?"

I force a smile and drop my hand, exchanging glances with Bennett. Izzy doesn't know the extent of my pain, and I made him promise not to tell her because it would just serve to worry her. She doesn't need that, especially in her current condition.

"I'm fine. Just a little discomfort."

She frowns. "Still? I thought the medication was helping."

"It does. It's not so bad." The look she gives me is full of doubt, and I roll my eyes playfully, hoping to ease the suspicion from her face.

"Have you gone back to playing the cello?"

"Not yet." My jaw clenches as I grab my beer from the table and gulp the liquid, feeling it chase frustration down my throat.

Bennett looks at me, then tugs Izzy's hand trying to catch her attention, but my sister pats him on the hand and murmurs, "Hold on, baby." She leans across the table and takes my hand into hers, giving it a little squeeze. "You will," she says in a firm voice. "You've been playing since you were five, following Dad around as he played his cello. Surely, God wouldn't take that from you. You were born for this."

He would. He already *did*.

Shit's about to fly out of my mouth, but my brother-in-law's warning glare shuts me up. So I down more beer, my gaze distractedly straying past the dark glass wall encasing us inside this booth. The view of the stage is clear from here. I can see the artists performing on the stage at the Talent Night below us. The space has been built in such a way that one can faintly hear the sounds from outside the four walls. Music filters in through the glass enclosing us. At this moment, there's a girl gesturing animatedly with her hands and making weird faces on the stage. I wonder what her talent is, maybe scaring the hell out of everyone?

I'm about to call it a night when she waves to the crowd and steps down. A vision in a plum dress holding a cello climbs on the stage. I take in the way the dress drapes that body like a second skin, and my eyes drift down to her black heels, which do wonderful things to her calves. Red hair in loose waves rests on her shoulders, spilling down her back.

Red hair.

Heat gathers in my groin, my cock twitching as Elon's face flashes through my head.

Proof number one why I should get the hell out of here. . . I'm becoming increasingly obsessed with my student. Everything reminds me of her, yet, she shouldn't be anywhere in my thoughts.

Taking in the woman's round ass and legs that make my mouth water, I stand up, ready to thank my sister and her husband for coming to celebrate with me.

And freeze.

My lungs deflate as air rushes out of my gaping mouth. Elon—my unhealthy obsession—turns around and takes a seat gingerly as if she's afraid the dress will tear, then kicks off her heels from her feet. Back straight, she parts her legs at the same time positioning the instrument between them, and I find myself standing in front of the glass walls. She turns and nods to a blonde guy—one of Reed's waiters sitting in front of a piano in the dim area of the stage. It's obvious they had discussed which song they'd be playing, given the knowing glances and nods they pass each other.

"Planning on leaving without telling us, Nate?" Bennett asks from behind me, but I can't be bothered right now. My attention has already been stolen by someone else. The constant calm, the simmering fire, the woman on the stage.

The second her bow kisses the strings, I'm out of the booth, muttering the words, "Be right back." I bound down the stairs, my good judgment no match for my feet.

On the ground floor, I position myself next to a wall, making sure my view of Elon is not obstructed, and cross my arms on my chest. I listen as she soars through the *Mission Impossible* tune, her head rocking with each beat. Goosebumps form on my skin, my breath suspended inside my chest. She stumbles on some notes but quickly recovers, but it doesn't matter. I'm spellbound, hypnotized by the beauty of both the music and the player. In the two weeks I've been here, I never bothered to wander further than my Music Theory classes and my office. Never the practice rooms. Now I know what I've been missing. *Christ*, I'd listen to this girl play from sunup to sundown and never get tired.

My gaze flicks back to where the cello rests between her thighs, roving over her creamy skin where the plum dress ends. Visions of me standing between those legs instead of the instrument fill my head. Her legs wrapped tightly around my hips as I rock into her. Her fingers, like a bow, strumming my body with reckless bliss as we compose a symphony: moaning, screaming, harsh breathing. Reaching a crescendo as she comes around my cock and I come inside her. A masterpiece.

Our masterpiece.

Quick pants leave my mouth just thinking about it.

Fuck. The things I would do to her, places I would take her with just my tongue. Places no man has ever taken her.

Yeah, I'm confident about that.

I've got three years of pent-up sexual frustration on my side boiling inside me; hands and mouth that know how to please a woman, make her keep coming back for me.

The stirring in my groin has grown into a full-blown arousal. My cock is *hard*. So fucking hard it's pressing on the front of my pants. Every molecule inside me sways with the music. I can't even remember the last time I was this aroused. It's a fact my student is beautiful, but seeing her in her element is so goddamn sexy.

She ends her performance, and air rushes into my lungs. I feel giddy, high as a kite. Could be the pain medication or the alcohol, or the woman sitting fifteen feet away.

Christ, there is no way I'll let her leave without saying something. My feet propel me toward the stage just as Miss Blake's long lashes flutter open, and the loud applause threatens to bring the house down. She smiles to the crowd, slips on her heels and stands up, holding the neck of the cello with one hand and bows her head slightly to acknowledge her audience. Her usually shy demeanor is gone. Standing there is a woman full of confidence. As soon as her eyes find mine, the air around us crackles with tension. Her gaze widens as she watches me stride toward her in determination.

She backs away, looking like she's about to flee, then changes her mind and stops. She lifts her cute chin. If what I'm feeling right now is written all over my face, then little Miss Blake has a reason to run and hide. She licks her lips when I halt in front of her, nearly blowing my load in my pants just watching her tongue brush across those red-painted lips.

"Professor Rowe." She regains her pose fast and smiles, even though her teeth skim her lip as if she wants to bite it.

I want to bite it.

"We are not in class. You can call me Nathaniel." Anyone who can play as brilliantly as she can has the license to call me by my first name. "Stunning performance, Miss Blake." My voice comes out gruffer than I intend.

"Thank you, Prof—Nathaniel." She directs her gaze to the floor, her cheeks flushing prettily. Disappointment about losing her eyes cuts through me. I want those hazel eyes on me again.

I wonder if she hears the loud thumping of my heart as it tries to break free of its cage. Does she feel this raw current that connects us, or has loneliness finally won and the attraction is all in my head? Maybe sitting around my sister and her husband, watching them moon over each other, intensified my usual warm attraction to Elon Blake. I've seen the way she looks at me when I catch her unguarded. The only way to know for sure would be to test that theory.

She's your student, jackass.

Breathing out a sigh, I run my fingers through my hair and squeeze my neck with my left hand while eyeing our surroundings.

Shit.

Miss Blake and I have unknowingly managed to attract an audience.

"Well—" she says, lifting her eyes, looking around and she stiffens. Her nervous gaze slides back to my face, then down to my crotch and she freezes. I can hear her sharp intake of breath as her eyes dart up to meet mine again.

I was so focused on getting to her that I forgot my dick had a mind of its own, practically waving at her.

Groaning inwardly, I murmur, "Excuse me," subtly readjusting my stance to allow myself relief, before striding to the hallway that leads to the bathroom.

Too bad, even after jacking off in the bathroom, my dick is far from waving the white flag. He's found something that fascinates him.

Something dangerous, forbidden. Beautiful tranquility to my raging storm.

Now I know how Adam felt lusting after the prohibited fruit in the Garden of Eden.

CHAPTER ELEVEN

Elon

HOLY. *FREAKING*. WOW.

Wow. My cheeks are on fire, and my nether regions are blazing with lust and need. I'm wearing a stupid-ass grin as I hurry toward the bar, my cello grasped firmly in my hand.

Crap. Even my nipples are hard as rocks. I've seen my share of penises in my twenty-one years. Well, maybe two penises. They were not as impressive as the bulge I spied tenting the front of my professor's pants. Honestly, there's no way I'll be able to face Amber and Alex without blurting out everything, which is why I'm dashing toward the bar to buy some time to gather myself together. I'm not a kiss-and-tell kind of girl, but I feel high, drunk from the way he was looking at me. So much passion, lust, hunger.

Need.

My brooding professor has feelings. Was I responsible for that hard-on? And why am I giddy about that fact?

I need to savor the knowledge for a minute. Or five. It's not every day I get to see my crush, my professor and boss all rolled into one, sporting a boner. King of the Bulges.

Then I remember Nick, and guilt cuts through me.

Why can't I have these feelings for Nick instead? He has had a crush on me since we moved in next door. To me, he was just a kid I used to babysit. I used to think he would outgrow his feelings, but time only served to make his crush stronger, worsening the constant guilt I have for not feeling the same way as he does.

At the bar, I choose a vacant stool located at the far end of the counter where my cello will be safe and prop it in a corner. Carefully, I slide onto the stool, making sure not to flash the patrons and give them an encore performance. A guy tending the bar sidles closer, pushing his ruffled, dark blonde hair back with a smile and leans forward, winking. "What can I get you?"

"Seriously? The wink?" I ask.

He grins. "One of the weapons in my arsenal. Did it work?"

I laugh and shake my head. "What else is inside your arsenal?" I ask jokingly.

"You'll have to come with me in the back to see for yourself." He winks again.

I giggle, enjoying this interaction. I can't even remember the last time I went out and had this much fun. "Just stop winking and serve me my drink. What do you recommend?"

He laughs, eyeing me up and down languorously. "The Cosmo. Hell yeah. Definitely the Cosmo."

"Dude. You're my spirit animal. Cosmo me up."

He shakes his head with a chuckle and goes about preparing my drink. "You're really, *really* hot."

"Um. . .thank you," I reply. What should I say? You too?

"Do you have a boyfriend? You know, a girl like you—" His words die abruptly, his gaze moving to my left shoulder.

Shifting slightly on my seat, I follow his gaze and find Professor Rowe, Sir Scowl-A-Lot, openly glaring at Sir Wink-A-Lot across the counter. The bartender clears his throat, choosing to finish preparing my drink in silence while the man beside me angles his body toward me, his shoulder brushing mine. And I die.

God, how I *die*, yet, it feels like a miracle I'm still standing here breathing his scent, a feather-light caress to my senses bringing me back to life. I run my hands up and down my arms, soothing the wild goosebumps on my skin. Being so close to him like this, knowing the effect I have on him thrills and frightens me. He does some pretty wickedly delightful things to me, stoking the fire in parts of me that crave attention, the parts that have forgotten how it feels for a man to look at me like I'm something precious. The only thing holding him back from devouring me is his control, which seems to be wearing off by the second.

He's your professor, Elon. Remember the 'no fraternizing' *rule set in stone at Rushmore? Remember your dreams? Playing with the Vienna Philharmonic or London Symphony Orchestra?*

For as long as I can remember, I've always strived to be the best in what I do. I've fought for my dreams and refused to allow my past to interfere with my future. How can I let something as simple as lust destroy what I've built so far?

"Cosmo for the lady," the bartender says, interrupting my internal turmoil.

"Thanks!" I pick up the glass and gulp down half of its contents.

"Easy, Little Wolf," Nathaniel's deep voice washes over me, sending shivers down my spine. He's close now, his ragged exhales brushing across my arm. So close I'm sure if I turn my head I would breathe his air. I can't face him though, because I'm terrified that he'll read the mayhem setting fires inside me.

Placing the glass down on the gleaming, dark wood counter, I gather my hair with my hands and pull it atop my head to keep it out of my face.

"Leave it." His voice is dark chocolate, sultry nights and dark silk sheets. "You look beautiful with your hair down."

Without a second thought I open my hands, letting my hair fall back into place, pooling over my shoulder.

Unable to postpone it any longer, I face him. I suck in a deep breath when I meet flinty eyes with specks of gold staring at me like I'm enigmatic or something.

You know that little voice that pleads with you not to do something, but you end up doing it because it's against the law of physics or something not to obey? Like trying to defy gravity but you know your butt will be hitting the ground sooner rather than later? That little voice is screaming at me, *Don't look at his crotch, Elon. Don't you dare look.*

My gaze drops to his crotch like metal being pulled to a magnet, then I grab my glass before my uncensored thoughts can slip through my lips, and I down the rest of my pink drink. It's kind of overwhelming to see your professor—who is also your boss—with tented pants.

A smirk curls across his face at my reaction, then he shifts in his seat and crosses his right leg over the left. Crap. He knows what I'm thinking.

I roll my eyes and dip my head to hide a grin. "Do you always pay compliments to your students like that?"

"No." He's still smirking, one side of his mouth curled up, and I'm melting. "I don't make a habit of cornering my students in a bar."

"Yet, here we are." The words tumble out my mouth without my permission.

One dark brow shoots up. "Yes, here we are. There's just something about you, Miss Blake. I can't seem to shake you off," he murmurs distractedly, as if he's mulling over the words.

His words knock the wind out of my lungs. I'm not about to attempt dissecting that comment, so I challenge him in a stare down, my eyebrows raised.

God, he's so hot. Why does he have to be my professor?

He chuckles. "Sometimes I think I've figured you out, but then you surprise me over and over again."

He has been trying to figure me out? Wow.

"Did you like it? The performance?"

Our bartender sidles close and sets a glass of amber liquid in front of Nathaniel. I didn't even notice Nate ordering a drink.

"Your Scotch, Sir."

Without taking his eyes off me, he lifts the glass to his lips and drinks deeply. I take in his strong jaw, watching as the muscles on his neck move as he swallows his Scotch. My thighs clench together, that single action more erotic than anything I've seen in a long time.

"Needs improvement."

Um. . . okay. "So, what would you suggest?" I ask a little too sarcastically.

He narrows his eyes in a glare, sensing my tone before saying, "Loosen your grip on the bow and the notes will flow softer."

I nod and stand up abruptly, causing him to lift a dark brow at me. "I will take that into consideration. I hope the rest of your evening goes well, Professor Rowe." I stress the latter more to remind myself of our respective positions at Rushmore.

He sets his glass on the counter, then tangles the fingers of his left hand around my hair and moves the tresses over one shoulder, exposing my neck. His chest rises in a quick inhale as he leans into me. His scent swaddles in its intoxicating warmth, and I swear he *breathes* me in.

I'm uttering Hail Mary in my head, the words *now and at the hour of our death* resounding over and over inside my head. It feels like the appropriate moment in time to pray for my poor soul because I feel like I'm dying. I'm sure coveting and fantasizing about your professor can be classified as a sin, since it's against Rushmore's law, right?

"Good evening, Miss Blake." And he pulls back, his fingers falling away, leaving me cold.

With my body buzzing with want, I let my legs carry me back to our table where Alex is sitting, his full attention on his girlfriend. Belatedly I realize I missed his performance, so I scramble to come up with an excuse.

A lie.

His eyes momentarily leave Amber on the stage and move to me, and he frowns. "You okay, Freckles?"

"Yeah—yeah, I'm fine. Why do you ask?"

He waves a hand around his face and says, "Your face is red."

"Oh," I force a laugh while rubbing a hand down my cheeks. "I think I need air. It's too hot in here."

He shoots me a weird look. "You missed my performance."

"Shit. I'm sorry." I point in the direction I came from. "I needed a drink—" His head turns toward the bar, and my heart drops to my feet when I see that Nathaniel is still sitting there.

"No worries, guess you'll never know if you won our bet or not. Dude. What the hell were you two talking about over there?"

I choke another awkward laugh. "He talked about my performance."

"And?"

"He enjoyed it, I think." Judging by the fact that his dick gave me a standing ovation, I'd say he enjoyed the performance just fine.

Alex nods, mutters something about giving me the Amazon gift card the following day, then turns his full attention to Amber, who is finalizing her violin performance.

Nathaniel and I have crossed an invisible line. I need more than a lie to forget this evening. But the truth glares at me in the face: My crush for Professor Rowe is now something more. A burning mutual attraction.

Shit. I'm in so much trouble.

CHAPTER TWELVE

Nate

THE LECTURE HALL IS EMPTY WHEN I STRIDE THROUGH THE DOOR thirty minutes before the class starts. I toss my bag on the desk, pissed off at myself for my lack of control over my fucking emotions, and start pacing while squeezing the tension coiled in the base of my neck. I spent the entire night thinking about *her*, tossing and turning in bed, frustrated, my balls tight and aching just thinking about Little Miss Blake with her pouty mouth and those damn freckles. And that *neck*. Eventually, I stormed out of my room and sat on my balcony with my vape case in one hand and a joint in the other. I spent the rest of my night until the chilly hours of dawn soothing my nerves.

I haven't been interested in any other woman like this since Camille. What makes Elon so special? Why can't I stop thinking about her?

I shake my head, dragging my fingers through my hair in frustration.

From the corner of my eye, I catch movement, followed by a soft giggling sound. I stop pacing, spin around, air catching in my throat.

I can't fucking *breathe.*

There she is, my Little Wolf, sitting at her desk with her knees pulled up. Her head is bowed low, hair in a meticulously tied-up bun on top of her head. Her chin is partially tucked inside the neckline of her oversized, black sweater. She's utterly immersed in whatever she's reading from the book propped on her knees that has her cheeks flushing prettily and her chest rising and falling rapidly. A set of pink earbuds are stuck in her ears, and one small hand clutches the earphone wires tightly while the other holds the book in place.

I suck in a deep breath through my mouth, unable to look away from the girl sitting several feet away, looking untouchable and so put together.

I want to undo that bun, rip off that damn sweater that's hiding the curves I saw last night, then do very dirty things to her. Ruin her perfection.

Fuck. I'm still high from smoking weed and imbibing Scotch to drown any thoughts of Elon and the constant guilt that followed every time Camille's face flashed in my head.

Suddenly she moans, then mutters a muffled, breathless, "*Oh God.*"

I'm standing in front of class, unable to take my eyes off her gorgeous face. Her perfectly styled hair. Her mouth, which is all kinds of innocent, sexy and sweet, purely made for kissing, and all I can think is *fuck me.* I want to kiss that mouth, undo that bun, wrap her red hair around my fist and then stand back and watch as fire flashes across her face.

What the fuck, Nathaniel?

Why her?

My mind shuts down and my body takes over, coiled tight with tension and violent need. Between one breath and the next, my legs are swallowing up the distance between Elon and me, and I halt in front of her, my breaths rough and fast in my ears. Her head jerks up, seeming to sense the shadow looming above her.

Ah, there's that pretty mouth I was missing so much.

She yanks the earbuds from her ears, the book slipping from her knees to the floor with a *thud* as she drops her feet from her seat.

"Professor Rowe." Her voice is soft, her eyes wide and her neck long and elegant as ever. "Sorry I didn't know the class has started." Her eyes dart around, and upon finding the lecture hall empty, they snap back to meet mine, a little frown marring her smooth forehead. "You're early."

"So are you," is all I can say because I'm out of breath from all the hunger for her clouding my fucking brain.

Why her? Why do I have this sheer fixation with this girl?

She leans to the side and picks up her book from the floor before straightening up and trapping my gaze with hers, and I see why I seem to be fascinated with her.

That *look*. The fire flashing in her steady gaze right now even though calmness surrounds her. She's quite a conundrum, and it makes me want to discover the true Elon hiding behind this quiet girl.

"I wanted to catch up on my reading before class started," she says, tapping the book that's now on her desk. "What about you, Professor? Did you have some reading to catch up on?" She stares up at me through her lashes, a small, teasing smile on her lips.

Oh, she's a playful little thing, isn't she? Placing my hands on her desk, I lean forward, aligning my face with hers. She gasps softly, but she doesn't pull back.

Bravo, Little Wolf. " I wanted to watch you as you walked through the door." My voice is low, barely masking the yearning wreaking havoc in me.

Those words seem to catch her off guard, but she doesn't back down.

Again.

Jesus. Why did I ever think this girl was shy?

"Lie to me, Nathaniel," she says in a conspiratorial whisper, my name husky and so damn hot on her lips. Me? I'm so hard and ready to drag her inside one of those cupboards in the front of the classroom and do things to her that will have her squirming every time she thinks about me.

My brain catches up with her words, and I frown. "What?"

"A lie." She licks her lips, hypnotizing me. Slaying me. "One sweet little lie."

I'm not sure what game she's playing, so I take a wild guess and push my face forward, staring at her parted lips. Her quick breaths softly blow against my nose and mouth. The only thing separating us now is the desk. "I really don't want to kiss you right now."

Her eyes fall shut, her head slanting forward bringing her mouth so close to mine. She inhales deeply as if she's taking in my scent and in one long breath says, "I really don't want to kiss you, too."

Lifting one hand from the desk, I brush my thumb across her full bottom lip, pressing it gently. A gasp falls from her mouth as her long lashes flutter open.

Fuck me. She's so hot with her hungry gaze, dark and needy. The craving to taste her burns through me like fire. One kiss. One taste. They're all it would take to cross the line. She's temptation and calm, wrapped in one hot package that could send me to Hell, but I don't really give a fuck right now. I've spent the past three years in purgatory. Maybe kissing her will stop the chaos in my head.

She stiffens, her gaze darting to the door, and mutters, "Shit!" She looks at the door, then back at me with a desperation that cuts through me like a knife. "Someone's coming!"

The haze in my head clears, and I hear the sound of feet shuffling and loud heckling in the hallway outside the class. I straighten and spin around, bounding down the steps that lead to the podium. Lowering my body into the chair behind my desk—more to hide my arousal—I school my features to an inscrutable expression and watch the students as their steps falter on the threshold when they notice me, then proceed to shuffle toward their respective seats. My gaze subtly drifts to Elon currently arranging her pens in order, but her hand is shaking so badly that she has to curl it into a fist before starting all over again. Her flushed cheeks puff as she blows a breath through her mouth before sneaking a look in my direction but quickly looks away when our eyes meet, worrying her lip between her teeth just as her friend Amber takes her usual place next to her, then scoots closer to the red-haired temptation at her right and says something.

Elon

My heart is beating out of my chest, and I'm out of breath. My entire body is shaking like a junkie in need of her next fix, and the whooshing in my ears makes it impossible to hear anything other than the panic tearing me apart. Amber's mouth is moving, but I can't figure out what she's saying. She snaps her fingers in front of my eyes to catch my attention, but the only thing running through my head is, *oh God, oh God, oh God, my professor almost kissed me and he smells like an invitation to the wild side.* And holy shit how I wanted to take him up on his offer. I wanted to press my lips to his so badly. I flirted back, so wrapped up in the ever-present force that seems to bind us whenever we're in the same radius.

The thudding in my ears seizes immediately at that revelation, and Amber's urgent whisper finally penetrates through my panic.

"Earth to Elon!" I blink, and her worried face comes into focus. "What's going on with you?"

"Nothing." *Think, Elon. Freaking think.* "When did you get here?"

Good one. Now she'll know something is *really* going on.

Her eyes widen, quickly filling with tears. "Is it Josh? Oh gosh, is he—"

"No! No, no." I'm quick to reassure her. "Josh is. . ." I let the sentence trail off, unable to formulate the right words. When I spoke to Nor last evening, she told me Josh's condition hadn't changed. It was just a matter of time before death claimed him.

My chest twists painfully just thinking about it. Thinking about Nor and my nieces. Any lingering thoughts of my professor momentarily taking a back seat in favor of my current fears.

"Josh is not doing great," I finally say, feeling my throat tighten and my eyes burn with tears. "I'm afraid to think of what might happen after he's gone. How will Nor and the girls move on from this?"

"You think she'll start cutting again?" she asks quietly.

I shrug. Honestly, I have no idea what will happen. I trust my sister implicitly.

When I was nine years old, I asked her if she felt weird when people stared at the scars on her arms. Her answer has stuck with me through the years, guiding me. Reminding me, no matter how big our problems are, everyone has the option to choose to survive or give up.

"No. I have a feeling she won't relapse this time. Not like after Cole left."

"She will not," Amber declares vehemently. "She might be tiny, but she's so strong. You girls are survivors."

We exchange a smile as she covers my hand with hers, giving it a quick squeeze of comfort, before pulling it away again.

I tilt my head back and close my eyes to ward off any thoughts of Josh dying. When I open them again and look around the class to make sure the lesson hasn't started yet, my eyes collide with Professor Rowe's searching gaze. A little frown has formed between his eyebrows now, which makes me wonder how long he's been looking in our direction. I swiftly look down at my hands on my lap, feeling my cheeks heat up, and clear my throat.

Amber bumps my shoulder with hers and whispers, "Hot Professor is staring at us. He's got that scowling thing down pat. I'd date him if he wasn't against the rules." She adds the latter jokingly.

Heat pools in my tummy, just thinking of that scowl. At the same time, this weird feeling slices through my chest, and suddenly I want to punch my best friend. *Hard.*

"Remember Alex? Your *boyfriend*?" I question a little too forcefully, glaring at her.

"*Sheeesh*, E. Possessive much?" She narrows her eyes at me, probably wondering where the animosity is coming from.

The bell rings again, signaling the lesson is about to begin and saving me from reacting to her question.

Thank *God*.

Turning my tense body from her to avoid any more scrutiny, I inhale deeply to calm my nerves before turning to face my hot professor in front of the class.

Nate

If I don't stop staring at Elon like a worried, lovesick puppy, someone is bound to notice. I can tell from the way she and her friend are whispering and their body language that whatever it is they are talking about is serious. The moment our eyes meet, heat slams into my groin as I remember how close I was to tasting that sweet as sin mouth of hers.

The first bell sounds, pulling me away from my staring. When I scan the class, I meet several pairs of eyes bouncing between me and where Elon and Amber are sitting. From the look in my students' eyes, I can only imagine their assumption that the two girls are in trouble or something. I guess wearing a permanent frown has its advantages.

They turn their heads downwards when my expression turns into a glare, which gives my mind a few seconds to drift back to Miss Blake before the lesson officially starts.

From what I've learned so far about Elon Blake, she's a hardworking, determined student. If she and I were found in a compromising position, she would end up being expelled and I'd lose my job. The last few weeks, my new job has been a welcome distraction from the restlessness I had been feeling these past years since the accident.

As Miss Blake's professor, I should be a better role model, not trying to seduce her.

I really don't want to kiss you, too.

Her response to my lie. *Fuck.*

I need to get my shit together.

The second bell rings to signal the start of the lesson. I ignore her for the rest of class, and as soon as the time is up and I turn my back on my students, my lungs deflate as air leaves them. Attraction and lust are two vicious beasts, and trying to ignore Elon while feeling her heated gaze on me is exhausting.

By the time I'm packed and ready to leave, the classroom has already emptied out. I sigh, relieved, before heading to my next class.

My last class of the morning ended an hour ago, which is why my ass is parked behind my desk at one o'clock in the afternoon, going over the printouts in front of me. I'm eager to put a distance between myself and Elon, and hopefully the weekend will help clear my head of the infatuation I have with her.

Adjusting the glasses on the bridge of my nose, I scan the printouts in my hands, taking in Miss Blake's meticulous work. The rows and columns are broken down into sections, showing the students who have been confirmed and are waiting to be auditioned for the two-week Strings Master class I will be teaching in the summer with three visiting professors from San Francisco and London. I'd had the pleasure of working with the latter on several occasions during my master's degree in performance at Royal College of Music.

Shouldn't there be more names here? From the list that was handed over to me after Professor Harris's sudden retirement, there was an overwhelming response for this class, and we were hoping to get in as many students as possible from local communities and Rushmore to join the lecture.

I pinch the bridge of my nose, weighing my choices: I could

either pull up the file from my computer and scour through the notes and end up spending more time in the office, or I could summon my fixation and check with her, saving time.

"Miss Blake!"

She walks into the room and stops a few feet from me, fixing her wide-eyed gaze on me. How can she look so calm and unaffected, when I feel every fucking single emotion tearing through me, reminding me of what being hopeful feels like? How feeling my heart racing like it is right now is like no other high? Ever. No one would believe she and I had a heated moment before class. Hell, I'm beginning to doubt we ever did, which pisses me off. For some stupid reason, I want to remind her how *hot* we can be.

"Is this the finalized list? Shouldn't there be more names on it?" I bite out the words and instantly regret the harsh tone.

Her eyes flicker to the papers in my hand before meeting mine, chin raised. "I went through the information the applicants provided to make sure they were qualified to take the class. Fifty-five percent of the applications didn't make the cut."

I glare at the report. "Is there any chance of getting the number to fifty percent?"

"We could try." She points to the right side on the printouts. "These are the names on the waiting list numbered according to their qualifications. I'll prepare the invitations."

I scribble some notes by hand below the waitlisted names, then glance up. "Great job."

She blinks, then stares at me like I'm a ticking time bomb. Or maybe she expects me to take back those words. Her lack of confidence in me leaves a sour taste in my mouth. She is a quiet, little thing, but her eyes. . .they say everything her mouth doesn't. And right now, she doesn't trust me.

Good girl.

Even *I* wouldn't trust me.

I clear my throat and allow my lips to lift in a minuscule smile. The change in her is like the sun breaking through stormy clouds.

Her features relax, and a smile lights up her face. If I thought she was beautiful before, she's stunning when she smiles like that.

"Thank you, Professor Rowe."

My name rolls off her tongue, and a high close to that of my nightly joints hits me hard. I shouldn't yearn to hear her say it over and over again, but I do. That thought brings everything to a screeching halt.

"You can go." I dismiss her abruptly, unfeeling even.

She flinches, her smile disappearing from her sweet face. Her fingers subconsciously move to tuck invisible strands of hair into her tight bun. Then she turns and walks toward the door with her head held high, as if I didn't just rain on her parade with my foul mood caused by my lack of control. Just before she walks out, she stops and turns to face me. Her eyes shine with something like. . .courage? Defiance? I can't put my finger on it, but it's damn arousing.

"What happened in class today?" she asks, as if wanting to reaffirm that that little scene actually took place.

"A mistake, Miss Blake," I answer back, my left hand gripping the edge of my desk to remind myself the girl standing in front of me is forbidden.

She nods, color rising to her cheeks, her lips slightly tightening. "Right. It will *not* happen again."

She turns and walks out of the room, her hips swaying gently. Even that gigantic sweater doesn't hide her full hips and sexy round ass.

Her scent floats in the air around me long after she's gone. I lean back in my seat, readjust myself in my pants, grunting in frustration when my dick hardens further just thinking about her tight little body beneath those fitted jeans and bulky sweater.

Looks like my hand and my dick have another hot date tonight with a dose of cold shower. Just like last night and every other night before that.

Great.

CHAPTER THIRTEEN

Nate

SATURDAY MORNING, I PARK THE JEEP IN A SPOT IN FRONT OF IZZY'S house and step out of my car. I promised my sister I would take my niece and nephew to the zoo, just like I've been doing every Saturday for the past couple of months to give her some alone time. My chest fills with warmth when Matthew rushes out the door, dressed in a white, short-sleeved T-shirt with the word *Pokémon* on the chest. He bounds down the steps, waving his arms wildly as he makes his way toward me.

"Uncle Nate!" he shouts, grinning wide. I scoop him up in my arms, that simple action sending a sharp pain through my shoulder and down my right arm, forcing my eyes to tear up.

Motherfucker.

"What's wrong?" Matthew pulls back, his eyebrows scrunched up in a worried frown.

Shaking my head, I force a laugh and shift his squirming body to my left arm. "Just a little sore spot on my shoulder. Ready to go?"

He beams up at me and wraps his little arms around my neck in a tight hug, nodding vigorously. He wiggles in my arms, eager to get loose. As soon as his feet touch the wet asphalt, he dashes toward the house mumbling something under his breath. I stand there, trying to regain the wind Matthew knocked out of me.

"Matthew Thomas Reed!" Izzy's voice fills the air, causing Matthew to freeze mid-run. My sister steps out the front door, one hand resting on her swollen belly, the free one holding a jacket. "Get back here and put this on."

"Oh shit," I hear him mumble under his breath before he yells, "Yes, Mama!"

"Matthew," I chide him in a low voice, half-amused. "Do you know what will happen if your mom hears you say that?"

He turns his big, brown eyes up at me and whispers, "Don't tell her. She's already mad at me."

I dart a look at my sister, then back to my nephew and fight a chuckle as I watch the mischievous twinkle in his eyes. "What did you do?"

He kicks the gravel with his boot. "I broke Kaylie's doll."

"Why did you do that?"

"She broke my Pokémon ball. So I wanted to hurt her the same way she hurt me." His eyebrows deepen a little. "Tit for tat."

We climb up the porch steps, and he takes the jacket from his mother and slips it on. Then I crouch down so that he and I are on the same eye level.

"Did you talk to your sister about it?"

He shakes his head, his curly hair bouncing around every which way.

"You think she did it on purpose?"

He shrugs and scowls harder, if that were possible.

I swear this boy reminds me of myself when I was his age. I'm two years older than my sister. She and I used to pick fights with each other at the tiniest provocation. As much as I adored her, I also wanted to declare my dominance and remind her I was the oldest between us and that she should treat me with the respect I deserved. Our mother never let us go to bed without apologizing to each other."

My gaze darts up to Izzy and we exchange a smile, her eyes gleaming with mischievousness so similar to her son's. I chuckle and look down to Matthew.

"Maybe you should talk to her first, before we leave."

He blinks, the mischievous look gone now. He folds his arms over his chest and pushes out his bottom lip in a pout. "But she started it!"

I nod and push the locks of hair off his eyes. "I know. But as her big brother, it's good to set the right example so she can learn from you."

He bites his bottom lip, the frown on his little face disappearing, and he huffs an exaggerated sigh. "Fine. Can we go to the zoo after that?"

"Sure, buddy."

And with that, he spins on his heel and darts inside the house while yelling his sister's name. I straighten from the crouched position and tuck my hands inside my jeans pockets.

"Wow. Impressive. I wish you'd have given yourself that advice when you were his age, big brother," Izzy grumbles as she turns and waddles inside the house.

I follow her and close the door behind me. "What would have been the fun in that?"

"Jackass. Leave your shoes at the door."

I do as I'm told before walking into the living room. "Short Legs," I mutter loud enough for her to hear from across the room, using her childhood nickname.

She shoots me a glare, but I see her lips twitch as if fighting a smile.

Bennett walks in from the kitchen and folds Izzy into his massive, inked arms, then says, "He's just jealous of your legs, baby. Have you seen his skinny legs? One word: Spongebob." He smiles evilly at me.

"Fuck off," I say with a laugh just as Matthew returns with

Makayla trotting after him as fast as her four-year-old legs can carry her, shouting "Uncle Nate! Uncle Nate!".

My heart tugs just hearing her call me that. So cute. She skids to a stop in front of me and waves her little arms and fingers letting me know that she wants me to pick her up, unable to resist.

She waves a pink and blue bracelet in my direction, similar to the one I've been wearing that she gave me for my birthday last year. I help her put it around my wrist, then hold out my arm for her approval. Her eyes light up, and just looking at her beaming at me like I hung the moon and the stars tugs at my heart.

"Girls are gonna fall at your feet," Bennett singsongs in his deep voice, causing my niece to giggle.

Yeah, I'm not taking that bait. Not in front of Kaylie. I have a reputation to live up to as the best uncle in the world.

"Oh hey, Nate. What happened on Thursday at Reed's?" Izzy asks.

I turn to meet her curious gaze, my chest tightening as I remember Thursday night's events at Reed's Lounge.

"What do you mean?" I ask

"You left without saying anything to Bennett or me."

I exhale a sigh of relief. She must not have noticed my strange behavior. I'm about to open my mouth and answer her when she says, "Was it that girl? The one who was playing cello?"

Shit. "I wasn't feeling too well." Bennett's brow arches up, and I decide to back up my claim and shut this down completely. "My shoulder was acting up again."

Bennett snorts, then tries to cover it with an awkward cough when my sister shoots him a frown.

You know what the worst thing is about having your childhood best friend become your brother-in-law? His ability to read you like a fucking book.

I shoot him a glare, my hand twitching to wipe the knowing grin from his face, but Izzy watches me with a worried look.

"You okay?" she questions. "You don't really need to take the kids to the zoo if you're not feeling well."

At the same time, Bennett asks, "Your shoulder, huh?"

What the fuck, Ben? What happened to the bro-code? It's like he cannot understand the look I'm giving him, you know, the look that lets him know we'll talk about this later. Or he's so blinded by his love for my sister he can't see straight.

Pussy-whipped fucker.

"I'm good." I fire another warning look at Bennett. He seems to take the hint this time.

Matthew starts jumping up and down, impatient to leave. Makayla frames my face in her tiny hands and kisses my cheek repeatedly.

Bennett turns Izzy around to face him, looks into her eyes as if she is his entire universe and says, "Why don't you get the snacks I made for the kids from the kitchen while your brother and I finish getting the kids dressed?"

She nods, smiling, and pecks him on his lips, then trudges toward me. "Thanks for taking the kids, Nate," she says, smiling through the tiredness heavy in her eyes that I hadn't noticed before now.

I shift my niece in one arm and pull Izzy close with my other hand, then kiss her forehead. I meet her drained gaze. "I'm making up for lost time. Sucked that I couldn't spend time with them while living in Chicago."

"Can we go now?" Matthew asks, tugging at the leg of my jeans.

"Yeah, Uncle Nate. Can we go now?" Makayla yells.

"Hey, Matt, buddy. Do me a favor? Can you go upstairs and fetch Lily for your sister, please?" Bennett says to his son, referring to Makayla's cuddle bear.

Matthew props his hands on his hip and says, "Dad! They're going to close the zoo before we get there."

"No, they won't. Just run upstairs and get it for her, will you?"

He scowls and stamps his foot, then scampers toward the stairs.

As soon as he's out of sight and Izzy goes to grab the snacks for the kids, I shoot Bennett a glare. "Why the hell does my sister look like shit?"

He runs both hands through his hair and sighs. "Low iron count. She's taking all kinds of supplements the doctor prescribed for her to bring it up to the normal level." He waves at me to follow him as he turns and walks toward the front door. He grabs Makayla's jacket and hands it over to me. "So, who's the girl?"

I set Makayla on the floor and proceed to dress her with my back facing Bennett. "What girl?"

"The cello player last night."

"Just some girl." My tone of voice should warn him not to push it.

Apparently, he ignores the proverbial red flag and says, "Huh. Some girl? Must be one lucky girl because you were staring at her like she was some kind of miracle-delivering goddess or something."

I don't even attempt to dignify that with an answer. When I'm done zipping up the jacket, I grab the red boots with yellow daisies on them—her favorite—and slip them on her socked feet. I straighten only to find Bennett staring at me through narrowed eyes.

"Drop it, Ben," I say firmly, sending him a glare.

He lifts his hands in surrender and says, "Fine. Can I give you a piece of advice, though?"

"No," I growl, making little Makayla's head snap up in shock.

He ignores me and forges on. "I'm just going to rip off this Band-Aid. If you focus on the past, you'll never find a reason to move forward. I saw the way you looked at that girl. Follow this—" he thumps the left side of his chest, "instead of this—" his index finger taps his temple. "Your ass is too good-looking to go to waste."

"Thanks."

"My pleasure, darlin," he says in a teasing voice. "Now get your fine ass out of here. Time for me to spoil my wife."

With Makayla's tiny hand in mine, we step out to the porch and wait for Izzy and Matthew to return. Bennett's unwanted advice rings through my head, and as much as I'd like to ignore it, I can't. But at the same time, I'm not ready to move on from the past. I seek absolution in everyday life. I look for signs to show me that I deserve to move on.

Maybe someday soon I'll be able to do that, but for today, for now, I'm going to spend the weekend with my family and fucking spoil them. Life is unpredictable, a lesson I learned cruelly.

CHAPTER FOURTEEN

Nate

By Monday morning, I have managed to convince myself the almost-kiss was a mistake, and the reason why I couldn't breathe properly whenever Elon is near, or whenever I think of her, was just my lungs playing tricks on me.

Until she walks through the door, her nose buried in a different book from the one she was reading last week, earbuds stuck inside her ears. She doesn't even look up as she climbs the stairs to the third row and shuffles to her seat without stumbling or checking where she is going. My heart does this little dance in my chest, and there's this awful thrill in my stomach.

It's so pathetic the way I'm staring at her right now. If Bennett were here, he'd be laughing his ass off at my expense.

One thing is for sure. Nothing about Elon is a mistake, and my lungs aren't playing tricks on me. It's simple. She takes my breath away without even trying.

The bell rings, and the most torturous class I've ever taught begins, launching an internal battle of staring versus not staring at Miss

Blake. I lean my ass on the table behind me and wait until everyone is seated before picking up the sheet music next to me and turning to face twenty pairs of eyes in front of me. My eyes momentarily hold Elon's wistful gaze—looking a little dreamy probably from whatever she was reading—before moving to the rest of the students.

"If you haven't submitted your assignment yet, you have until two o'clock this afternoon to bring it to my office. Any paper delivered after that time will be disqualified." Disgruntled murmurs sweep across the room. I lift my hand and hold it up, effectively stopping the noise, then sharpen my gaze. "You had two weeks to finish your work," I say, leaving no room for discussion.

"Before we move on to the next chapter, who amongst you brought their instruments with them today?"

A few hands go up, including Miss Blake's. And because I'm a sucker for pain, I call her name along with Amber and Joseph, a black-haired kid who plays the oboe, and motion with a slight nod for them to come down to the podium. I point to the three chairs I set up when I got here, then pass the music sheets to the three players, making sure to brush my fingers on Elon's. She jolts in her seat with a gasp. Heads turn in her direction, and she fakes a cough to cover her reaction. I'm an ass for doing that to her, but I can't help it. She brings out the best and worst in me.

Elon

Shiiiiit.

What the hell is he doing? One wrong move and rumors will spread like wildfire.

Inhaling deeply, I watch my professor as he explains the exercise to the class, then turns and instructs Amber, Joseph and me to take ten minutes to study the sheet music he gave us. The sleeves of his pristine, white shirt are rolled up to his elbows, exposing his strong forearms. I zone out a little, mesmerized by the lines of veins that run down the back of his hands. The dark hair scattered down his forearms, the cute purple bracelet on his wrist—

"*Miss Blake!*"

And I jump again in my seat, my cheeks and ears on fire because *ohmygod* I totally want to lick his strong wrists.

I focus on Professor Rowe. He's wearing his signature closed smirk, as if he knows I was ogling him. "Are we keeping you from anything important?"

I straighten, try not to die in my seat, and attempt to pretend I'm not this close to having an orgasm just thinking about *those* veins. He knows exactly the effect he has on me.

Jackass. "No, sir."

"Good." His impressive chest expands as he takes in a deep breath. "You have ten minutes to go over the fugue. After that, decide who plays first, then who joins after that. Then present this piece to the class."

We nod, and I drop my gaze to my sheet music, but not before catching a glimpse of his tight butt in those fitting grey pants.

When the time is up, I reposition the instrument between my jean-clad thighs, my bow posed above the strings ready to play.

Damn it, my palms are sweating hard, and the bow keeps slipping from my fingers. I've never been this nervous in my life, not even when I auditioned for Rushmore. That was a cake-walk compared to this: playing a four-minute fugue while Professor Rowe's unnerving gaze is on me.

I search for the culprit, find him sitting in *my* seat, his long legs parted in a casual pose. One arm rests along the back of the vacant chair next to him, while his free hand taps idle staccato beats on his thigh.

His head moves in a curt nod, a sign for us to continue. I glance at Amber, then Joseph, and they return the look. Amber nudges me with her elbow, her eyebrows raised in question. We agreed I'll be the first to play, but my muscles aren't cooperating.

"Any day now, Miss Blake," Professor Rowe says in an almost bored voice. I inhale deeply, ready to play, but he speaks up again. "Imagine I'm the judge and you just have one chance to impress me. Play for me. Enthrall me. Seduce me. Win me."

How am I supposed to regain control when all I can think about is seducing him?

"Play for *me*." His eyes move from Amber, then Joseph, and lastly to me, lingering longer than would be deemed appropriate. I swear the way he stresses those words, his eyes pinning me where I'm sitting, it's like he's speaking to me. When I look at Amber, she doesn't seem as affected as I am.

Taking a deep breath, I pose, ready to play, my eyes fixed on his. He wants a show, I will give him one. The urge to shock him flows through me. I drop my gaze to the sheet music.

I let the notes flow from my fingers to the bow. I break eye contact and sink into the music. I'm in the zone where nothing matters, where music is the only thing that exists. No pain or suffering. No anxiety. Just me and the notes. I'm completely engrossed in the music, the depth of the notes.

After the little performance and a round of applause, we return to our seats, adrenaline rushing through my veins.

Holy shit. That felt good.

When the bell rings to signal the end of the lesson, I tell Amber and Alex I'll catch up with them shortly, that I want to discuss some last-minute details with Professor Rowe regarding some work in the office. As soon as the class clears, I sling my cello over my shoulder, grab my bag, then descend down the stairs.

"Great performance, Miss Blake," he says without looking in my direction.

Was his voice like this before?

I wait for him to stop packing his things inside his bag, to look at me at least.

When he doesn't, I march forward until I feel the heat coming off his body wrap around mine. His head snaps up to look at me, then his eyes do a quick sweep around the class before focusing on me again.

We are so close, I can see the gold flecks in his grey eyes. He really does have beautiful eyes. I bet they'd be more noticeable if he didn't scowl so much.

"You touched *me*," I whisper, tossing a quick scan toward the door to make sure we are alone.

His brow goes up, his eyes studying me for several seconds. "I did."

"Why?" I'm trying to keep my cool, but—"What the frigging hell?"

His eyes narrow to slits. "Watch your tone, Miss Blake," he sharply scolds under his breath.

I take a deep breath and bite my cheek to collect my scattered thoughts, but his scent overwhelms me and I feel myself being drawn to him like I'm Earth and he's my axis. I'm spinning and spinning, tethering him to me, and him touching me will be my undoing and—"You can't touch me like that." My thoughts spill out of my mouth.

"Stop," he growls, sending my heart somersaulting inside my chest.

"What?" I breathe.

"One sweet little lie, Elon."

A lie. Is he serious right now? He wants to play this game when I feel so nervous I'm about to puke all over his well-fitting pants?

And the smirk is back, challenging me, spurring me on. Teasing me.

My hands flex, fighting the stupid nerves. "I don't like the way I feel when you are close to me. Or when you touch me."

He snaps his bag shut and within seconds, his face is right there in front of mine, eyes dark, his jaw clenched as if he's barely holding onto his control. "Run, Little Wolf. Run before I ruin you. God, how I want to ruin *you*."

At first, I don't move. I just stand there, my brain yelling, "*Ruin me!*" As if he can read my thoughts, his head moves down an inch and

I push myself up on my toes, my chest slightly pressed against his, our breathing ragged. His nose brushes the length of my neck, and I swear I feel his tongue skim the vein pulsing there.

"Leave. *Please.*" He sounds pained, his grip on control barely there. His voice snaps me from the trance I'm in, reminding me where we are and that anyone could walk in and find us in this standoff.

I've been following rules and always do my best to stay out of trouble, which is why this big shift inside me, this rebelliousness so alien and exhilarating and *scary*, is giving me a thrill and before I know what I'm doing, I'm blurting out my phone number in a rush.

"*What?*" And now he's staring at me as if I'm crazy.

Adrenaline courses through me, injecting boldness into my blood. "Call me if you want to. . .um. . . kiss. Do more than kiss—"

Shut up, Elon.

I see the second the shock wears off. His eyes turn dark, his body locks as if he's ready to pounce and mine uncoils ready to flee.

One. Two. Two and a half.

It only takes two and a half seconds, then he's moving forward and I'm stumbling back, back, back until the cello hits a wall and he's standing in front of me, his large frame blocking my view. He unhooks the straps of the cello case and sets it aside, taking my backpack along with it. Then his chest is pushing against mine, his left palm braced flat on the wall on the side of my head. He's touching me everywhere without really touching me, and I'm melting, dying, breaking, tasting pandemonium. His mouth hovers above mine, his breath fanning my lips. I'm a star, burning through the sky. I'm falling, plummeting to Earth faster than gravity. I'm smiling now because this feels like being adored, appreciated. Wanted. Something I've never experienced before. My eyes fall shut as his lips brush my brow, cheek, jaw, whispering words that mean nothing and *everything*, and I'm no longer dropping. I'm flying, breaking gravity.

Suddenly the heat of his body on mine disappears, and a harsh "*Fuck!*" leaves his mouth. It's like someone dumped cold water down the back of my shirt. My eyes fly open and find Nathaniel pacing a tight line between his desk and the lectern, running his fingers through his hair. He stops and turns to face me, his face unreadable.

And I hate it.

"Elon—"

"Don't ruin it," I beg quietly, cutting him off.

He moves closer, his steps faltering a few feet away from me as if he's terrified of being close to me. "I *ache* to do so much more than kiss you, Elon. It's driving me fucking insane. If we—" He stops talking and rubs his neck with his left hand, and declares in a rough voice, "I *crave* you."

Well, knock me over with a feather and color me speechless!

The world could disintegrate beneath my feet, and I wouldn't even feel it.

Laughter drifts from the hall just before the bell sounds. I jolt upright, pushing away from the wall where I'm stuck trying to catch my breath and cool the fire raging down under. I reach for my cello and bag where Nathaniel set them against the wall and swing them both over my shoulder, then head for the door. On my way out, I quickly turn around and repeat my phone number because now I know. Now I know he *aches* to do more than just kiss me, too.

Take a chance, Nathaniel. Take a chance on me.

Amber and Alex are long gone when I finally emerge from the lecture hall.

For once since school started, Professor Rowe doesn't show up in the office that day. I try not to be too disappointed, justifying this might be the right way to handle this.

Once my lunch break is over, I head to my next class. I'm nervous as hell, and I find myself walking around with my nose buried in a book just to avoid making eye contact with anyone, afraid they will easily see the guilt, excitement, fear, and lightness exploding inside me.

The thing is, I don't regret my feelings for Nathaniel. Maybe a little trepidation, given my history with men, but remorse?

None.

The worst thing is I want more.

More of him, more of the way his eyes light up when he looks at me.

More of the way my heart misses several rhythms before it picks up a million beats, trying to catch up with my breaths.

More of the way he makes me feel so good, wanted.

By the time I get home that evening, I'm dizzy from the emotional rollercoaster I've been on since morning. Thank God Amber is staying over at Alex's place three floors up.

Tonight I need to relish this feeling and carefully plan my next move.

Professor Nathaniel won't know what hit him. I just discovered my favorite drug, and I *need* more.

CHAPTER FIFTEEN

Nate

WEDNESDAY ARRIVES AND I'M STANDING IN FRONT OF MY CLASS, watching as the students shuffle in.

Subtly, I shake a pill from each of the two bottles in my bag and throw them inside my mouth to stop the minor tremor and pain already building in my upper extremities. I grimace as the bitter taste spreads across my tongue before swallowing them dry. Then I turn my attention to the class again.

After that little standoff with Miss Blake a few days ago, I made sure our paths didn't cross. I've resulted to going to the office after four o'clock in the afternoon. Not that I'm afraid of her.

I'm terrified of myself, scared of what I might do to her if we're alone in the same room again. I can't look at her without wanting to kiss her, to touch her. I've stayed away to keep her safe from me, knowing full well if given the opportunity, I'd end up destroying her with this volatile need I have coursing through my veins. Case in point, she probably has a boyfriend—Mr. New York. Plus, she's my student, something I've told myself over and over to convince this stupid heart. I'm starting to sound like a broken record.

It doesn't stop me from darting glances at the door, waiting for her to appear. My breath is stuck in my throat like a fucking teenager before his first prom, waiting for his date to climb down the stairs.

The bell rings, but there's still no sign of Elon. I glance at Amber. She is staring at the door with a little frown on her forehead. She leans to her right and whispers something to Alex. He shakes his head, his gaze flickering over to me before pulling out his cell phone. For just a second, my chest tightens, wondering if he is aware of my transgressions. His eyes didn't have any curiosity in them, so I assume he is unaware of my feelings for his friend.

I stride to the door and grasp the knob, ready to push the door shut when Elon appears in front of me a frazzled mess. I frown, taking in her messy hair and attire. It is as if she grabbed whatever she could find and threw it on before rushing to class.

"Miss Blake?"

She freezes mid-step with her head bowed down, her cheeks flushed and her nose red from the chilly morning outside.

Standing next to her, with his arm wrapped tightly around her shoulder, is a tall boy I've never seen before. He drags his fingers through his messy brown hair, his blue eyes lighting up on Elon like she is his world. He's too pretty. I want to smash my fist into his perfect features.

"You're late," I bite out the words. She flinches at my harsh tone but quickly recovers her pose.

Her back snaps straight. She lifts those goddamn beautiful eyes, rimmed with dark circles as if she hasn't had a good night's sleep in days. Blood thrums in my veins, the need to comfort her clawing at me. I want to hurt whoever made her cry.

"I'm sorry for being late," she apologizes in a flat voice.

Pretty Boy clears his throat and says, "Sir? I'm sorry—"

I round on him, glaring, and spit out, "Who are you?"

His eyes widen, taken aback by the threat in my voice. "Um. . .Nick Holloway."

"Do you go to school here?"

He shakes his head. " I attend the University—"

"Then I suggest you leave," I cut him off, dismissing him with a look. *Clearly, I've gone mad.*

Pretty Boy sends me a death glare before taking Elon's shoulders in his huge-ass hands and turns her around. "Call me if you need anything, and I'll be here as fast as I can."

She nods, and he wraps his arms around her. I avert my gaze, my stomach churning with. . .I'm not sure what. I just know I want to do some major damage.

As soon as he walks away, my attention reverts to Elon. Fire has replaced the gloom in her eyes, chin raised, lips pressed into a stubborn line. Her fingers grip the strap of her cello case as if it's a lifeline.

I scowl down at her cute, upturned nose. "Punctuality is a virtue. 8 a.m. is *my* time. Whatever you do before that is your own business." I cock my brow at her in question, some kind of sick thrill rushing through me as I watch the flames lick through her cool facade.

She squares her jaw, narrows her eyes. "Fuck you," she hisses passionately under her breath, in a low voice that doesn't travel far, knocking me flat on my ass. Then she steps around me and marches to the third row and takes a seat next to Amber.

Fuck me sideways. What a little firecracker! I should punish her for her insubordination. Thing is, I can't find it in me to douse the fire in her eyes.

I bite back a grin, shut the door, and retrace my steps to the podium, belatedly realizing the little altercation has managed to gain an audience.

"Open your books to chapter thirteen," I order the class, effectively breaking the tension and sending hands scrambling to pull textbooks from inside of their bags. I dart a look to Miss Blake and find her talking to Amber in hushed tones. Alex cranes his neck in their direction as he tries to eavesdrop. The conversation stops the second they catch me watching them.

After instructing the class to read through the chapter before our discussion begins, I take a seat behind my desk, my stubborn brain choosing that moment to analyze what happened.

I was a dick. My harsh behavior was unnecessary, but seeing Elon with Pretty Boy turned me into the Neanderthal Camille used to accuse me of being, albeit playfully.

Nothing could explain my actions, other than I was jealous.

Shit.

I was fucking *jealous*.

Surprised by this revelation, my jaw tightens until I feel my teeth crack. My gaze wanders around the class, drawn in by temptation in the third row. I catch her swiping her cheeks with the sleeve of her bulky, black sweater before Amber pulls her in for a quick hug. I want to be the one holding her, offering her comfort.

Elon

I should have called in sick today and stayed in Willow Hill with my family. After my last class yesterday, I drove straight to the hospital to visit with Josh.

Unfortunately, his condition has gotten worse, and it's so hard to watch him suffer. We were just talking, and the next second the monitors attached to his body started beeping wildly, then he flatlined. Within minutes of me being shoved out the door by a nurse and the horde of doctors working hard to save him, the machines stuttered to life, racing to catch up with his heartbeat. I've never been so emotionally exhausted in my life. Every time I think about it, telling Nor and her daughters that the man who had taken care of them, the man they loved so much, has passed away, makes me tear up.

Right after leaving his side, I went to the hospital's chapel and prayed for God to take him just to stop all the suffering he's going through. Does that make me a bad person?

The doctor says he's not ready to leave us yet. I don't know what to think. Damn it, every time I close my eyes, Joce and Cora's identical, scared little faces flash inside my head.

What the hell am I doing here?

I should be with my family.

I start packing my books when I feel someone staring at me. I glance up and meet Professor Rowe's gaze searching mine, his brows creased in what I assume is worry.

He summons me with a subtle nod of his chin. I stand up and make my way toward him.

I hate how weak I feel right now, hate that I can't control the tears falling down my cheeks. So instead of heading left where the professor patiently waits for me, when my foot hits the last step, I mumble, "Excuse me" and stumble out the door into the hallway and duck into the girls' bathroom. I lurch inside the first stall near the door and flip the lock shut, turn around and slam down the toilet seat before collapsing on top of it.

I take in deep breaths, trying to calm down while asking myself if I should leave the school grounds, then call Amber to grab my things and bring them home.

Crap. My car keys are in my bag.

I could walk back in class and politely excuse myself, pick up my stuff and leave with my head held high.

The sound of the restroom door squeaking pulls me away from my thoughts.

"E? You in there?" Amber's voice shatters the silence. I straighten from the seat and open the door. "I brought your things. I spoke to Professor Rowe, so you're excused—Oh, babe!" she exclaims when she sees my blotchy face. Amber props the cello on the wall, then pulls me into her arms. "I'm coming with you."

I move out of her arms, shaking my head. "I'll be fine. I just need a few hours to rest and decompress. I guess yesterday's experience with Josh affected me more than I thought."

She bites her lips studying me, then says, "You sure?"

"Yes." I smooth the frown marring her forehead with my finger. "I'll be fine."

"Okay. I'll pick up whatever notes I can get my hands on from today's classes for you. Here's your bag and keys." She slides it along my arm and drops the keys in my outstretched hand.

"Thanks. I really appreciate it."

She bumps my shoulder and quickly reaches behind and tugs my bun. "That's what I'm here for. Are you driving to Willow Hill?"

"I'll need to check with Nor first."

She nods, gives me another quick hug and leaves the restroom.

I hurry to the sink and splash water on my face, then grab a few tissues from the dispenser and pat it dry. Picking up my cello from where it rests and stepping into the hall, I'm almost at the practice rooms when I hear someone call my name.

"Miss Blake?"

I tense when I realize that deep voice belongs to none other than Professor Rowe.

What is he doing in here? "Professor Rowe?"

He strides toward me, watching me intently. He stops in front of me and shoves his hands inside the pockets of his pants.

"What are you doing here?" I ask, my breath stuck in my throat.

"Is everything okay?" His worried gaze searches my face and he curses under his breath, taking a step forward with his hands lifted, as if to cup my face. He catches himself and drops his arms, shoving his curled fists inside his pockets.

I nod and at the same time say, "Yes."

"You've been crying."

I force a laugh. Isn't that what happens when your heart bleeds? When you feel like your world is falling apart? "You should be in class teaching."

Besides, won't other people wonder where he went?

"I'm concerned about your well-being as my student." Silence. Deep breath. "Don't worry. Your classmates are occupied having group discussions."

It occurs to me I probably look like I spent the night drenched in tears, and I avert my face. "Shit. I'm such a mess. You shouldn't see me like this."

"You think seeing you cry bothers me?"

"It should." Some people look pretty when they cry. Me? "Not a pretty sight. There are tears and snot everywhere."

He chuckles softly. Then, he scans up and down the empty hallway before reaching down for my hand and dragging me toward practice room number three.

"What the hell are you doing?" I whisper, trying hard to catch up with his long strides.

He doesn't answer me, just opens the door and pulls me deeper into the dark room. I hear the sound of the door closing as my feet scramble to match his pace.

Moments later, the sound of a switch being flipped on fills my senses right before a door clicks shut and bright light threatens to blind me. My hand flies up to shield my eyes from the harsh light.

"Jesus. Warn a girl before you blind her," I mutter in a disgruntled voice. "How were you even able to navigate the way in the dark?"

"I know these rooms like the back of my hand." He answers in a matter-of-fact voice.

When my eyes finally adjust to the light, I see Professor Rowe looming above me. He's still wearing his impenetrable gaze, but there's something fighting to break free.

A flicker of heat.

Lust.

I glance around the room filled with music instruments and music stands before looking up at him. Now he's looking at me again with that unreadable expression that I loathe.

"What are we doing in here?"

He ignores my question and asks, "Tell me what happened?"

He risked being seen and dragged my ass in here to ask me that? Wow.

"Do you really want to know?"

He nods, crossing his huge arms over his chest—and lets out a wince probably from pain on his right arm—and looks down at me earnestly.

"Well, my brother-in-law almost died yesterday while I was staring at him helplessly. I wish I could save him. But like you said, this is *your* time, so I'll deal with this during my own free time." I throw the words back at him.

His gaze softens as he takes a step forward again, crowding me, his wide shoulders blocking my view. "I'm sorry. I had no idea. I'm an asshole."

He leans his head down a notch, and instead of pulling back, I sway toward him as his lips brush my cheek, skimming my skin, sending a shiver down my spine, and I have to curl my hands into fists around my sweater to stop myself from touching him. "Tell me what you need," he murmurs.

I'm shocked by those words, mainly because he is the first man to ever say them to me. My head slants back and I blink up at him, searching for the right words. "I'm fine."

He lifts his hand and, without warning, runs his fingers through my hair, pushing the loose tresses behind my ear. He grasps my chin between his thumb and index finger, lifting it up and bringing his face close. So close I can smell his minty breath. His cologne, something like bergamot and the woods.

My breath hitches, the thudding in my ears deafening.

"What do you need?" he asks, but there is more force, more passion behind the words this time. More fire and concern in his grey eyes.

Panicking because of the massive amount of emotions ripping through me, I pull my chin from his grasp. "Why do you care?"

He scowls down at me but catches himself, and the look is swiftly replaced by an impassive one.

"Go home. I will speak to your professors to let them know you're not feeling well."

He turns around to leave.

"But—"

He stops and looks over his shoulder. "That's an order, Miss Blake. Go home."

Who does he think he is ordering me around? I shake my head and step forward, but his next words stop me.

"Just go, Elon. All right?" His gentle voice strokes the syllables in my name like a lover's caress, his eyes soft.

I feel the anger simmer down a bit, and I nod.

His fluctuating moods confuse me. One minute he's warm and gentle, and the next he's scowling at me—which is kind of hot. It's like there's battle tearing him apart, pulling him in different directions.

I want to be the one who tapers that war inside him.

That thought shocks me, causing me to take a step back, but there's no place to go. He's everywhere: his scent, his dark eyes now smoldering with a feral look that reminds me of a predator, sending my heart into overdrive.

One. Two. Three sprinting heartbeats.

"You have a free period, right?" I ask quickly before I have a chance to change my mind.

He doesn't answer, because he knows I know his schedule, so my question was rhetorical.

He's still staring at me and I can't read him, and it makes me nervous.

But I've subconsciously made up my mind, and before I can back out, I open my mouth and blurt, "347 Bridget Way. House number 44. Apartment 5. No one is around during the day." I add the latter in a quiet voice, feeling stupid and second-guessing myself.

I gave him my number.

He never called. So why am I giving him my address?

One dark brow goes up.

Ohmygod!

I mentally slap my forehead.

He probably has a girlfriend, and I keep throwing myself at him—

"Shit. I'm sorry."

"Why are you sorry?" he asks without preamble, a frown on his face.

I lick my lips, trying to collect my scattered thoughts. It's almost impossible with him standing so close to me. "You probably have a girlfriend or a wife or whatever."

"No girlfriend or wife or whatever," he murmurs, and suddenly I have wings and I'm soaring at that revelation. "Be careful of what you are asking for, Miss Blake." His words sound more like a threat than a warning.

"I've been careful my whole life, Professor. Sometimes you just have to take a chance."

He studies me, eyes full of questions. "Is he your boyfriend?"

"Who?" I ask, frowning. "*Alex*?"

He shakes his head, and I'm wracking my head wondering who he means. The only other person who seemed to bring out the worst in him was—

"*Nick? No.* No, he's my friend. He's Josh's brother."

"Josh?"

"My brother-in-law. We've been close since my family moved next door to the Holloways—" *Shit.* "Sorry. I'm rambling. Anyway. He's not my boyfriend. I don't have a boyfriend, and *please* make me stop talking before I start rambling again."

He laughs softly and dear God, that *sound*! It's unexpected, warm, real. Coming from those lips of his, it's like a promise of dark, sultry nights. I watch it take over his body, his brooding demeanor changing to *breathtaking*.

"You're cute," he says with a chuckle.

"Wow, thank you," I mutter under my breath. "*Cute*."

He rolls his eyes, his lips twitching, and I know he's suppressing a smile. He lifts my chin with a finger. "Unusually stunning. Quirky." He brushes the tip of my nose with the tip of his finger, drops his hand and shakes his head. "I shouldn't be drawn to you like this, but I am. The worst thing is I have no fucking clue how to stop feeling this way."

His head dips and my breathing stalls in my throat, my eyes falling closed and my head tilted up. Waiting, waiting, waiting.

But his lips never find mine.

I open my eyes to find him staring at my mouth, the look in his eyes feral. Yet, he won't kiss me.

He draws in a deep breath, his body visibly shaking with the effort of holding back. Nathaniel steps away from me and says, "See you tomorrow." Then he unlocks the door and leaves.

I'm smiling wide because dude, he touched me. He's losing control, and *he has no fucking clue how to stop feeling this way.*

I did that to him.

Cute, unusually stunning, quirky, *me.*

I wait until I hear his footsteps fade, then the sound of a door closing before ducking out of the cupboard..

After switching off the light, I step into the empty hallway, darting a look in the direction of the lecture hall. My heart misses a couple of heartbeats when I see my cello tutor, Professor Masters, talking with Nathaniel. They seem to be having an intense conversation given the deep frown on Professor Rowe's face and the angry look on Elizabeth's.

I spin around and stride toward the exit door without looking back.

Nate

My heart literally screeches to a halt when I find Elizabeth leaning on the doorway of the lecture hall, her arms folded on her chest. There's no way I can walk into the room without manually uprooting her from her spot and pushing her aside. So I stop in front of her out of respect for her daughter and meet her hate-filled gaze.

"What do you want, Elizabeth?" I ask, choosing to be the first to attack in this silent battle.

Before she can answer, I hear footsteps echoing down the empty hall in the direction I just came from. My breath catches like it does every single time Elon is within my vision. Even standing next to danger, knowing full well she could destroy me, my body can't hide the pull toward the woman walking in the opposite direction.

Elizabeth flicks a glance over my shoulder, surprise flickering in her gaze, then looks at me.

Fuck.

Her warped brain must be formulating all kinds of scenarios right now. What the fuck does she want? I thought after our exchange in my office a few weeks ago, she'd never talk to me again. From the way she walked past me every time our paths crossed after her visit, you'd think I was nothing but air. At some point, I believed I no longer existed in her world.

Yet, here she is.

I'm quick to wipe off any feelings I have for Elon, while my brain searches for a way to get us out of this predicament. The morbid curiosity in her eyes sends shivers down my spine. She saw me leave the practice room for fuck's sake, Elon following behind in the space of a few minutes.

"So you conduct private music theory lessons in the practice room these days." It's more of a statement than a question.

Apparently, I wasn't quick enough in hiding my reaction to Elon. If she's trying to bait me, then she's barking up the wrong tree.

"Did you need anything?" I question in a bored voice.

Her eyes narrow, her mouth twisting in an ugly sneer. "Stalking students, I see."

My temper flickers to life and I get in her space, looming above her, my eyes narrowed. "I'm going to ask you again. What do you want, Elizabeth?" My voice is low, barely hiding the anger brimming beneath the surface. She blinks up at me, and I can see she's trying to hold on to the nonchalant facade. "Now, unless you have more bitchy commentary, I have a class to teach."

Her arms drop to her sides as she straightens, a calculating look in her eyes. "You seem quite fond of her."

I ignore her, snake my left arm around her, and open the door.

"You were looking at *her* the way you used to look at Camille."

Every part of me locks as I turn around to stare at her coldly.

"You have no fucking clue about how I *looked* at Camille, how I felt about her. You lost that right when you left her to fend for herself. She was mine. My responsibility. *Mine.*"

The disgust on her face morphs into guilt and something like regret, but swiftly disappears, replaced by impassiveness.

"And Elon Blake is *my* responsibility. Remember that," she throws the words in my face, and a knot coils in my gut.

She turns and walks down the hall, the sound of her clicking heels fading as she rounds the corner and disappears from sight.

This time the pain coursing through me is more intense, slicing through my heart as my two worlds collide.

Guilt from my past consumes me. Desperate craving for my present burns hot in my veins.

Camille.

Elon.

Straightening my shoulders, I school my features to my usual unreadable expression. I stride into class to face my students.

As soon as the lesson ends, I leave Brown Hall with my bag gripped in one hand and stride out to the parking lot to my car. I have a free period, and I know exactly how to make use of that time.

When I'm seated inside my car with my windows up, I pull out the bottle with my pain medication and uncap it. Holding a pill in my hand, I do something I haven't done for almost two years. After peeling the coating on the pill, I break it into pieces, place them in a piece of white paper and fold it. Then I pull out my phone from my pants pocket and crush the pieces further, using the screen of my phone as a flat surface. After making sure the powder is the right consistency, I pull my credit card from my wallet, open the paper and make a perfect line. I reach up and flip the mirror above my head and pull out a crisp dollar from the little pocket there. I lean forward with my index finger holding my nostril down.

And freeze.

What am I doing?

This is wrong. So wrong.

If I take this path again, I might not be able to stop this time around.

My family's faces flash inside my head: Mom, Izzy, Bennett. After my rehab stint two years ago, I promised I'd stay away from snorting medication. The thought of seeing disappointment in their faces has me throwing the crisp note on the floor and crumpling the paper with the powder inside it in my hand, then shoving it inside my bag. I shake two pills from the bottle and pop them in my mouth, then roll my head on the headrest and close my eyes, waiting for the soreness in my shoulder and bicep to fade.

It takes several minutes before the pain fades. I'm tempted to pull out the paper and unwrap it, finish what I started, craving the immediate effect of crushed medication as it shoots through my veins.

Chasing the pain away.

Making me forget for just a little while.

My therapist would drag my ass back to his office if she suspected what I was considering, but the elation coursing through me would be worth it. I know what would follow after I came down from my high: the need for the next hit. And before I know it, I'm back to square one.

I push the craving aside and search my mind for something to latch on to.

Elon.

Quirky, sexy as fuck Elon.

CHAPTER SIXTEEN

Nate

TWENTY-EIGHT MINUTES PAST ONE O'CLOCK IN THE AFTERNOON. I got here at 1 p.m. but couldn't bring myself to leave the car. I look at the three-story building. Earlier on in my car, I awoke the sleeping beast. It's getting harder and harder to not think about taking a hit.

The worst thing is that my body now remembers how good it feels to be on a forty-five minute high, all physical and emotional pain gone. Forty-five minutes of sweet surrender, until the euphoria fades and I'm back to wanting to forget again. Wanting forty-five more minutes of pure ecstasy where nothing matters, where I can forget the fact that I couldn't save Camille when she needed me the most or that my arm will never play the cello again.

The number on the clock on the dashboard changes to thirty after one. My fingers slide inside my bag and wrap around the paper, already tasting rapture on my tongue. I meant to dispose of it, but I couldn't bring myself to do it.

Elon's eyes flash in my head, looking at me as if I'm more than my useless arm, more than my medication. I remember the hunger warring with uncertainty in her face, the smell of lime crowding my senses when I pinned her against the wall in class, her soft panting, the little moans. . .

I pull my hand out of the bag with a groan and glance down at my lap.

Fuck, I'm so hard.

I press my palm flat on the front of my pants and grit my teeth, imagining those pretty lips of hers around my cock. That thought has me exiting the car, slamming the door shut and crossing the street with one target in mind.

Elon Blake.

Her invitation to her place, her beguiling eyes, her pouty lips and neck I want to bite.

I glance around for any potential witnesses before scanning the numbers on the buzzer in front of me, pressing number 5, and waiting. Several seconds pass, and it feels like I've been waiting for hours. I almost give up and return to my car when a female voice accompanied by loud music in the background speaks through the intercom with a cheery, "Elon and Amber's humble dwellings."

I blink at the numbers in front of me, half-amused, half-surprised by the greeting.

"Hello!! Anyone there?"

I hear someone yell in the background, "Who is it?" Miss Blake's voice. Then, a distinct male voice yells, "Margaritas for my ladies."

She's not alone. Coming here was a mistake—

Elon's voice joins the cheery female. They talk rapidly for a few seconds. Silence follows, punctuated by soft footfalls fading away before Elon whispers, "Prof—Nathaniel?"

The barely-hidden surprise and excitement in her voice sends blood rushing into my groin, and I know I have to see her or I'll *die*. A little dramatic, but it feels that way right now.

Elon

"Nate?" I call out in a low voice, my eyes on Elise's retreating back. My heart's racing so fast I can't breathe properly. "Is that you?"

Several seconds of silence pass, then, "Yeah. You have company. I'll—"

"No! *No*, I'll buzz you up." I press the button quickly before he has a chance to protest, then grab a pair of flip flops at the door and duck my head around the corner. Elise and Nick are arguing over what to watch on TV: *Game of Thrones* versus a live car racing event in Monaco.

Perfect. That will keep them busy for a while. "Guys, I'll be back in a sec. Keep those margaritas coming, Nick. And we're watching *MI Rogue Nation* when I return!"

"Where are you off to?" Nick asks at the same time Elise yells, "Who was that at the door?"

Think fast. "Alex. He needs the keys to my locker—"

I'm dismissed quickly when Nick grabs the remote control, muttering "*Rogue Nation*, my ass" and starts flipping through the channels.

I quickly straighten my white tank top and plaid shorts, turn around and dash out the door, pulling it shut behind me. Everything around me sways a bit when I move too fast, feeling the lovely effects of the margaritas I've had the past hour.

I'm surprised Nathaniel is here. I didn't even think he'd show up. When I got back to my apartment, I changed into my tank and boxer shorts, wanting nothing more than to crawl into bed with a book and read my heartache away. Instead, I called Nor to check on Josh. She informed me he had stabilized, and there was no need for me to drive down to Willow Hill. So I texted Nick and Elise to let them know I was home and needed company. Within a few hours they were here, hanging out with me. Elise is doing her residency at St. James Hospital where Josh is currently admitted.

I round the corner just as the door to the stairwell swings open. In walks in my professor in all his brooding glory, long toned legs in black pants, broad shoulders draped in a white button-down shirt and a blazer. His eyes snap up to mine, the frown on his forehead vanishing.

"Hey," he greets in that deep voice of his, his gaze searching mine, taking in my features.

"Hey." A shiver trails a hot path up my spine. Even tipsy, my body still reacts to his addictive voice, basking in the concern in his tone.

We stare at each other, his eyes roaming over me, pausing on my thighs where my checked boxer shorts end. He swallows hard before lifting his darkened gaze back to mine.

When he doesn't say anything, I whisper, "I didn't think you'd come."

He shoves his balled up fists in his pants pockets. "Feeling better?"

I snicker, not sure why I find his question hilarious. "You came all the way to ask me that?"

He blinks, probably wondering why I find his words funny, steps closer, his head tilted to one side. "What do you think?"

"You tell me." I move forward, and I can smell his cologne and him.

He narrows his eyes. "You're drunk."

I roll my eyes. "Just two margaritas."

"Isn't it a little early for margaritas?" he asks, tucking stray hairs on my forehead into the lopsided bun hanging over my shoulder.

"It's five o'clock somewhere." I grin at him, feeling high because of *him*.

He studies me, a frown forming on his face, changing to a deep scowl. "He's in there with you," he growls, jaw tight.

Is he jealous? Even after telling him who Nick was to me, he's *jealous*.

And why does that make me feel giddy?

I choose not to answer his question, just to see where he's going with this.

"Go back inside." He jerks his chin in the general direction I came from. "I'll see you tomorrow."

He turns and stalks back the way he came.

"Why are you here, Nathaniel?" I ask, crossing my arms on my chest.

He stops and turns to face me, and I can't read his expression anymore.

Damn it, I really hate seeing that look on his face.

Being here is dangerous. Anyone could walk in on us, yet, I'm rooted on the spot, staring at this siren of a girl. A woman. I'm nine years older than Elon, but when I'm around her, I feel like I'm back to when I was fifteen, trying to impress a girl. Trying to be cool and lock my gaze with hers, jealous of the boy in her apartment. My body hasn't gotten the memo though. I'm rock hard to the point of pain.

Jesus, those tiny shorts were made for her. Seeing her wearing those boxers makes her even more sexy. I've seen her wearing dresses and jeans, and they look great on her, but those shorts, my fingers itch to rip them off her body, bend her over on the stairs and pound into her hard and fast.

She steps closer. I take a deep breath as a tangy scent hits me hard. Orange? Lime? I'm too intoxicated to tell the difference. All I know is that she smells like something I want to eat, preferably not here. If I'm going to eat her, it has to be in private. No witnesses. All fucking *mine*.

"I feel better," she says in a low, husky voice, answering the question I almost forgot I asked. "You're looking at my mouth. Want to have a taste?" She bites her lip, moves forward but wobbles a little, trying to right herself, then stares at me through her lashes.

She's drunk, you idiot.

"You are inebriated. You'll regret this tomorrow," I say sternly.

She rolls her eyes. "Not too drunk to know what I want."

I raise a brow. "And what do you want, Miss Blake?"

Her mouth pulls into a coy smile. How is that even possible?

"To feel the shape of your mouth with my lips. I want to know if they are as firm and cruel as they look or if they soften when you kiss."

Christ. This girl.

Those words send heat rushing through me. It takes a lot of effort to take a step back from her just to save my sanity.

She smirks and says, "Lie to me and tell me you don't want to kiss me right this second. I see the way you look at me. I know you feel this." She points the space between us.

"You do, huh?" I wet my dry lips, then swallow hard. "How do I look at you?"

She slightly dips her chin and looks up at me through her lashes. "The way you're looking at me right now."

If what I'm feeling inside me reflects on my face—the sheer need to consume her whole—then I know exactly what she sees.

She places her palm flat on my chest. I feel her touch seep through my shirt and into my bones, searing heat to the part of me that hasn't seen light in three years. It scares the shit out of me, makes me lose my breath.

"Elon," I groan, pressing a hand atop hers and opening my eyes. "This should be the end of you and me. I shouldn't want you like this, craving you, aching for you. But here I am, standing in front of you, wanting this. Wanting you any way I can get you." I release a long breath, knowing what I have to do. It's wrong, but I do it anyway.

Tossing the code of ethics out the proverbial window, I grasp her wrist with my left hand, pull her toward the stairs, away from the hallway and push her against the wall. I drop my arm around her waist and yank her to me. The chaos, the hunger for medication has been replaced by the need to consume and be consumed.

"Little Wolf has come out to play, hmm?"

Her eyes widen at the pet name. She recovers quickly and smiles. "Are you finally going to kiss me?"

Christ, that mouth. "Just so we're clear, if we cross this line…" I squeeze her ass like I've wanted to do for weeks now—tight to the point of pain—moving my palm in firm caresses up her stomach, her tits, her neck, stopping at her mouth. "Every part of you will belong to me from this point forward until we fuck each other out of our systems. This—" I stroke her full top lip with my thumb. "—And this—" I move my hand down, cup her between her legs. "Mine. You okay with that?"

She nods, watching me through hooded eyes, quick pants rushing out of her parted lips. "All yours. Just kiss me before I die," she says desperately.

A sound between a laugh and groan escapes through my lips. My head dips, catching her off guard. She gasps, tangles her fingers in my hair and tugs hard.

I pull back. "Easy. I know what you need. I'll give it to you. Just let me enjoy this fucking moment."

She huffs, her nostrils flaring. "Are you serious right now? Someone could walk in on us."

My head jerks upright at her words. I glance around, then feel my body relax a little. We're squished in a small alcove where the window dips in. Besides, the floors in this place have a way of announcing someone's arrival before their appearance.

I lean down and run my tongue along her bottom lip, letting myself be swept away by this moment, this thing, whatever is happening between us, this force field pulling us together. A moment to remember who I am and who she is to me. This feeling, so fragile, yet powerful at the same time. A dissonance of notes.

She wiggles, grinding her pussy on my cock. Her breasts are pressing into my chest now, her nipples hard, her breath fanning my lips. Her eyes are dancing with mischief and promises of making me forget.

"Stop it," I ground, ready to come in my pants.

"Are you going to punish me for disobeying?" she asks playfully.

Elon has a wild streak, and I cannot wait to discover what it is.

"You know, the first time I met you I thought you were a shy, quiet little thing."

She raises her chin in that stubborn way. "Let's get one thing straight. I'm not shy and never have been. Just because I don't talk a lot doesn't mean I'm shy. Or stuck-up."

My eyes leave that mouth and rove all over her face, taking in the sultry look in her eyes, then wander back to those lips I just tasted and want to destroy with my own. "Oh, Miss Blake. Stuck-up is not a description I would use for you."

She bites the corner of her mouth, cups my jaw in her hands, forcing me to meet her gaze, and says, "I'm going to kiss you now, Professor."

Fuck. Me.

She smiles before leaning forward and pressing her lips to mine, and the world falls away from under me.

"Fuck the rules," I grunt, grip her hips, and pull her flush to me. My body tenses as pain rushes from my shoulder, forcing my hand to relax and let the pain pass. I shift her weight to my left arm, grasp that obnoxious, lopsided bun that still makes her look so goddamn hot, holding her to me as my mouth descends.

"Shit, your arm," she says, attempting to move away, but I circle my left arm around her waist and pull her to my chest.

"It will pass," I say, breathing in through my nose, my eyes falling shut.

I feel soft lips on mine, and my eyes snap open to find hers locked on me. Her teeth come out to play, nipping my bottom lip, still watching me. I'm waiting, the need to kiss her driving me crazy, but I want to see how far she will take this. A moan slips through her lips, and my grip around her tightens as her hands move restlessly, like she can't get enough of me. She kisses like dynamite: starts out slow, the fire building up before everything around us detonates as soon she bites down on my lip, hard.

Our mouths mesh into an explosive kiss full of need and want, a little ungraceful as our lips learn each other's shape and pressure. Then I'm pulling my arm from around her, pressing her tight little body into the wall behind her while pushing my hips into her to support her body. My tongue greedily seeks hers, wanting inside her mouth. Thank fuck she opens up for me and I shove inside, circling my hips in the same rhythm as my tongue. She sighs and moans low in her throat as if she has been waiting for this kiss her entire life, and my fingers tighten around her hair.

Hot *fucking* damn.

This kiss makes sense, the dissonant notes from before turning into a harmonious tone, a prelude to a deeper kiss. Darker, sweeter notes and even darker, addictive depths.

My arm could fall off and I wouldn't even care. This girl, this perfection in my arms, reminds me how it feels to want someone with a ruthless hunger, wanting them like they are your next breath. And being wanted in return.

I squeeze her thigh and skim my hand up, then dip it under those insanely hot shorts to cup her ass. I sweep in front and land on her pussy. She whimpers, urgently rubbing herself on my fingers.

She's wet, so fucking wet. My cock is pressing against my zipper, wanting inside her heat.

"I need inside you, Elon," I murmur between kisses.

She groans and mumbles inaudibly through her panting.

"What?"

"I want to feel you so badly." Her hands leave my hair and are now rubbing my swollen cock through my pants. "I can't tell you how many times I've thought about this moment. In class, at the office, every freaking single time."

I snag her wrists to stop her. With my eyes closed, I pull back, our inhales and exhales rough, hot. Trying to catch our breath.

"God," she moans and my eyes open.

"Was that firm and cruel enough for you, Miss Blake? Soft enough?"

"Oh, God," she whispers, brushing her fingertips on her swollen lips. "I knew it. I knew it would be perfect."

The sound of feet padding hits my ears, right before a male voice—Nick—yells Elon's name, jolting me.

Shit.

I set her down, making sure her feet touch the floor before dropping my hands. A primal part of me wants to continue kissing her until I make my point clear to Nick that she is mine now. Elon says they are just friends, but I saw the way he was looking at her earlier today.

He is crushing on her. Badly.

Common sense kicks in and I step away from Elon.

"I'm not done with you," I say gruffly, pulling my phone out of the pocket of my pants. I scroll through my contacts and pause on the name "Red", which is the name I used to save her number. Let's face it: I'd never be on the list to receive awards for coming up with the best nicknames.

Quickly, I open a new text and shove the phone in her hands, then rattle my address for her to type in. If fucking her will get her out of my system so we can go on with our lives, then so be it.

She wants it.

I want it.

Two adults. One goal. A goal that could get her expelled and me fired.

Fucking each other's brains out.

When she's done, I take my cell phone and tap *send*.

"You have my address now. I want to finish what we just started. Today."

"Um. . .Elise is sleeping over," she says, looking dazed. She straightens her tiny shorts and licks her lips, as if to remind herself what I taste like. "Tomorrow after my tutoring class? Around seven-thirty in the evening?"

I nod curtly, partly focused on the footsteps drawing closer. "You look so hot with your lips swollen and cheeks flushed." I duck my head and steal a quick kiss that has her moaning deep in her throat.

I pull back, watch her face while her eyes blink open. No chaos in my head. No heaviness in my heart. "I don't feel it when I'm with you."

She blinks at me in confusion. "Feel what?"

"The darkness. The pain." I hear the wonder in my voice. "I feel—" I try to look for the right words. "A sense of calm."

She swallows visibly, tears forming in her eyes. "Nathaniel...Nate." She opens and closes her mouth, shakes her head and smiles through the wetness falling on her cheeks. "I'm glad." She swipes her cheeks with the back of her hand, still smiling, and says, "*Go.* I'll see you tomorrow."

I swipe a thumb under one cheek then the other, the tears making my chest hurt. I want to ask her why she is upset, but that fucking Nick sounds closer now.

I turn and jog down the steps, wincing when my arm jostles, sending pain skittering down.

When I climb into my car, I pull out the bottle with my medication and toss a tablet in my mouth, then lean my head back and close my eyes, waiting for the pain to pass. Still breathing hard. Heart racing fast inside my chest. My mind replays the kiss on loop. I can't remember the last time my knees felt this weak after a kiss. My entire body feels like I'm floating on air. I wouldn't be surprised to see rainbows and glitter shooting out of my ass.

I open my eyes and glance at the clock.

Five minutes until two o'clock. I restart the BMW, roll out of the parking spot and drive off toward Rushmore.

I search through my brain for any traces of regret. I've always been mindful of other people's well-being. I've never done something so reckless, stupid even. But today, I crossed a line that could get me fired and Elon expelled, destroying her dreams in the process.

I regret putting her education in danger, but I don't regret that life-altering kiss.

Best fucking kiss. Ever. With my student.

Fuck.

Elon

I still can't believe Nate actually came to visit me. I swear the moment I heard his voice on the intercom, my heart sped up so fast I thought it would rip through my chest. Then he backed me against the wall at the stairs and kissed me as if he has been waiting for *years* to ravish me.

God. Fireworks exploded behind my eyes and—

"Nick!" I screech, almost tumbling backward down the stairs when I see my best friend standing two feet away. My arms wheel about, seeking purchase. My hand finds the banister and grasps tightly while my free one clutches my chest. "You scared me."

Nick is standing there, his head tilted up toward the ceiling, eyes wide. His face has gone pale, mouth gaping.

"What's wrong?" I ask, dropping my hand from my chest and hurrying forward. His focus doesn't waver. In fact, the way his throat is bobbing as he swallows, I think he's going to vomit. Panic tightens its fist around my neck. "Is everything OK? Nick, talk to me. You're scaring me."

His head drops, his eyes meet mine, anger brimming in their depths.

"*What the hell*?" His voice is tortured, full of disbelief.

"What?"

Surely he couldn't have seen Nate and me sucking face.

He takes a deep breath, releasing a gush of air through his mouth. "You and *him*? What the actual fuck, Elon?"

Shit! Shit! Shit!

"What?" I ask dumbly. *Think. Damage control!*

He lifts his arm and jabs a finger at the ceiling, then glares at me accusingly.

My gaze darts in the direction he pointed, and my world splits in the middle, pushing out panic, sucking out all the air in me when I realize he saw me on those surveillance hall monitors.

Three months ago, the management of this building installed surveillance cameras in the halls and stairways after a freshman was found unconscious, frothing at the mouth on the staircase. They wanted to make sure it was possible to monitor the public spaces at any given time. The little screen in the corner on every floor ensures the security guard is able to see if there's anything going on as he patrols inside the building.

The cameras never bothered me before. In fact, I completely forgot they existed because I've never been one to fool around in hallways and staircases.

Until now.

I look away from the tiny surveillance monitors propped where two walls meet, then back at Nick. My mouth feels like it's filled with sand, my breath stuttering in my throat.

"I can explain—" I choke on the words because this is *Nick*, my best friend and one of the sweetest guys I know. The boy who has had a crush on me since we moved in next door to his house when I was nine.

My throat feels tight now, and I have to bite my bottom lip to stop it from trembling.

"You were kissing that asshole?" A vein ticks furiously on his temple. "Your *professor*?"

Lie, Elon. Freaking lie.

I kill that thought quick. I'm the worst liar ever. When I lie, my lips start to wobble and my eye twitches.

So I nod, forcing the panic back down my throat with a quick swallow. "But listen—"

His nostrils flare, his face, bordering on too pretty, now twisted with anger.

"Why was he here? Is he forcing you to do something you don't want to do? Because if he is, you have to report him to the head of school. I can be your witness—"

"Nick, stop!" I yell, the sound ringing up the stairs and down the hall.

He stops, his chest rising and falling with exertion.

"*I* kissed *him.*" I press my palm flat on my chest.

"*What?*"

"I kissed him," I repeat in a firm voice.

He shakes his head emphatically, stepping closer. "You're lying. You are one of the most level-headed people I've ever met. You wouldn't risk being expelled because this has always been your dream. You are one of the good girls, Elon. For fuck's sake, why are you lying for him?"

I'm one of the good girls.

In other words, I'm boring.

Unadventurous.

His words make my insides twist with irritation.

I cross my arms on my chest and stare down at my flip flops. "I'm not lying."

"Look at me." His tortured voice has my head snapping up, obeying his command.

Then he poses a question that has me wishing the grounds would open and swallow me and dump me in Hell. Surely there must be a special chamber made for people like me.

"Why not *me*?" He thumps his chest, eyes gleaming as if he's holding back tears. "Why *him* and not *me*?"

Because—"Because you are—" *like my little brother.* I finish that sentence in my head. I can't hurt him like that; he is already hurting. Uttering those words will only make things worse.

I can't lose him.

He drags his fingers through his hair in agitation and asks, "Because what?"

Because I want someone to look at me like I'm one of the bad girls. Someone who looks at me as if he'll die if he doesn't kiss me or touch me or breathe the same air as me. Someone who looks beyond the walls I've built up and sees me. Really sees me.

And Nate looks at me that way.

"What's taking you guys so long?" Elise's voice precedes her, and my body tenses.

Shit. She can't find out about Nate.

"Nick—" I try again, reaching out to touch his arm, but he stiffens and steps back. "Please, don't tell Elise—"

Elise's face pops around the corner, all smiles and twinkling eyes, her gaze bouncing between Nick and me. It drops as soon as she enters the palpable field of tension surrounding us. "Whoa! What's this? Couple conflict?" she jokes. "I know a thing or two about conflict management, so if you guys need a—"

I glance at my sister and subtly shake my head to let her know this is not the right time to make jokes. Clearly, she doesn't seem to catch my warning.

"What's going on?" She sweeps the blue dyed bangs off her forehead, looking at Nick, then me.

Nick's eyes haven't left mine. I can still feel the fiery anger in them licking every inch of me.

He shakes his head, and without another word, spins around and storms back to my apartment.

"Elon?" Elise prompts, and my gaze swings back to hers. "What the hell is going on?"

"Nick and I had a little disagreement—"

"Bullshit. You and Nick have never disagreed on *anything*. So whatever it is must be pretty huge."

I exhale in frustration, then turn around to keep her from witnessing the tears fighting to fall, and follow Nick. "Leave it, okay?"

Her bare feet pad softly on the cement floor behind me, but she doesn't press me on it. Thank God. I only have enough strength to deal with Nick at the moment, and I can already feel exhaustion settling in my bones as the adrenaline cools off.

Before we reach our apartment, Nick shoots out the door while shrugging on his navy blue jacket. He gives my sister a quick nod of goodbye, then mumbles a "bye" without even looking at me. I turn to watch him, my chest aching. I listen to his fading footsteps descend the stairs, hear the door open and slam shut. I raise my hand and wipe my cheek. Elise wraps her arms around my shoulders, pulling me in for a tight hug.

She shoots me a sympathetic look. "Whatever it is, it's going to be okay. He won't stay mad at you for long. It's *Nick*."

From your lips to God's ears.

Then she pulls back and guides me inside the apartment and points to the couch for me to sit down. "Now let's cheer you up." She grabs a stack of DVDs on the table and pulls out *Game of Thrones*. I swear my sister is the only person on earth who still collects DVDs in this age of Netflix and Amazon Prime.

She waves the DVD in the air. "*Khal Drogo*. Enough said."

I choke out a laugh, then groan. "I really don't want to watch anything." I just want to go to my room and curl up in bed, feel sorry for myself.

"Come on. I know you have a thing for his arms. Such a fine specimen of a man." She sighs dreamily. "I need a *Khal Drogo* in my life."

Knowing Elise, she won't stop bugging me until I agree. She is already in "big sister" mode, and when she gets like this, it's always easiest to let her take care of me. I desperately need it right now.

So I settle down on the couch without another word. She heads to the kitchen and returns with two margaritas and shoves one in my hands. She curls up next to me, then grabs the cream knit afghan from the armchair and drapes it around us. No matter how much I pretend to watch *Khal Drogo* prowling stealthily and beating his chest, my brain keeps replaying what happened. My breath accelerates remembering that kiss. The moment Nate's lips touched mine, I was done for. It's like I've been waiting for that kiss my whole life. Then images of Nick's angry face flash in my head. My stomach ties itself in knots. I have to look for a way to talk to him. Maybe I should give him some space. Hopefully time will ride out his anger.

But I won't regret kissing Nate.

Ever.

CHAPTER SEVENTEEN

Elon

RIGHT AFTER MY TUTORING CLASS AT STUDIO 22, WHERE I WORK three days a week—Thursdays, Fridays and Saturdays—I drive to the address Nate texted me last night, then park my Jetta outside the building.

My phone beeps twice, alerting me of the incoming text. I dive down on the floor below the passenger seat, grab my bag and dig out my phone, hoping it's Nick finally texting me back. I've texted him several messages and called him double that number of times. He hasn't replied to any of my messages or returned my calls. Before Elise left this morning, she pulled me into her arms, hugging me tightly, then told me to give Nick time. She said things will work out in the end. I just hope she is right, because losing Nick's friendship was something I never thought would happen.

Thank God she did not insist that I tell her what happened between us. She knows me too well to persist or question me. Being known as the quiet girl has its perks. No one knows exactly what you are thinking.

There are things even my sisters or Amber don't know. Like that one time when I was nine years old and our PE teacher had fallen ill, so the afternoon class ended early. The principal's secretary called the kids' parents to let them know they were free to pick up their children early. She couldn't reach Nor on the phone though, so Mrs. Spritzler, who lived a couple of houses down from ours, picked her daughter and me up from school. When I got home, I paused outside the path leading to Mrs. Spritzler's house when I saw the door to our house was slightly open. So instead of following her to her house and waiting until Nor or Elise came home, I dashed inside our house. I heard moaning coming from upstairs, as if someone was in pain. With my heart racing in my chest, I followed the sound and immediately froze at the door to my mother's room, unable to take my eyes off what I was seeing. My mom was bent over on the edge of the bed with her head facing the door where I was standing, her eyes closed tightly, tears streaming down her face. Above her was my father, making fast work of yanking her panties down her thighs, then fumbling with his zipper. I must have made a noise because his head swung in my direction, and I saw the glazed look on his face, a look I had seen so many times. He was drunk.

He glowered at me at the same time my mom's eyes snapped open and met my frightened ones.

"Please, don't do this, Stephen," Mother whispered on a sob. "Not in front of her."

He yanked one of the hands that was holding Mom down by her shoulders and jabbed his finger at me. "Get the fuck out of here, you worthless piece of shit."

I whimpered, scared shitless. I'd already seen him in a violent rage before, and from the way he was looking at me, I thought he was going to kill me.

"Stop hurting her!" I shouted in a trembling voice, hands fisted at my side. "I hate you! I wish you were dead!"

His face got red and his eyes bulged from his head. Dropping his hands from my mom, he zipped up his pants while stalking toward me. I should have run, but my feet were like lead on the floor. Even when he raised his arm, his hand descending to my head, freezing for a moment before making contact with my chest, my legs still couldn't move. Between one second and the next, I was lying on the floor, pain ricocheting from my ribs. Too intense. I blacked out. The next time I woke up, I was lying on a white bed in a white room, and a doctor was hovering above me. I survived the incident with only a few bruised ribs. I could see my mother and the doctor talking in low, urgent voices on the other side of the room. I'm not even sure what she told the doctor. So when the doctor asked me what happened, I stared long and hard into my mother's eyes, taking in the terrified expression in her gaze.

Then I opened my mouth and said, "I tripped on my toys and fell down on the porch steps."

From the way the doctor studied me, she didn't believe me. But I didn't care, especially when I saw my mother's relieved expression. I knew I had done the right thing. She huddled me in her car and drove us home. Given my quiet nature, my sisters didn't notice any change in me. I stayed in my room most of the time, as usual, playing my cello or burying my nose in a book.

And that was the day I really, really started despising my mother for a weakness that I later on inherited, I suppose. And I hated her more for that. Well, not really hate her, but—-ugh! I can't afford to think about all the shit that went down in the past.

I retrieve the message, my heart dropping lower in my stomach when I realize it's Elise, asking me if I'm okay and if Nick contacted me. I reply, letting her know that he hasn't, then toss my phone back in my bag and psych myself up about this sex-meeting with Nate.

When I was eleven years old, Nor arrived home and handed me a letter and asked me to open it, then sat on my bed and put her palms on her swollen belly as if protecting her unborn babies. My tiny fingers paused long enough to notice the Music & Co. stamp on the back of the envelope. My excitement spiraled high. I'd been dying to enter the Junior Classical Music Award competition. Even at that age, I knew we didn't have enough money to waste on things like competitions. It would cost a lot to drive to Miami, where the competition was being held, which is why I didn't attempt to enter. My mom didn't have a job and mostly stayed in her room the whole day, rocking on her chair, zoned out, ignoring us. My loser of a father hardly ever came home. And when he did, he was a looming cloud of misery and pain, using his words as a tool of abuse. He did leave money, but it wasn't much. Somehow Nor made it work.

I was so excited, so nervous to be part of something as huge as that competition. I came in third, but I'll never forget that feeling.

Sitting in my car, the same feeling twists inside my stomach. I glance out of the car to the row of windows on the building, which is located two doors down from Reed's Lounge. There are lights on in four of them, but the others are unlit. I'm anxious about what will take place when I enter his apartment.

Am I ready for this?

Yes.

Am I scared that I may not be able to blow his mind?

Hell *yes*.

I met my first boyfriend in high school. We only fooled around and never had sex. Then Rick came along and swept me off my feet with his charming and dominant ways. Older guy, more experienced, both sexually and life wise. Thing is, he just focused on fulfilling his urge to fuck. To own. Me? I was only something to get his dick wet, which I realized much later. That and the fact that he had a violent nature. I shudder, feeling sweat pepper my hairline just remembering that part of my life.

I jerk my head from side to side, scattering those thoughts and forcing myself back to the present. My phone beeps again, and I dig it back out of my bag, read the text, this time from The King of the Bulges himself, Nate.

Get your sweet ass up here.

I duck down and dart a look at the windows, noticing a silhouetted figure behind white curtains.

I turn my attention back to the phone, smiling.

He's waiting for me.

I wipe my palms on my skirt before letting my fingers hover above my screen for several seconds. But before I can reply, my phone starts to ring. *Mr. Scowly* flashes on my screen, the name under which I saved his number last night after he sent the text message with his home address.

I answer the call and stick the phone to my ear.

"You have two choices." His voice is a husky sound that has my thighs clenching. "Come upstairs and I'll make you come hard over and over. Or turn around and leave, but then you will never find out how good my mouth and cock can make you feel." He pauses, inhaling unevenly. "Which one will it be?"

Holy shit!

My tongue is stuck on the roof of my mouth, and I can't form any coherent words. No random thoughts running wildly in my head. His bold declaration short-circuited my brain. The image of his mouth on me sends my thoughts scattering, and I end up uttering a string of letters that sound like this: "agagag."

Very attractive, Elon.

"What was that?" He sounds amused. I close my eyes and picture him smirking, eyes heavily hooded.

I clear my throat, then cough a little. "Yeah? How many times?"

He laughs softly, and my head spins, my skin tingling. I'm beginning to like *that* rare sound a little too much. "Why don't you come upstairs and find out?"

I let out a long exhale, letting my head fall back on the headrest. "Be there in a bit."

He chuckles deeply, darkly, sinfully before disconnecting the call. Shit.

Am I in way over my head here? There's only one way to find out.

I toss my phone inside my bag and jump out of my car with an extra spring in my step. I button up my jacket to ward off the late-January chilly breeze before grabbing my cello from the back seat—I never leave my baby in my car. I've heard horror stories of students leaving their instruments in vehicles but finding them stolen when they return.

After making sure the car is locked, I cross the street.

I step inside the lobby and halt in front of a dark brown, hardwood counter being manned by a portly old guy in a black uniform, shock of white hair combed back on top of his head. My gaze flickers on the silver nametag, noting the name Geoffrey.

I smile, straightening to my full height of five feet two inches. "Good evening, Geoffrey."

"Elon Blake?" He smiles back, lines fanning at the corners and bracketing his mouth. "He's waiting for you." He motions for me to follow him to the elevator.

I jerk back in surprise, feeling even more nervous than before, but my heart is dancing inside my chest just thinking about the fact that he told Geoffrey to expect me.

Hiking my bag higher on my shoulder, I follow Geoffrey to the elevators. As soon as the doors slide open, he gestures with his arm for me to enter. I do, then turn around just as he steps back and nods once, and the doors slide closed.

God, my heart's beating out of my chest, and I feel the sudden urge to pee. I need to focus on something else before I back out, like maybe do something that will shock him. Be one of the bad ones instead of the good ones. And damn it, I want to be bad. Naughty.

I shove my hand inside my bag and pull out a half-eaten Snickers bar, then unwrap it quickly and shove the entire thing in my mouth. The taste explodes on my tongue, giving me an immediate sugar rush and courage. Glancing down, I study my white lace, button-up shirt, black jacket, black skirt that stops a few inches above my knees, black stockings and a pair of dark brown lace-up booties.

Not so shabby, I think. But it needs a shock factor.

I press the *stop* button on the console, halting the elevator's upward ascent. I set my cello and bag on the floor, and with shaking fingers, unclasp my bra and pull it down and out of the blouse and jacket sleeves. When I'm done, I unlace the booties and step out of them, lift the black skirt up and roll down the stockings, hook my fingers around the band of my hot pink, cotton panties and slide them down my legs. I quickly shove the bra, stockings and panties inside my bag before shoving my feet back inside my shoes and straightening to my full height.

Cool air sweeps up my legs, brushing the heated, sensitive skin of my thighs. A sound between a whimper and moan leaves my lips as air caresses my pussy. I wiggle my ass and boobs a little to loosen up, tug the hairband holding my hair in a high knot, then shake my head, sending my hair tumbling down my shoulders to the small of my back.

Perfect.

If I'm going to be *one of the bad girls*, I'd better act the part. At least for tonight.

By the time I exit the elevator with my cello slung back behind me and my bag grasped against my chest, my body is humming with anticipation. Every time the material of my blouse brushes against my nipples, I groan, and when a slight breeze brushes my mound, I clench my fist to fight the urge to touch myself. I walk toward door number 9, my footsteps muted by the blood red, wall-to-wall carpet and halt in front of my destination.

I take a deep breath, raise my hand to push the bell but stop when I realize that the door is slightly open. So I knock softly, still wondering what the heck am I doing. Still wondering how many times he'll make me come. Hell, the last time I came in the hands of a man was. . .never.

I always made noises while having sex with Rick, then lied to him after we fucked, telling him I'd orgasmed to pacify him and also so he could leave me alone. Always afraid of what he'd do if I told him I didn't come.

I'm here now, waiting to be allowed entry into my professor's den and collect the orgasms he promised me.

"Come in," a deep voice commands from the other side of the

white door.

I do as I'm told, stepping through the threshold. I suck in a breath, almost getting knocked over by the scent of him that welcomes me.

His presence fills this space like a glove. Anticipation builds in my chest, my stomach, my bones.

CHAPTER EIGHTEEN

Nate

The second she walks through the door, I almost leap out of my seat in the living room where I've been sitting for the past several minutes waiting for her. I'd made sure to position the chair so that I could see her as soon as she stepped inside my apartment.

I grab the tumbler of Scotch from the table and down the amber liquid, then I set it on the table.

Holy *fuck*!

I cannot stop staring at her: crimson hair forming a curtain around her shoulders, slight sway of her hips as she walks inside a few steps and looks around. The shadows that sometimes tarnish her beautiful eyes have been replaced by desire.

I know she's not mine to tease and touch. She's my student. I'm her mentor. I'm supposed to be taking care of her.

Sure. I'll take care of her, but not as my student.

Tonight, I'm a man who is about to stake claim on a young woman who drives him insane with need, both in and out of class. A starved man who's about to lay her on the table and feast on her like she's his last meal.

She pushes the door closed before setting the cello on the floor next to the small table by the wall, then drops her bag beside it.

"Nate?" she calls out while shrugging off her jacket and hanging it on the hook behind her.

Then she raises her arms up in a stretch, a little moan slipping out of those lips. Her blouse rides up, giving me a glimpse of that soft-looking skin I crave to bite and lick so bad. But that is not what makes me hard. It's the graceful innocence surrounding her. She's so unaware of how attractive she is.

She drops her arms and begins to walk toward me, her head focused on something to her right, probably the view of the St. John's River outside the floor-to-ceiling windows. Her eyes widen, a squeal popping out of her parted mouth. And I know she has spotted the Montagnana. *Christ.*

I rub the front of my pants with my left palm, then groan when my balls pull even tighter.

As if sensing me, Elon turns her head, locking her gaze with mine. She stumbles when she realizes I've been there all along.

Watching her.

Her giddy smiles falters. I wonder if I'm competing with the cello for her attention.

Seriously. If you don't think too much of my right arm, I'm actually a very capable man. A fine specimen at that.

"You're nervous."

"Very," she admits in a breathless whisper.

"Don't be. I'm a generous lover." I watch her intently, ready to prove my point if need be.

She rolls her eyes. "Feeling confident about that, aren't you?"

"When I set my mind on doing something, I give it my everything. When I finally have you in my bed, you will have all of me. All my attention. Mind, body and soul."

"Holy. Shit," she mutters under her breath, squeezing her thighs together.

My body sinks lower in the seat, my legs spreading a little further apart. She inhales sharply as she blatantly stares at the bulge in my pants.

Damn right, sweetheart.

"Come here, Little Wolf." My voice is low, firm.

The corners of her mouth lift in a smile as she bravely makes her way toward me.

"Hello, Professor," she greets, *that* skirt swaying with every step. She stops in front of me, her gaze falling on my crotch. Her mouth parts on a breath, her eyes bugging out a little. "Wow."

I raise a brow, smirking. "Yeah."

Deep lines form on her forehead as she bites the corner of her bottom lip in contemplation, as if she's working on a difficult math problem, her eyes narrowing. If my guess is right, she's attempting to calculate the size of my cock. For just a second, I contemplate putting her out of her misery and just telling her when she blurts out, "Monster penis."

I blink at her sudden outburst before barking out a laugh.

Christ, this girl.

The more I'm in her presence, the more I find myself laughing or smiling at her unpredictability.

That's *it.*

I've been trying to figure out what's so special about her that has my head screwed on crooked, what makes me catch my breath whenever she walks into the room. Every night when I close my eyes, she's right there watching me with those big hazel eyes.

This may sound cheesy, but I really don't give a fuck. Elon is my ray of sunshine, punching holes through my armor with gentle blows I hardly saw coming until now.

She shifts on her feet, rubbing her flushed cheeks with her palms in obvious mortification, looking so cute all flushed and turned on.

"I have this thing I do where my thoughts just tumble out of my mouth—"

"I know." I smile, interrupting her rambling. I noticed that little quirk of hers a few weeks ago. Such a turn on. "It's one of the things I like about you."

She freezes, eyes wide.

What the actual fuck?

I just told her I *like* her.

I groan inwardly. I should ask her to leave, stop whatever this is before we go further. I wonder if she expects us to be a couple after we fuck.

I watch her face intently, hoping to catch a glimpse of her thoughts, but all I see are *those* eyes.

"Your eyes are incredible," I murmur. "The second you lifted your head and looked at me on my first day of class I was done for."

"Bullshit." Her lips tighten, her nose flaring. Her gaze shifts to the space over my shoulder as the blush on her cheeks deepens, almost covering the freckles scattered on her nose and cheeks. "You don't have to offer me compliments to have sex with me." Then she looks at me again. "It's a one-time thing, right? Just to get this sexual energy out of our systems?"

I don't think I've inhaled air since she walked in. I'm stunned, speechless at her sass and sporting the motherfucking boner of the century.

Again, I wonder how I ever thought Elon was shy or quiet. Maybe because the only people she allows in her orbit are Amber and Alex. She ignores everyone else as if they don't exist.

One-time thing? Is that what she thinks?

A growl leaves my mouth. I expect her to run out the door at that sound. Instead she stands there, chin lifted, staring down at me.

I reach for the glass of Scotch, gulp down the rest of its contents, then set it back on the table. I swipe my bottom lip with my thumb before turning to face her, then crook my finger, motioning for her to move closer. A few more steps and she's standing in front of me. I lean forward and place my palms behind her knees, tugging her forward, bridging the small space between us.

"You are beautiful." My voice is firm, my hands squeezing the back of her thighs hard when I see she's about to roll her eyes. I'm about to add this is *not* a one-time thing, but I bite my tongue. Let her believe whatever she wants. I don't want to scare her yet, given that she hasn't even seen my monster penis. Maybe that will give her reason to run.

I chuckle under my breath, shaking my head.

"What?" she asks, lifting her hands and threading her fingers into my hair, sifting through.

"I know for a fact that having you once will not be enough for me."

Her hands halt on top of my head. "You sound sure of yourself."

I shrug confidently, almost arrogantly. "It's the truth." She lifts a brow at my nonchalance. Her thighs clench, her arousal slamming into my gut. From the heat in her eyes, I have a feeling she's enjoying this a little too much. "Fucking *me* once will not be enough for you either."

Her bottom lip quivers, but she quickly mutters, "Cocky asshole." She attempts to wiggle out of my grip, probably to hightail it out of here, but I tighten my hold to stop her.

"So which one is it going to be, Little Wolf? Staying or leaving?" I challenge her. I should stop taunting her. This is what I wanted, as well, right? Just a night of blissful fucking to get each other out of our systems so we can both go back to normal.

Right?

Then why am I am trying to convince her otherwise?

Her eyes fall shut, her tongue peeking out to lick her lips. Fuck, those lips, around my cock—

"Staying," she says, opening her eyes and meeting mine head-on. Her mouth curls up to one side, her eyes gleaming with mischief. "Shut up already and make me come."

I laugh, pressing my forehead on her stomach, grinning like a teen who's browsing his stash of porn.

Holy hell.

My girl has spunk and a backbone. If she's like this in bed, I might end up blowing my load even before my cock is buried inside her.

Nudging her blouse up with my nose, I press my mouth on her skin and suck hard. My tongue circles her navel, my teeth nipping gently.

She gasps, followed by a sigh, my name sounding breathless passing through her lips, her fingers gripping my hair and knees buckling. But somehow she straightens, whispering my name again in that voice that has me groaning, craving to flip her on her back on the couch and fuck her mercilessly.

"So soft," I murmur, rubbing my nose on her stomach. My hands skim her thighs, sliding up, up. She groans just as my fingers glide between her legs.

I freeze when my fingertips graze the bare skin there, my head snapping up. Her head is thrown back in bliss, her mouth parted, little pants of need escaping her mouth.

"No panties, Miss Blake?"

Her head rolls forward and she smiles. "Surprise."

"Fuck, yeah." I chuckle. "Surprise indeed."

Unpredictable as ever. Naughty, Miss Blake.

A thought occurs to me, and my body tenses. "Wait. Did you walk around like this the whole day?"

Her lips twitch as she says, "Yeah. Why? Oh my God! Do you think people could see my butt?"

I grit my teeth, her words casting images of hungry-eyed ass-holes jerking off to her ass. My hands curl into fists.

She snorts, escalating quickly to a full-blown laugh. That sound sinks into my chest, and just for a moment, everything around me disappears. Just me and her. She looks so carefree, happy.

For the second time since she walked in, I'm at a loss for words.

She's *breathtaking*.

When she's calm enough to talk, she says between a burst of giggles, "Calm down, Conan. We don't want that throbbing vein on your forehead exploding."

Slowly, I move my hands up to cup her breasts through her

blouse and squeeze them together, then bury my face between them to hide my grin, inhaling that lime scent and groan, "Did you go commando the whole day?"

She doesn't answer immediately, and I'm going crazy. *Why the hell does it bother me so much?*

After what feels like hours and I'm two seconds away from flipping her on her back, injured arm or not, and fucking the truth out of her, she whispers in a shaky, husky voice, "No."

"Good." My body relaxes.

Shit. I've got it bad for this chick.

I grip her hips and yank her down on my lap at the same time, pain shooting through my shoulder and settling heavily on my right arm.

"Goddamnit!" I yell.

She flinches, her body tensing, her eyes flying to mine. What I see in their depths freezes the blood in my veins.

Panic.

Then her eyes slam shut, and she inhales a shaky breath.

"Did I hurt you?" I ask, air locked in my throat. The thought of causing her pain makes my chest tense up.

She opens her eyes, attempts to smile. But I can still see the lingering panic in them. I wonder who put that fear in her eyes.

Who the hell hurt you, Little Wolf?

"We don't have to do this," I say gently, trailing a finger on her top full lip. "I really enjoy kissing you. We could just hang out. And kiss. And cuddle."

She eyes me as if I've suddenly gone crazy. "Cuddle?"

I flash her a wolfish grin, and her body practically melts on my lap. "I may not look all fuzzy and warm, but I love to cuddle."

She snort-laughs, then murmurs, "Who would have thought?" Then loudly, she declares, "I *want* this. I haven't stopped thinking about you. About having sex with you. I just panicked a little, but I'm fine now. I promise—"

I cut her off with a quick kiss. She gasps into my mouth, but before she can deepen the kiss, I tear my lips from hers and fight the urge to ask her who did this to her. I have a feeling if I voice my thoughts, she will run. So I don't. Instead, I cup her face in my hands and pull her mouth down to mine. This time, the kiss is soft, my eyes never leaving hers. Air rushes out of her mouth, her eyes never leaving mine.

"Thank you," she whispers against my lips.

I have no idea why she's thanking me, but I don't want her to regret her words.

My mouth leaves hers, trailing kisses along her jaw, her cheek. Her body starts to tremble, her fingers sliding up to grab my biceps so hard I have to bite back a wince. I don't stop her. The heat and wetness soaking the front of my pants is worth it.

When my lips brush her earlobe, her thighs clench around mine, her breathing erratic.

"I'll never hurt you, Elon. Trust me. Open yourself up for me. *Trust me*," I whisper in her ear, then lean back to meet her eyes. "Can you do that for me?"

She studies me with those big, expressive eyes, her chest rising and falling fast. She nods, smiling shyly, and my poor heart flips inside my chest. "I trust you."

I breathe out long and hard, shifting my body and aligning my cock to the heat between her legs.

"You're so wet," I murmur hoarsely in her ear. "I need to make you come before I blow my load in my pants. I'm going to make this so good for you, Elon."

She lets out this cute little moan that has my hand grabbing the hem of her skirt and lifting the material up. With shaking fingers, I trace her inner thigh and growl when my fingers find her pussy.

"Shit, Miss Blake. I want to see you," I growl, stroking the trimmed hair down there. "Hold on tight," I warn before reaching to the side of the recliner and pulling the release handle.

CHAPTER NINETEEN

Elon

ONCE THE CHAIR ARCHES BACK, I UNLACE MY SHOES AND SLIP THEM from my feet. They fall to the carpeted floor with a soft thud.

Nate shoots a heated look between my now-parted thighs. He makes this sexy sound in the back of his throat that has more wetness pooling where I want him to touch me.

When he lifts those dark eyes to mine, hungry fingers tug the hem of my shirt, my heartbeat reaches a crescendo, but then he grimaces, dropping his right arm down at his side with a hissed "*motherfucker*."

I freeze. "Crap! Your arm." I scoot down lower, and he winces. Belatedly, I realize his very hard cock is wedged between my butt cheeks. "Sorry!"

"Don't *move*," he commands, eyes flipping shut.

I stop, my palms pressed flat on his thick torso, our breathing mirroring each other's as it fills the room, erratic, needy. My body is ready to worship on the altar of this man because *holy shit*. Have you seen the cock on him?

I force myself to calm down and scowl at Nate. "Why didn't you say something?" His cock twitches, and I jerk in surprise. "I was about to ride you like a cowgirl, and you were in pain the whole time."

His eyebrows jump to his hairline before he guffaws. "Ride me like a cowgirl?"

Heat slaps my cheeks, but I don't let it distract me. I mumble, "I subscribe to an online magazine. . .hey! Don't change the subject."

He shakes his head, still chuckling. "It's not so bad. It will pass." Inhaling deeply, he asks, "So what else do you want to do to me?"

Eyeing him beneath my lashes, I grin, move down his legs and start unbuckling his pants and pulling down the zipper. He sucks in an inhale when I push his pants and boxers down his toned thighs, reach inside and take out his cock.

Without pulling my gaze from his, I lower my head. "This." My lips circle the tip. My tongue sweeps the length of his impressive cock, trying to remember what comes next. I've never done this before. Rick loathed oral sex.

I must be doing something right because Nate growls deep in his throat and yells, "Fucccck! I knew your mouth would feel perfect around my dick."

I feel strong fingers grip my head, and his hips jerk up as he shoves himself inside my mouth, groaning with every thrust. His hold tightens almost painfully as he lifts my head.

"Enough," he shouts gruffly. I lick my lips, smiling, proudly watching him. "I want you on the couch." He jerks his chin to the right, releases my hair and sits up. After zipping up his pants, he stands up in one swift move with his left arm around me. "Legs around my waist."

"But the pain—"

"I will live," he grunts, strong jaw clenched as he strides forward but seems to change his mind and stalks toward a darkened hall and stops in front of the first door on the right.

He pushes the door open with his foot, enters and murmurs, "The switch is on your right."

Immediately, the room is bathed in soft lighting. Quickly I take in the passing scenery as his long legs eat up the distance between the door and the large, black bed in the middle of the room. When we reach the edge of the bed, he tosses me on it. I land on my back, a yelp escaping my lips, bouncing a few times. I'm glad he doesn't handle me like I'll break. He said he'll never hurt me, and I believe him. It's weird since I have known him for only a few weeks.

Since meeting him, I've come to realize Nate loves it when I surprise him or challenge him. So I sit up quickly, crawl forward and tug the zipper down, then slide down his pants and boxers. He lifts his long legs and steps out of his clothing without a word, then he removes his watch and sets it on the dresser.

I unbutton his shirt, eager to touch him, but his fingers close around my wrist. His stares at me keenly, the heat from before replaced by something I can't put a finger on. Uncertainty? Vulnerability? I cannot imagine why he'd feel this way. He oozes perfection. He's hot beyond words.

He eyes me, his grip on my wrist tightens a little, then loosens. Exhaling a long breath through his mouth, he nods.

The second I push the material over his shoulders, I gasp. My hand flies to cover my mouth as I take in two pink scars on the right side of his upper body: one on his bicep and another on his right shoulder below the clavicle.

Now I understand the look on his face.

"Oh God, Nathaniel," I whisper. I bring my hands toward him but stop when he winces and pulls back. "C-can I touch you?"

His throat moves as he swallows audibly, watching me apprehensively. I wait, air suspended in my throat, hoping he'll say yes because dear God, the need to soothe him with my touch surpasses wanting him inside me. Or even breathing.

After what feels like years, he licks his lips nervously and nods. My palms hover on top his chest, moving up without touching him. The second my finger brushes the scar on his right shoulder, his body shakes violently.

"Elon," he hisses under his breath, his eyes shutting tightly.

I don't stop though, even when he breathes my name in a broken whisper, still shaking. My hand glides over his chest, over his shoulder and pauses when I feel a soft scar.

Exit wound.

His eyes are no longer focused on me when I pull back, so I cup his strong jaw, angling his face to mine and kiss him. My lips move against his, softly, then insistently. At first he resists, then he gives in, parting his mouth, allowing me entrance.

"Don't kiss me out of pity, Miss Blake," he mutters against my lips.

"Pity?" I press my forehead to his. "Do you know how long I've wanted to bang your brains out?"

He blinks in surprise, then laughs.

Mission accomplished.

"Allow me to show you how much I want this." I kiss the side of his mouth. Kiss the two scars on his shoulder and bicep. His body arches up, chasing my lips as his fingers grip my hair. "With you."

He's looking at me like he's seeing me for the first time. "You're something else, Elon." He flexes his thighs and smirks. "Bang my brains out."

I tug the shirt down his shoulders and arms and fold it on top of the pants and place them on top of the nearby chestnut brown two-seater. I feel his eyes on me the entire time, the heat coming off him palpable.

I guide him to the bed, gently shoving his chest to lie on his back, making sure to take care of his shoulder, then I slowly pull down my skirt.

My fingers grip the hem of my shirt, ready to pull it over my head.

Shit. Can I really do this? If Nate sees what's on my back, he'll either (1) be appalled or (2) start asking questions I'm not ready to answer.

He senses my hesitation, grasps my thigh and gives it a squeeze. "Take off your shirt."

Maybe I can switch off the lights. Or maybe if I am on top, he won't be able to see *it*. Just one night of pure pleasure, that's what I need. We need.

He frowns. "Do you have like three nipples or something? Or two belly buttons?" His eyes go wide. "Holy shit! You have triple nipple? That is so hot—"

"Oh my God! You are a freak!" I cut him off with a laugh. Seeing this easy-going side of him is so refreshing. Adorable, actually. But from the concern he's trying to hide behind that smirk, I won't be able to keep this up. So I grab the hem of my shirt and slide it over my head, fold it and set it beside his clothing.

"Condom in the first drawer." He points at the nightstand with his chin. I retrieve it and tear the foil, then dart him a questioning look. He nods, and I roll the condom around his cock.

His hands land on my hips, and he yanks me up his chest. I almost topple over. My gaze flies to his determined one. If he's experiencing any pain in his shoulder, I can't tell. His eyes are darker, hungrier, his mouth parted, teeth bared as if he's ready to eat me whole.

Jesus.

I've never seen anything sexier in my life. The reason I wanted to be on top, other than making sure he doesn't see what's on my back, was to make sure he doesn't strain his arm too much.

Once Nate positions me where he wants me, my pussy hovering above his mouth, he lets out a satisfactory grunt, muttering, "Fuck yeah. I knew you'd be so beautiful like this." Hot air from his mouth brushes across my sensitive skin as his tongue flicks out to lick down my slit. My head falls back, eyes shut tight, whimpering, moaning, my thighs clenching in anticipation.

If I continue looking at him, his gleaming eyes, that wicked mouth, I might come before I'm ready. I want to prolong this for as long as possible.

I can feel his teeth now, teasing my clit. His tongue again, thrusting into me. His fingers replace his teeth, rolling the little bud of nerves between them, before pulling out his tongue and shoving one finger inside me.

"Look at me." His words, the hoarseness in his voice, send another wave of bliss through me and I almost shatter. *Almost.*

I do as I'm told, forgetting to breathe when my eyes collide with his. I take a mental picture of him like this—smiling languidly up at me, his face flushed, need pouring out in waves—and save it for later.

He shoves a second finger inside me, pumping in and out, deeper, faster. My hands fly to my breasts, but his hand is already there, pushing mine aside. His fingers roll my nipple hard, causing a cry to fly out of my lips. Pain, pleasure. I feel all of it. His teeth graze my inner thigh and bite down hard. I clench against his fingers and come apart in his mouth so hard, shouting his name. He pulls his fingers from inside me in time to catch my slumping body before my full weight lands on his shoulder, and he lays me at his side, then licks his fingers clean. I can't look away.

I've died and gone to heaven. Seriously.

"God, you're even more beautiful when you come," he declares, lifting his head and kissing my shoulder, edging down, down—

I flip around on my back, ignoring the confused look in his eyes and take his face in my hands and kiss him, opening my mouth, allowing him entry. He takes my cue, crawls on top of me, nudges my legs apart with his knee and plants his body between them. A groan rumbles in his chest as his cock comes in contact with my pussy, that sound sending more heat between my legs.

Without his eyes leaving mine, he enters me slowly. I hold my breath, trying not to wince as I do my best to accommodate him.

When he's fully seated inside me, Nate grasps my face in his large hands, crashes his lips to mine without warning, thrusting his tongue into my mouth, tangling with mine. He kisses me, a short snarl pouring into my lips like he's angry, punishing me and fucking my mouth all at the same time. God, he's addictive. The need to make him feel what I'm feeling shoots through me. I sink my fingers into his hair and pull. A sharp hiss leaves his mouth and pours into mine. Then he chuckles that dark sinful laugh from earlier before biting my lip.

He starts to move inside me, our mouths still connected, our fingers still clutching onto each other. He pulls out, then pushes inside me. In and out. Slowly, torturously.

My hands leave his hair and land on his tight ass. The way he's moving, the way he's making me feel, I just want him to ravish me without holding back. I want to watch him as he comes apart.

"Don't hold back," I utter when he lifts his head to stare down at me, sweat peppering his forehead.

I trust him, I remind myself.

He's not that asshole Rick. Nate would never hurt me. I feel it in my bones every time he looks at me.

"I want this to be perfect fo—"

"Nathaniel," I cut him off and his eyes narrow, a muscle ticking in his jaw. That look! I've never been so turned on. "I don't want perfect right now. I want you. All of you, whatever way I can get you. Do. Not. Hold. Back."

Those words seem to do the trick. Nate drops his body on top of mine, tilting a bit to the side to give me some breathing space.

"Hold on to the headboard."

I do, then take a deep breath. He's taller and heavier than me, but somehow, we fit perfectly. Hip to hip, my breasts against his chest. Then his hands are moving up my arms and linking with mine on the headboard. His head drops in the crook of my neck. He peppers kisses along my collarbone at the same time as he's thrusting into me.

His hips lift, then lower as he plunges into me without notice with enough driving force to cause my body to slide up the bed, sending my thoughts scattering and turning my brain to mush. He's fucking me like he's on a mission to free me from my demons, and I'm loving it.

"Feel that, Elon?" His voice is muffled in my neck. "I'm about to fuck the bad memories away. By the time I'm through with you, the only thing in your mind will be me. Understood?"

I nod, feeling hot tears in my eyes. He knows. He knows I've been hurt before, probably got a hint when I froze up on the recliner in the living room.

His body stops moving on top of mine. "*Understood*?" he asks again softly.

"Yeah," I whisper, hoping he can't hear the tears in my voice.

He starts moving again, muttering into my neck, making promises to "replace those assholes". He circles his hips, then thrusts deeper inside me than I thought possible. I close my eyes, feeling my orgasm rushing forward, threatening to kill me. Revive me. Then I'm propelled into the skies shouting his name; I'm soaring. My heart fights to catch up with my breathing. I let myself be swept into this place that doesn't have rules, just pleasure.

When I finally come down and open my eyes, Nate is watching me with something like awe while thrusting languidly inside me.

"Beautiful," he says, increasing his strokes, making love to me with heartbreaking gentleness. I'm useless beneath him.

I try to wrap my limbs around his torso so I can return the favor, but they won't cooperate. He doesn't seem to care though. He continues driving into me with single-minded determination, his eyes never leaving mine, bottom lip caught between his teeth.

He pumps a few times, then I feel his body stiffen above mine. He growls my name, the sound ricocheting around the room. He's still uttering my name in soft pants when he drops his head in the crook of my shoulder, placing wet, hot kisses on my jaw, my neck, behind my ear.

He rolls to the side using his left arm to take me with him. He tucks me to his side, reaches down and pulls the sheet to our shoulders. He kisses the top of my head and rests his palm flat on my chest possessively.

The room smells of sweat and sex. So intoxicating. So *us*.

He pulls out, leaves the bed and removes the condom while heading to the bathroom. He returns moments later and pulls me in his arms again.

Silence envelopes us as we just lie there, enjoying being in each other's arms, his hand drawing patterns on my arm. I'm basking in his heat, my brain subconsciously following his finger's movements. His finger moves on my skin and I concentrate on following the letters he's tracing on my back.

MINE.

Mine.

And I'm flying again, reaching for the stars.

You don't even have a future with him, Elon. He's your professor, a voice rudely snaps me out of my languid bliss.

As if I need a reminder.

I shove that voice to the back of my head and snuggle closer into his warmth.

Right now in this room, he's mine. I'll think about the rest once I walk out the front door.

My head jerks up, and I stare at his handsome, scruffy jaw, taking in the satisfied look on his face.

"Are you sure you are okay?"

One eye pops open. "I've never been more okay in my life." He closes his eye and says, "Sleep, Little Wolf. I need you well-rested for the next round."

I nod, still wanting more of him, but he probably needs to rest his body.

I giggle, letting my eyes fall shut, feeling his semi-erect cock on my back as he spoons me.

CHAPTER TWENTY

Nate

I wait until her breathing evens out before carefully shifting her out of my arms and sit up on the bed.

Holy hell.

My arm is throbbing, and my head feels like it's about to explode. I should have admitted to Elon when she asked me if I was in pain, but I was beyond stopping it. Not with the way she was making me feel like I'm whole. Then she kissed my scars and right there, I could have laid the world at her feet if she'd asked me to.

I pull the covers up over her, covering her shoulder, and go to the bathroom across the room and shut the door. Anxiously, I grab one of my prescription bottles from the cabinet above the sink and toss two in my mouth. I return to bed just as Elon releases a loud snore and stretches in her sleep, letting out that sexy-as-hell moan. That sound should bother me. Instead, it comforts me, thrills me, having her here in my bed.

The sheet slides down her chest, revealing her breasts. Even with pain crushing my senses, my shameless cock responds to her. Then she curls into a tiny ball of red hair and tight little body, before falling back asleep.

I'm about to cover her again when I notice her inked torso. Is this the reason why she kept squirming away or flipping around whenever her back was on me?

My gaze lands on the tattoo of a cello on the right side of her torso that wraps around to her back, dark against her pale skin. Musical notes float above the cello, giving way to birds in flight, stopping slightly above her right shoulder blade.

It's beautiful.

Unable to resist, I bend down and softly kiss the cello, the notes, the wings of one of the birds. The slight curve of her spine calls to me, and I softly kiss the little dimples on her lower back.

Fucking sexy.

I growl just thinking about taking her from behind, my thumbs digging into her creamy, dimpled flesh.

I frown when I see a fine, line scar on the left side of her lower back, about twenty centimeters long.

What the hell?

Forgetting the fading pain on my shoulder, I lean closer and brush the tip of my fingers on her skin. A cold sweat breaks out on my hairline.

My fists clench, the vein in my temple throbs.

Who the fuck did this to her?

I want to rip the world apart until I find the shithead responsible for hurting her like that.

My body trembles with anger, and there's no way I can lie near her and not wake her up.

I kiss her shoulder, then pull the sheet up to her jaw. After throwing on a pair of pants and a T-shirt, I turn off the light and leave the room.

Elon

I wake up to a dark room, feeling a little disoriented. Then, I remember where I am and jackknife on the bed, the sheet pooling around my waist. Heat fills my cheeks, and my thighs clench as memories of what happened in this bed flash inside my head.

Was that really me? Those sounds leaving my mouth, my body arching wantonly as Nate fucked me like he was going to war, and he was taking a piece of me to remember me by? Me screaming his name over and over as I came? If it weren't for the evident pain on his shoulder he was trying to hide, I'd have claimed a few more orgasms.

Damn, Elon, you little harlot.

I fall back on the bed and turn to look at the alarm clock on the nightstand on Nate's side of the bed.

Twenty minutes past midnight.

Moving my head, I press my face on the pillow where Nate had been four hours ago, inhaling his scent. I could get used to this.

Shit. Just one round of great sex with one of the hottest men alive, not to mention a great lover, and I'm already thinking of getting used to this. To him.

Time to leave before I start planning on having his babies.

I reach to my left and switch on the lamp before rolling out of bed, snatching my clothes and tossing them on. Then, I grab my booties and tiptoe out of the room.

Nate is not in the living room or the kitchen. I risk a glance over my shoulder, beyond the glass balcony door. The lamp on the wall above him casts his side-profile in shadows. I feel those tiny butterfly wings beating wildly inside my tummy as I take in his tousled hair, strong jaw, wide cheekbones.

I also notice again how sexy he looks wearing his reading glasses.

He scrolls the lit-up screen of his phone, a small frown forming on his face. Seconds later, he sets it on the table and picks something from the table and puts it between his lips. His cheeks hollow as he sucks on what looks like a cigarette between the tips of his index finger and thumb of his left hand, then exhales again. He then tilts his head back. Wisps of smoke leave his lips, vanishing into the cold air.

Nate smokes? Not that I have anything against smoking, but I never pictured him to be a smoker.

God, even smoking looks good on him.

This man who rocked my world, ignoring whatever pain he was going through just to make sure I was satisfied.

I can't sneak off like I'm ashamed of what we did. If anything, I'm grateful to him for giving me something I thought I'd never feel with any man.

Feeling adored and the out-of-this-world orgasm.

Dropping my shoes next to the cello, I join him on the balcony, rubbing my hands along my arms to ward off the chill. The smell of weed hits me in the face, causing me to stagger a bit.

"I wondered if you would leave without saying goodbye," he says without looking at me, rolling the joint between his fingers before taking a quick drag.

When I don't answer, he looks up to find me staring at the joint.

I'm a junior at Rushmore, and while some students make a point to enjoy college, maybe try everything once, I've never felt the urge to try recreational drugs. Even Amber, who grew up in a sheltered household, has smoked a joint or two.

So, when Nate smirks at me and says, "You've never smoked one of these before?" I shake my head and cross my arms on my chest tighter and say, "There's always a first time, right?"

He chuckles deeply and sets the joint on the glass ashtray on the table in front of him. He snakes his left arm around my waist and pulls me on his lap, my back to his front.

God, even on resting mode his dick is huge.

"You okay?" he whispers, nuzzling his nose along the column of my neck, and I let my head fall back as his teeth nibble the skin there.

I nod, shivering, snuggling closer. "Yeah." I glance at the ashtray, suddenly feeling reckless. "Can I try that?"

His head comes up and he narrows his eyes, studying me for several seconds before nodding once.

Reaching forward, I take it and hold it the way I saw him doing, put it between my lips and take a quick hit.

And then I start coughing, my nose and mouth fighting to exhale the smoke.

"Shit," he mutters, taking it from me and grinding the end on the ashtray. He starts to rub my back soothingly as I cough my lungs out. "Breathe, sweetheart."

When I feel well enough to speak without tears spilling down my cheeks, I giggle at my inexperience. He joins in, laughing softly.

"You okay?"

I nod, my head feeling lighter than before. "Is it weird I feel a little high right now?"

He tucks my head under his chin, kissing my hair, a laugh rumbling in his chest. "You're so cute."

Silence falls between us for several minutes and the effect of the drug loosens my thoughts, causing a mayhem inside my head. Doubts creep in.

Did he enjoy what we did? Was I good? Did I satisfy him? Shit. Maybe—"This was a huge mistake."

His body stiffens beneath mine, the hand on my stomach tensing. "What did you say?"

I lick my lips and close my eyes. "Was this a mistake?"

He is quiet for several seconds. "Do you regret it?"

"God, no," I admit quickly, shifting on his lap to straddle him. "Honestly? It was the best night of my life. Best sex I have ever had."

He grins wide, flexing his thighs. I gasp when I feel him thickening between my legs.

"Then what is it?" he inquires, kissing my shoulder.

This is awkward. Doubting myself makes me feel weak, and I hate it.

"So, you smoke," I say instead, praying he'd follow my lead and forget about what we were talking about.

He watches me intently, then says, "Helps with the pain. Helps me forget."

I drop my gaze as his words make my stomach lurch. "Is that why you are smoking now? To forget?"

"Jesus, fuck. *No*." He cups my cheeks in his big hands. "For the first time in three years, I feel alive. What we did in there–" he points inside the house with his finger "–you have no idea what you did for me. You gave me something I thought I would never find again. You gave me *me* back."

I want to ask him what happened to him, what did he lose. But I have a feeling that's a sore subject, and he might end up shutting down on me. Besides, I want him to tell me when he is ready.

So I nod. He seals his lips over mine, kissing me so softly but passionately nonetheless.

He leans his forehead to mine, eyes holding mine captive and whispers, "Stay."

"Okay." How can I refuse him when he's looking at me like I'm the next best thing since oxygen? Besides, Amber is out with Alex and will probably be back on Sunday.

He stands up, making sure my feet are touching the ground before removing his arm, and we head back inside. He pulls me toward the kitchen.

"Come on. Let me get you something to eat."

The next twenty minutes, we spend eating ham sandwiches. We don't talk much, though.

When we are finished, Nate guides me to his room, his hand teasing my lower back.

He removes his glasses and sets them on the nightstand before stripping off his clothing, never looking away from me while I remove mine. He watches me as I reach for his and fold them, neatly setting them on the couch next to mine.

"I'll be on edge if I don't do this," I explain.

"I know." And he does. I can see understanding in his eyes. "Get on the bed."

I literally skip to the bed and crawl on it. He's on me within seconds, kissing my neck, breasts, lips, jaw, taking his time like we have eternity on our side.

"Tell me something dirty," he whispers in my ear hotly. "Something you have never admitted to anyone. Something that turns you on."

His words send heat spearing between my legs. Like every woman with a pulse, I have fantasies, but I've never spoken them aloud.

"Blindfold." I pant just as his tongue slowly moves across the sensitive place between my neck and ear.

"Kinky." He moves, flanking my back. "Why blindfold?'

My back arches as he curls his body around mine, his arm curling around my waist and pulling me back to his hard body.

The way he is working me right now, it will be a miracle if I remember my own name.

"Elon." He bites my shoulder, and I squeal at the unexpected pain. "Blindfold."

"I—I don't know," I pant. "I've never done it before. Maybe the not knowing what my partner is going to do next. . . oh God! Nate!"

His mouth is grazing my spine, making this sound in the back of his throat as if he's eating his last meal. The tip of his tongue traces a hot trail down, down, down until it's too late, and his lips are skimming the knife scar on my torso.

Shit!

My body jerks in shock and I flip around, almost clocking him on his nose in the process.

"Sorry!" I mumble, sitting up and pulling the sheet around me, my body trembling. "I really think I should go."

He sits back on his heels, fully erect and hands outstretched toward me. "I shouldn't have done that. I'm sorry."

Regret and concern swirl in his eyes. My vision blurs, and I turn away before he sees the tears building in them, then pull my legs up and fold my arms around them.

He must have seen the scar while I was asleep, the sign of my stupidity.

"I met him three years ago when I started school here at Rushmore," I start telling him without preamble. "He was older than me, handsome and the way he used to look at me." I face him again and swallow hard, then force a laugh. "I have no idea why I am telling you this–" He moves so fast and before I know his intentions, he moves behind me, pulling me between his legs and hugging me so tight, I can feel his touch in my bones. Never in my life have I been held this way by someone who knows how it feels to be inside me.

"Tell me," he murmurs into my hair, and more tears stream down my face.

"Sorry. I'm not always such a mess," I apologize. "At first he was exceedingly nice to me. And I let myself believe that there were men out there who were not like my father. One month into the relationship, he changed. He became volatile and moody." I pause, realizing Nate has gone still behind me.

"One night I went to his place just in time to find him trashing everything, a bottle of vodka in one hand. He accused me of cheating on him with Nick. Said he was going to teach Nick a lesson."

My lungs are starved for air, I need to breathe. Every time I close my eyes, I feel the knife slicing into my skin, cutting me open, marking me as his without my consent.

"He did that to you?" His voice is laced with fury.

I turn to face him. "I tend to attract the wild kind," I chuckle, trying to soften the tension cracking the air around us. "I should have left him the second I realized he was violent."

Nate grasps my face in his hands. "Everyone is born with a clean slate. What we do with it is up to us. Just because your ex-boyfriend got off on hitting you doesn't mean you are to blame. Real men don't hit women, no matter how angry or frustrated they are. Real men do everything to protect them."

I'm about to open my mouth and tell him that Rick was a coward and a manipulative asshole, but his words stop me.

He's right.

Tears roll down my cheeks, and I wipe them away with the back of my hand.

"That's really sweet," I whisper, as I look up at him, his eyes calming me as my breathing begins to even out.

He ducks his head to meet my gaze. "I want you to do me a favor."

I nod, forcing a smile.

"I need you to trust me and know that I will never hurt you intentionally. As long as we are doing this. . . whatever this is we are doing, I hope you will consider letting me in. Let me take care of you."

I squint at him, wondering what it is about him that makes me believe his words. "I already trust you. I have told you things my own sisters don't know about me. I never told them about what Rick did to me because I was so humiliated."

Growing up, I vowed to myself I'd never let any man lay a hand on me or hurt me with words like my father used to do. I'd failed miserably when I started dating Rick and also my boyfriend before that.

After the incident with that bastard, I signed up for counseling sessions with Rushmore's therapist. It took me a long time to stop excusing him for what he did.

"Where is that son of a bitch now?"

I shrug. "I don't know. I filed a restraining order seven months ago." I don't tell him what Amber told me about Rick being back. He already knows that part of my life that I didn't intend to share in the first place.

But then he held me.

Made me feel safe.

He takes my hands into his. "You mentioned your father."

I stiffen in his arms and close my eyes. "He was a bastard." The words are harsh and final.

He doesn't say anything after that, just lets go of me and pushes me gently to lie down. Then, he straddles my hips, kissing every inch of my back. "Beautiful tattoo. Any special meaning behind it?"

I nod, my fingers curled around the sheets. "When I was little, I used to feel trapped in my own existence. My life. Playing the cello makes me feel free, like I'm soaring through the sky. Every time I feel like I'm tethered to this earth, I remind myself that anything is possible and that one day I'll find my wings and fly."

"You already found your wings, and they are beautiful," he says into my skin. "You're fierce and brave, Little Wolf."

"Why do you call me that?" I ask, looking over my shoulder at him, moaning when his hand skims my inner thigh.

"You're not afraid of talking back to me, especially when I'm being an asshole. God, do you know how stunning you look when you are angry and fire flashes in your eyes?" He bites one cheek, staring at me under his lashes. "Quiet, until provoked."

Then, Nate drapes his body over mine, his left elbow propping his upper body up, keeping most of the weight off his right shoulder and at the same time pinning me on the mattress with his lower body. I'm at his mercy, writhing beneath him as he plays me like a cello, strumming me with his tongue and teeth. His fingers lock around my hair, firmly tugging me back to meet his mouth.

God, this man can kiss. And he does it like he was born to make love to my mouth and only mine.

Suddenly he is on fire, greedily kissing me everywhere, as if he's apologizing for my past, showing me how being treated right feels like.

A sob slips from my mouth, but it doesn't stop him. In fact, it seems to fuel his ministrations, altering my reality and rearranging my thoughts. It's kind of scary because, after Rick left and before Nate's arrival, I never thought any man would make me feel like this.

He pauses long enough to pull a condom from the nightstand.

"You okay, sweetheart?"

I nod. "Yeah."

He's back behind me, thrusting into me, groaning, his lips on my ear telling me how good it feels to be inside my tight pussy, how tight I am. He knows what I need, and he's going to give it to me. His arm circles me and he clutches my boob in his hand. Shifting to the left, he anchors our bodies with his hip before he makes love to me excruciatingly slowly, his grip on my hair hovering between gentle and rough. His scruff, his teeth, his mouth. . .he's consuming me, making me realize I hadn't lived until his mouth was on mine, until he was buried inside me.

"Nate!" I breathe.

"Give it to me," he growls into my ear, thrusting with gentle, deep strokes as he makes love to me.

"Oh God! I'm coming!"

His hand moves to my hip, grips hard as his thighs flex, and I'm spiraling out of control, shouting Nate's name, soaring across a star-kissed sky. He's still murmuring encouragement when I finally come down from my high, staring at me like. . .like I'm his *forever*.

Before I can collect my thoughts, he's pumping into me viciously, then stiffens, his warm breath feathering my neck, calling my name over and over in a husky voice, his body shaking from the force of his orgasm.

When our inhales and exhales are in synchrony, he pulls out of me and kisses my shoulder. He grimaces as he gets on his feet, favoring his right shoulder as he heads to the bathroom. After disposing the condom, he returns and *spoons* me.

He buries his face into my neck, inhaling deeply, then says in a sleepy voice, "After three years of feeling as if my lungs would never consume oxygen again, I can finally breathe."

My body stills. My thoughts freeze.

Seconds later, he exhales slowly as his breathing evens out.

My thoughts burst into chaos, flight mode activated, but he's holding me like he's never going to let me go.

I'm terrified out of my mind because stuff like this only happens in my dreams or in fiction. The man draped all over me with his big hand clutching my boob is too real, too good to be true. He's also my professor. And he just rocked my reality with a few simple words.

God.

Being here, being in his arms is everything.

Before my sensible brain sabotages my reckless heart, I snuggle deeper into him and savor his scent, his closeness, knowing that tomorrow morning, this will be over.

"Shit. shit shit!"

The whispered words in a panicked voice rouse me from my deep sleep. Elon is no longer nestled in my arm like she was two hours ago when I woke up to make sure she hadn't made a run for it while I slept. My poor ego wouldn't have survived the blow. And also, for some weird reason I cannot explain, I wanted her face to be the first thing I saw when I opened my eyes.

Whatever has her freaking out must be colossal to make her thoughts spin around inside that pretty head of hers.

Finally, I pop my eyes open, and I'm met with a round ass covered in hot pink, cotton panties pointing to the ceiling. I imagine climbing out of bed, yanking the material down and taking her from behind, and my dick responds like a champ.

"I hope you're not planning on sneaking out without a goodbye, Miss Blake," I say.

She squeaks and spins around, her hair flying to her face, blocking her view. She tucks a lock behind her ear and greets me animatedly. "Hey! Hi, you're awake."

Her eyes scan the room before zeroing in on the couch. Relief washes over her face as she practically sprints forward.

"What's going on?" I ask, swinging my legs out of bed.

I have a rough idea why she looks like she's about to jump out of her skin.

She is spooked. Scared as fuck. Just like last night when she told me about that little shit excuse of an ex-boyfriend. And when I spouted those words about finally being able to breathe, I could swear if I wasn't caging her with my arms, she'd be gone by now. I won't even begin to evaluate my reasons behind speaking those words, otherwise I'll just be as spooked as she is.

After Camille, I never thought I would ever feel that kind of pull with someone else. Something beyond mere sex. It's terrifying, but more than that, it gives my heart that extra beat, just enough to make me feel alive.

I watch her for a few seconds before standing up and walking over to her. I block her path with my body and take her hands in mine.

"Take a deep breath, okay?" I instruct her. She nods and sucks a deep breath, blows it out through her mouth. "Now, tell me what's going on."

"I'm running late for my tutoring class. I'm never late for class."

"What time is your class?"

Her head whips in the direction of the alarm clock. "Nine-thirty. I have less than thirty minutes to go home, shower and change."

She pulls her hands from mine, grabs her skirt and wiggles her sweet ass into it and zips it up, but then her face suddenly goes pale and her body sways. Her stomach grumbles, causing her eyes to widen. Her cheeks flush with embarrassment.

I walk over to the dresser, pull out a pair of faded jeans and T-shirt, and slip them on, then take her hand and leave the room.

We enter the living room, which is designed in an open-plan style. I point to one of the chairs in the living room. "Sit."

She doesn't argue with me and sits primly, drumming her fingers on her thighs.

I watch her for a few seconds, wanting more than anything to comfort her, but I have a feeling she needs distraction more than being reassured.

"Coffee or tea?"

She blinks at me, surprised by my question. She answers, "Coffee. With cream."

I head to the kitchen, feeling her eyes on me the entire way. When I glance back, she's practically drooling at my ass.

"That look could get you into a lot of trouble," I tease.

The flush already on her cheeks deepens as she wipes her mouth with the back of her hand and brings her eyes to mine. I could swear I hear a sigh when I smirk at her.

I return with a mug of coffee and a plate of Nutella bread cut in the middle like I've seen her eating at the office.

"Here you go."

She beams up at me as she takes the plate from me. She plows through the bread like she's starving, then gulps down the coffee

Christ, I can't stop looking at her. Disheveled hair or not, she's beautiful.

"Come back after your class?"

She shakes her head while hopping up from the chair. "I'm driving home later. I'll see you in class Monday."

Last night, we were passion and heat. Now, she is distant and edgy. Seeing her like this leaves a bad taste in my mouth. She's already in my blood like a drug that won't be drained.

As if reading my mind, she doubles back, stands on her tiptoes and seals her mouth over mine. The kiss is short but hot, knocking the wind out of me.

I watch her as she slides her cello to her back, grabs her bag and rushes out the door.

I could have easily hauled her ass back to bed and given her something to remember me by. But from the speed her legs were carrying her to the door, I couldn't chase her. Not yet anyway. I know she will be back because, like me, she wants more of last night.

From the moment I laid eyes on Elon, I knew I was in trouble. And if what I'm feeling right now shows on my face, then Elizabeth was right. I did look at her the same way I used to look at her daughter.

I need to be careful.

The sound of a phone ringing in the direction of my room jolts me from my thoughts. I walk back to my bedroom and answer the phone, catching Bennett's name flashing on the screen.

Shit. I forgot we had plans to take Matthew to drafting day for the Burlington Little League at the Burlington Sports Club.

"Yo," he greets. "You coming or what?"

"Give me ten minutes."

He grunts something under his breath, before saying, "Make it five. I need you to hold me back before I murder the coach."

I laugh and end the call.

After a quick shower and downing coffee, I shoot a quick message to Elon to check if she got home safely, then grab my keys, shove my medication in my jacket pocket and head out.

CHAPTER TWENTY-ONE

Elon

THE SECOND I WALK INSIDE THE APARTMENT, AMBER DASHES OUT OF her room and throws her arms around me, knocking me back a couple of steps. She mutters, "Thank God, you are okay."

I hug her back tightly, feeling guilty and trying to come up with an excuse for where I spent the night. Last night she and Alex were supposed to go to a party, then she was going to spend the weekend with him at his parents' house.

Crap.

She pulls back, her eyes roaming my face, the worry in them cutting through me like a knife. "Where have you been? I tried calling you several times and your phone just kept ringing, then going to voicemail." She stops and inhales deeply. "I thought something happened to you. You better have a good excuse, E."

I checked my phone for any missed calls or messages after leaving Nate's place, but it had already shut off. The battery must have drained again, even though I'd charged it during my tutoring class. I've been saving to get a new phone for a while now, but between

Josh being sick and helping Nor with the bills, and also paying half of the bills for this apartment, a cell phone wasn't high on my list of priorities.

I can't tell her I was at Nick's place. She already knows what happened between us.

My heart races at the thought of her finding out about Nate. I move away from her arms and hurry toward my room. "Can we talk about this later? I'm late for my class."

"*Elon.*" I've never heard her use that tone of voice before, which is why I stop and face her again, trying hard not to squirm under her concerned gaze. "I was *worried.*" Her voice breaks as she wipes her cheeks with the back of her hand.

I'm a world-class jerk.

"I'm so sorry for worrying you. I didn't mean—" She suddenly leans forward, sniffing me. "What are you doing?"

She narrows her eyes at me. "You smell like sex."

"What?" I blurt out in a nervous squeak.

Of course she'd know what sex smells like since she gets laid on a daily basis. I'm sure the blush on my face is a level-ten alarm right now. I curse my phone for dying on me.

Outwardly, I roll my eyes and mumble while continuing my journey to my room. "Yeah, like I'd be so lucky. I thought you were supposed to be with Alex."

"Elise called me when she couldn't get you on the phone, so I told her I'd come home and check if you were okay," she explains, staring at me as if she's trying to read me. "Holy shit! You totally got laid!" She hoots loudly, clapping and jumping. "Was it Mr. Crotch Grabber? Dude, this is *good.*"

I show her my back as I prop my cello and bag against my desk, hurry to the white dresser and pull out a black T-shirt, bra and panties and leave the room again. Amber's feet pad behind me as she rambles on about making up for all the times I've gone without sex. I stop abruptly at the bathroom door, causing her to bump into me, and turn around.

"Unless you want to join me in the shower, then by all means come in and strip." I raise a brow in question.

She takes a step back, snickering. "Someone is letting their freak flag fly. Okay, first tell me who's ding dong you rode all night."

"I can't do this right now." My voice comes out harsher than I intend. She flinches, the smile fading fast. "Shit, I'm sorry. Look, can we talk about this another time? I'm almost late for class—"

"Fine. Whatever." She flicks her blonde hair back, turns and marches away with her shoulders curled around her as if to protect herself from a blow.

"Amber—"

She pauses long enough to look at me over her shoulder and mutters, "It's okay," before disappearing into her room.

I rub my face with my hands, groaning under my breath. Not only am I breaking the rules and endangering my position at Rushmore, I'm the worst friend ever. First Nick and now Amber.

The thought of my friends being upset with me makes my nose sting and my eyes burn with tears. I don't have many friends, and losing the few I have makes my heart twist in my chest.

I've played by the rules my entire life, and the second I step out of line, pieces of my life start collapsing like dominoes.

How the hell am I going to sort this out?

Pushing those thoughts to the back of my mind for now, I strip off my clothes and toss them in the hamper before hopping in the shower.

After taking the shortest shower in the history of showers, I rush out of my room, dressed in my T-shirt and faded jeans with my towel-dried hair pinned up in a bun. I duck my head inside Amber's room to say goodbye, but it's empty. She must have left while I was in the bathroom. I grab my cello and bag and leave the apartment, the tightness in my chest getting worse as I hop inside my car.

Seven minutes later, I pull into the parking lot Studio 22 shares with Burlington Sports Club. I hop out, grab my stuff and dash into the building. I arrive in class with only two minutes to spare, plug my phone into the charger and concentrate on teaching two different classes filled with ten-year-olds for the next three hours, momentarily distracted from the issues plaguing my life.

Nate

"It's about time you got your ass here," Bennett declares as soon as I sit next to him on the bleachers.

"Yeah, yeah," I mutter under my breath, propping my elbows on my parted knees and clasping my hands between my legs. "How's the game going?" I ask, searching the field for Matthew.

I spot him running around in circles in his white uniform, his cap barely sitting properly atop the massive curls on his head. The coach yells his name, waving animatedly, but two more boys join my nephew and run off in the other direction

"Jesus," I chuckle under my breath. "No wonder the coach looks like he's about to have a fit."

"He can't seem to control the kids. He's as useless as tits on a nun."

I turn to look at him, my brow raised. "Ouch. Someone's grouchy this morning. Did Izzy forget to kiss your boo-boos today?" I flash him an evil grin.

"Shut up, asshole." He rubs his face, then glares at me with blood-shot eyes. "Izzy was having pains last night, so we went to the hospital to make sure everything was okay. The doctor put her on bed rest for at least two weeks."

"Shit, I'm sorry. Why didn't you call me?"

He shrugs and says, "She threatened to cut off my balls if I called you. I happen to love my balls where they are." He inhales deeply. "My mom drove over and stayed with the kids until we came back around three in the morning."

"Christ." I drag my fingers through my hair, massaging my neck as I worry. Unlike previous pregnancies, this one seems to be taking a toll on Izzy, and I'm worried about her.

"Yeah," he murmurs. "I told her I'd tie her to the bed if it comes to that."

I laugh and ask, "What did she say?"

This time his huge-ass shoulders shake with laughter. "She'd kick my ass before I even had a chance to tie her." We fall silent for a few seconds, staring out into the field just in time to see the batter, a scrawny boy around Matthew's age, hit the ball and send it flying across the field. Matthew, playing center field, runs as fast as his small legs can carry him. Just as he's about to catch the ball, the two boys playing right and left field dash toward him aiming for the ball, too, and they all collide, rolling around on the grass.

Chaos erupts, and at some point, the coach looks like he's about to cry.

"Your sister is quite a handful. But one look from my mother is enough to set her straight," Bennett says with a soft laugh.

"Good," I say, relieved. I know Izzy; she has always been stubborn.

She needs someone who will not let her get away with a lot. Gladys, Bennett's mother, is the right person for this job. Mine would just let my sister do almost anything as soon as she bats those baby blues at her.

"I wouldn't trade her for anything though," he adds, pointing at the field, and we watch his spawn dusting his pants while scowling at his teammates. "She gave me the world. She gave me life."

"If you traded her, I'd kill you." He turns to face me, probably gauging how serious I am. Whatever he sees on my face has him raising up his hands, palms facing me as if in surrender. "Besides, after what you two put me through while dating and after getting married, I'd lock you both in a room until you sorted out whatever shit was going on, making sure you stayed true to your vows."

"I knew there was a reason I love you," he teases. "Such a romantic."

I shake my head and chuckle under my breath.

I love Izzy and Bennett, but Jesus. These two give a whole new meaning to love and marriage. But they gave me a nephew and a niece, so I forgive them for the headaches.

I have always wanted children. I've dreamed about having enough kids to fill a soccer field.

That being said, as much as I'd love to see my woman barefoot and pregnant, I'd also respect her wish if she wanted to work.

"Camille never wanted kids, you know," I say quietly, remembering how many times we argued about it.

"Don't look back, Nate." Bennett says. "Focus on now. The present. Otherwise you'll always be trapped by your past."

He's right, and I know that. I have no idea why I brought it up. Maybe because after the last few weeks, something has changed in me. For the first time in as long as I can remember, I feel hopeful.

Elon makes me feel alive. And from what I have seen so far, she has a stubborn streak in her and enjoys a good challenge.

I feel my lips pull upward in a smile, remembering the loud snores and waking up to find her cute ass pointing at the ceiling.

"You are weirding me out, man," Bennett says, pulling me out of my thoughts. "What is going on with you?"

I school my features to unreadable before facing him.

"I'll be damned," he mutters under his breath in fascination. "Let me guess: Cello Girl?"

I'm about to snarl at him, let him know she has a name, but I change my mind because it'd only make him more interested. Right now, I need him off my ass.

My gaze snaps to his and I frown.

Nosy bastard.

"Back off, Ben."

Laughter booms out of his mouth as he slaps my shoulder, sending pain shooting down my arm.

"Fucking *hell*, Bennett," I grit the words, my eyes watering.

"Shit." He scoots away quickly, turning to face me. "I'm sorry."

I pull out the plastic bottle from my jacket pocket and toss a pill into my mouth, then grab the bottle of water he's holding out in my direction. "Just keep those large paws to yourself, Goliath."

I close my eyes and wait for the pain to pass.

"Has Dr. Rosenburg contacted you yet?" Bennett asks quietly.

I nod, remembering the email I was reading last night before Elon joined me on the balcony. "He wants me to fly to Chicago for some tests." In the past three years, I've been through several tests and undergone two surgeries. I never wanted to see the inside of a hospital again after that. "He's proposing a different kind of surgery now. Tendon transfer to restore muscle function, and hopefully fix the injured nerve in my bicep."

I blow out a long breath, open my eyes and watch his as they shift to my right arm, then back to my face. "Tendon transfer?"

I didn't really understand the mechanics of the whole procedure while I was reading the email, given that I was a little high from the weed. So I say, "He'll explain everything when I get there."

"When do you leave?"

"He'll be out of the country for at least three weeks, so probably at the end of February."

Bennett looks at me with sympathy in his eyes.

I grimace. "I hate it when you look at me like that, Ben."

He licks his lips, the look replaced by a wicked glint in his eye. "So, have you proposed to her yet?"

"Proposed to whom?"

He laughs. "Her. Cello Girl." He narrows his eyes. "If I remember correctly, you have a habit of proposing to women—"

"Oh fuck *off*." I roll my eyes. "I've proposed to only one woman in my life. And she turned me down every single year."

Until three years ago when she was taken away from me.

The memory of proposing to Camille on the same day we first met in Rushmore and then consequently every year after that makes me smile but at the same time forms a lump in my throat.

The laughter in his face fades, his brows dipping a little. "Nothing is stopping you from having that again. Sometimes—"

"Daddy! Daddy!" Matthew's shout interrupts Bennett, and we turn our attention to the field.

Baseball practice seems to be over.

"Did you see me catch the ball?"

Bennett unfolds his bulky frame from the seat and grins wide, arms outstretched as his son runs toward him. Matthew doesn't even wait for his father to answer his question. He hops into Ben's arms and excitedly talks about the game while his father tells him that he saw everything.

"Acting is not for you, my friend. Stick to running Reed's Lounge," I say loud enough for my words to reach Bennett as we walk out of the sports center, heading to his car. Matthew hops inside the passenger seat as soon as his father opens the door.

He smirks and says, "Look at you making jokes. You should get laid more often." He slides inside his truck and slams the door in my face before I can form a rebuttal, leaving me glaring after him.

I'm about to turn around and walk to my car when I see Elon marching across the parking lot, carrying a plastic bag in one hand. At the same time, she lifts her head in my direction. Her steps falter before halting altogether.

"Hey," I greet, my feet finally finding the strength to walk. "What are you doing here?"

She smiles, and I shove my balled fists inside my pants pockets to stop them from reaching out. Touching her.

"I'm done for the day—" she points at Studio 22 on her right, and I notice her eyes do a quick sweep of our surroundings, as if checking if we are being watched. "So I went to buy some yarn for Joce from the shop over there," she says in that soft voice that sends blood straight to my groin, and she points to some shops behind her. But I'm too busy being sucked in to those eyes of hers. "My niece enjoys knitting. School project. I help her whenever—"

"Relax, Elon," I say in a low voice, cutting her off.

The sound of a car door opening and slamming shut reminds me my nosy brother-in-law hasn't driven off.

Footsteps thump closer, then, "Hey Nate, I forgot to ask you—" stops, then, "Oh, hi there. I'm Bennett Reed. His brother-in-law." He jerks his thumb at me, side-eyeing me while smirking. "And you are. . ."

Elon's smile widens. "Elon Blake." And then she innocently adds, "I saw Professor Rowe standing here and thought I'd say hi."

"You're his student, huh?" Bennett asks, his voice laced with curiosity.

She nods, looking from me to Bennett. "Anyway, I'd better get going if I want to make it to Willow Hill before nightfall."

She says goodbye and walks past me in the direction where I assume her car is parked. As much as I want to turn and stare at her, I can't. Not with Bennett standing beside me, vibrating with questions.

He rounds on me, eyebrows raised. "The fuck, Nate? Your student?"

"You've lost your mind if you think I'd mess around—"

"Your face lit up like fireworks when you saw her. Have you already fucked her?"

Those words sound crass coming from his mouth, rubbing me the wrong way. I pull my clenched fist out of my pocket, ready to slam it into his face. He seems to notice my stance. His eyes widen, and he takes two steps back.

"Daddy you said a bad word," Matthew's voice interrupts the staredown, and his little face appears behind his dad's legs. "Grandma Gladys says it's a bad word, and if I ever say it again, she'll wash my mouth with soap and pray for me."

Bennett groans and looks down at his son. "Let's make a deal, buddy. You don't tell Grandma Gladys, and I'll get you the Pokémon game you wanted. Deal?" He holds out his hand to Matthew, who stares at it for a few seconds before nodding quickly.

"You're worse than my mother," I tell Bennett as I ruffle my nephew's hair and turn to leave.

"We need to talk about this, Nate."

I pause long enough to scowl at him and say, "No. We don't. Forget this happened."

I continue walking, his laughter following me to my car, and by the time I slide inside the driver's seat, my jaw is clenched so tight that I feel a migraine forming.

CHAPTER TWENTY-TWO

Elon

I CLOSE THE BOOK THAT I'VE BEEN READING TO JOSH THE PAST thirty minutes, place it on my lap and cover his cool hand with mine. I take in his relaxed features as he sleeps; the dark circles under his eyes, bald head, gaunt face and pale skin. I blink a few times to keep the tears at bay.

We are not ready to lose you, Josh.

I wish there was a way to make you better. Fucking cancer and its greedy tentacles.

"Is everything okay, Elon?" Nor asks without pausing from whatever she's working on in the sketchbook propped on her knees.

Her question throws me off and sends my heart racing. I roll my eyes. Every time someone stares at me for more than three seconds, I start hyperventilating, wondering if they know I slept with my professor. Seriously, I need to get my act together.

"Yeah. Why?"

"You just seem distracted. Is everything going well with the new professor?"

Poker face, Elon, I remind myself.

"Everything's peachy," I gush. She studies me while biting the end of her pencil. "How's your drawing coming along?" I point at the sketchbook, hoping to change the subject. "You should totally publish them as coloring books."

Nor has been doodling for as long as I can remember, which is like therapy for her, just like reading is for me. Drawing helps her escape into another world that she creates using pen and paper.

She frowns at me, but seems to let it slide when she looks down at what she's currently working on. "I don't know if I want to. I've never thought about it before."

I set the book on the nightstand, stand up from my seat and crawl up next to her on the cot that has become a permanent fixture in this room. I study the drawing, the word *Courage* flanked with hearts and flowers doodles stands out in all its magnificent beauty.

I bump her shoulder with mine and smile. "It might be a way to share your gift with the world."

She sighs, her eyes on the drawing. "I'll think about it."

The door opens and Nick strides in with Cora and Joce, each holding one of his hands. The second our eyes meet, his body tenses and a scowl replaces the huge grin on his face as the tension between us sky rockets.

I exhale a frustrated breath. He still won't talk to me. I cornered him yesterday when he brought take out to Nor's house, but all he did was walk away.

"Hey, Nor. Is it okay if I take the girls to the movies?"

"Oh, that would be amazing." If she notices any weirdness going on between Nick and me, she doesn't say anything.

I give her a quick hug, then hop down from the cot and slip on my shoes. Five minutes later, I leave the room with my nieces as they debate about which movie we are going to watch.

I arrive for my class on Monday morning with fifty minutes to spare. Things are still a little awkward around Amber, and I have this ever-growing need to tell her everything. Thing is, I'm afraid of what she'll think of me, my choices. That's why I've been spending most of my time away from the apartment and coming in to class much earlier than usual.

But the main reason I'm here before class begins is to have my fill of Nate before everyone else steals his attention. I missed him badly. And after the weekend I'd had in Willow Hill, I just wanted to see him.

Seeing Nick and not being able to talk to him because he ignored me most of the time and only spoke to me when necessary sucked big time.

After grabbing my cello from the backseat, I lock my car and head for Brown Hall. I'm smiling at the thought of seeing Nate when my stomach twists suddenly and the hair on the nape of my neck rises as the feeling of being watched heats my skin.

I stop and turn around, scanning the parking lot. Given that classes haven't started yet, there are not many cars parked.

A white truck pulls into a spot next to some bushes to my right, and seconds later, a man dressed in black hops out and briskly walks toward Sebastian Hall.

Taking a deep breath to slow my racing pulse, I scan my surroundings again, then pick up my pace, unable to shake the feeling of being watched.

Right before I walk inside the classroom, I see Nate standing a few meters away, talking to Bennett, and I completely forget the uneasiness I felt a few minutes ago.

Holy shit.

Bennett is huge, easily four inches taller than Nate, who himself is six feet of lean muscle. If it weren't for Bennett's friendly smile and handsome features, I'd be running in the other direction.

I take a moment to study him.

Dressed in grey pants and a long-sleeved, button-down shirt, he looks amazing. Even the tattoos peeking out from the collar don't do anything to tarnish his striking looks.

Standing side by side, Nate and Bennett are the most beautiful men I've ever seen. They shouldn't be allowed in the same room. There's just too much maleness surrounding them, which could cause spontaneous combustion to the entire female population.

What is Bennett doing here so early in the morning?

As if sensing me, Nate's eyes snap up in my direction. Heat flashes through them before quickly shifting to an indecipherable cursory glance that weighs nothing other than disinterest and boredom. My heart drops to my stomach. Bennett, on the other hand, waves his hand in my direction in greeting, a wide grin on his face, white against his mocha skin. That is, until Nate says something in a low voice, causing Bennett's smile to vanish quickly.

What crawled up my professor's ass this morning?

The thought of turning and heading back the way I came crosses my mind. But instead of doing that, I walk inside the room, set my cello and bag next to my desk and take my usual seat, then wait for Sir Scowl-A-Lot slash my lover slash my boss.

He doesn't disappoint.

He enters the class in long, purposeful strides, his presence filling the room, sending tingles down my spine. His scent reminds me of Friday night and Saturday morning.

My thighs clench, my breathing comes out a little fast.

He's back to his brooding self and doesn't even spare me a glance. I have to remind myself this is the same man who fucked me like his world was ending and beginning at the same time, then made love to me like he was making up for lost chances.

I've gotten to know the other side of him: the passionate side that makes me want more of him.

And damn it, I want to crack that impenetrable armor he's wearing right now. "Hey."

He's standing with his ass propped against his desk, his legs crossed at the ankles. "Hey."

"About Friday," I start to say and pause when his eyes narrow at me.

"*Elon.*" My name is a warning on his lips, his tone sending shivers down my spine. He tilts his head to the side toward the door as if he's listening for something, before turning his attention back on me.

"About *Friday.* . ." I repeat, stressing the last word.

His gaze sharpens on me, and my words trail off as he strokes his lower lip with the index finger. "Yes?"

"I want more of that," I lower my chin, staring at him through my lashes. "With you." Something about Nate makes me brave. He makes me want to explore that adventurous part of me I've hidden for so long.

His expression shatters, his flinty eyes turning dark and smoldering. He seems to be holding himself back though.

"This is dangerous, Miss Blake." His voice travels across the space between us in a low, seductive rumble. "We could get caught. We both know how it would end for both of us."

I frown, wondering what happened between Saturday and today.

I clear my throat and lift my chin. "We'll be careful. I just—" I stop in order to collect my thoughts. I'm about to lay it all out there, risk being rejected. "After, you know, um—" I glance at the door quickly, then say, "the horizontal tango—"

He lets out an honest to God laugh, shoulders shaking, eyes alight with mirth.

"Horizontal tango?"

"Yeah." I smile, enjoying seeing him like this. Happy.

"I remember us being more than horizontal. In fact, we vertical fuc—"

"*Jesus*, Nathaniel. Someone could hear you." My cheeks are on fire now.

"Okay. Being inside you?" he prompts, smirking.

"Yeah. That."

"Get down here," he orders in a soft voice.

The clock on the wall in front of the room indicates we have about twenty-five minutes until class starts. Given how many times I've arrived to class early in order to catch up on my reading and conquer my ever-increasing pile of books to read, I know for a fact that the first student will probably stroll in at least seven minutes before class starts.

I step around my desk with my eyes fixed on his intense gaze but drop my stare when I get to the steps on shaking legs. Seconds later, I'm standing in front of Nate, making sure to keep a healthy distance between us in case someone walks in. I lift my head to look at him.

"I have wondered so many things from the first time I saw you," he starts to say in a husky voice, sending a shiver through me, and I wonder if he can see my heart frantically beating through my blouse because I feel like it's about to rip through my chest.

"And?" The word leaves my lips in a breathless whisper.

His Adam's apple bobs as he swallows, and he lets out a shaky breath. "After kissing you and burying myself inside you, it's everything I had imagined and more. It's very distracting, addictive even. I can't look at you without wanting to take you back to my place and spend hours worshipping you like you deserve and making you come. I'd live in your mouth if this wasn't what it is. You have a beautiful, talented mouth Little Wolf."

He stops talking, and I take a long, shuddering breath, the *tick, tick, tick* of his watch causing my stomach to tighten with need even more.

"We can't do this—"

"You want this as much as I do," I cut him off as the rejection slams into my gut. "But you realized whatever this is between us is bigger than we both imagined and now you are scared. . ."

I'm rambling. I'm desperately clawing at whatever I can get to latch on.

How did I become this person? Wasn't I the same person who wanted this to be a one-time thing?

"You are scared," I tell him, shooting him a challenging look and waiting for him to deny my claim.

He holds my gaze, leaning closer. "Aren't you?"

"Of course I am. I'm really terrified!" I exclaim, adrenaline pumping through me like I've been sprinting. "I've never done this before."

Oh my God. This is not me.

I'm a calm person. Quiet. I rarely let my emotions run away with me. I'm level-headed. Yet, here I am, trying to lure my reluctant professor into my proverbial web.

Shit.

I need space to think. I need to collect my thoughts and strategize. If he's thinking I'm going to just let this go, he hasn't met me yet.

"Excuse me." I climb down the last step and march to the door. Strong fingers grasp my wrist, spinning me around. The heat of his body slamming into me.

"Where the hell are you going?" he questions, seeming perturbed by my sudden exit.

"I need a few minutes to think."

His eyes narrow with suspicion. "About what?"

I sigh. "Look. I get it. *You* can't do this—"

He grunts in frustration, dropping my hand and starting to pace. "You didn't let me finish what I was going to say."

I shake my head. "I'll be right back. I just—"

"Miss Blake," he warns in a soft, yet lethal voice that has my knees trembling.

"Oh, don't 'Miss Blake' me." I turn and head for the door, wondering how I became this person. This desperate creature. My body is literally firing up with emotions I've never experienced before.

My feelings for this man are all over the place. I need a few minutes away from his intoxicating presence to compartmentalize everything so I can deal with each emotion individually before I explode.

"*Elon.*"

Goosebumps spread across my arms. Did he just growl my name?

"Bite me," I mutter under my breath, equally frustrated by this situation, by my inability to sort through these feelings. I reach for the doorknob, ready to pull it.

He curses under his breath, the thumping of his feet on the wooden floor getting closer behind me. Before I can open the door, his hand flies over my head, slamming it shut.

"Abso-fucking-lutely," he growls. His arm leaves the door and slides around my waist, flips me around and yanks me flush to his hard body, knocking air from my lungs.

"What are you doing?" I shriek, trying to push away from him with my hands on his chest.

"Obeying your command."

"Command? What th—" I cut myself off as panic replaces the anger. "Are you crazy?"

"I'm fucking hungry, and I need my high." His head lowers to the crook of my neck and his nose skims along my skin, inhaling deeply, humming at the back of his throat. At the same time, his left hand leaves my waist and slides down to the hem of my dress and tugs it up.

"Oh my God. Stop it. Anyone could walk in—" my eyes fly to the clock. Twenty minutes until class starts. "—any second."

He lifts his head from my neck and smirks. "Then we'll have to be fast, won't we? You think I'd let you walk out that door then have you go change your mind about this—whatever this is?"

"But you said we couldn't do this," I squirm as his fingers skim my inner thigh, causing my eyes to roll back in my head.

"You didn't even let me finish what I wanted to say."

"Then what did you want to say?"

"We can't do this here. That's what I wanted to say."

My chest is pressed against his and we are both panting, the air around us crackling with tension.

"Come," he commands, taking my wrist abruptly and dragging me with him.

Before I can ask where he's taking me, he pulls me inside one of the built-in cupboards in front of the class and lets go of my hand. He drops to his knees in front of me, sending me a heated, hungry gaze in the process. Then he hooks his left hand around my panties and pulls them down, with me helping him on the other side.

"What's with you and cupboards?"

He chuckles and mumbles something under his breath.

My head falls back, a moan rushing from my lips.

He's officially gone bonkers. Insane.

I might be riding the same crazy train, too, considering I'm so close to wrapping my legs around his neck and holding on for the wild ride.

He pinches my ass and says, "Look at me. Look at what I'm about to do to you."

With a deep moan, I return my focus to his dark head as he lowers it between my legs. His tongue thrusts inside me without warning, and I gasp. I slap a hand over my mouth to block the sounds.

Voices drift in from the hall, and my body ignites as danger looms closer.

I'm terrified of being caught with my professor's mouth on me.

I'm excited because this is so scandalous.

Holy shit, I must be a closet exhibitionist. How can I be enjoying this so much, knowing that things could go sideways fast?

"Oh, Miss Blake. You love a little danger, don't you?" He nips my inner thigh, and I try to stifle my ragged breathing, my little cries of pleasure. He swats my ass cheek, the sharp pain spreading all over my body.

I choke on a groan, and he rumbles his approval.

"Good girl," he murmurs. "I bet I can make you come in under one minute."

And I don't doubt him.

I can feel my orgasm building, higher, hotter, stronger. With one last swipe of his tongue, I fly, soaring through a dark sky behind my closed eyelids lit up by a million fireworks. I'm breathing hard, trying to catch my breath when I hear Amber's voice in the hallway.

Nate straightens to his feet while pulling my panties back up. I rearrange my skirt and blouse, then look up at Nate, who's looking at me like I'm the one who made him see heaven instead of the other way around. His thumb strokes across my bottom lip.

"Look at you. I love this look on you. Sit tight. I'll go out first, you can come out after a few minutes."

"Don't you think people will—"

"You are my assistant." His eyes scan the room, and he points at something on the shelf. "Bring out the projector and a bunch of those textbooks and place them on the table." He turns to leave but stops and twists around to look at me. "And Elon? Let your hair down for me."

"Okay, Professor," I whisper in a shaky voice, and his eyes darken even more than before. He strolls out of the tiny room and lowers his long, fairly built frame on the chair behind his desk, then subtly rearranges the bulge in his pants with his left hand.

I hear the sound of feet shuffling on the floor a few seconds later, followed by mumbled greetings.

After lifting the projector and some textbooks from the shelves, I stride out, hoping no one notices the flush on my cheeks or the way my body is vibrating like I'm a junkie in need of another fix.

Because that's what I'm feeling right now. Like I need more of my professor.

I don't spare Nate a glance as I place the stuff on his desk, then head to my seat. Amber is already sitting at her desk, texting on her phone, while Alex is busy chatting with one of his friends.

"Hey," I greet her.

"Hey." I can feel her eyes on me, studying me, probably trying to figure out what's going on with me. Then, her gaze falls away, the awkwardness digging a rift between us.

I turn my attention to the front of the class and find Nate's eyes boring into me. His gaze subtly flicks on top of my head, and I remember the order he gave me before he left the cupboard. His gaze, unreadable as ever, moves back to mine, and he tilts his head slightly.

And I obey him, pulling out the hair band and letting my hair fall around my shoulders. He sucks a sharp inhale that ricochets around the room, before he quickly covers it with a little cough and turns around, showing us his back.

I duck my head to hide my grin.

Gotcha, Professor.

The lesson starts, but my thoughts keep wandering back to Amber. This strain in our friendship is killing me to the point of wanting to just come clean. The problem with being a loner like me is that you want to hold on to the people you've allowed to see the real you. And when something threatens to sever that love, that bond, all bets are off.

I clear my throat and eye Amber sideways. "I think I'm being followed," I whisper.

She lifts her head, angling her body toward me. "Oh God. Do you think maybe it's Rick. . ." she trails off, speaking my thoughts out loud.

Hearing his name sends my stomach plummeting, and bile burns my throat.

I nod, then shake my head. "I don't know. Maybe?" I rub my face in frustration. "I got this weird vibe. It's the same feeling I used to get when I was around him."

"Shit. You have to go to the police, E." The tension going on between us vanishes as concern for me fills her face, making me feel even more guilty for not telling her what's going on.

"We can't. Not unless we have proof or he threatens me."

We fall quiet, lost in our own thoughts.

Moments later, I clear my throat again, taking in a big inhale. "Can we talk later?"

She casts a surprised look at me, the corners of her lips lifting in a smile. "I would love that."

My body slumps back in relief, and I watch, distractedly, as Nate continues to teach the class, looking unaffected as always. At one point his gaze lingers a little too long in our direction. At me. I feel heat crawl up my neck and spread across my cheeks, just remembering what he did to me only moments ago.

"You've got to be shitting me!" Amber whispers under her breath, but it's loud enough to make a couple of heads snap in our direction. Even Professor Rowe pauses long enough to raise a dark brow at her.

She apologizes, but the second the lesson resumes, she grabs her notebook and scribbles something, then slides it in front of me.

You're totally flirting with him!

Oh shit. I glance up and meet her shocked look, shake my head to deny it but stop when she narrows her eyes. She grabs the notebook again, writes quickly, then pushes it in my direction.

Is that why you're wearing your hair down today?

I clench my hand into a fist to stop it from shaking and whisper, "Talk later?"

Amber is looking at me with wide, excited eyes. She reaches her arm to the notebook and writes, *Yes. Today you and I have a lunch date, you little slut.*

Sex? Please tell me he's just as intense between the sheets.

I grin at her and wink, before quickly scribbling, *beyond intense.*

She squeals, causing several heads to turn in our direction, including Nate's. His narrowed eyes move from me to Amber.

"Miss Jordan." Amber's head jerks up as she sinks deeper into her chair. "Do you have anything to share with the class?"

My fingers inch toward the notebook, slide it toward me and tuck it under my arm just as Nate's gaze flits to the desk, then back to my face. His lips tighten in obvious annoyance.

Oh shit. I'm so in trouble!

"Nope. Nothing to share here!" she announces in a high pitched voice.

"All right, everyone. Let's get back to work," Nate's voice booms across the hall as he switches on the projector.

The class resumes and I exhale in relief, feeling as if a huge weight has been lifted off my chest.

Right after the bell rings to signal the end of the lesson, Nate looks in my direction and nods.

"Miss Blake."

Ah, Lord have mercy.

That voice of his destroys me.

I pause mid-step and give him my attention.

"May I have a word?"

Beside me, Amber mutters under her breath, "I can't believe I didn't see the clues. I'll be outside if you need backup. Or maybe not." She chortles while scooting away from me.

As soon as the last student leaves, that look on his face falls away, replaced by the hooded eyes and sexy smirk.

"What's up," I whisper, not ready to tell him Amber knows about us.

He pulls out something from his pants pocket and hands it to me.

"I won't be home until seven this evening. You can let yourself in and wait for me."

I raise an eyebrow, my eyes on the key. "Isn't it too early to exchange keys and shit?"

He scowls at me. "I'm not asking you to move in with me. Take it."

I wet my lips and take a step back. "This is too much, Nate. I can't—"

"Elon," he says, sounding annoyed and impatient.

I sigh and take the key from his hand.

"I want you naked and waiting for me," he orders, then adds, "Things seem to be working out between you and Miss Jordan."

I nod, smiling.

"I'm glad," he says, his eyes going soft. "See you tonight, then." He gives me his back without another word, effectively dismissing me. Before I walk out the door, I hear him warn, "No more mischief in class, Miss Blake."

"Yes, Professor." I say the latter in a low sultry voice as I walk out the door. Behind me, Nate lets out a noise that sounds like a low growl, sending heat between my legs. I grab the doorframe to support my trembling body.

"I can't wait to hear you say that while I'm buried inside you." His voice rumbles across the space between us, leaving me breathless.

Shiiiit.

Breathe.

God, this man is lethal.

Taking in a deep breath, I look over my shoulder, and say, "I can't wait." Then I stride out the door armed with a secret grin and the key he gave me gripped in my hand.

Nate

I turn and watch Elon leave the room, swiping my tongue across my lips for the hundredth time this hour. I swear I can still taste her.

Goddamn it.

I had no intention of dragging her into the cupboard. But then she said that she needed to think and I panicked.

I fucking *panicked*.

Christ.

The only thought playing on a loop in my head in that moment was that she was going to change her mind about us. I was going to lose her, which activated a primal part of me to conquer, claim and convince, eliminating any rational thoughts.

Then after that, I found myself opening my mouth and my home to her. I gave Elon a spare key to my apartment. No wonder she stared at me like I'd lost my damn mind.

I rub my neck, still trying to wrap my head around my actions and end up with one conclusion.

This woman is driving me to the edge of insanity. The worst thing is I'm loving it. She brings out the wild side in me.

If Bennett got wind of my current state of mind, he'd have a field day roasting me to death.

After packing my books in my bag, I head for my next class, already fantasizing about getting home and finding Elon naked, waiting for me.

Elon

I spend the next forty-five minutes in practice room three, working on perfecting the piece we will be playing for the fundraising ball concert. When I can no longer focus, Nate having completely wreaked havoc on all of my rational thoughts for the day, I give up and head to the café on campus. I order a hot chocolate, curl up on the seat by the window and pull out the novel I'm currently reading.

I pull out my earbuds from my bag and plug them in, then scroll down my playlist. Before I can tap the play button, my phone starts to ring in my hand, Elise's name flashing on the screen.

Taking out the earbuds, I answer the call.

"Cole came home." Those are the first words that leave her mouth.

"What? When?"

"He arrived last night. He's on his way to the hospital right now. Josh was asking for him," she sniffs, then adds in a shaky voice, "I think Josh might be leaving us soon."

"On my way." I end the call, jump from the seat and leave the warmth of the café with my bag slung over my arm. My entire body is shaking, and I wonder how I'll make it to Willow Hill without crumbling into pieces.

Once I'm seated inside my car, I roll down the window, letting the cool air wash over my face. I dig out my phone from inside my bag and quickly type a text to Amber letting her know what's going on and that we'll talk when I get back to Jacksonville. Then I type another to Nate informing him that I have to leave town and will call him later.

When I'm calm enough to drive, I start the car and pull away from the parking spot.

CHAPTER TWENTY-THREE

Elon

By the time I arrive in Willow Hill, my stomach is wrought with nerves. Once I was on the road, I called Elise to find out more information about what was going on. She had slept over at Nor's house to help with the kids, so she was right in the middle of everything that had been happening. Cole was already in the hospital visiting his brother.

When I arrive at the hospital, I rush inside and only slow down when I reach the waiting area. I take in the scene before me. No one has to tell me what is going on. I can see it in their faces that death finally won the war.

Elise runs toward me with her arms open and pulls me into a tight hug.

"He is gone," she whispers into my neck in a broken voice. "Josh is gone."

I hug her tighter, letting the tears I've been holding back the past few hours fall. I'm not sure if I'm sad or relieved that he is gone. He was in so much pain for so long, and the only thing that made it bearable for him was the pain medication.

Each day, he'd wake up and ask if Cole had finally returned home.

Each day, his face would fall when he realized his brother wasn't coming home, but he'd wipe the disappointment clean off his face and put on a front for everyone, especially Cora and Joce. I guess now that Cole made it home to see him, Josh found the much-needed peace he had been waiting for. So I guess I'm relieved he's in a better place.

At least I hope he is. He was always cheerful and tried to make everyone laugh no matter how much pain he was going through. The thought of never seeing Josh again is like a punch to my gut, and his death leaves a huge hole in our hearts and lives. He will be missed and remembered for being such a wonderful husband, brother and son.

My thoughts are cut off when Nor stumbles out of a pair of sliding doors that lead to the ICU, with Cole in tow carrying the twins in his arms.

I break into a sob as I rush toward them. I hug Nor first, who literally collapses in my arms, sobbing like her body is breaking. We hold each other until she pulls away, wiping her cheeks with the back of her scarred forearm. Then, I turn to Cole, tears streaming down my face as I take him in. He's no longer the boy that left town nine years ago, thinking that his girlfriend and brother betrayed him. Instead, I'm looking into the face of a man ridden with guilt and loss. And from the way his eyes stray toward my sister, he never stopped loving Nor.

He lowers Joce and Cora to the floor before bridging the distance between us and pulling me into a tight hug. His shoulders shake with silent sobs as his tears soak my shirt.

When he finally steps back, I sign, *"It's good to see you, Cole."*

He flashes me a sad smile that doesn't reach his blood-shot eyes. *"A little too damn late."*

When Cole was five years old, he had bacterial meningitis, which led to hearing loss. His life changed after that, and he has been communicating through ASL ever since.

We break our stare and he steps around a chair, walking over to where his parents, Ben and Maggie, are huddled together. Maggie tells me that Nick went to the chapel and he will be back soon. Minutes later, Nick comes running through the hospital doors, his eyes widening when he sees Cole's stricken face. Then we're all crying quietly as they embrace each other. Then Nick pulls back and scans the room. The second his gaze lands on me, his face tightens with anger, but it disappears just as fast. He barrels toward me and snatches me in a hug. I bury my face into his chest and cry for Josh. For Nick's friendship, which I feel like I've lost. I miss him so much, and the fact that he put aside our differences at this time of grief makes me love him even more.

After we pull apart, I join Nor, Elise and the twins on the couch, then I quickly check my phone, which had been pinging the entire way home. But I wasn't sure if I'd be able to speak to anyone without breaking down.

Ten missed calls from Nate and almost the same number of texts from Amber.

I toss the phone back inside my bag without answering any of them and turn my attention to my family, making a mental note to return their calls when I get home.

Later on, after we are allowed to pay our respects, I head to the chapel in the hospital and light a candle for Josh.

He deserves more than a candle. He deserves a bonfire for being brave and selfless.

Elon

I'm lying in bed after dinner, when my phone vibrates. I tap the pause button on the music player on my phone when I see Mr. Scowly flashing on the screen.

Warmth spreads all over me, just knowing that he is on the other side of that incoming call.

I answer the call on the fifth ring, a huge smile on my face.

"Nate," I whisper, scooting down on the bed.

"Hey. I got your message. What's going on? Are you all right?"

I look up at the ceiling and blink quickly to clear my vision. "Not really." I sniff and wipe my cheeks with the back of my hand. "I feel like my heart is bleeding on the inside. So much pain."

His sigh travels across the line, sending shivers down my spine. "Are you going to be okay?"

"Not for a while."

"I wish I could hold you. Comfort you," he says in a tortured voice.

I wipe my eyes with the back of my hand, then sniff. "I'd love that."

Silence falls between us, but it's not a bad silence. I know how weird this is. I sense that this is more than just him checking on me. There's a long pause, and I hear Sinatra playing in the background.

We remain quiet. There are no words exchanged between Sinatra crooning the end of "Witchcraft" and Coldplay picking up. I snuggle deeper into the comforter as the lyrics of "Fix You" trail across the line.

"It's almost ten o'clock. You should get some sleep," I say giving him an out.

"I'm not good at obeying orders," he says. "Besides, sleeping is overrated."

"Insomnia?" I joke.

He's quiet for a few seconds before he exhales. "Yes."

I bite my lips between my teeth, wondering how far or deep this conversation is allowed to go. He called me. That should be some kind of green light to ask questions, right?

"Why?"

Nate doesn't answer. I pull the phone from my ear to check if the connection is still there.

It is.

"You don't have to talk about it if you don't want to."

"This is not about me. Tell me about your brother-in-law. This might be the only time I get to speak to you."

I know what he means, and sadness cloaks me. I shake it off and focus on now.

"Josh?" He makes this sound in his throat in confirmation; it's sexy. "He was a hero."

"Was?"

I nod, tears once again stinging my eyes. I let them fall down freely.

"Yes. He died earlier on today."

"I'm sorry, Elon."

I sob quietly into the phone and he listens to my silent cries, never cutting me off or talking. Just letting me be. Then when my tears dry, I tell him about Josh and Cole. I'm not sure what it is about him that makes me open up like this, but I can't stop myself. When I'm finally done, I lay back on the bed, my eyes drooping closed.

"Elon?" he calls out softly, and my eyes bounce back open.

"I'm here."

"Get some sleep. I want you to do me a favor."

I cover my mouth to stop the yawn threatening to drug me with sleep. "Sure."

"Keep the line open. I want to hear you." He sighs. "It might be my only chance to ever hear you breathe while you snore."

I laugh abruptly, caught off-guard by his words. "You're weird."

He chuckles, and I hear something rustling on the other side of the phone. I imagine him sliding his long, toned legs beneath his sheets, and I sigh and curl on my side.

"Would you prefer if I said I wanted to hear you breathe?"

I snort then giggle. "That's just creepy."

He laughs. "I know. Just humor me."

I lay the phone down on the pillow and pull the blanket up to my shoulders and bring my knees up to my chin. He's humming to the song playing in the background now.

"Which song is that?" I ask sleepily.

"'You Got What I Need' by Joshua Radin," he says in an intimate voice that has me rubbing my thighs together in need.

"You have an eclectic collection over there."

He chuckles and murmurs in a low voice, "Sleep, Little Wolf." Then he continues humming, setting my soul on fire.

Giving me the peace I crave right this second.

CHAPTER TWENTY-FOUR

Elon

It's been five days since Josh passed away. The mood around the house is subdued. I returned to Jacksonville two days after his death in desperate need of diversion. One day later I was in my car, driving back to Willow Hill. I couldn't stay away from my family, which is why I'm sitting with Nor and the twins in the living room, knitting up a storm. This is something Joce and I do whenever I'm in Willow Hill. Cora is more interested in painting, which is what she's doing right now at the desk in the corner of the living room.

My phone starts to ring, and I see Amber's name flashing on the screen. As soon as I answer the call, she demands, "I know this is probably not the right time but oh my God, girl. I'm dying over here."

I laugh at her dramatic tone, causing Nor to look at me. We've been talking every day, and she never even once asked me about Nate. I love her for giving me the time and space I needed to mourn Josh without pressuring me about the details of my love life.

"Give me a minute." I prop the phone between my shoulder and ear, then gather the knitting project I've been working on with Joce and put it inside the basket at my feet. Then, I head to my room and climb on the bed.

"Once upon a time," I start, bracing my shoulders on the headboard.

Amber squeals on the other side of the phone. "This is going to be good."

Then, I start from the beginning and tell Amber about Professor Rowe and me. When I'm done, I inhale a deep breath. "Aren't you going to lecture me on the hazards of dating my professor?"

"I could, but I won't," she says after a few moments of silence. "You know what will happen if this gets out and. . . " she trails off with a sigh.

"Yes, I do," I tell her. "I wish I didn't feel this way. I wish it was someone else. . . like Nick."

"A heart wants what it wants," is her answer. "Just be careful, okay?"

"I will. Thank you for being cool about this. I don't know what I'd do without you."

She sighs. "You're stuck with me, E. But you know Nor is going to freak if she finds out," Amber whispers, as if she's afraid of being heard.

I pull my legs up and rest my chin on my knees. "God, don't even say that. She'd skin me alive if she knew."

"Are you happy?" she asks quietly.

I don't even have to think about the answer. "Yes."

She inhales a deep breath, then says, "You could use a little happy in your life, babe."

At her words, tears spring to my eyes. I let them fall and whisper, "Thank you, Amber."

I deserve to be happy. What Nate and I have might be frowned upon, but he's giving me what I need.

Every time I see a happy couple looking at each other with so much love, I covet what they have; I want to experience that. Whenever I think about how much Josh and Cole loved and adored Nor, I yearn for someone to look at me the way they did her.

I want someone who will treat me like I'm his Jupiter in a galaxy full of planets.

His lucky penny.

My phone beeps, alerting me of an incoming call. I pull it from my ear to check the screen, and my heart beats faster when I see 'NR' flashing.

"Hey, um. . .he's calling. We'll talk later, OK?"

"Yes! Oh, say hi to him."

I roll my eyes and snort-laugh. "No, I won't."

"You're no fun," she says.

We say our goodbyes, and I switch the calls, then slide from the headboard and flop over to my stomach on the bed.

"Hey, lover," I whisper. He's been calling to check on me at least three times a day since my abrupt departure from Jacksonville.

"Hey," he greets in that deep voice of his, sending goosebumps all over my body. "Can you take some time away this weekend?"

"Why?"

"I want to take you somewhere."

"So mysterious," I mutter under my breath, grinning. "Sure. When?"

"Saturday," he says, then gives me the address of where we should meet in Ocala.

We chat for a few minutes before saying goodbye and hanging up.

The rest of the day seems to drag as anticipation of where Nate wants to take me continues to build with every hour.

By the time I slip between my sheets, I'm vibrating with the need to see him. Unlike the past few days after Josh left us, sleep seems to come easy tonight. The last thing I see before falling asleep is the memory of Nate's eyes, looking at me with soft eyes, one side of his mouth curled up in a sexy smirk.

CHAPTER TWENTY-FIVE

Elon

I'M SITTING INSIDE THE STARBUCKS WHERE NATE AND I ARE SUPPOSED to meet, when I see him stride through the door. His gaze roams the room until he finds me.

My fingers threaten to drop the paper cup when he makes his way toward me, his eyes never leaving mine.

It feels wonderful to be the center of his attention.

Before he sits down, he scans our surroundings carefully, then lowers himself into the seat next to mine. He slides his left hand around my knee possessively under the table but doesn't attempt to kiss me, even though I see in his eyes how much he wants to. The heat from his touch sears through the thin material of my black stockings and I moan softly, feeling his touch everywhere, calming me, *claiming me.*

"Hey," he murmurs, sitting back in his chair. "How are you holding up?"

"Better."

His gaze wanders around us again, on alert. Then his hand leaves my leg. "I've missed you. Class hasn't been the same without you there."

My heart soars at his words, absorbing them like they are the very air I breathe. "I missed you, too. It feels good to be this close to you in public without worrying someone will see us."

His gaze intensifies. Different emotions flash in his eyes. He opens his mouth like he wants to say something, but stops and shakes his head as if he's breaking free from a spell.

"Ready to go?" he asks, and the breath trapped in my lungs rushes out as disappointment cuts through me.

What did he want to tell me?

"Sure," I say, closing the book I was reading while waiting for him. I shove it inside my bag before returning my focus to him. "Where are you taking me?"

"Patience, woman," he says with a playful glint in his eyes, holding his hand out for me. "Come on."

His long, strong fingers close around mine, infusing warmth and sending shivers ricocheting all over my body. He doesn't let go as we step into the cool February morning embraced by a sun-kissed blue sky. He guides me toward a black Wrangler with massive wheels, pulls his hand from mine to retrieve the keys from his pants pocket and unlocks the car. A beep sounds across the parking lot.

"Is that yours?" I ask, unable to hold back my excitement.

He glances down at me with a smirk and nods as his fingers tangle with mine again.

"Sexy."

One dark brow shoots up. "Should I be jealous?"

I giggle and say, "Someone is afraid of a little competition."

When we reach the car, he turns me around and pins me against the passenger door before taking my mouth in a skin-tingling, heart-stopping, knees-melting kiss.

His lips leave mine, and he brushes his nose against mine. "Damn right, I am. Get your sexy ass inside the car."

I laugh, turning around and opening the car door when I'm

suddenly hit with the fact that he *drove* all the way here.

"Wait. You drove almost two hours? What about your arm?" I nibble the edge of my lip nervously, worried.

His usually firm lips soften, and he kisses my hair before opening the door wider and pointing in the general direction of the dashboard. "It has a few adjustments."

He goes ahead and explains the Wrangler is an automatic, fitted with a steering spinner to give his left arm a sufficient grip. The indicators are on the left side, which allows easier access without releasing the steering wheel.

"See? I'm covered." He moves aside for me to jump inside the vehicle. "I usually use this car if I'm driving long distances."

Soon we're pulling out of the parking lot, the silence in the car charged with a tangible energy filled with excitement and expectation. His driving speed is still steady, but I notice he stays mostly in his lane and doesn't overtake other cars on the highway.

He lifts his right arm in my direction but lets out a wince and drops it on his thigh.

"*Fuck*," he swears harshly under his breath.

"Are you okay?" I ask, moving to touch his hand but stop when he flinches.

"I'm fine," he says in a snappish voice.

"I could drive so you can rest," I offer.

Those eyes of his leave the road long enough to shoot me a scowl before facing forward again, his jaw clenched.

I sigh and sink lower in my chair, casting subtle glances at his prominent side profile.

We drive in uncomfortable silence for almost ten minutes. I squirm, unable to bear the tension any longer, inhale deeply and take his hand in mine. He sucks in a sharp breath but doesn't pull away. I can feel his gaze on me, but I don't look at him.

Gently, I unfold his fingers from the loose fist and attempt to massage his fingers in light movements, starting at the center of his palm to the tip of each finger. They twitch a little followed by light spasms traveling up his arm, but other than that, he seems to be relaxing under my touch.

"That feels fucking amazing," he says with a sigh.

I smile. "Yeah?"

"Yeah." I hear a smile in that word.

After a few minutes of driving in a steady pace, his hand moves from mine and wraps around my thigh. The touch is not as firm as his left hand, but I still feel it down to my core.

"I didn't mean to snap at you. I'm sorry." His voice is soft, sincere. "I hate that I can't reach over and hold your hand or touch you whenever I want," he says in frustration.

"I know." I can't even begin to imagine how it feels not having full use of your arm, wanting to do something but your arm and pain standing in your way. My fingers weave with his as he slides them to cup my knee.

He's quiet for a few seconds, then clears his throat and asks, "So, books and music?"

The change of subject catches me off guard, but I catch up quickly. I'm grateful because I hate the weirdness and tension from before. "Yeah. Reading sets me free and music makes me soar. There's no me without those two things. You?"

"I do enjoy reading on and off, and music always."

My ears perk up and I grin. "Who's your favorite author?"

"Azariah Hunter."

"Oh." That name doesn't ring a bell. "Which genre does he write in?"

"Thrillers mostly." He darts me a look. "What?"

"Nothing," I mumble, and his brow arches up, obviously not believing me. "It's kind of hot."

He gives me a skeptical look. "Thrillers?"

"Reading."

His fingers tighten on my knee. "Looks like I need to up my game then," he winks at me. I've never seen him wink until now. But wow, I think he might actually control the rhythm of my heartbeats with his left eye, because one wink and I'm out of control.

Breathe, Elon.

"You look really hot when you're wearing your reading glasses, too. Just saying." I wink at him, biting my bottom lip.

He gives me a look that has me melting on my seat. Maybe I could convince him to ditch his plans so we can shack up somewhere and get down to business. We haven't had sex since the first time I went to his apartment. I miss feeling him inside me, setting me on fire.

"Elon?" His concerned voice penetrates my lust-filled thoughts, and I wonder how many times he's called my name.

I look at him, my cheeks burning at the images still flashing in my head.

The curiosity in his face melts, giving way to a wolfish smile. "You're thinking about us. Me inside you."

"What if I am?" I peek at him through my lashes in what I hope is a sultry look, then slide one of my hands over his toned thigh. "We could take a detour somewhere…" I trail off, letting the words hang in the air suggestively.

I feel the muscles beneath my palm tense as my fingers explore his inner thigh.

He groans low, shifting on his seat. I drop my gaze to his lap and notice the bulge already forming there.

"I'm seconds away from pulling over, hauling you onto my lap and letting you have your way with me, but we'd end up getting arrested." His chest expands as he takes a deep breath. "It would definitely put a damper on my plans."

We stop at an intersection and wait for the light to change.

I waggle my eyebrows playfully at him and say, "Or I could just suck you off while we wait for the lights to change. I promise I won't bite."

"*Elon*," he warns in a hoarse voice, sending me a glare, which makes me want to climb all over him.

"What?" I ask him innocently. "You want me to bite?"

"*Christ.*" He lets out an exasperated breath. "Are you trying to kill me?"

"Admit it. It would be a great way to die."

He makes a noise that sounds almost like a frustrated laugh. "You don't know the kind of power you have over me, Little Wolf. Your lips on me right now would be my undoing."

His words leave me speechless for the next minute. I had no idea I have that kind of power over him.

I swallow hard to get rid of the dryness working its way up my throat.

"When did you know that cello was your thing?" I question, still flustered by his words and eager to move to a safer zone.

His heated gaze skims my face, a slow smirk gracing his before he turns toward the road.

He purses his lips, eyes narrowed on the road. "I've loved music for as long as I can remember. My father bought me my first cello when I was five," he says fondly, his expression soft. "By the time I was seventeen, I was playing on and off in the Jacksonville Symphony alongside my father."

I wonder what my life would have been like growing up with a father who loved me. Growing up in a family where both parents gave a shit about their children. I can't help the feeling of envy creeping up inside me. That feeling hits me swift and sharp, causing tears to leak from my eyes.

I jerk my head to the side, watching the trees zoom by outside the window, and force myself to shake off that ugly feeling.

When I feel brave enough to face him again, I say, "He sounds like a good father."

He's quiet for a few seconds before he says in a wistful voice, "He was. He died of a heart attack six years ago."

"God. I'm sorry." I lean down to kiss his palm, feeling guilty for being envious when he lost a person he loves and that matters to him.

He shifts on his seat as if being consoled makes him uncomfortable. "So what do you want to do after school?"

"Tour Europe. Hopefully play in the London Symphony or Vienna Philharmonic."

"Why?

"Why what?"

"Why not a symphony here in the US?" I don't sense a challenge in that question, just curiosity.

"It's something I've wanted since I can remember. At first it was a way for me to escape my past, a way to start over in a new place far away from home. One night while I was talking to Nor, she whole-heartedly agreed that I should follow my dreams. I couldn't help but feel guilty. This girl had done so much for me and was always there for me, putting her feelings aside, as well as putting her life and dreams on hold for me and Elise. My sister who was part of my past. I couldn't just pack up and leave and forget about her or Elise.

"My past was and is who I am. What I am. You can't just for-get the very thing that molded you and gave you strength to beat the odds. As much as the past shapes us, we can choose to let it define us or we can carve a different path and define it ourselves."

I look up when I feel his eyes on me, wondering why the car is not moving, then look out the window and see a board with the words *Jeep Trail Off-Road Park*

I turn back to face him, ready to unbuckle my belt. "Are we here?" He doesn't answer, just continues to watch me with something akin to admiration. "What? What is it?"

"You are incredible."

"Um.. okay."

Oh, Jesus, Elon. Is that all you could come up with? Um. . .okay? Really?

Inwardly, I roll my eyes and say, "Thank you?" like it's a question, making me cringe.

He laughs, shaking his head.

"Thank you." This time it comes out with more certainty. And because I'm still feeling awkward after the compliment, I say, "Oh hey. A group of us will be playing at the Women Against Violence fundraising ball on February twenty-eighth. Would you like to come?"

He squeezes my hand. "I won't be able to."

I lick my lips to crush the bitter taste of disappointment on my tongue.

His mouth pulls into a frown. "I am scheduled for a doctor's appointment on the first of March in Chicago. I could move the appointment date though."

"Is it for your arm?"

He nods. "The doctor is considering other options to try and get my arm working again, which means more tests." He recites the words in a monotone voice, which makes me wonder if he wants to do this.

"Don't you want to explore the options?"

He grimaces, his gaze wandering out the window before he admits, "I've been through several tests. I just don't want to get my hopes up and have them crushed again." I can hear the pain, the helplessness in his voice.

I blink in surprise at his confession. I'd have never thought this strong, proud man would ever admit something that makes him vulnerable.

He exhales a long breath. "I never thought I'd be returning to Chicago so soon after—" he cuts himself off, his features hardening. A vein ticks furiously in his jaw.

Before I can open my mouth to speak, to ask him what exactly happened in Chicago even though I know bits and pieces of what transpired, he turns to look at me. Whatever emotion was there three seconds before has faded, replaced by a neutral look.

Damn it.

"I'll move the appointment. What time does the ball begin?"

"Don't do that, Nate," I say, shaking my head. "You should consider meeting with your doctor. This could be the one chance you've been waiting for to make your arm better. I won't even pretend to understand what you are going through. You need to go, Nate," I implore him.

"Elon—" he starts to say, and from the look on his face, I know he's about to argue with me. "I'm so fucking scared," he whispers in a hoarse voice.

I lean forward and press my lips to his in a soft kiss. "Being scared is a good thing." Nate's dark brow goes up as he waits patiently for me to continue. "It's how we become better fighters in life, gain more courage to try something that scares us shitless. Besides, we can only let our demons rule us for so long."

Nate rubs his hand down his face. His tense shoulders seem to relax as he takes in a deep inhale before shifting his body to focus on me, the intensity of his gaze knocking air from my lungs. The large palm of his left hand cups my jaw, his thumb brushing the apple of my cheek.

"What is it about you that makes me want to destroy everything in my path just to have you?" His brows are pulled down in a little frown, his eyes roaming my face as if he's trying to unlock that part of me that makes me who I am.

I'm not sure if he intended to speak those words out loud, given the lost look in his face. Like he's in his own world, trying to figure out his thoughts. Or maybe he doesn't want to talk about his appointment anymore.

So I lick my lips and smile. "My sense of humor?"

His gaze bears down on mine, trapping me with honesty and sincerity. "I find myself wanting to spend more time with you—"

"Nate—"

"I have never done this before," he continues, cutting me off. "What are we doing, Elon?"

"I don't know yet. We are at the Jeep Trail so I guess—"

"No. What are *we* doing?"

I know what he meant before, but I'm not ready to analyze my feelings for him that have taken root inside my heart, growing with each second.

What I want to do is enjoy this moment. No promises, no guarantees, but Nate seems to have other plans, still watching me closely, waiting.

I gnaw my bottom lip with my teeth, searching for the right words to explain how scared I am of what we are doing but want to do it anyway. So I say, "Breaking gravity."

His eyebrows dip a little in confusion. "What?"

I stroke a thumb along his bottom lip, his square jaw, then smooth his furrowed brow. "This is new for both of us. We're breaking rules. When I'm with you, nothing else matters. Nothing can touch me or pull me down. Not even gravity."

"Huh." His mouth curls on one side, the beginning of a smile, giving him a boyish look. "Breaking gravity."

"Yep." I grin wide. "Now, can we stop overanalyzing everything and go?"

He chuckles as we get out of the car. We head toward the registration office and once our entrance fee is sorted out, Nate guides me back to the car, a playful glint in his eyes.

"Are you ready for this?"

I glance around me, watching as people jump inside their Jeeps while others high five each other excitedly. There are posters showing vehicles teetering dangerously on rocks with only two side wheels keeping them on the ground, while others show cars rushing through bumpy trails.

"Is it safe?"

He chuckles, taking in the look of horror on my face. "Where's your sense of adventure?"

"At the moment, quivering in fear. Do you do this often?"

"Not as often as I used to before this." He jerks his chin to his right arm. "I usually take Bennett with me. Driving on those trails can get intense."

I dart a look at the banners again, and it dawns on me. Bennett is *not* here. My eyes go wide as I take in his full grin. "Are you serious? I'm likely to throw us over the edge of some rock!"

He lets out a deep laugh that has my tummy tingling, and the desire to do anything he wants swells in me.

He pulls me to his side, and for the next half an hour, he explains

to me what I need to know to operate the Wrangler. Then we get inside the car and attempt to put theory into practice, which I fail at
miserably at first. But knowing me and the fact that I love a good
challenge, I eventually get the hang of it after almost two hours of
driving into rough terrains and screaming my poor heart out when
we get to the rocks.

CHAPTER TWENTY-SIX

Elon

AFTER ANSWERING THE TEXT MESSAGES FROM NOR AND ELISE AND letting them know I'm sleeping over at my apartment in Jacksonville, I take one last look on the hot guy lying on the bed.

My professor, my lover.

Nate.

He wasn't feeling well, so we had to cut our off-roading trip short and head for the first bed and breakfast we could find. When we got here, he took his pain medication and laid on the bed to wait for it to work, which is why he's fast asleep, snoring softly. He's lying flat on his back on the bed, his chest rising and falling in a steady rhythm, his right arm lying on his side, his left folded behind his head. He looks peaceful, the worry lines faded in sleep.

I head for the bathroom and close the door softly before stripping down and hopping in the shower.

Ten minutes later, I join Nate on the bed with only a towel wrapped around me. Since we didn't have any plans of staying at a motel, we didn't bring a change of clothes.

Nate stirs awake as soon as my head hits the pillow. He turns his head to face me.

"Feeling better?"

"Yes." His eyes wander down my neck, his gaze darkening when they reach the little cleavage showing above the towel. "What a beautiful sight to wake up to."

I scoot up and lie next to him, placing my head on his good shoulder. "Today was perfect. I really needed that after everything that has been going on. Thank you."

"Yeah?" he asks, wrapping his left arm around my shoulder, pulling me up to him and meshing his lips with mine.

I nod and laugh. "I can't even remember the last time I had so much fun, even though I literally screamed the whole time."

His body shakes with laughter. "Damn, Little Wolf. I wouldn't be surprised if the entire state of Florida heard you."

I swat his chest, which only makes him laugh harder as he tucks my head under his chin.

God, I could listen to him laugh the whole day.

We sprawl on the bed in a comfortable silence. All I can hear is the rhythmic *thump thump thump* of his heart where my ear is pressed on his chest.

He sinks his fingers into my hair, sliding them to the back of my neck and squeezing me gently in a command.

"What's wrong?" I ask, lifting my head from his chest to meet his gaze.

"I have been selfish and didn't think to ask you what you expect from this. . . whatever this is." He points at the space between us.

I touch his cheek, caressing his stubbled jaw. "This is whatever we want it to be."

"I just want to make sure we are on the same page. I can't offer you more than this," he says, moving his hand on the nape of my neck. "No happily ever afters. Just this. Enjoying each other's company."

I sigh, relieved. If he thought I was in this for an HEA, I'm about to shock him. Growing up, I dreamed that one day I'd meet a man who would sweep me off my feet and spoil me. Love me. Give me something to believe in. As much as I yearn for such a life, my past has tainted my perception of happily ever afters.

He must see the relief evident on my face. His gaze sharpens in curiosity, his head subtly arching to the side and the fingers on my neck squeezing, demanding my attention, sending shivers down my spine.

"Some women would be storming away after what I just said. But you're still here."

I shrug. "I am."

"Why?"

I look at him, debating how much I should tell him. I could lie and tell him something like, "I've always wondered what dating my professor would be like" or "I was dying to get in your pants." Something sassy to make this seriousness that has suddenly entered our conversation disappear.

I decide to go with the truth. "I'm not sure happily ever afters are in the cards for me. If you'd met Stephen Blake, you'd understand."

He blows out a slow breath through his mouth, as if my answer offers him some kind of relief, but the way he's looking at me right now makes me think otherwise. I keep asking myself why he's here since he traveled all the way from Jacksonville to Ocala. That's some dedication unless. . .my heart skips a beat.

No. *No.* I can't afford to make assumptions.

"Why did you do this, Nate?" I finally ask the one thing that has been on my mind since he called me last night.

"What do you mean?" His warm breath tickles the hair on my temple, causing me to shiver in delight.

I lift my gaze to his. "I thought this was just, I don't know, a lust-only arrangement?" I mutter, spellbound by the depth of the emotions swirling in his eyes.

His eyebrows dip a little, as he searches my gaze and murmurs, "I changed my mind. I wanted to spend more time with you *out* of bed."

His voice is so low, I wouldn't have caught the words if my senses weren't on high alert, breathlessly waiting. I'm not even sure he meant to say the words out loud, given the mystified look on his face.

"What did you say?" I whisper now, wanting him to say it again.

He pulls his arm from around me and sits up, then drags trembling fingers down his hair before gripping the nape of his neck like it's a lifeline. "I changed my mind."

"Nate," I start to say, but stop to gather my thoughts.

"Look. Let's just enjoy whatever this is. At least for as long as you want me." He reaches for my hand on top of the sheet and kisses the knuckles, his eyes locked on mine the whole time. "I'll go clean up."

He stands and strides to the bathroom, closing the door behind him. Seconds later, I hear the sound of the shower running. Images of him leaning his forehead on the wall while rivulets of water cascade across his broad shoulders and down his strong back flash inside my head. I moan and punch the pillow twice in frustration. I hop out of bed and march to the bathroom door, then remember that hours ago he was in pain and needs to rest.

I spin on my heel and take my lusty ass back into bed and pull the sheet up to my shoulders, then wait for him to finish taking his shower.

Nate

After the shower, I leave the bathroom, rubbing my hair with a towel, and return to bed to find Elon lying on her stomach, her loud snores filling the room.

After toweling myself dry, I unhook the one on my waist and toss them on a nearby chair, but they slide and fall on the floor. My Little Wolf would have a seizure if she saw that.

I crawl on the bed, feeling refreshed and my body free of pain, and lie on my back, then pull Elon to my side. The towel she had wrapped around her after the shower now lies beneath her body. She burrows her face in my neck, curling her tight little body around mine and throwing a shapely leg over my thighs. My cock, already semi-hard, rises eagerly to the occasion.

"God, you smell so good, I could eat you right now," she says in a husky voice, lifting her head and giving me a sleepy look that's all kinds of sexy with her hair mussed up and falling around her shoulders. The tip of her tongue peeks out as she licks her lips, and that primal part of me imagines grabbing her head and guiding her down between my thighs.

Something holds me back though. My head and my dick are at war, and as much as I want to spend the night inside her and make up for the last few days, I can't. Not when my feelings have been all over the place from the moment I stepped into Starbucks and our eyes met from across the room, sending shocks of awareness all over my body.

Seeing Elon waiting for me was like inhaling a lungful of air after being underwater for years. At first I thought I was going through the motions because I hadn't seen her since she left Jacksonville. But after spending the day with her and watching her eyes light up and hearing her addictive laughter, chasing the traces of shadows in her face, I knew I was screwed. I realize that "*Whatever we want this to be*" just got really fucking complicated.

"These are so cute," she says, tracing her pinkie along the purple friendship bracelets Makayla made for me.

My lips pull in a smile, remembering her delighted face every time she sees her gift around my wrist. "My niece made them for me."

"What's her name?"

"Makayla. Or Kaylie." I reach for my phone on the nightstand and notice several messages from Bennett—nosy fucker—and two missed calls from my mom. I make a mental note to call back my mother tomorrow and ignore my brother-in-law's messages for now.

I tap the screen and pull up a couple of images, then angle the phone so Elon can see the screen. I point to the ray of sunshine with curly hair framing her cherubic face sitting next to Matthew, who is staring at the camera with a smirk similar to my own, his hair a riot of wild curls. "Here she is. And that is her brother, Matthew, next to her. Izzy would likely kill anyone who tries to cut Matthew's hair." I chuckle. "There's this one time Bennett wanted to take his son to get a haircut. My sister stopped him with just a look."

She snort-laughs, and my arm instinctively tightens around her. I've fucking missed that sound.

"They are so adorable! How old are they?"

"Matthew is six and Kaylie is four." I swipe a finger across the screen and a different image appears. "That's Izzy, and of course you know Bennett," I point to the second, and then the third one. "And my mother and father."

In the photo, Izzy's lying on a couch and Bennett is leaning forward, his lips pressed on his wife's swollen belly while flashing a thumbs up to the camera.

"They're a goofy pair," I say with a chuckle.

She laughs softly, the sound a siren's song to my soul.

My gaze wanders to my mom. Her chestnut hair is littered with white streaks, grey eyes like mine staring into the camera, smiling. Standing behind her with his arms around her waist, hugging her to him, is my father. Tall, dark-haired, greying on the sides. People say I resemble my father, which is true. He was one good-looking man.

Elon flashes me a cheerful smile, but I see the lines straining the corner of her eyes. "You have a beautiful family."

After everything she has told me about her family, I now understand the glimpses of sadness I see in her eyes. She doesn't talk about her mother a lot, which gives me the impression that she is much closer to her sisters than the woman who gave birth to her. Then there's that twisted motherfucker of a father and the shitty ex-boyfriend.

I pull her tighter into me, my chest burning with a powerful need to protect her from anything that could harm her. I lift her chin, slanting her face up and kissing her savagely, pouring my feelings in the way my tongue tangles with hers. She moans, her breathing growing erratic.

I slow down the kiss and take in her flushed cheeks, her swollen lips. "Now that's the look I was going for. Look at the camera for me, sweetheart."

Slightly, I lift my left hand holding the phone and take a photo of us, then toss the phone on the nightstand.

We settle back in the bed, and she pulls the sheet to cover our naked bodies.

"Can I ask you something?" she inquires in a timid voice, which is unlike her. My Little Wolf is quiet, but never shy.

"Sure," I agree, feeling uneasiness slither down my spine. I shake it off, kiss her hair and squeeze her ass. Christ, I love her ass. "Go ahead."

She clears her throat. "Um. . .Camille—" She stops abruptly, probably feeling my body tense beneath hers.

I squeeze my eyes shut as the guilt and pain that has been simmering just below my skin explodes to life. After the last month and few weeks, I thought I'd managed to sort out those feelings.

I was wrong. They just boiled over at the mention of Camille, scorching my veins, tearing down every single barrier I'd put up the past three years. My head starts to pound with the restrained memories until I feel as if it will split in two.

My hand leaves her ass and I rub my temples, hoping to ease the pain. Behind my closed eyes, I see *her*.

No, not Camille.

Elon.

I see her terrified face as she opens herself to me, telling me about her life, her pain. And yet, she still manages to stand strong and positive, even after everything she has gone through.

I open my eyes and stare at the ceiling.

"What would you like to know?" I find myself asking her.

"Whatever you are comfortable telling me."

I blow out a deep breath and wet my lips, not sure where to start.

"The first time we met, I just knew she was who I was meant to be with. She was my first. . ." I trail off as I try to gather my next words.

"We were inseparable. Elizabeth—her mother—despised me from the beginning."

She looks up at and murmurs, "Elizabeth. . .Elizabeth Masters. Camille's mother." Understanding shines in her eyes. "I saw the two of you talking in the hallway a few weeks ago. It looked intense."

"It was. She said I looked at you the way I used to look at Camille."

She jolts up on the bed and quickly sits up. "*What*? Mrs. Masters knows about *us*?"

"No. But I have a feeling she suspects something's going on."

"Shit," she mutters under her breath, hopping out of bed.

"Elon."

She starts to pace as if she didn't hear me, halts next to the towels scattered on the floor and starts folding them into a neat pile. Then, she places them on the chair, marches to the bed, snatches her towel and walks to the bathroom.

Elon strides back, paces up and down twice before stopping and facing me. "Okay, I'm calm. I'm *calm*. Continue, but let's leave Mrs. Masters out of the story for now, please."

I nod and hold out my hand to her. She crawls back on the bed and curls her soft body into my hard one.

Once she's settled down, I let myself go back in time for the first time since the night my life changed.

Three years ago

"*Stop scowling, Nathan.*"

"*I'm not scowling,*" *I say, swiping the screen with a finger to exit the message on my phone, then lift my gaze and meet Camille's bright blue eyes while shoving the phone inside my pants pocket. Her eyebrows bunch up in concern.*

I planned this evening down to the tiniest details. Now, just one small issue and everything is unraveling fast. I clench my fist, annoyed. I should have planned everything myself before we left home.

"Uh-uh. That look on your face can only mean one thing. Something beyond your powers of control happened, and you have no idea how to fix it."

I wipe the irritation off my face and smile at her. Then I slip my arm around my girlfriend's waist and pull her flush to my body. Automatically, she angles her face to mine and lifts on her tiptoes with her lips in a pout, waiting for a kiss.

"Do you know how beautiful you are when you smile?"

I roll my eyes, my lips twitching, unable to fight the smile. "So I've heard. Happy birthday, Camille. Did you enjoy the opera?"

She hums softly under her breath. "It was perfect. Thank you for this, Nathan. I'd been dying to attend La Traviata."

I grunt. "You really loved it?"

She nods, grinning.

"Even though she dies in her lover's arms in the end?"

"Don't you dare spoil it for me. It was rather romantic, you know." *She smiles shyly before brushing her mouth to mine in a kiss.*

Unable to resist her sweet mouth, I wrap my fingers around the nape of her neck and claim her lips. She melts into me like she always does, kissing me like the fucking world is ending.

"Good enough for me to make you come over and over tonight?" *I mumble against her mouth, moving my lips down her cheek, her jaw. She inhales sharply when I nip her neck with my teeth.*

Her cheeks turn pink, and she buries her face in my chest. "Oh God, Nathan. We're in public. People are looking at us."

I chuckle, cupping her face in both my hands. "Still so shy, even after all this time."

"And you love me for that. Come on. Let's go home so I can thank you properly."

"Fuck, yeah," *I agree, linking my fingers with hers and tugging her* toward the cloakroom. I subtly slide my right hand inside my pants pocket and wrap my fingers around the velvet box in there.

Tonight, I plan on asking her to be my wife, just like I've been doing every year since we first met when we were nineteen. My gut tells me she'll finally accept my proposal.

After putting on our coats, we leave the Chicago Opera Theater. Flurries of snow swirl downward as we step into the December evening. I wrap my arm around Camille's shoulder and pull her close to me as we hurry toward my car parked two blocks away.

Minutes later, we're standing in front of my silver BMW. I pull the keys from my pocket and drop my gloved hand to quickly brush the snow off the windshield.

Behind me, I hear Camille's teeth chattering as she mutters, "It's freakin' freezing today."

I unlock the passenger door and turn around. "I could warm you—"

My blood freezes in my veins as stare at the man standing five feet away with a gun aimed toward us.

"You couldn't wait until we got home to make some dirty remark, could you?" Camille giggles, swatting my chest, unaware of the looming danger. Her smile fades when she notices I haven't moved. "What's wrong?"

"Your purse, lady," the man dressed in a long, black trench coat demands in a slurred voice. "And you." He points the weapon at me. "Don't fucking move, or I'll put a bullet through your little lady over there."

Camille gasps and spins around, her eyes wide.

"Get behind me," I whisper, my gaze never leaving the asshole in front of us.

She doesn't. Her breath is coming fast, and she whimpers.

"Cami—"

"I want the fucking purse!" The man shouts, the hand holding the gun trembling in his unsteady grip. He shakes his head, then squints as if trying to focus on us.

Shit. I need to keep his focus on me.

After quickly glancing up and down the deserted walkways, I turn back to face him.

"Easy there, buddy," I say in a soothing voice while raising my hands in the air. "I'm going to bring the purse to you, all right?"

He licks his lips and then uses his free hand to steady the one holding the gun. "Your wallet, too, mister." His jittery gaze jumps to the car behind me. "And the keys."

Not on his fucking life.

"The purse and wallet first, right?" I subtly lower my hand and pull my wallet from my coat, then Camille's clutch from her hand.

He nods, taking a step forward, his greedy eyes focused on the items I'm holding in my hand. Suddenly he stops and glares at me.

"Throw them in the car and give me the keys."

I nod, shifting my body around while shielding Camille, then toss the items inside the car. My mind is racing, calculating the ways I could disarm him without his drunk ass killing us.

He's holding the gun loosely now, probably more focused on the purse and wallet.

When he's two feet away from me, I launch myself on him and grab the wrist of the hand with the gun. The smell of stale alcohol and unwashed body slams into me, causing me to gag. His eyes widen in surprise before he begins to fight back, twisting his arm and trying to get out of my grip. He's surprisingly stronger than I thought.

Swinging my arm, I grab him in a choke hold with my back on Camille, grip the hand with the gun and twist it around on his back, hoping to disarm him. I hear her fumble with something inside the car, and seconds later, she's talking to the police.

I tighten my hold, but the asshole's hands flail around as he tries to remove himself from my grip. The hand holding the gun slips from my grasp, and I watch in horror as it forms an arc toward my face.

One. Two. Three.

Three seconds filled with uncertainty of what is going to happen next. Three long, life-altering seconds for the wild look in his eyes to shift to resolution. He staggers back as the gun fires two shots before he falls down on his ass.

That's when I feel a burning hot sensation rip through my shoulder and right upper arm.

Fueled by adrenaline and the need to protect Camille, I dart forward and bend over him. I lift my right arm and land blow after blow with one thing in mind: decimate the threat. Then, I step around him and kick the gun, sending it sliding across the snow and stopping several feet away.

I spin around and see Camille standing behind me with her hand clasped around the side of her neck, looking at me with so much hope, love and trust in those baby blues. I exhale in relief, but my reprieve is short-lived when I see blood running down her fingers. She lets out a choked sob threatening to split my world in two.

"Nathan," she whispers in terror. Her knees buckle and her fingers leave her neck. She falls to the ground and blood spurts over the snow around her shoulders and head.

Ignoring the pain tearing through my body, I sprint toward her, adrenaline and the fear of losing her fueling my body. I drop to my knees and lift her head into my hands.

"I'm sorry, baby. I'm so sorry. Stay with me, okay? The paramedics will be here soon." Her eyes fall shut and panic shakes me to the core. "Please look at me."

Her eyes flutter a few times before they open again and lock on mine.

"Don't cry, baby," she whispers before her eyes fall shut again.

"Open your eyes," I roar. "Look at me, Cam. Please. Stay awake for me," my voice breaks as I desperately try to think of something that will make her stay here with me until the paramedics get here.

Carefully, I shift her head on my lap and support it with my left hand, then dig the little velvet box from my pocket. "See? I never gave up even when you turned me down every year. Camille Masters, will you marry me?"

The corners of her mouth quirk in a smile or maybe it's my imagination.

"My p—purse. Check. . .inside."

"What's inside your purse, baby?"

Her mouth parts, but no words come out. "Check. Now," she insists. Begs.

Carefully, I shrug off my jacket, wincing as I pull it down my right arm. I fold it and place it under her head, then stumble toward the car. Just when my fingers wrap around the purse strap, pain shoots up my arm. My knees buckle, sending my body crashing on the ground. A dark cloud of nothingness threatens to render me unconscious.

Camille's heartbreaking sobs tear through my head, and I inch up on all fours and crawl toward her.

If I had known the night would be ending this way, I'd have done everything in my power to stop it before it even began.

"Don't leave me," I beg, my gaze fixed on hers, watching as life waxes and wanes in her blue eyes.

She blinks once, then blankly stares at the starless, dark sky. For just a second, I think I've lost her, and my heart stops beating.

I can't breathe.

I can't imagine living without her.

But then she smiles. Air rushes into my lungs, and a sob bursts through my lips. Even looking like this, she's just as stunning as the first time I laid eyes on her.

"Don't you fucking leave me," I plead again in a hoarse voice.

"Never," she vows in a fading whisper. "I'll always be with you, my love."

"God. Please don't take her away from me," I pray under my breath, muttering the words over and over, hoping someone will hear me. Hoping for some sign that everything will be okay.

I glance down at her neck.

Christ, the blood.

So much blood, and there's more still trickling from the gaping neck wound.

I need to get to her.

I climb on my hands and knees and attempt to crawl to her but fail *and fall flat on my face on the dirty snow, crippled by the pain slicing through my shoulder.*

"Keep your eyes on me, OK?"

"So cold—," she says, her teeth chattering, then she coughs.

Through my blurred vision, I see her face has gone extremely pale, her breathing shallow.

"Baby, stay with me," I plead. More hacking coughs and my desperation drives me forward. "Come on, fucking stay with me!" My voice is weak and hoarse from all the screaming I've done.

Sirens wail through the silent, chilly air. Snowflakes continue to fall like ashes after a volcano eruption.

Her chest rises once and then falls. I'm watching her now, waiting for her next breath to assure me that she's still here with me.

Her eyes remain unfocused as life fades from their depths.

"No!" I scramble up, but my feet are too weak, causing my body to slump back down. Darkness swirls in my vision, threatening to pull me under.

I can't black out now, damn it. She needs me.

"You'll always be my hero," she once told me.

The last thought that fills my head before my world turns dark is that heroes are supposed to do everything to save lives.

I've let her down. All it took was three seconds to bring my world crashing down around me.

I'm no one's hero.

Elon

By the time Nate is done telling me what happened three years ago, my face is drenched in tears.

No wonder this man is drowning in guilt. He believes she died because he couldn't save her.

I wipe my eyes with the back of my hand. "What was in the purse?"

A sad smile flits across his face, and he clears his throat. "A marriage proposal. And a ring," he laughs, shaking his head.

I run my fingers along his jaw, forcing his eyes on me. "You tried, Nate. But that doesn't mean you failed to save her."

He glares at the ceiling, tears swimming in his eyes. "I could have tried harder." His gaze moves to me. "I was supposed to save *her*. I'd always been there for her. Always. She didn't have anyone else to turn to when her mother threw her out of her fucking house. I promised her I'd always be there to save her."

"Oh, Nate." I wrap my arms around him and just hold him.

We stay like this until I feel his body relax and his breathing even out.

The last thought running through my head before I fall asleep is that Nate and Camille, they were each other's first love. They shared a love so powerful. How good it would feel to be loved by someone so much that you can feel it beyond death.

I wake up some time during the night to find Nate thrashing in bed. Sweat rolls down his face as he tries to fight whatever demon is hunting him in his dreams.

"Nate!" I shake his shoulder gently at first. "Nate! Wake up!"

His eyes snap open. He glances around wildly, then sits up, still shaking. He drags his fingers through his hair and stands up but doesn't turn to face me.

"Are you okay?" I ask, wanting more than anything to go to him and comfort him.

The muscles on his broad shoulders and tight butt flex as he shifts and looks at me over one shoulder. I gasp as his bloodshot eyes roam my face.

He shakes his head, grabs his dark jeans and Henley shirt from the neat pile I folded while I was on panic mode. He puts them on and faces me again.

"I'm going out for some air." We study each other from across the room. "I have these nightmares often. Please don't worry about me, okay?"

How can I not worry after everything he told me?

I walk over, cup his jaw and press a kiss on his lips. "Take all the time you need. I'll be here when you come back."

He stares at me for several seconds. Then, he lifts his left hand and runs his knuckles on my cheek before he walks out the door.

After waiting up for Nate, wondering if he's okay, wondering if I should go out and look for him and deciding against it, I eventually fall asleep.

I snap awake to the feel of the bed dipping under a heavy weight. Nate's scent embraces me as his head hits the pillow. He lets out a breath, then calls out in a raspy voice, "Elon?"

I turn to face him and wait for his next move.

"Come here. I want to hold you."

I do, scooting up next to him and tucking my head under his chin with his arm holding me to him. His heart beats steadily against my cheek as we lie there in silence. Soon I'm pulled in to a dreamless sleep, and I go willingly.

CHAPTER TWENTY-SEVEN

THE NEXT DAY, WE HEAD BACK TO OCALA. NATE HAS BEEN MORE subdued than usual during the entire trip. I have a feeling he needs space after last night, so I let him be.

We pull up into a free parking spot outside Starbucks, and he cuts off the engine. Then he angles his body to face me. I notice the dark circles around his eyes, a sign that his night didn't go well.

"Thank you for yesterday," I say when the silence becomes unbearable. "I had a wonderful time."

He watches me, his lips pressed in a tight line, chaos playing in his stare. Finally, he says, "I had a great time, too."

Silence descends, threatening to suffocate me. Without another word, I hitch the strap of my purse higher on my shoulder and swing the door to my side open. I hop out of the Wrangler and slam the door, then squint against the harsh sunlight to get my bearings. I sigh in relief when I see my car parked two rows away.

"Elon!" I stiffen when I hear a familiar voice call out my name.

My gaze zooms in on Elise, who's grinning widely several feet away. Behind her, Nick stops mid-step, scowling in my general direction, his eyes focused on something behind me.

"Elon, wait!" Nate calls out, his jogging footfalls getting closer while my sister retraces her steps and grabs Nick's hand. She turns and starts to drag him toward me.

"This is getting ridiculous," I hear her mutter and click her tongue. "I don't know what happened between you two, but you need to kiss and make up."

Oh, shiiiiit.

Wiping my clammy hands on my jeans, I shut my eyes and start counting down from ten under my breath, praying for the ground to open and swallow me.

Strong fingers wrap around my bicep in a gentle grip, and my eyes fly open. Goosebumps wash over my arms at his warm touch.

"What?" I ask in a harsh voice full of panic and irritation.

Before I guess his intentions, Nate's fingers wrap around the nape of my neck and grip my hair. His mouth slams down on mine in a hot kiss. I don't return his kiss at first, but then his tongue traces the seam of my lips, begging for me to open for him.

I press my palms on his chest and try to push him away, but he's like a brick wall. "You can't just—" And his tongue is inside my mouth, dueling with mine, claiming me. I moan, and suddenly my protests vanish and my hands are all over him, pulling him down to me. Everything else falls away as his kiss consumes me. Right now, it's just him and me and the roaring sound of blood pumping in my ears.

"Holy shiiiiiiiit!" a voice shouts excitedly, yanking me from the drugging kiss. "Did you know about this, Nick?"

I feel as if someone dumped ice cold water down the back of my shirt. I pull back from the kiss and stumble a few feet away from Nate and turn to find Elise grinning wide a few feet from me.

"Well, aren't you full of surprises." She scoots closer and whispers, "Who's the tall drink of water?" She tears her eyes away from Nate long enough to raise her brow at me and asks, "Aren't you supposed to be spending this weekend in Rushmore catching up with your homework?"

My heart has never beaten so fast in my life. Nick stands several feet away from us, wearing a pained look. Nate looks like he's two seconds from pouncing on me.

Then Nate's hungry eyes leave mine as he strolls forward. He holds out his right hand to Elise in greeting, even though I know how much he must be hurting just lifting it that high.

"Elise, right? I'm Nathaniel Rowe. It's great to finally meet you."

Elise beams even brighter as she takes his hand. "You seem to know me, yet I don't know a thing about—" Her eyes widen as something clicks inside her head. She lets go of his hand, and his face relaxes as his arm hangs loosely at his side. "No way! *The* Nathaniel Rowe? The cellist?"

Nate darts me a surprised look before looking at my sister.

"Sorry. I know you from hearing my sister talking about you. How did this happen? When did you two meet?"

I share a lot of information with Elise. She knew my old professor retired unexpectedly and that we had gotten a replacement. I'd avoided telling her about Nate being my new professor. I can't pinpoint the reason for holding back. Maybe it was a gut feeling that he and I would be crossing lines, and I didn't want anything spoiling what he and I have?

Nick clears his throat, and we all turn to look at him. "He's her professor," he says bitterly. "Come on, Elise. We need to go before Nor calls to check on us."

He spins on his heel and stalks in the opposite direction, which I assume is where their car is parked.

Dammit, Nick.

Elise's eyes have taken a suspicious look. "Is it true?" she whispers. "This is dangerous, Elon."

"Can we talk about this at home?" I ask, eyeing Nate as he watches us.

She nods, thank God.

I walk toward Nate and stop in front of him. "See you on Monday?"

He nods, presses a lingering kiss on my forehead, then strides to his car.

"You are the most sensible person, Elon. You should break it off before you get expelled from school." Elise rumbles as we walk toward my car. "Nor is going to freak out. Please. . .You can't do this. You're destroying your life—"

I swing around and grab her shoulders. "Don't you think I know that? Please, *stop*. I can't. . ." I don't even know what I want to say.

"Is he the new guy who replaced Professor Harris?" she asks. I nod. "You've fallen for him, haven't you?"

I drop my hands from her shoulders, open my car door and slide in the driver's seat. "Just leave it, okay?"

"Elon—"

"*Please*, Elise." I can't meet her gaze, because she'll see the tears and helplessness I feel burning in their depths. "Don't tell Nor. I'll sort this out, okay?"

"Yes. OK," she says quietly. "I'll see you at home."

As soon as her feet disappear from my line of sight, I drop my head on the steering wheel and squeeze my eyes tight until I feel the burning behind them recede. Only then do I close the door and drive to Willow Hill with my heart in my throat, my emotions scattered and my lips still burning from Nate's kiss.

CHAPTER TWENTY-EIGHT

Elon

A WEEK HAS GONE BY FROM THE TIME WHEN WE BURIED JOSH. LIFE hasn't been the same since he's been gone. I miss him so much. His goofy smile, his calming presence, his unfailing love for both my sister and her kids, so many moments and memories he left behind. But having Cole there seems to ease the pain. When I spoke to Nor on the phone last night, she mentioned that she was planning on telling Cora and Joce that Cole is their father. I can't even imagine how difficult it is for her to do this. It's for the better, I guess.

After the funeral, Nick made a point of avoiding me as much as he could without causing suspicion. Everyone probably assumed he was standoffish because he'd just lost his brother, which may have been true. However, it was that fact alone that made it so much harder not to be able to be there for him. To comfort and support him the way he has always done for me.

I was mad at him when he told Elise about Nate. I should have been the one to tell her.

The more I thought about how much I had hurt Nick and I

realized he probably wanted to hurt me in return, the more my anger diminished. It's obvious he acted out of anger and pain. Partly, I blame myself for not telling him about what was going on. I have never, in any way, flirted with him, encouraged him or given him hope that we'd one day be a couple. I loved him and still do, but he doesn't make my heart beat faster or make me lose my breath the way Nate does. Selfish of me or not, I just miss my best friend.

Now, sitting in the third row on Wednesday morning, I watch Nate shake a pill from his bottle of medication and pop it in his mouth. That's when I notice his right hand spasm more than normal, and his body is tense. Seconds later, he starts the lecture. He leans his butt on the desk behind him with his hands shoved inside his pockets. He seems to be favoring his right side more than usual. Other than that, his expression is indecipherable. His gaze flickers to mine every so often. I can't tell what he is thinking, but I see something akin to pain in his eyes before he looks away.

I've missed him so much. We've talked on the phone only twice since that trip to *Jeep Trail.* It was nice to know he was thinking about me, even though we left things feeling a bit uncertain, because I was sure as hell thinking about him whether I liked it or not.

I push thoughts of him to the back of my mind and focus on other things. The rehearsals for the fundraising ball are held every day now, other than Sundays since we are so close to the event, which means I need to reorganize my schedule.

I'm caught in my own thoughts when Amber nudges me with her pointed elbow. I wince and scowl at her, but before I open my mouth, she tells me the lesson ended a few moments ago, then jerks her chin to the front of the class. I glance around the emptying room before sneaking a look at Nate. The second our eyes meet, the air around us crackles with tension. I'm the first to look away. I gather my books and shove them inside my bag, then duck down and grab my cello at my feet and follow Amber down the stairs.

"I could wait outside if you two need to talk," she whispers from the corner of her mouth.

I already filled her in on what happened during our trip. She has been encouraging me to call him to talk or go to his place since I have his keys and surprise him. But I couldn't bring myself to do it. At this point, I'm not sure how I'll handle rejection.

"It's fine," I say, my gaze straying one last time to Nate, whose back is to us now, shuffling papers and putting them in his bag. "I'll talk to him in the office."

And I do intend to talk to him on neutral, yet private grounds, and the office should be the best place.

Just before I walk out the door, I feel my neck heat up and I know he's watching me leave. As much as I wish with every breath that he'd call my name and ask me if he could have a moment like he used to do a few weeks ago and pretend that he needs something sorted out, I know he won't do it.

I don't look back though. I'm so fucking tired of looking back, and if this is it, if that confession at the bed and breakfast was our end, then so be it. As much as my heart breaks for what happened to him and Camille and as much as I want to be there for him, I know he has to sort everything out on his own.

Nate

"Stop growling at me, you cranky bastard."

Those are the first words Bennett throws at me the second I answer his call.

I stop outside the head of strings department, Professor Kraft's, office to discuss the upcoming Strings Masters class scheduled for summer. I rub my eyes to lessen the exhaustion that has been riding me for days.

"Bennett," I snarl impatiently.

"You haven't called me in the last three days. I'm worried. You know I'm needy, honeybunch."

I take a deep breath, then squeeze my eyes shut to fight the nausea rising in my throat. When I woke up today, I thought the excruciating pain in my right arm would fade once I took my medication. Five hours later, it seems to have worsened. I can't remember the last time I was in so much pain.

"I'm fine, Ben—"

"Is it Cello Girl? Did you two have a fight or something?"

I grind my teeth. "My fucking arm is killing me, and I'm not sure who asked you to analyze my relationship."

"Ah, so there *is* a relationship," he chortles but quickly catches himself. "You need to go home and rest, man. How can you be helpful to the students if you are in pain?"

"I'm just about to go in for a meeting, then I'll take the rest of the day off."

"Good. I'll bring soup."

"No soup. I just need to rest."

"Fine. But if Izzy asks—"

"Just tell her I said no." I press my head on a wall and close my eyes. "Can I ask you a question?"

I expect him to be his usual smartass self, but he surprises me when he says, "Of course."

I wet my lips while trying to assemble my thoughts through the throbbing echoing down my arm. "Do you think it's possible to love two people equally?"

He pauses long enough to ask, "*Love?*"

"You know what I mean," I say, wondering if it was a good decision to talk to him about this.

I don't have anyone else to talk to though. Bennett has always been there for me since we were kids, just like I've always been there for him.

He's silent for several seconds when his sigh travels through the connection, and he says, "In the grand scheme of things, I think it's possible to love two people equally. The heart is a strange thing, my friend. It wants what it wants. And if yours wants Cello Girl, is there a chance of talking you out of this?"

"No." My answer comes out as a growl, which causes him to let out a chuckle.

"I was just checking. You've always been a determined fucker. What about your job? Cello Girl could be expelled if this comes out."

"She has just one year left to finish. We could keep this on the down low until she finishes. Or," I add.

"Or what?"

"I could quit."

He's quiet for what feels like years. Finally he asks, "Are you really sure about this?"

I grip the nape of my neck while studying the empty hall. "I have to go."

"Great chat, honeybunch," he says cheerfully.

"Fuck you," I say, my lips already forming in a reluctant smile despite the soreness wracking through me. After disconnecting the call, I scroll through the photos in my gallery and tap the screen when I find the one I'm looking for. The picture of us lying in bed at the bed and breakfast a few weeks ago.

Christ. She's beautiful. This is the only thing that has kept me going since that day. When I woke up from the recurring nightmare— Camille shot and dying in my arms—I cringed at the thought of Elon seeing me like that. Weak. Trapped in my own existence. My feelings for Elon were developing into something that scared me. Something I never thought I'd feel again after Camille.

What if I let her in and I lost her?

And so I ran, scared like a coward. But the more distance I put between Elon and me, the more I'm pulled into her. It's like we were always meant to be, and I am fighting a losing war.

I chuckle to myself and shake my head.

She's stealing pieces of my soul, replacing them with hers, awakening parts of me I was certain had died when I lost Camille. I never thought I would know what it felt like to be wanted again, but Elon seems to have taken my heart captive, and I'm her willing victim.

It was obvious from the start, but I was blinded by my own fear and guilt. I didn't stand a chance.

Professor Kraft isn't in his office yet. I pour water in a plastic cup from the water cooler, down another pill, then settle down in one of the chairs at the reception area as instructed by the receptionist and wait.

CHAPTER TWENTY-NINE

Nate

THE STAFF MEETING TOOK LONGER THAN I THOUGHT IT WOULD. Two hours later, I stumble inside my office and collapse on my chair. The pain escalated throughout the meeting, and by the time I walked out of Professor Kraft's office, I could barely move my right arm.

I loosen my tie and then contemplate calling Bennett to come and get me. The sound of the outer door opening and closing interrupts my train of thought. I gather whatever energy I have left and straighten on my seat while schooling my expression to impassive.

"Professor Rowe?" Elon's sweet voice calls out, sending relief coursing through me.

She peeks around the door before she steps in looking apprehensive. Her gaze roams my face, and her expression instantly shifts to concern as she hurries toward me.

Elon

I round the desk, taking in the pained look on Nate's face, the light sheen of sweat on his forehead and locked jaw.

"Do me a favor," he says, panting. "Grab my phone from my bag and call Bennett. He'll take it from there."

I shake my head. "I'm on my lunch break. Come on. I'm taking you home." I toss whatever I can find and he'd probably need inside his bag before snapping it shut. "Didn't the medication help?"

He grunts. I assume from his response the medication didn't work.

I grab my bag from behind my desk and turn to face him. "Maybe we should go to the hospital. They could give you something stronger for the pain."

He jerks his head adamantly in what I assume is a negative. "They won't be able do anything for me."

I feel his body tense next to mine as soon as we step into the empty hall. He scans our surroundings, and then I see his features relax. He stops to adjust his weight from his right, leaning more to his left side.

"I'm going to go ahead first and bring the car to the back of the building," I whisper, looking up and down the hall, then holding out my hand, palm up. "Keys?"

He pulls them from his left pants pocket without a word and drops them in my hand. I spin around and hurry down the hall. Moments later, I walk toward the lot allocated for staff, find his car and jump in. He's waiting on the other side of the building when I pull up. He quickly gets in the car, eyes clenching shut in pain as he settles into the seat.

Right before I drive away, I feel eyes watching me. Us. Upon taking a quick inventory of our surroundings, I don't see anything or anyone suspicious.

Ten minutes later, Nate and I walk inside his building. His face is paler than before, and his eyes are bloodshot. Veins pop out on his neck.

As soon as we get to his room, I toss our bags on the loveseat, then order him to sit down while he instructs me on what he needs. I rush to the bathroom and open the cabinet above the sink and gasp.

The space is filled with yellow and white bottles of medication. I catch words like Oxycodone, Lyrica, Vicodin and other names I can't even pronounce. Then there's his trusted little bag on the top shelf where he keeps his weed. I grab the bottle of Oxy and a bottle of water from the fridge in the kitchen. Then I rush back to the room. He's already lying on his back, breathing heavily. He demands two pills, which I notice is higher than the prescribed dose. He tosses them in his mouth and downs them with the water from the bottle.

He frowns. "You could have left me there writhing in my pain, especially after the way I've behaved toward you, but you didn't."

I'm not sure if that's meant to be a question, so I shrug and say, "I could have, but I didn't want to. I don't like to see you suffer."

He relaxes his frowned eyebrows and clears his throat. "Thank you."

"You don't need to thank me."

He sighs, yawning. "I do. You are so good to me," he murmurs, his eyes falling shut at the same time he holds out his left hand in my direction. "Come here."

I crawl up on the bed and cautiously curl my body next to his. He sighs as his arm comes around my shoulders, pulling me tighter into his warmth.

"Stay with me."

"Okay," I whisper, curling my fingers around his shirt, trying to get my emotions for this man under control. "Sleep, baby. I'll be here when you wake up. I'm going to take care of you."

His arm tightens around me. He releases a long breath, his body relaxing on exhale.

I wait until his breathing has evened out before slipping out of bed and pulling the sheets to his chest. I sweep the hair off his damp forehead, so soft I could run my fingers through it the whole day.

I chew my bottom lip as I study his face, the chiseled jaw and stubborn chin. He looks so peaceful in sleep, his face free of scowl and frown lines.

Standing up from the bed, I move to remove his shoes and socks and put them on the floor next to the dark brown dresser. Then, I straighten and glance around, searching for something to pass my time when I notice a silver photo frame lying face down at the corner of the dresser. Curious, I inch my hand forward, looking over my shoulder to where Nate is still sleeping soundly on the bed. Then I pick up the metal frame and turn it around.

Astounding blue eyes shining with pure love meet mine. Blonde hair styled into loose curls, falling around a heart-shaped face. A smile so beautiful it would make angels weep aimed at the person holding a camera.

Camille.

She was *gorgeous*.

Jealousy coils in my belly. How would it feel to be loved so fiercely, the way Nate loved Camille? Before my mind can wander any farther, I set the frame back down and drop my head on top of the dresser in shame.

Gosh, what kind of person am I? How can I feel jealous of a woman who's long since gone? A woman whose death still haunts the man I'm beginning to feel all sorts of crazy feelings for.

I take deep breaths to pull myself together, then push off the dresser before I start loathing myself.

The sound of a phone ringing offers me reprieve. I spin around and follow that sound to Nate's bag. As I dig out the phone, I notice Izzy's name flashing on the screen. The ringing stops before it picks up again seconds later. All I can do is stare at the display, worrying my bottom lip between my teeth.

If I answer the call, she'll want to know who I am. I don't think telling her I'm his student would bode well for him. And I don't think Nate has told her about us. He would have clued me in if he had.

What if it's an emergency? I remember Nate mentioned that his sister was expecting soon. I spend the next two minutes arguing with myself before concluding that Bennett would definitely call if something happened.

Right?

Right.

The ringing stops. When it doesn't start again, I sigh in relief. I set the phone on top of the dresser and turn to face the beautiful man on the bed. Despite the insistent sound from his phone, he slept through it all. The medication must have knocked him out properly.

I rotate on my heel, taking in Nate's bedroom: the massive bed built from the same wood as the dresser, deep grey sheets that remind me of his eyes when he's aroused, warm brown wooden floorboards. Weak sunlight filtering in through wide windows flanked by light grey curtains, which also remind me of his eyes. The room is masculine and welcoming.

I didn't get a chance to check it out the last time I was here since we were too busy screwing each other's brains out. A shiver trails up my spine, spreading across my scalp just thinking about Nate and me on the same bed he's lying on. God, this man turned my world on its head and then proceeded to make me feel wanted and adored.

Too anxious to explore my growing feelings for Nate, I walk to the windows overlooking the St. John's River and take in the beauty of the skyline before me. I stand there just enjoying the sight and try hard not to think too much about whatever this is between Nate and me.

CHAPTER THIRTY

Nate

I BLINK AWAKE TO A DARK ROOM ILLUMINATED BY THE MOONLIGHT streaming in through the window. I lazily roll to my side and switch on the lamp on my nightstand, then swing my legs to the edge of the bed. I run my fingers through my hair as the memories of the past few hours trickle through my head.

Elon.

My sweet girl.

Is she still here or has she left already?

Disappointment slices through me at the thought of her gone. After the past few weeks of awkward silence, I miss feeling her soft skin beneath my fingers. There's no chance in hell I can go on pretending she means squat to me. I miss the way she looks at me, I miss her quirky sense of humor, I miss burying myself inside her and finally feeling like I'm home, where I belong.

Home.

Where I belong.

I need to talk to her.

I stand from the bed and scan the room in search of my bag where I left my phone. I stop when I see the petite body curled up on the couch, dressed in one of my white T-shirts. She must have changed into it while I was sleeping.

My gaze slides down the curve of her hip, catching a glimpse of lilac panties with lacy edges.

All this beauty, this perfection in front of me.

She's still here, like she said she would be.

By the time I'm standing in front of the couch, my fingers itch to touch her, my mouth watering at the mere thought of kissing and tasting her. My cock is straining in my pants, wanting inside her badly.

From the corner of my eyes, I glimpse the frame lying face down on top of the dresser. I'd moved it from my nightstand several weeks ago to ease the ache, the guilt that had become a constant companion.

The past few years, I felt like I'd been treading in deep waters, afraid to look down because I'd lose my balance and sink, never come up for air again.

I'm tired of feeling empty, feeling like it's wrong to want someone else. Tired of wanting Elon and denying myself what she's offering.

I still blame myself for not saving Camille, and I hope one day I'll find it in myself to forgive and let go. But right now, Elon gives me what I need. It's terrifying and freeing and addictive.

As scary as it is, I'm willing to go all in.

I'm about to drop to my knees and give Elon something to wake up to when the sound of the doorbell ringing fills the air. I straighten and glance at the alarm clock on my nightstand.

7:30 p.m. Have I been sleeping that long? I must have gone completely under after taking the medication.

The bell rings again five seconds later. Irritation flares through me at the interruption.

I gently sweep the tresses of her hair off her forehead with my fingers before kissing the freckles scattered on her nose. Then I stride out of the room, closing the door behind me, turning on lights along the way while heading to the living room.

As soon as I open the door, Izzy waddles in with my mom in tow, arguing about some shit. It's like they didn't see me standing at the door, but my thoughts are proved wrong when Mom abruptly stops talking and wields her blue eyes so similar to Izzy's at me.

"Why didn't you pick up the phone?" Mom asks in a worried voice.

I blink, attempting to wrap my head around the fact that two of my favorite women are in here, while the girl I was about to devour, my *student*, is in the other room. Who am I kidding, make that *three* of my favorite women.

Fuck. This is *not* good.

"What are you two doing here?" I glance between Mom and Izzy, who is now making her way to the living room. She tosses her bag on the coffee table, then grabs the arm of the couch and lowers herself onto it. Mom rounds the couch and stops in front of me, her brows furrowed in concern, before she opens her bag and pulls out a round Tupperware container.

"I made you chicken soup. Bennett told Izzy you weren't feeling well." She hands it to me, then feels my forehead with her palm as if checking for fever. "Are you feeling better, honey?"

Fucking Bennett.

"I'm good. You didn't have to come—"

"We called several times. We got worried, and Mom drove us here to check if you were okay," Izzy says, patting the space on the couch for me to sit.

I set the container on the table then cross my arms over my chest, subtly checking the hall that leads to my room, hoping Elon is still asleep, before turning my attention to my mother and sister. I can't ask them to leave without raising suspicion, so I ask, "Shouldn't you be resting, Izzy?"

She waves her hand. "I'm fine. Baby's fine," she sighs and leans back on the couch. "I was going crazy inside that house, so I asked Mom if I could tag along. Ben's mom dropped by to watch Kaylie and Matthew."

Shit! Usually I don't mind when they drop by unannounced, but today—

The sound of a door softly opening and closing has Izzy and Mom cutting their eyes to where I'm standing, body tense, mind scrambling to find a viable explanation when their heads turn simultaneously toward the hall, following the sound of feet padding softly on the tiles.

"Nate?" Elon calls out in that I've-just-woken-up husky voice that makes my toes curl.

She appears at the mouth of the hall, still wearing my shirt. Relief washes through me when I notice she's wearing a pair of my boxer shorts.

She squints against the light, running her fingers through her messy hair.

I swallow hard at the vision wobbling sleepily toward us. Another emotion different from the lust coursing through my veins hits me hard in the gut, stealing my breath.

I love seeing her in my clothes.

I love her chaotic hair.

I fucking love having her in my home. Somehow I sleep better when she's in my space.

I can't fucking *breathe.*

Her body stills suddenly. Her face pales and eyes widen as she takes in the scene before her.

I know that look. It's the same look I saw when I mentioned that Elizabeth suspected something was going on between Elon and me. There's no way I'm letting her run.

"Um. . .sorry—" she starts to say with her hand gripping the front of her shirt.

"Elon," I command in a gentle, yet firm voice.

Her gaze swings to where I'm standing, and she wets her lips.

With my eyes locked on hers, I hold out my left hand to her and dip my chin slightly. "Come here."

I wait, watching indecision play across her face. Then her fingers drop from my T-shirt. She walks toward me with her head high, eyes never leaving me, and takes my hand.

Finally, my lungs deflate as air rushes past my lips. When she's secured snugly next to me, I turn to face Izzy and my mom. They're wearing identical facial expressions: wide eyes, jaw dropped.

Mom speaks up first, breaking the charged silence.

"Nate?" she questions in a hopeful, confused whisper.

I squeeze Elon's shoulders, and I feel her body relax further into mine.

"Mom, Izzy. This is Elon." Then I turn to the woman at my side. "Elon, meet my sister, Izzy and my mom, Grace."

My girl shifts and moves from under my arm and bravely walks over and holds out her hand to Mom, then Izzy, before making her way back to me.

"I think I need to go and change," she whispers when my mom and Izzy exchange glances, still speechless.

"Okay," I murmur.

Elon hurries back to my room without looking back. Mom's narrowed stare follows her until she's out of sight before cutting to me.

"She looks awfully familiar," she mutters to herself.

Shit. Is there a chance she has seen Elon and me together before?

Mom shakes her head as if to disperse that thought and asks, "Is she. . ." She trails off, her face filled with hope.

"I'll be damned," Izzy exclaims, grinning wide. "The girl at Reed's Lounge? I'd know that red hair and those freckles anywhere. Tell. Us. Everything. Does Bennett know?" She wiggles on the couch to get comfortable, then puts her hands on her belly. "Oh my God. I haven't been this excited in a long time."

"Stop looming and sit down, Nathaniel," Mom orders softly.

I continue looming, waiting for Elon to return to my side.

Mom sighs when I don't do as she asks, then folds her hands on her lap. "Who is she?"

My student. The girl stealing pieces of my heart. "Elon Blake."

"Annndddd?" Izzy asks, looking unbelievably happy. "Stop being stingy with the info, bro. Lay it on us, Romeo. I can't remember the last time I saw you glow."

I scowl at her. "No, I'm not glowing."

"You so are," she sing-songs, a mischievous look on her face. She studies me with narrowed eyes, as if she's trying to figure out what's going on.

I shut my eyes and inhale a deep breath, rein in my frustration and force my expression to neutral, before peeling my eyes open.

My mom snaps her fingers, her face lighting up. "That's it! I knew I had seen that face before." My eyes go to her. "The Swan Girl."

"The what?" Izzy and I ask at the same time.

"The Swan Girl," Mom repeats again. "Caroline Turner."

I blink.

Mom's gaze scans my living room before asking, "Where's your laptop?" She doesn't wait for the answer. She digs her phone out of her bag and hands it to me, literally vibrating with excitement. "You two are better at this than I am. Type her name. Caroline Turner or The Swan Girl."

I walk over, take the phone and hand it to Izzy, who seems as curious as I am.

Moments later, Izzy's brows shoot up as she looks up at Mom, then me and mutters, "Wow. I wish I could do *that*."

Frowning, I take the phone from her and glance at a girl who could pass for Elon's sister, apart from the green eyes. She's dressed in a white ballet outfit, long elegant neck arched to the side with eyes staring into the camera, arms stretched above her head.

"I could never forget that face or the performance," Mom says fondly. My head twists to her, taking in the reminiscing look on her face. "Your father took me to New York to attend the opening of *Swan Lake* on our fifth wedding anniversary." She frowns, lips pursed. "She got married and stopped performing after that. Last time I heard, she had two children and was living in Ohio."

Just then I feel the hair on my arms curl in awareness. My heartbeat accelerates like it always does when Elon is close. My body is so attuned to her. Whenever she walks into a room, every part of me gravitates toward her.

She's like my personal satellite, signaling me and drawing every part of me into her radius.

She halts and adjusts the strap of her bag on her shoulder, her gaze going to my mom and Izzy before *those* eyes find me. She's back to Perfect Elon: perfect bun with not a single hair out of place and a face that doesn't reveal a lot.

She clears her throat and smiles at me. "I'm heading out. It was great meeting you." She says this to my mom and Izzy.

I nod, my throat tightening. My gaze moves from her face to her fingers curled tightly around the strap on her shoulder.

Fuck. I'm crushing hard on this girl.

"Wait!" My mom shoots up from her chair when Elon takes a step toward the front door. "You don't need to leave. Izzy and I were just about to go."

"No, we were not," Izzy protests. "We just got here."

Mom ignores my sister and asks, "Are you Caroline's daughter by any chance?"

Elon's eyes widen in shock. "Yes. You know my mother?"

"I once saw her perform in New York years ago."

At those words, Elon's shoulders seem to relax a little, and something like longing flashes across her face. She never talked a lot about her mother, so I got a feeling they were not close.

They continue talking about The Swan Girl for a few minutes. Izzy keeps tossing me curious looks, and at one point, she mouths, "I like her."

I roll my eyes, my lips twitching.

Of course she would. She's been worried about me since Camille's death, so I imagine how seeing a woman in my house makes her happy.

"So, how did you two meet?" Izzy finally asks, waving her hand to the space between Elon and me.

The smile on Elon's face drops as her eyes snap to mine. Subtly, she shakes her head, a panicked look on her face.

I take in Izzy and Mom's expectant looks, then back at Elon, holding her gaze.

"At Rushmore," I finally say, breaking the heavy silence.

"Oh, you teach, too?" Mom asks, although she's frowning now. "She looks so young to be a professor."

Elon's chest rises and falls with quick breaths, shoulders raised, ready to take flight. My heart clenches as I watch her as if she's waiting for hell to break lose.

She's begging me with her eyes to lie.

I can't do that.

I won't lie.

Not when I'm standing in front of the first woman that has made me feel something else other than guilt, grief and self-loathing.

I'm not ashamed of my feelings for her.

Plus this is my family. They know *me*.

"She's in my class." I pause, watching shock wash across her face. "Elon's my student."

Someone gasps. I can't tell if it's my mom or Izzy because I'm too busy being sucked into those eyes of my little wolf staring back at me.

"What?" Mom asks. Finally, I look away from Elon and meet my mom's stunned gaze. "What did you just say, Nathaniel?"

I blink at her, not repeating my answer.

"Are you out of your goddamn mind?" she yells, causing Elon to flinch and inch toward the door.

I pin Elon with my gaze, and she freezes mid-step.

"Please tell me you're joking," Mom whispers, shutting her eyes tight and inhaling a sharp breath.

My lips press into a thin line, and my jaw clenches. Seriously, doesn't she know me by now?

Izzy bursts out laughing, holding her belly. We all turn to look at her, her body shaking and tears running down her face.

Trust Izzy to diffuse a tension-filled situation.

When she's calm enough to talk, she looks at my mom. "Don't you know your own son by now?"

Mom glares at her daughter, then gives me the same look. "This is preposterous! What do you think people will say if they—"

"I don't give a fuck about what people say," I clip out, and Mom's face turns red. "I'm sorry for the language, but I'm not sorry for the way I feel about her."

Izzy laughs once more and shakes her head. "You don't do things half-assed, do you? Does Bennett know?"

I don't answer, just stare at her.

"That bastard!" she groans, struggling to get on her feet while Mom protests about all the cursing going on. I reach down and help my sister up and only let go when I'm sure her footing is steady. Then I reach down, pick up her purse and hand it to her. "I'm going to kill him. Mom, call Gladys and tell her to say the last prayers for her son. Lord, I'm going to murder his ass."

Mom doesn't even blink at this threat, obviously used to Izzy's melodramatic ways.

Izzy lumbers toward the front door before turning to seek me out, winks at me with a huge smile, then says to Mom, "Gladys mentioned she had a thing at her church to attend to at eight thirty."

Mom huffs and mumbles under her breath as she moves toward Izzy. She pauses where Elon is standing, holding her ground—damn, I'm proud of this girl—and glares at her.

I expect my mom to rip Elon a new one. Instead, the anger on her face disappears as her eyes cut back to me. She shakes her head, returning her gaze to Elon, and says, "I suppose you know what you're doing. Both you and my son."

Elon swallows nervously, then nods her head.

I join them at the door, hug my sister and my mom, pressing a kiss on their cheeks. "I need this to stay between us," I warn them.

They nod and walk out the door, pulling it shut behind them.

Elon lets out a huge breath, the weight of it almost knocking her off her feet.

"*Shiiiiiitttttttt!*" she exclaims, giving me all her weight as soon as my arm slides around her shoulders. "Oh man. That was just intense.

Oh my God! My stomach feels funny."

I chuckle under my breath, which results in her swatting my chest. "I'm panicking here," she whispers in a shaky voice.

I move back and tug her chin up to meet her tear-filled gaze. "Are you okay?"

She shakes her head and sniffs. "It's just a little overwhelming. Do you know how amazing and badass that was? You stood up for *me*, Nate."

Christ. The way she's looking at me right now, like I gave her a reason to breathe. To live. I'd gladly do it all over again.

I kiss her forehead, then brush my nose against hers. "I stood up for *us*."

Her mouth forms an O. Her eyebrows scrunch up seconds later. "Us?"

Since I decided to go all in, I nod. "Us." I take a deep breath and forge on. "You were so brave. For some insane reason, I like you more than it's legal for a professor to like his student. You are afraid, but you don't let that stop you from pursuing whatever this is between us. You make me laugh. I've been a dick the past weeks after that trip, yet, you helped me today and refused to leave my side." I pause, trying to read her. I can't tell what she's thinking.

"Go on." Elon nods and narrows her eyes. "Keep them coming. I like where this is going."

I laugh, holding her tightly to my body. "I've never met anyone like you. You're like—" I dig around inside my head for the right word,"—this magical, mythical creature."

She arches her head back to meet my gaze, her lips twitching. "Mythical creature?"

I smirk down at her. "Yes." I press a kiss on her forehead, then tug the strap on her shoulder lightly. "Stay."

"Okay," she agrees, linking her fingers with mine and guiding me to the kitchen. "I'm going to make you dinner, then thank you properly. In bed."

"I love that plan." I slide the bag off her shoulder and toss it on the couch.

"Are you feeling better?" she asks.

"You're here." I smile down at her and run my knuckles down her cheek. "I'm feeling fucking fantastic."

"You needed me," she says, her concerned eyes searching mine.

There's something else in her gaze, too, which makes me pull my hand away from her soft skin.

"What is it?" I question, bracing myself for whatever it is that has her looking at me differently than usual.

"Um. . .I saw the um. . ." She clears her throat and averts her gaze from mine.

"Yeah?" I prompt.

"The medication in your cabinet." She rubs her forehead with her hand before looking at me. "I'm not judging you or anything. I just got a little worried when I saw them, there was just so many of them, and I wondered. . . if it was a little, um, too much and I am so sorry I don't want to jump to conclusions and—my God! Please stop me before I say something stupid." She slaps a hand on her mouth and covers her eyes with the other one. "Stupid traitorous mouth," she mumbles into her palm, her ears and cheeks flushing in mortification.

I take deep breaths, trying to leash the sting caused by her words.

"Look at me," I order in a soft, firm voice.

She does, worrying her bottom lip between her teeth.

"I would give anything to stop feeling the pain. Those pills are my salvation until my doctor finds another option." Which means it could be a long time. Forever even. "It bothers you, doesn't it?"

Without a second thought, she nods. I exhale in relief. Right now, I'm not sure I could handle any lies. I love that she trusts me enough to be honest with me.

"I'm worried *for* you." Her features soften, the truth in those eyes.

Finally, I kiss her forehead and say, "You *care*. You're *here*. That means everything to me."

She raises up on the tip of her toes and gives me a closed-mouth kiss, then pulls me toward the kitchen.

After explaining where everything is, I grab two wine glasses and open a bottle of Chardonnay. After a quick toast, I park my ass on one of the stools along the kitchen island and watch *her* ass as she makes herself comfortable in my home.

We chat a lot about her family, my family, her life, my life. Just enjoying each other's company. The tension between us builds, the heat off our bodies fusing, melting whatever lingering awkwardness my mother and Izzy left behind.

At some point after dinner, my girl rises up from the couch and leaves the room with a little sexy sway in her hips and mischievous twinkle in her eyes. By the time she walks back into the room, my cock is hard and I want that naughty minx beneath me. She slides the black silk tie she brought back with her between her hands before throwing a leg over my thighs and straddling me.

"I can't stop thinking about you, Miss Blake. Your mouth. Your neck." I flick my tongue along her skin, licking the vein thrumming wildly at the base of her throat. "And your quietness and smart mind, your stunning eyes when they catch fire, the freckles on your nose. . ."

I rub my nose along her jaw and inhale deeply. "You smell like something I would gladly eat for breakfast, lunch and dinner. Scratch that. You smell like something I would gladly eat every second of the day. Baby," I bite her earlobe, and I feel her legs tighten around mine. "You make me want to do things that will likely not earn me a place in heaven."

Her back arches as a whimper leaves her parted lips and her nails dig into my bicep.

"You had plans to go to heaven?" she asks with a little snort, a little moan. "Imagine how disappointed the devil will be if you denied him your presence."

A laugh bursts out of my lips. Christ, I'd missed that smart mouth of hers.

She grinds her pussy against my cock. She pushes her hair back over her shoulders and arches her back, giving me a hooded look.

I slide my palms under her skirt, brushing them up to cup her ass, then raise a brow at her. "No panties, Miss Blake?"

"I thought I'd save you the time and removed them while I was in your room." She grins sweetly at me.

I laugh. "So considerate of you." My hands skim along her inner thighs, trace my fingers along her wet opening, then slide a finger inside her. She sighs, biting her bottom lip between her teeth, whispering, "Yes, *yes*. Right there, Nate. Please make me come."

And I do, adding another finger, my gaze never leaving her flushed, beautiful face as she pants, grinding her hips against mine as soft moans leave her mouth.

"Scream for me, Little Wolf. We both know how loud you can scream, sweetheart."

She obeys, screaming my name over and over, her body shaking as she comes down from her high. She collapses on top of me, quick breaths from her lips fanning my chest. We stay like this, my hand rubbing circles on her back as she comes down from her orgasm.

"I've missed seeing this look," I tell her when she raises her head to face me.

Her fingers move down my abs and unzip my pants. I lift my hips as she slides them down my legs. Her hands are warm when she takes hold of my cock and starts to stroke up and down in firm strokes. I groan and a shuddering breath leaves me and my hips buck, my body strung tight with need. The way she's looking at me right now, this is not a "whatever this is" relationship. I'm trying to figure it out, but all the blood has rushed down to my dick, my body bowing as her fingers slide, squeezing me. She lifts up and rubs the head on her pussy, and I almost explode.

My gaze flits down, and I watch as she pumps her hand up and down my cock.

"Look at me, Professor," she orders in a husky voice. My head jerks up, and *those* eyes catapult me into another universe. "I love the way you're looking at me right now. I love having your eyes on me, Professor," she says, looking at me beneath her lashes. "Nevertheless, I'm going to blindfold you, then have my way with you."

I sink into the couch, my legs spread, and push my pelvis up. "God, I'm so wild for you. Take whatever you need. It's yours."

The last thing I see before she blindfolds me is her saucy smile. Then I feel her lips wrap around my cock. The world falls away after that as Elon thanks me, rocks my world, burrowing herself deeper under my skin and stealing another piece of my heart.

CHAPTER THIRTY-ONE

Elon

THE FOLLOWING DAY, I WALK IN CLASS WEARING A SECRET SMILE AND Nate's silk black tie in a bow around my neck. The second he darts a look in my direction, his eyes grow wide when sees his tie, and I know he is thinking about last night and this morning. We are playing a dangerous game, but oh my God, it feels freaking amazing. He and I share a little secret. Well, Amber is in it, too, but yeah. What Nate and I have is dirty and sweet. It is us.

Earlier today, I woke up with Nate's lips on my neck and his hands skimming my inner thigh. Then he proceeded to make me come with his fingers. By the time he was buried inside me, every part of me was on fire. He made love to me quietly, intensely. The silence shattered when he shouted my name as he came.

Right before I took a cab to my place to shower and change, Nate and I agreed to stay away from each other as much as we could. Today in class, he didn't look in my direction except when he noticed I was wearing his tie. At one point, Amber asked me in a concerned voice if something happened between us, so I told her what our plan was.

Apparently, Professor Masters had confronted him again three days ago and threatened to have him fired when she had proof that he and I were involved.

Professor Masters has been watching me since practice started. So, as soon as my time is up, I make a quick job of packing my cello inside its case, then grab my bag and fly toward the door.

"Miss Blake?" Her voice stops me cold in my tracks. Taking a deep inhale to steel my nerves, I spin around to face her, pasting a smile on my face.

"Yes, Professor?"

She folds her arms on her chest as she studies me, then takes a step forward. My brain screams at me to flee, but my feet haven't gotten the memo yet. Plus I'm freaking terrified.

"You are one of the most talented students I've ever tutored. With the kind of education you receive here at Rushmore, you could go places, Miss Blake. Take the world by storm."

I hope the smile still frozen on my face doesn't reveal how nervous I am. I feel like I'm about to hyperventilate.

"Thank you, Professor," I say, and I'm shocked by how strong and calm my voice sounds.

"Tell me something." She tilts her head to the side. "Why do you want to destroy that?"

I blink, forcing a confused frown on my face. "What?"

Her gaze sharpens on me. "Do not take me for a fool. I wonder how things will go for you if President Bowman finds out about you and Professor Rowe."

Blood drains from my face and I feel like I can't get enough air, but still I manage to say, "What are you implying, Professor Masters?"

The confident look on her face wavers as she searches mine for secrets and truths. I'm not sure what she sees there because moments later, the confidence falls back in place. She smiles triumphantly.

"Is he forcing you to do this?"

I huff a breath, remembering Nick thought the same thing, too. I bite my cheek to keep myself from blurting out the fact that I invited him to my place. I kissed him. I welcomed his attention. I'm sure she's waiting for me to slip and say something that will incriminate Nate.

"I really don't know what you're talking about, Professor Masters." I make a show of checking the clock hanging in front of the practice room. "I really need to go. My tutoring class at Studio 22 starts in half an hour."

Anger flashes across her face, her lips curling into a sneer. "What did he promise you? A good grade?"

I lift my chin, meeting her gaze without flinching. "With all due respect, I don't appreciate your insinuations, Professor Masters." My voice is quiet and respectful, but firm. "Professor Rowe is just that. My professor and my boss. That is all."

She sucks air through her clenched teeth, her eyes burning in determination and hate. "I'll get him one way or another."

"Professor Masters?" I prompt.

"That man turned my daughter against me. I lost everything when she left with him."

Biting my cheek to stop myself from blurting out that she threw her own daughter out of her house, I glance down at my boots and wait for her to calm down.

When she stops talking, I lift my head and meet her gaze. "I don't know what happened between you and Professor Rowe in the past," I say calmly. "All I know is that he's an inspiration to the music community and a well-loved professor. Good night, Professor Masters."

Then, I march out of the room. Outwardly, I might look like I just kicked some major ass, but inside every part of me quivers with nerves and all the injustice Nate has gone through at the hands of this woman.

As soon as my feet hit the hallway, I charge for the bathrooms and into one of the stalls. After propping my cello on the door, I flip the toilet seat down and collapse on it.

Breathe in.

Out.

Breathe.

This is bad. I hate confrontations and do everything to avoid getting involved in one myself.

I drop my face in my hands and replay the conversation in my head. I'm certain I didn't say anything that would incriminate us.

After a few calming breaths, I dig out my phone from my bag, intending to call Nate to explain what happened, but then realize I'm five minutes late for my tutor class.

Moments later, I dash out of the bathroom door with my cello on my back and drive to Studio 22 like the hellhounds are after me.

CHAPTER THIRTY-TWO

Elon

FEBRUARY TWENTY-EIGHTH. I'VE BEEN WAITING FOR THIS DAY WITH bated breath.

Not only is the WAV fundraising charity ball something I wholeheartedly support, it's also a huge chance for me to really show what has lived inside of me from the time I held my first cello in my hands. It's a chance for me to prove to myself that I can beat the odds. And I just did. We just did.

Nate flew to Chicago for his doctor's appointment last evening. I haven't heard from him since we spoke on the phone at eight this morning. I'm anxious to hear his voice and know that he's okay, which is why I keep checking my phone every few minutes.

I glance at Alex, who is proudly grinning down at me, then he folds those lanky arms around me and hugs me tight. He pulls back and takes my hand, twirling me around as he takes in my floor-length gown that hugs my curves. It is black with nude-colored sequined mesh long sleeves. The flow of the dress reminds of me a bird in flight.

Alex whistles softly. "Damn, that dress."

I roll my eyes and smile, eyeing his dark suit, white button-down shirt and black bowtie. "Thank you. You clean up nice too."

Alex drops my hand and says, "You and me. We should form a band."

I pull back and cock a brow at him "Totally. *Elon and Alex. The Cello Whisperers.*"

"Right." He laughs. "Alex and Elon. I am the man here."

I glare at him, pretending to be offended. "Male chauvinist."

"Yeah, yeah. You love me," he says as he drops his hands and begins packing his cello. "Ready for the auction?"

"Not really. I don't want some guy donating money to have dinner with me."

"Why? You are gorgeous."

"Have you met me? Awkward Elon."

"Maybe Nick will show up." My face falls, pain cutting through my chest. "You two haven't kissed and made up?"

I wish it was that simple. Alex knows we are not on good terms but not the reason why. I shake my head and focus on packing my cello.

"He will come around," he says with enthusiasm.

I wish I was as sure about that as Alex is. So I say, "Yeah."

After calling home several times, I decided to give him space, hoping that time would help ease the pain. But it seemed the more we didn't speak, the more we fell from each other's radar. My nose starts to sting, and my eyes burn with tears.

I can't lose him. I need to talk with him again.

The past week, since my confrontation with Professor Masters, has been nerve-wracking. Grueling. How I managed to survive that long with tension coiled inside me without exploding into pieces is still a miracle. That night, after my tutoring classes, I went to my place, grabbed a change of clothes and drove to Nate's. He was visiting with his sister and wasn't home. I let myself in, took a shower and put on his T-shirt and boxers. Having his clothes on my body calmed me a bit. It almost felt like he was holding me.

Then I settled on the couch in front of the TV and accessed the recorded episode of *Game of Thrones* I missed.

Ten minutes into the episode, Nate arrived. The second he saw me sitting on the couch, he grinned wide and I melted like always. He kicked his shoes off and climbed on the couch, curling his hard body into mine. Then when he was satisfied, he tucked a thumb under my chin and kissed me slowly. I thought I'd combust from the mere taste of him and the heat of the kiss.

He pulled back and ran his nose alongside mine. "What is it?"

"I want to be *Khalesi* when I grow up," I announced.

His brows shot up, his gaze moving from the TV, then back to me. "Yeah?"

I nodded. "I want dragons. And unicorns."

His lips twitched. "Noted. Anything else?"

I shook my head and patted his chest. "I have my own *Khal Drogo* right here."

He threw his head back and laughed, his entire body shaking against mine. I loved this about him. He never did anything half-assed. It was all or nothing with him.

"Who pissed you off?" he asked, tucking the loose tendrils of hair on my forehead behind my ear.

"Professor Masters," I muttered, meeting his gaze.

Then I told him what happened. By the time I was done, his body had gone still behind mine, the fury rising off him, a force all its own. Knowing my professor, he would be having words with Masters soon.

I twist my torso to face him. "Promise me you won't go Khal Drogo on her." He blinked, a vein ticking dangerously in his jaw. "Nate?" I pressed.

Eventually he agreed. During dinner the following evening, he surprised me with a white gold necklace with little dragon and unicorn pendants. It was one of the sweetest gifts anyone has ever given me.

Safe to say, working with Professor Masters the past week has been extremely challenging. She didn't mention Nate again I hated the tension between us, which made for exhausting cello lessons.

"Freckles!" Alex yells, snapping me out of my thoughts. "Come on. The auction is about to begin."

"Coming!" He hooks his arm around my shoulder, turning to wave his other hand at Amber, who is sitting in the audience.

After putting on a white and pink sash with numbers tagged on it, Alex and I take our seats at the allocated spot on the stage with the other twenty volunteers and wait for the auction to start. Apparently the winning bidder gets to have dinner with one of us. Who'd want to pay money to take me out to dinner? What if I end up sitting up there on the platform with zero bids? I would die of humiliation. As much as the idea of having dinner with a complete stranger, especially for money, irks me, the idea of no one bidding on me makes me break into a sweat.

Twenty minutes into the auction, Mrs. Delamont, the president of the WAV organization, calls out number twelve. Alex stands and walks confidently to the center of the stage, running his hand through his dark, wavy hair and flashing the audience a wide grin. The hall explodes with bids as women try to top each other, but only one woman wins him. My best friend, Amber.

Mrs. Delamont calls out the next number into the microphone. I zone out, my thoughts wandering back to Nick and how I can make things better between us. He has never missed any of my performances before.

I did this to us. It ends tonight, even if it means pitching up a tent and camping outside his dorm until morning. I have to talk to him.

I'm yanked out of my reverie when the middle-aged woman sitting next to me nudges me with her elbow and points to the stage.

A couple of men stand up and raise their paddles, placing the first of their bids. I clutch the pendants on the necklace Nate gave me as my stomach coils with trepidation.

That is, until a familiar, high-pitched voice announces a higher bid, which sends disgruntled murmurs across the hall.

Izzy?

I scan the audience and see a very pregnant, very adorable Izzy waving at me.

My grip around my necklace loosens as my lips spread into a huge grin.

Izzy wins, of course. I make a mental note to always stay on her good side. She's one determined woman.

"I'm so confused right now," I whisper when I reach her side. She hugs me without warning, then pulls back and hooks her hand around my arm as we leave the hall.

"My brother sent me." She looks so pleased with herself. "Well, he asked Bennett, but I guilt-tripped them and complained how I never get to do anything fun. Eventually, they let me do this," she says unrepentantly and pats my arm. "He's waiting for you over there."

She points to Nate's car parked under a large tree, several feet away from the main entrance. I squint, but only make out a dark silhouette of someone sitting in the driver's seat.

My shock fades and I smile, my gaze fixed on the car. "I thought he wasn't flying back until Sunday."

She snickers. "Knowing Nate, he probably glowered at the doctor until he agreed to finish everything in one day."

I laugh. I really like rebellious Izzy.

"Why are you doing this for us?"

"You make him happy," she says, slowing down next to the car and turning to face me. "The past three years have been hell for him. I know he still has a long way to go before he sorts himself out, but you make him smile. I see hope in his eyes again. That's *everything.*"

My fingers wrap around my necklace, and I smile. "He's a wonderful man. He deserves to be happy."

She pulls me into her unexpectedly and whispers in my ear, "Thank you for bringing him back."

I blink hard to keep the tears from falling as Izzy takes my cello from me, opens the back door and props it on the floor before scooting awkwardly inside.

Seconds later, I'm sitting in the passenger seat, staring into the eyes of the man who's changed me. Changed my life. He pulled me from the shadows and into the light just by opening himself up to me, giving me his pain and taking mine. We might be broken in places, but somehow we heal each other.

"Hey," he whispers as he leans into me and presses a kiss on my lips. Then, he brushes his thumb across my cheek to wipe the tears I didn't know had fallen.

"Hey," I greet, sliding my hand against his and lacing his fingers with mine while kissing his knuckles.

"God, you two are so cute," Izzy exclaims from the back seat.

Her words rip me back into reality. I laugh, my face heating up in embarrassment. As soon as my gaze meets Nate's, everything else around me fades away, like always when we're together. It is just him and me.

Without taking his hand from mine, Nate pulls out of the parking spot and drives his sister to Reed's Lounge where Bennett is waiting for her. Then he parks his car in his building's underground parking. He laces his fingers with mine as we head toward the elevators.

"What's wrong?" Nate asks, pulling me to a stop and ducking his head to meet my gaze. "You've been quieter than usual."

"Nothing," I mutter, clutching the strap of my cello around my shoulder. I force a smile through the pain in my chest. I've tried to push thoughts of Nick to the back of my mind, but somehow they keep creeping back, taunting me.

He tugs my chin with his thumb, and my eyes meet his. "I think I know you by now. The way your brows furrow slightly when you're contemplating something. Your eyes turn more brown when you're sad. I know you, Elon. Come on. Talk to me."

I gape at him, floored by the fact that he noticed all those things in the short time we've known each other, something no one has ever mentioned before.

I huff a breath and shrug. "It's Nick." His body tenses, his gaze sharpening, but he doesn't say anything. "He was supposed to be there tonight. It just stings a little. That's all, I promise." I inhale deeply, but the ache in my chest blooms instead of going away. "How did your appointment go?" I ask, changing the subject eagerly. The more I talk about Nick, the worse the guilt and pain become.

Nate's watchful gaze roams over my face. Then, he exhales deeply. "Everything went well. The doctor wants to consult with a neurologist before he can confirm the date for the surgery in May."

I frown. "Can't they do it earlier?"

"He could. But I don't want to stop teaching in the middle of the semester." He kisses my forehead, his fingers sliding up to my hair. With quick movements, he pulls the pins holding my bun up, causing my hair to spill around my shoulders and down my back. He grunts, satisfied, then tucks the pins inside his jacket. "Tell me about Nick."

I sigh, taking in the determined, yet gentle look on his face. We pick up our steps toward the elevator, and I tell him about the sweet boy who lived next door in Willow Hill.

My feet halt mid-step suddenly when I feel like we're being watched. I scan the deserted, dimly-lit space. Nate stops long enough to trail my gaze before looking back at me.

"What is it?" he asks, his brows pinched in a frown.

I force a laugh and shake my head quickly. "Nothing. I'm just being paranoid."

He nods, tucks me under his left arm and kisses my hair. I don't miss the way his eyes sweep the parking lot before he steers me forward again.

"Elon?"

I freeze at the sound of my name. Nate's body tenses next to mine.

That voice.

Oh God.

Oh God.

No.

No.

Nate's arm falls off my shoulder as I whirl around, eyes wide, air sawing in and out of my chest in painful gasps.

Oh God.

Rick.

Bile rises up my throat, and I blink several times to stop the dark spots dancing in front of my vision. My instincts tell me to run, but my feet are frozen on the spot as fear settles in my bones.

"Baby, it's you." My skin crawls at his words. His head goes up a notch as his hand lifts the bill of his red cap, then he steps toward me, smiling. "I wasn't sure before. You look beautiful."

Behind me, I hear Nate inhale sharply and mutter, "What the fuck?" But I'm too busy trying not to hyperventilate to turn back and look at him.

I shut my eyes and try to recall what the school counselor told me during the time I was attending therapy after Rick was arrested on the school grounds.

Be strong. Don't give him or the memories the power to rule me. It's the only way I can defeat him and what he did to me.

I need to calm the hell down. I'm no longer the girl he left behind. I let this bastard rule me and that gave him the power to destroy me. And now it's my turn to take that power back.

"Rick," I whisper, then curse my shaky voice. "What are you doing here? How did you find me?"

"I saw you leave the opera hall. I wanted to talk to you."

He followed us.

Shit.

He must have been following me around. How long has he been keeping track of me?

Nate steps forward while pushing me behind him. "Son of a bitch. What the hell are you doing here?"

Rick's eyes widen as they move to Nate. Something like recognition fills his features. His lips pull back in a sneer, eyes moving from Nate to me.

He points at Nate, anger lacing his features. "You! What's going on here?"

How in God's name do they know each other? "Nate?"

"The fucker almost ran me off the road," Nate bites out without taking his eyes off Rick. "How do you two—" He stops mid-sentence. I know the second he makes the connection. His body vibrates with heat and fury as he stalks forward with his hands clenched into fists.

Worried about what he's about to do, I quickly step around him and cup his face, forcing him to look at me.

"I got this," I whisper. His jaw twitches, and he gives his head a sharp shake.

"Get behind me, Elon," he grits out, attempting to push me behind him.

"Please stop," I plead, grabbing his face again. "You're going to hurt yourself."

"I fucking don't care—"

"I. Got. This." I inhale deeply and wait until he reluctantly nods, then I spin around to face Rick. "Leave, before I call the police."

Rick's eyes narrow and his lips flatten. "Are you threatening me?"

"Leave," I order, surprised at how strong my voice is.

Suddenly, he throws his head back and laughs. All I want to do is rip my ears from my head so I never have to hear that sound again. "And tell the police what? This is a free country, baby doll."

"I could get you arrested for stalking me."

Rick stretches his arms wide and slants his head to the side. "Go ahead. Call them."

His eyes travel down my body slowly, then back to my face. Nate growls behind me but doesn't make a move. In this moment, I feel this overwhelming love for him even more, for trusting me to handle this.

"You've changed," Rick says, eyebrows bunched up in a displeased frown.

I tilt my chin up boldly. "What doesn't kill you makes you stronger."

"We were good together, baby doll." Rick's gaze flicks to Nate, then back at me. "I want you back. You belong to me—"

Before he has a chance to finish the sentence, Nate is looming above him, left arm raised. He gets in two blows on the bastard's face before I'm at his side, pressing my palms against his hard chest.

"Nate!" I cry out. "Stop. Please *stop*."

"I'll kill the son of a bitch." He pushes against my hand, his body vibrating with anger.

"No, you will not," I whisper, tears running down my face. "Nate. . . I—just stop, okay?"

"Motherfucker!" Rick screams in a muffled voice from the floor. "You're going to pay for this!"

I ignore Rick, my entire focus on Nate as he shuts his eyes and takes deep breaths to calm down. He opens them again and meets mine, the sheer emotion shining through them making my heart clench and warm up at the same time.

"Okay?" I question.

He nods. "Okay."

I exhale. "Okay."

At the sound of feet shuffling on the cement floor, I turn around. Rick hobbles away with one hand clutched over his bleeding nose. He looks over his shoulder and yells, "I swear you will regret this."

"If you come anywhere near me again, I'll file a complaint of harassment," I tell him, sounding braver than I feel.

Inside the elevator, I take Nate's hand in mine and check it for injuries. The skin around his knuckles is raw and scraped, but other than that, it doesn't look broken.

"I'm fine," he murmurs. He winces as he rolls his right shoulder. I know he's in pain, but he's putting up a strong front for me. "Are you okay?"

I inhale a deep breath. Adrenaline has left my body shaking and my knees weak. I unhook the cello from my shoulders and prop it on the steel wall, then crouch down on my heels with my head down and take deep breaths. Nate follows me and slides his strong fingers around the back of my neck and pulls me to him. I go willingly, burying my face into his shoulder.

"You were amazing out there. I'm so proud of you," he whispers hoarsely against my hair.

"Why can't he just leave me alone?" I ask no one in particular in a broken whisper. Why can't I catch a break with that bastard?

Nate pulls back, the fingers on my neck moving up to gently grip my hair. "Something is seriously wrong with him. I could see it in his eyes. I don't want you walking alone. Always with me or Alex or Amber. Never alone."

I nod, wiping my wet cheeks. The scar on my lower back burns at the memory of the knife slicing through me and a sob escapes through my lips.

"I never told my sisters what he did to me. I was so embarrassed, Nate," I say. "I mean, they knew about him but not what he did to me."

"From what you've told me, it sounds like your sisters love you."

I nod again. "And I love them so much. But. . .after growing up with a father like mine, how could I tell them I was involved with a man who abused me? Nor was already neck deep in medical bills and dealing with Josh having cancer. I just couldn't."

He nods in understanding. Then I notice something else working its way in his eyes. He seems torn about something as he studies me intently. His gaze fills with resolution and his jaw clenches. "I'll kill him if he comes near you again." He moves his face closer to mine, pressing his lips to mine in a feather-light kiss. "I fucking love you, Elon."

I stop breathing.

My eyes widen.

The thudding in my ears intensifies.

"Nate," I breathe.

He told me he loves me in the same breath he used to utter words about killing Rick. I'm utterly and irrevocably in love with this man. I should tell him that, like I've done so many times in my head. Then why the heck am I scared to say those words?

As much as I've yearned to hear those words from a man I totally adore, I'm not prepared to hear them right this second. It's too good to be real, which scares me. His fingers uncurl around my hair as I straighten on my feet, my eyes darting around the small space, looking for a way out. I need air. I need to sort out everything that happened today first.

"Elon." His voice melts me, kick-starting my breathing. "I don't expect you to say those words back to me. I know how you feel, and that's enough for me. I just want to let you know where I stand. I also want to let you know I'm never letting you go." He smirks at me, his eyes turning playful. "One sweet lie, Little Wolf."

"One sweet truth," I correct him. "You own me. You own my universe." I inhale a deep breath, feeling each piece falling into place.

Him.

Me.

Us.

I have no idea what happens from this point forward. I'm scared of what this means for me, school and my dreams. Nate's job. But I'm more terrified of losing him.

A ping echoes inside the small space, and the doors slide open. I can't move because those last words are still soaking inside my heart. His eyes locked on mine tell me his truth, calming my racing heart.

I don't want to run anymore.

I want Nate to show me how fucking much he loves me and how much he wants to keep me, never let me go.

With my cello in one hand, I lace my fingers with Nate's and step out of the elevator silently, my knees quivering in anticipation.

As soon as we step inside and he kicks the door to his apartment shut, he pins me to the wall next to the door while taking the cello and expertly leaning it against the wall while kissing me, consuming me.

"Show me how much you love me," I whisper hoarsely.

His heated gaze on me sends shivers up my spine. He reaches for my hand as we walk into the living room, grabs a chair and drags it to the middle of the room. "Are you hungry? Bennett sent one of his guys to bring dinner up here while I was picking you up."

Pulling my eyes from Nate's smoldering dark gaze, I glance at the table, my mouth falling open when I see it laid out with various foods, all covered with huge steel bowls to keep them warm. I swallow and shake my head.

"My appetite lies elsewhere." I drop my gaze to his crotch. Heat spears between my legs, and I rub my thighs together. He releases a sound between a growl and a groan.

"Strip and take a seat." He points his chin to the chairs. "I'll be right back."

He heads to the bathroom. The sound of cabinet doors opening and closing reaches me. He walks back moments later and grabs two bottles of water from the fridge, uncaps one of them and gulps it down, chasing the painkillers he tossed in his mouth.

I quickly do as I'm told, then perch my naked behind on the cool, dark wood, squirming a little to get comfortable.

"Water?" Nate holds out the second bottle to me.

I shake my head, too anxious to see what he plans to do with me.

He eyes me slowly without a word, appreciation, lust and hunger dancing in his eyes. He strips his clothes off, then leaves again. I can't stop tracking that ass, those broad shoulders. He comes back with my cello in his hands and motions for me to stand up.

Once he takes my place, he taps his thigh twice for me to sit before handing me the cello. I moan as his now hard dick snuggly wedges itself between my butt cheeks, my back flush to his front.

By now, my heart is beating a rhythm I never thought possible, a prelude of what I know will be the most mesmerizing symphony he and I have ever created.

"I never thought to ask before. Are you on the pill?" he asks, running the tip of his fingers down my spine, then his lips following the same path.

"Yes."

"Good. I want to feel you." His left arm circles my waist tightly and lifts me while his other hand teases my pussy with his cock. I feel the head push slightly into me, but I can't move. He's holding me secure, so we're moving at his speed.

Gently, he lowers me on his cock, and I almost loose grip of the cello in my hands.

This is so good.

We groan, moan, grunt as we become one. When I'm deeply seated on him, I move my hips. His teeth on my shoulder dig into my skin as he growls.

"I'm so turned on, Nate," I say breathlessly.

"That's so sexy. Seeing you turned on like this and knowing it's all me. So. Fucking. Sexy." His tongue licks the bite marks on my shoulder. "Play for me, Little Wolf."

Oh God. How am I supposed to concentrate while he's circling his hips, his hands touching me, his lips leaving hot kisses on my skin?

"What should I play?" I pant, arching my back when his pelvis clenches, his dick thrusting deeper inside me.

"Whatever you want to play. Jesus, Elon. I'm inside you so deep. You feel so good." He rasps. "Play and try not to miss a beat. I'm listening."

And I do, slowly stumbling through the first arrangement of Debussy's *Claire De Lune*, even though my concentration is mostly on how he's playing my body.

His fingers on my hips grip harder, holding me down as his hips thrust up. Gosh, he's driving me wild, and I feel like I'm burning from the inside out. I scream, the bow slipping from my useless fingers, and I know the next thing to crash on the floor will be the cello.

"I can't. . .*ohmygod*, Nate."

He grabs the cello by the neck and props it on the edge of the table, before bringing his hand back to my skin.

"These hands have never produced a sweeter symphony than the sounds you make when I'm touching you," he growls breathlessly into my ear. "Mine. Every part of you belongs to me, Elon. Always. Never letting you go."

I nod emphatically, panting. "Yes, yes. I'm yours."

Then he shows me how much he wants me and I follow his guidance, and before long I'm gasping for air as I come. He pulls me tight into his chest, still pumping at a furious tempo as he comes, shouting my name.

He falls back on the chair, holding me close. Our sweaty bodies meshed against each other.

When I'm calm enough to speak and move, I lift my head and look over my shoulder, taking in the sated, hooded look on Nate's face. "Holy shit. That was. . .*holy shit!*"

"Phenomenal?" One side of his mouth curls up.

I nod, sighing. "Thank you."

His forehead crinkles. "For what?"

"For making me yours."

His face lights up brighter than the lights above us. "I'm more than happy to make you mine again."

I shake my head and laugh, shifting around to face him, my front to his front. "What happens now?" I ask, my mind pushing me back into reality.

One brow goes up as his dark eyes linger on my boobs, then climb back to my face. "Babe, I might look like Adonis and may be built like Hercules, but I kind of need to recharge."

I blink several times at the joke before bursting out laughing.

I adore this carefree part of him.

I swat his chest and glare at him, which is totally ruined by my lips twitching. "Focus."

He rolls his eyes and sighs. God, he looks so cute.

"I decided to follow up on some teaching offers I'd received before I joined Rushmore. Has Elizabeth spoken to you about us again?" he questions, his fingers squeezing my hip lightly.

I shake my head, my brows pinched together. "I expected her to report us to Mrs. Bowman by now. We've kept a low profile. Maybe she hasn't found any proof to tie in with her suspicions."

"Maybe. Until then, we have to be careful."

"Okay," I say, praying that everything works out without anyone else finding out about us.

"Okay," he murmurs. "Time to feed my woman. Nutella bread?"

My woman.

I kiss his chest, his scruffed jaw. Breathe in his cologne and his breath while basking in his warmth. I've always belonged to myself. Even when Rick tried to break me, I remained who I was.

Now, I'm Nate's. Every part of me belongs to him.

His woman.

I tuck my head into his chest and nod. "Nutella bread sounds great."

We don't move, though. He kisses my forehead, a satisfied sound rumbling in his chest as he settles back in the chair and just holds me like I'm something worth holding on to.

Something worth having and keeping.

CHAPTER THIRTY-THREE

Nate

I'M STANDING OUTSIDE *THE FORKS* RESTAURANT WHERE NICK WORKS, waiting for him to come out. His morning shift should be ending in the next few minutes. According to Elon, he works part-time here on the weekends, from 7 a.m. to midday.

After the awful day she'd had with Rick stalking her to my building, all I could think of after that asshole's visit was that I wanted to make everything okay for her. Later on after dinner, with her body curled into mine, she told me about Nick. I couldn't bear watching her go through so much pain. I still felt jealous each time she brought up his name, but even I had to man up and stop acting like a ten-year-old. I wanted my woman happy and smiling, which is why I'm waiting outside this swanky restaurant, hoping to have a chat with Pretty Boy.

My thoughts flit back on the second I realized that Rick was Elon's ex-boyfriend and the same fucker who almost ran me off the road. I've never been so consumed with fury like I was at that moment. Seeing how brave she was as she faced that son of a bitch, no matter how scared she was, made me proud. At that very second, I realized that not only had this girl gotten under my skin, she also owned my heart. My instinct to protect her rose, and I wanted to fight that monster for her, keep her safe. I saw red when that fucker opened his mouth, claiming she was his.

I haven't gotten a visit from the cops yet for busting Rick's nose, so I can only guess he didn't file a complaint, which makes me nervous. I have a feeling in my gut he's planning something. I wish I knew what it was.

I glance at my watch just to make sure I won't be late to pick up Elon from her tutoring class at Studio 22.

The door to the restaurant opens and Pretty Boy walks out, his attention on the phone in his hand. He doesn't see me until he's walking past me and I call his name.

His eyes widen at first before anger replaces the shock on his face. His hands form fists as he stalks toward me. "What the fuck are you doing here?"

I shove my hands inside my pockets, reminding myself I'm doing this for Elon.

I nod in greeting. He doesn't return it. Instead he glowers harder. "Can we talk?" I ask

The anger rolling through him momentarily stalls, and his eyebrows bunch in concern. "Is she okay?"

"That's what I need to talk to you about."

He gets in my face, jaw clenched and veins bulging in his temple. "If you've done something to hurt her, so help me God—"

"I'd never hurt her." I cut him off. He's panting, dragging his fingers through his hair. "You need to call her and talk to her."

He stares at the ground, a vein ticking in his jaw. "Look. She made her choice, okay?" He grunts, running his hands down his face. His shoulders slump forward as he exhales. "Just leave me alone."

He skirts around me, heading toward the white Peugeot parked a few feet away.

"Nick," I bite out, flexing my fingers, praying to God for patience.

He spins around, coming at me with the fury of a twenty-year-old.

"I've loved her for as long as I can remember. Then she got involved with that fucking psycho ex-boyfriend, Rick. He almost broke her. *Almost*. Then you roll into town, throw your professor mojo around and she chooses you over me? It should have been me." He thumps his chest with a fist. "I *loved* her," he declares in a broken whisper, tears brimming in his eyes. "God, I love her so much."

Christ.

I feel his pain as the words he's thrown my way cut through me. I'm such an asshole. "I'm sorry. It wasn't my intention to hurt you like this."

"So, what is she to you? A plaything? Someone for you to pass time with until you get tired of her?" he asks angrily, narrowing his eyes. "I should report you."

"I wouldn't do that if I were you," I say in a low, firm voice.

"Why not?" he shoots back.

"Because you'd be hurting her." Despite the fact that she didn't say she loved me, I know for a fact she does. It's in the soft way she looks at me and the way she smiles at me, her touch, her kiss.

I see the moment the meaning behind my words hits him. His eyes widen. He looks at the floor, then back at me.

We stay locked in a staredown for several seconds before Nick averts his gaze back to his sneakers.

"I love her, Nick." His head jerks up, his eyebrows raised.

"Yeah? So how's that going to work out with you being her professor?" He laughs bitterly. "You're just going to break her heart. I know it. But don't worry, *Professor*. I'll be here to pick up the pieces, just like I've always done."

"You don't get it, do you?" I shake my head and saunter forward. "I *love* her."

He scrutinizes me for several seconds. Then, he looks away and swallows hard. "Fucking perfect," he mutters under his breath. "If you ever hurt her—"

"Never."

His eyes meet mine. Whatever he sees there seems to placate him.

He nods, the anger he was carrying visibly tapering off. "I'll give her a call." He starts to turn away from me but stops abruptly, twisting his torso to face me. He studies me in contemplation, then huffs a breath. "I'll text you my number, in case you need to get in touch with me."

My eyebrows shoot up. Well, that was unexpected, but I'm not the one to pass up a chance like this. Besides, this is for her.

Seconds after giving him my number, my phone buzzes in my pocket. I pull it out and save his number, then nod in thanks. The phone beeps again with a new text. I tap the screen and a middle finger emoji stares back at me. I look up and catch a glimpse of Nick smirking before he stalks off with his head bowed and a hand rubbing the back of his neck.

I chuckle under my breath as I watch Nick get into his car. Then, I take off in the direction of my car and drive to Studio 22.

Elon

By the time my class ends at midday, I'm a complete emotional mess. My period is as usual playing havoc on me. I've had cramps since this morning when Alex and Amber dropped me in front of Studio 22. After the incident with Rick, Nate, Amber and Alex have been taking turns driving me wherever I want to go. Alex is still in the dark about Nate. I skirted around the truth when he asked about Rick stalking me.

Today, Nate and I had plans to spend the afternoon at his place. I texted him to let him know I wouldn't be good company. He said he wanted to take care of me. Honestly, feeling the way I'm feeling right now, I wouldn't mind him spoiling me.

As soon as he calls and lets me know he's waiting outside, I head out and spot the Wrangler parked further away from the main entrance. He has been using the Jeep on the weekends whenever we are together because it doesn't call attention as much as the BMW does. Besides, it makes it difficult for anyone to peek through the tint-ed windows.

I scan my surroundings just to make sure we're safe, then stride toward the car. Once I'm seated inside, he takes my hand and kisses my wrist, then leans into me for a quick kiss on the lips.

"Feeling better?" he asks as he pulls out of the parking area.

I shake my head, closing my eyes. "I want to punch someone in the face and at the same time curl up in a ball and cry."

He darts me a quick look before returning his focus on the street.

"You should just drop me at my place before I turn into The Hulk," I moan.

He chuckles deeply, causing me to open one eye. "You're cute."

"Not feeling cute at the moment," I mumble.

Nate pulls to a stop at the red light. His fingers gently rub circles on my thigh before resting possessively on my knee. Then I hear fab-ric ruffling, followed by beeping sounds of a phone, then silence.

Then, "Hey. Are you busy?" he queries whoever is on the other side of the call. My eyes flutter open and meet his. He has that unread-able look on his face. Seconds later, he ends the call and sends me a knowing smirk.

"Plans for tonight?"

He shakes his head. "Just a small surprise for you."

"I love surprises," I mumble. Did I say how much I adore him? I sigh, sinking into the seat and holding my hand in front of my mouth to cover my yawn.

"How was your morning?" I ask.

Nate continues to talk, but my eyes are heavy with sleep. I slide them closed while listening to his calming voice.

"Wake up, sleepy head." I jerk awake at the sound of that familiar voice and wipe the drool on the side of my mouth, then look around.

The Wrangler is parked in Nate's usual spot. My eyes widen when I see whose head is hovering a few inches from mine.

"Nick?" I squeal in surprise. I dart a gaze at Nate, who's grinning wide, then back to my friend.

Nick blinks twice, looking a bit apprehensive. He steps back as I open the car door and hop down to the ground. We stare at each other awkwardly. Then he takes the first step and I follow suit. Soon he's sweeping me into his arms in a tight hug and lifting me up.

"I've missed you," I say into his neck, tears sliding down my cheek. He sets me down and cups my face in his hands, brushing my cheeks with his thumbs.

"Shh. I'm here now, okay?"

I nod, and he pulls his hands away and shoves them in his jeans pockets.

"What are you doing here?" I offer him a shaky smile.

He rolls his eyes. "You missed me, so I'm here." He looks over my shoulder at Nate, anger momentarily flashing in his gaze. "He called me. Plus, I wanted to see you." He kicks the flecks of dust at his feet with his sneakered foot. He's nervous, I can tell.

"Thank you for coming," I say, lightly punching his shoulder with my loose fist, then smile when he meets my gaze.

My eyes drift to Nate, realizing it was Nick he called before.

"Thank you," I mouth, grinning wide.

He nods, his lips curved in a closed-mouth smile.

"Ready to go? You and I will be making up for lost time," he says as he grabs my cello from the back seat and then slips his arm on my waist. "I really missed you."

"I can't believe you are here. Give me a minute, okay? I'll be right back." As soon as he nods, I dash around the car and fling the door to the driver's seat open. I climb inside, crawl on his lap and grasp his stubbled jaw in my hands.

"You. . . you called Nick." He nods, his gaze soft, gentle. "You didn't have to do this, but you did. For me."

He nods again. "You missed him. I don't like to see you sad."

I kiss his mouth and pull back, remembering Nick is most likely watching us. I don't want to hurt him more than I've already done, so

I lean back. "Thank you," I whisper, blinking back the tears.

Saturdays and Sundays are our days. Nate and I make a point of spending that time together whenever I'm in Jacksonville.

He just forfeited today so that Nick and I can spend time together. God.

This man.

"Anything for you," he murmurs as he runs his knuckles down my cheek and kisses my forehead. "Go. We'll talk later."

I hop down from the truck and race toward Nick, happier and lighter than I've been in weeks as I get inside his car.

I don't know what I've done to deserve such a wonderful man. But I'm counting my blessings—and counting down the days until summer semester is over. Hiding our relationship and always looking over our shoulders is hard and frustrating.

CHAPTER THIRTY-FOUR

Elon

"WHAT THE HELL AM I GOING TO WEAR?" I ASK, FRANTICALLY running around my room and throwing clothes on my bed.

Three weeks ago, Izzy called me to invite me to her birthday, which is today, March twenty-ninth. Since then, I've been a nervous wreck. It's one thing meeting Izzy and Grace at Nate's house. It's another thing going to Izzy's place, where we'll probably sit down and have conversations and small talk.

Amber rolls her eyes dramatically and jumps on the bed.

"Relax," she soothes. "It's not like he's planning to ask you to marry him." Her eyebrows hit her hairline. "Or has he?"

This time, I roll my eyes and shake my head. She's such a hopeless romantic. "You need to stop this, A-Girl. You've asked me that question like every week."

"You know me. I need my dose of happily ever after." She sighs dreamily, then flips over on the bed to lie on her stomach.

"Amber—" I shake my head and inhale deeply.

Every time she says things like this, my hopes dash through the roof. Maybe I'm stupid for wanting what Nate and I have to last forever. I've had a lifetime of doubts and heartaches. Would it be such a bad thing to want more with a man who loves me? A man who put aside his pride and gave me back my friend, even though he knew Nick's feelings for me.

"Elon?" Amber's worried voice pulls me out of my thoughts. "You okay?"

"Yeah. . . sorry."

I hope Nate has enough words for both of us because I don't do small talk. While Bennett and Izzy seem to have given in to the fact that Nate and I are together, his mother has not.

I don't expect her to. Hell, if Nor or my mother knew I was dating my professor, all hell would break loose.

I'm considering calling Nate and telling him I'm not feeling well when my phone buzzes with a text. Amber leaps from the bed and grabs my phone from my desk before I can get to it. She grins as she swipes the screen.

"Izzy says she can't wait to see you!" She looks up at me. "If it were up to her, you two would have been married on the day she met you. She's so *into* you."

I groan, fighting a smile. "Shut up and help me choose something to wear." I'm usually confident choosing my own clothes, but this birthday invitation has my stomach twisting in knots.

She hops down from the bed and makes a beeline for the closet. Seconds later she pops out, holding a little black dress.

I shake my head. "Probably something that doesn't show too much leg."

"What's wrong with showing a bit of skin? I'm sure Professor Nathaniel won't mind." She wiggles her eyebrows, then ducks her head back inside the closet.

I groan. "I'm trying to make a good impression on the Rowes."

She mumbles something under her breath before jumping out, holding another dress. "Ta-da!"

I stare at the blush pink chiffon vintage dress with tiny silver buttons on the front and a black sash for a belt around the waist, one of the swanky dresses I own that I bought last year during a spring clearance sale.

"Yes! I love you." I take it from her and kiss her cheek. "This. . .going to this party. It feels like a huge deal, you know?"

"It *is* huge," she says thoughtfully. "He introduced you as his girlfriend to his mom and sister. Not every man would have done that." She folds her arms on her chest and slants her head to the side curiously. "You accepted the invite. Why?"

"I don't know," I mutter more to myself. Izzy invited me, and I agreed without a second thought. But deep down inside I know the reason why. And the reality of it terrifies me like nothing else ever has. "Truth?"

She nods. "Truth."

"It felt so natural. Nate cares. He puts my needs before his. He looks at me in a way that sets everything inside me on fire. Like I'm someone. Like I exist. It's hard to explain, but I feel like he is the one, which is insane, right? Girls like me don't get a happily ever after."

She scowls at me. "Stop talking crazy. What do you mean 'girls like you'? You're not any different than any other person out there who wants the same thing as you do. Just because life dealt you negatives in the past doesn't mean there aren't positives in your present and future. Fight for the fairy tale, E. Reach for the stars, and everything else will fall into place."

Blinking back tears, I open my mouth to speak, but she lifts her hand to stop me.

"The past few months have been nothing short of amazing to see you transform right before my eyes. You seem more. . ." She pauses and squints as if she's searching for the right word.

"More what?" I ask, wiping my cheek with the back of my hand.

"Peaceful." She quickly hugs me, then steps back. "Now, take deep breaths and get your ass in the shower. Everyone's going to like you."

"Everyone but Nate's mother," I mutter, walking toward the bathroom.

She trots after me and leans her hip against the sink while I lump toothpaste on my toothbrush. "You're his student. He's your professor." She shrugs. "Of course she doesn't approve."

I sigh. "Why does it have to be so complicated?"

"Good things don't come easy. Just remember that. Anyhoo, I need to return some calls. Mom's upset because I opted to spend spring break with Alex instead of going home."

She starts to turn away when I call out, "Amber?"

"Yeah?" She twists around to face me.

"Thank you."

She nods and winks, before stepping out of the bathroom and shutting the door behind her.

Thirty minutes later, I'm standing in front of the mirror, staring back at my own reflection, taking in my flushed cheeks that don't need blush and hair spilling past my shoulders in waves. After quickly applying mascara and nude lipstick, I step back and smile, pleased with the results.

Amber was right. I do look different. Happy. Nervous, but happy.

I'm meeting Nate at his house so we can drive to his sister's place in his car.

I grab my purse and Izzy's gift, then say goodbye to Amber before heading out.

The first thing Nate does as soon as I walk into his apartment is kiss me like he hasn't seen me in years and murmurs between groans, "I've been dying to do that since last night."

"We *were* together last night," I tell him.

"Exactly." He steps back, his eyes taking me in from head to my nude heels and then back up again. "Perfect."

"Separate cars or should we drive in mine?" I ask jokingly, just to see his reaction.

He screws his face in a grimace and says, "Mine."

I raise a brow at him. "Where's your sense of adventure, Professor Rowe?"

"In bed at the moment. I'd prefer if we arrived to Izzy's place today and not a century from now."

I laugh, falling in step as we walk toward the elevator with his hand pressed on the small of my back.

He jerks his chin at the bag in my hand. "What's that?"

"A little something for Izzy."

His eyebrows dip a little. "You didn't need to get her a gift. I did that for both of us. I put it in the car earlier today."

"I wanted to. It's more like a thank you gift anyway." I smile up at him, and his features relax immediately. I pray under my breath for the nervousness fluttering my tummy to cease. What was I thinking when I accepted Izzy's invitation?

The answer hits me like a punch in my gut, stealing my breath: I hope to prove to Nate that I can be more than just his student. Hope to stay in Bennett and Izzy's good graces? Maybe in time I could make a good impression on Grace, and hopefully she'd like me a little more?

God, I even sound pathetic in my own head.

Maybe going to this party was a bad idea.

By the time we get to Nate's car, I'm ready to call the whole thing off and go home.

He pushes me against the passenger door, pressing his body into mine. "What are you thinking about, Little Wolf?"

I huff a breath. "Maybe I should go home—"

"Why?" he questions, looking perturbed.

"I feel like I'm trying too hard for your family to like me." I wet my lips. I want him to understand where I'm going with this. "You know me and what happened with the last man I let into my life. You and me. . .it seems too good to be true. I feel like I'm holding my breath, waiting for the other shoe to drop." I press my hands against his chest. "I don't want to ruin this—"

"Elon, *stop*." He grasps my hand, stopping me and cupping the nape of my neck with his other hand. "You need to have more faith in us. There'll be no shoe dropping anytime in the near future, or ever, because you'll come out of this wearing both of them."

"Bennett and Izzy already like you. As for my mother, she's

worried, which is normal. She's a retired teacher, so I see where she's coming from. She needs some time to warm up to the idea of you and me. Us." He brushes his thumb across my bottom lip. "You're not ruining anything. I want you with me. I want you to sit next to me with my family. I just want you. It's as simple as that. Okay?"

"Okay." I smile, pushing whatever doubts I had before to the back of my mind. I push to my toes just as he leans down, taking my mouth in a sweet, languorous kiss before he opens the door for me.

Once we're settled inside the car, I lace his fingers with mine against his thigh as he pulls out of the parking lot and we drive off.

"They're here!" Izzy shrieks from the porch as soon as Nate and I get out of the car. "Just in time for lunch."

Grace appears in the doorway and takes her daughter's outstretched hand, then huffs angrily, shaking her head. "I wish you'd just follow the doctor's advice, Isabelle."

Izzy accepts her mother's help while grumbling under her breath as we step onto the porch.

After quick hugs, Nate presses his palm on my lower back in reassurance, kisses my hair and says, "Go ahead. I'll get our gift from the car."

I follow Izzy inside the house. We're met by two tiny balls of energy barreling toward us, and they screech into a halt in front of us.

"Grandma, can we have ice cream? We've been waiting for ages," the boy begs, his huge, brown eyes wide, pleading.

"Matthew, Makayla. We have guests. This is Elon, Uncle Nate's girlfriend," Izzy says.

Two sets of eyes focus on me.

"Girlfriend? Yuck." He screws up his cute face. "Girls suck."

"Matthew!" Grace reprimands her grandson. "That is very disrespectful."

"But Grandma, it's true! Even Uncle Nate knows they suck. Right, Uncle?"

We all shift around to look at Nate as he freezes in his tracks, eyes narrowed.

"What did I miss?" Nate questions as he strides past us and sets Izzy's gift on a nearby table.

"Apparently, you think girls suck, Romeo," Izzy snickers under her breath and winks at me.

"What?" he asks, looking flustered, which is really adorable. This man hardly ever loses his cool.

Grace shakes her head while turning to face her son and nods her head toward Matthew. "Nathaniel?"

Nate's lips twitch as if he's fighting a smile as he crouches in front of Matthew. "Why do you think girls suck, buddy?"

Matthew shrugs. "My friend Dave says so. Girls are crybabies. Like Kaylie."

"Kaylie is still young, you know." Nate sweeps back the massive curls on Matthew's forehead with his hand.

Nate's nephew's eyes narrow on him. "Yeah, but you don't have girls following you everywhere."

"I do now, but I'm the one following her around." He twists around, his eyes going soft when they find me. "That pretty girl over there."

Melt.

Matthew studies me for a few seconds, then smiles shyly, displaying one missing front tooth. "She's pretty."

"Yes," Nate murmurs, still watching me. "She is."

The discussion ends when Matthew's focus shifts to the Nintendo DS in his hands.

After we've all settled around the table, Nate's hand automatically finds mine and gives me a squeeze, his eyes roaming over my face fondly. He doesn't need to tell me I'm beautiful because I can see it in his eyes, the sincerity in them screaming like a thousand suns. And he doesn't seem to care who knows it.

Conversation flows as I sit back and just enjoy being here, the nerves I was feeling before fading. Bennett eventually shows up from his trip to town to get his wife jalapeño pizza, her favorite. Then he excuses himself and heads upstairs to make some calls about a property he's looking to buy in Miami to open another restaurant.

Grace excuses herself and walks to the kitchen to start preparing the food. I'm about to stand up and follow her, wanting to help, when Nate's fingers move to my knee to stop me. Then, he stands up and joins his mother in the kitchen.

Izzy pulls herself up and takes Nate's seat. "You're not much of a talker, are you?" Izzy nudges me with her elbow, smiling.

"Not really, but I could be. Just pour me some wine and you'll see my chattier side come out to play," I joke, then laugh nervously.

She chuckles, sitting back in her chair and wincing a little.

"When is the baby due?" I ask

"A week from now. I'm huge, aren't I? Just tell me the truth. We're like friends now, you know." She stares at me expectantly with big blue eyes.

I press my lips together to stop from laughing, then clear my throat. "You look gorgeous, Izzy."

She rolls her eyes. "I feel like a whale, but thank you for making me feel better." She flips the pizza box open and grabs a piece from inside, then takes a huge bite and hums in delight. "God, I love Bennett. And jalapeño pizza. Want some?"

I shake my head. "I'm good, thanks."

"Good choice. Pregnant Izzy doesn't share pizza."

I snort. "Then why did you ask?"

"I was just being polite and trying to be a good host." She winks at me, and I burst out laughing.

"So you and Nate, huh? Is it serious?"

I try to read her, but it's difficult when she's wolfing down pizza and smiling at me like I'm her best friend in the whole world. I shamelessly love that look. "What has your brother told you?"

"He's been overly quiet about you two. We can't get him to stop smiling these days. He walks around like he knows a secret none of us are in on. And I want in, so, tell me," she prompts.

I shrug. "We're just hanging out."

She rolls her eyes and snorts. "Riiiight. Nate doesn't just *hang out*. He wouldn't have even bothered to be with you if he didn't like you. He's a Rowe. Once we set eyes on someone, we never let go. They're *it* for us. We don't just like or hangout, Elon. We claim. My brother claimed you the second he laid eyes on you."

I suck in a breath, my heart beating fast. Deep down, I know she's right.

I've gotten to know Nate. He's intense, determined and extremely focused when he puts his mind toward pursuing something.

"He told me you know about Camille?" she asks in a hushed, reverent tone. I nod. "So you know he still blames himself. He's stubborn. He needs to work this out on his own and learn to forgive himself, even though what happened was an accident. Just be there for him. Be his guiding light."

"Izzy. . .don't you guys disapprove of him dating a student?"

She laughs, her entire body shaking with it. "Mom almost burst a vein when Nate introduced you as his student—" She stops talking, her face turning pale. Then, she drops the pizza crust in her hands onto the table and bends over, breathing hard. "Shit! Fucking shit shit *shit!*"

"Izzy!" Grace chastises her daughter in exasperation.

Matthew's head jerks up from his Nintendo, his eyes wide. "Mama said a bad word!"

"Mom. . . something is wrong." Izzy clutches her tummy and begins to breathe in and out fast. "I think the baby—is—*uggghh!*"

Grace and Nate hurry into the living room and rush to Izzy's side. Grace waves to Nate and instructs calmly, "Run upstairs and get her bag, honey. Tell Bennett we need to leave now."

"Is Mommy okay?" Kaylie comes running into the room, her

eyes wide, terrified.

Not sure of what to do, I pull her to me and reassure her. "Don't worry sweetie, your mommy will be okay." I'm not sure how much Bennett and Izzy have told their kids about this baby, but when I see her eyes swimming in tears, I pull her tiny body to me in a hug and reassure her that everything is going to be okay.

Nate returns downstairs with Bennett in tow. Bennett freezes, panic settling in his features as he takes in his wife's flushed face. "We still have a week before the baby comes. Are you sure—"

"Bennett," she grits between her clenched jaw, taking two deep breaths, then narrows her eyes at her husband. "You're not going to do that thing you do, are you?"

Bennett's gaze snaps up to Izzy's as she straightens. "Come on, baby. Don't be like that. I have grown a lot since the last time it happened."

I glance at Nate, who seems to be holding back a grin, and whisper, "What thing?"

Nate puts a hand over his mouth to hide a grin and clears his throat. "Passing out during the birth of his children. They had to carry him out of the room on a gurney."

I press my lips tight and look away, the image of Bennett fainting stuck inside my head.

"Shut up." Bennett glares at his brother-in-law, but I see his lips twitch with a smile. He mutters, "I thought I was going to lose Izzy both times. Baby, you know I'd wither and die without you," he says to Izzy.

Nate chuckles and slaps Bennett on his shoulder on the way to the door.

Grace scoops up the kids, and we all pour out the front door, hurrying to our respective vehicles.

Bennett helps Izzy into the passenger seat of his truck while Grace buckles Matthew and Kaylie into their car seats inside her Ford.

We arrive at the hospital in under ten minutes, and soon the nurses are taking Izzy in a wheelchair into the delivery ward while

Bennett fills out the forms.

Grace's forehead crinkles in worry as she watches them wheel Izzy away with Nate on their heels.

"I can stay with them while you go with Izzy and Nate since Bennett is busy," I tell Grace, reassuringly.

She shakes her head. "We will wait together. Nate will let us know what's going on."

"Is he allowed to go in there?"

She chuckles. "Nothing in this world could stop him. He has always been there for her, even when he moved to Chicago."

We settle on the plastic chairs in the waiting room and wait. When Bennett is done, he nods to us then sprints toward the doors that swallowed Izzy and Nate.

I steal glances at Grace holding a sleeping Kaylie in her arms, digging around my head for something to say. But it's a useless effort. I can't even come up with small talk to save my life.

Beside me, Matthew, wrapped up in his own world, nods and kicks his legs as he watches Pokémon in Japanese.

Frustrated, I roll my eyes and take a deep breath. We have to talk at some point. Right now, with nothing to do other than listen to women screaming in pain whenever the doors open, this seems like a great opportunity to talk.

Six months ago, I'd have excused myself and ran off to avoid facing the elephant in the room. Now I remember Amber's words: fight for the fairy tale. They fuel me on as I clear my throat and shift slightly, angling my body to Grace's.

"Mrs. Rowe." I pause, waiting for her to look at me. Then I continue, "I know you don't approve of me dating your son. And I really get it. It's unprofessional and dangerous for both of us. His career, my education. I just. . .it just happened. I can't explain how or why, but it did. It's like Nate and I are each other's compass. We weren't looking for each other, but somehow we were pulled into each other. Our paths crossed and. . . it just happened." I finish before I go on rambling into next week, then sigh, frustrated. "I'm not presenting a good case here, am I?"

Grace studies me with pinched brows and pursed lips for a few moments, then shakes her head. "I'm worried for both of you. You seem like a very nice girl. And from the way Nathaniel and you look at each other, you're in too deep. It would be so much easier under different circumstances.

"Your life has hardly begun. My son is just getting back on his feet after the accident. The teacher in me agrees that it's wrong for you to be involved, but I'm his mother, as well. Seeing Nathaniel smile after going through such a painful time in his life is everything I've been wanting for him."

She blinks and then looks away, but not before I see her eyes gleaming with tears. She wipes her cheek with her palm before turning back to face me with a watery smile.

"I'm sorry I haven't been accommodating. I'm just caught between what is ethically correct and what I want for my son."

Swallowing hard, I cover her hand with mine. "Nate is a wonderful man with a big heart, if you look beyond the scowls and glares," I add the latter with a chuckle. "I never thought I'd end up feeling the way I do about him."

Grace holds my gaze as she asks, "You love him?" From the neutrality in her voice, I can't tell if she's testing me or just curious.

I nod, feeling my eyes start to burn with tears and my chest swell with the feelings I have for Nate.

"Have you told him?" Again, the tone.

I shake my head and drop my gaze to my heels. "I'm scared." I wet my lips, ready to confess my inner fears to the woman who gave birth to a wonderful man. "I'm scared of failing at love. I know Camille was his big love and I'm not trying to fill in her shoes—"

"You won't be filling her shoes. Nathaniel and I have been talking a lot—or rather arguing a lot," she chuckles. "—Since I met you at his place," she admits hesitatingly. "True, Camille was Nathaniel's first love. But you gave him back things he thought he'd lost. Hope. Love. A reason to smile. My son thinks with his heart and not his head."

My heart is racing now as I worry my bottom lip between my teeth. When she doesn't continue talking, I look up and find her staring down at Kaylie in her arms as if in contemplation.

I clear my throat, and her gaze meets mine. "You said you attended one of my mother's performances." Immediately, her face breaks into a stunning smile as she nods. "How was she? Did you get a chance to meet her personally?"

Growing up, my mother never talked about her life before she met my dad. It was almost like taboo. I remember one time Elise asked her if she had pictures from any of her performances. Mom quickly shut down and went back to ignoring everything and everyone after that. Nor filled us in on some details of our mom's life, which she had acquired from my grandmother before she passed away. My mother's parents and her sister, Sabine, died in a cabin fire during winter years ago. We stopped asking her questions after that.

Grace shakes her head. "She was magnificent on stage." She continues to tell me about how she'd followed Mom's career, hoping that one day she would get a chance to attend another performance by *The Swan*.

Almost an hour later, the doors leading to the delivery room swing open. Nate steps out wearing a blue overcoat on top of his grey, long-sleeved Henley and dark blue jeans. I jump to my feet, and Grace leans forward as he shakes his head while wiping the sheen of sweat across his dark brow.

"Is she okay?" I ask, wringing my hands.

"Ben's out," he announces, wincing as he lifts his right arm outward slightly, then looks at me. "She's asking for you."

"Me?" I squeak, my eyes widening, then blurt out, "Are you sure?"

"She's chanting your name like you're the birthing deity or something."

I look at Grace. "Mrs. Rowe—"

"Please call me Grace." She nods toward the automatic doors, smiling softly. "Go."

Our gazes lock for a few seconds, and in them, I see acceptance.

"Thank you," I mutter under my breath, overwhelmed and grateful, but I know she heard those words when she subtly nods, offering me a small smile. I smooth my hands on my dress and turn to face my boyfriend. "Let's do this."

Nate's eyes dart from his mother to me as if sensing the shift between us. "You sure?"

"Yeah." I breeze past him confidently. "Let's go."

"That's my girl," he rumbles behind me in approval.

I walk in just as a couple of nurses wheel Bennett out on a gurney with an oxygen mask strapped on his face. A nurse hands me a similar overcoat like the one Nate's wearing. Moments later, I'm standing at Izzy's right side with her hand gripping mine tightly. I bite my lip to stop wincing and peek at Nate across from me.

She breathes a couple of breaths before letting out a blood-curdling scream.

Holy shit. Is this normal? No wonder Bennett passed out.

I've never really thought about having children, but after seeing Izzy in so much pain, I'm leaning toward never giving birth.

I'm not sure how much time passes when suddenly the doctor starts cheering Izzy on, urging her to push. Then the sound of a baby crying fills the room, and the doctor announces way too cheerfully, "It's a girl!"

Minutes later, the baby is cleared as healthy, and Izzy's holding her in her arms swaddled in blankets, tears streaming down her face.

Nate leans down to kiss her forehead, then gently combs the dark curls on the baby's head. "She's beautiful, sis."

"I know," Izzy whispers in a wobbly voice and kisses one rosy cheek, then pulls back to stare at the cute little pink face with little black curls framing her face. "Welcome to the world, Harper. I wish Bennett was here right now."

"He's awake. The doctor just wants to check his vitals before they bring him in," Nate says.

I try to speak around the lump in my throat, congratulate Izzy, but I'm too close to sobbing in joy, which would be embarrassing. Despite watching Izzy writhe in pain and swearing off ever giving birth again, my heart is just so full it could burst. This has been the most wonderful and scary experience I've ever had. I add it on my mental bucket list, then check it off.

How would it feel, holding our baby in my arms?

I peek at Nate, and for once, I allow hope to fill my veins as I imagine my life with him.

"Do you want to hold her?" Izzy asks me, but I'm a bit scared.

What if I drop her? Harper looks so tiny. I don't remember Cora and Joce being so small.

I shake my head. "Maybe later."

She hands the baby over to Nate, who accepts eagerly and cradles her in the crook of his left arm. His entire face transforms into this soft and gentle expression as he hums under his breath.

Right then and there I know I've never seen anything as beautiful as Nate holding a baby.

And yeah, I kind of want to have his babies.

I excuse myself, leave the room and head back to the waiting room. After letting Grace know everything went well, I dig my phone from my bag and pull up my mom's number. She picks up the call on the first ring.

"Elon?" She sounds surprised, which sends guilt spearing through my chest. We haven't seen eye to eye on things in a long time, but after talking to Grace, I want to make things better between us. So I figure calling her is a good start.

"Mom? How are you?"

She's silent for a few seconds, then says, "Good. Just a little surprised to hear from you. Is everything okay?"

I laugh under my breath at our reversed roles.

"I just want to tell you. . . I love you and I'm sorry I haven't been a good daughter—"

"Sweetheart. I love you, too. I should be apologizing for not being there when you and your sisters needed me the most."

I lean on the wall and talk to my mother in a way that I've never done before. After agreeing to meet when she flies to Florida in a couple of weeks, we say goodbye. I head back to the delivery room feeling lighter.

CHAPTER THIRTY-FIVE

Elon

May

"Hey, Elon. Professor Masters wants to see you in her office."

My gaze snaps up from the novel in my hands and collides with Valerie's dark brown eyes as I halt in front of the practice rooms. She's my tutor's teaching assistant and mostly keeps to herself.

"Hey, Val." I peek inside the class, feeling my heartbeat picking up, then look back to her. "Now? Why? Our lesson begins in like five minutes."

She shrugs while turning and heading down the hall. "I have no idea. But she's in an awful mood."

I run after her, my pulse pounding in my ears. "How bad?" I ask, worrying my lip between my teeth.

"On a scale of one to ten? Twenty."

Shit.

Since the time she asked me about Nate, my private classes have been nothing but awkward. At some point, I thought about requesting the Head of Strings Department as a new tutor, but I'd have to justify my request. Besides, it would take weeks before any of the others took me in last minute. I decided to wait until the semester ended so I could put in my request.

I wonder why she wants to see me.

We stop at the door to Professor Masters's office and Valerie whispers, "Good luck," then scurries to her desk.

I take two deep breaths and knock on the door. I hear her snap, "Come in."

I step inside, then close the door behind me. "You wanted to see me?"

"Sit down," she commands without looking up from the documents on her desk.

I do as I'm told, setting my cello at my feet. I wipe my sweaty palms on my jeans and try to breathe through my rising panic.

She looks up, her eyes boring into mine. "Several weeks ago, I asked you if there was something going on between you and Professor Rowe. I'm going to ask you again, and I want the truth. What is your relationship with Professor Rowe?"

My stomach clenches painfully as bile rises to my throat. Why is she asking me this? Does she have proof?

"He's my professor," I say with more confidence, but deep inside me, I'm quaking with dread.

Her nostrils flare in anger. She snatches what looks like papers on the desk and tosses them in front of me.

My heart ceases beating.

My breathing stops as I stare in horror at the proof right in front of my eyes. Pictures of Nate and me together. The top one mocking me shows us kissing inside his car in his underground parking. Another one shows him backing me up against his car and kissing me, his fingers buried in my hair.

"Let's do this again. What's your relationship with Professor Rowe?"

This time I don't answer. Instead, I focus on remaining calm, which is a huge feat. Where did she get the pictures? Was she that desperate to bring down Nate that she followed us and took photos of us?

"Good," she says when I fail to say anything. "Mrs. Bowman's assistant is a very good friend of mine. So when she found this among her mail, she forwarded them to me out of respect for my daughter." She lifts her chin, smiling triumphantly. "You can leave now."

I can't move. My body is still going through the shockwaves of what just happened. "Professor Mast—"

"Leave, Miss Blake," she snaps, turning her back on me. "You'll be assigned a new tutor."

Finally, I rise from my chair, taking my cello with me. "Please don't report this to Mrs. Bowman," I beg her. "Just give us until the end of the semester to sort this out."

She twists her torso to look at me with narrowed eyes. "I've been waiting for that man to make a mistake. I won't give this up for anything. So you can make your choice right now. Either you join me and save your place in this school, or you forfeit the chance and destroy your career, which hasn't even begun yet."

We eye each other for several heartbeats. I clear my throat, hoping to loosen the tightness there, but maintain eye contact.

"He loved your daughter. He still loves her," I start to say in a calm voice. "How can you hate him when your daughter, your own flesh and blood, was the center of his world?"

She blinks at me and then looks down at her desk, her chest rising and falling with quick breaths. "You think you know him, but you don't. He poisoned my daughter against me. He has to pay for what he did."

Right there, I know there's no way of talking her out of it. I know I have to choose between my heart and my waiting career. I also know that she and I won't be having classes today.

It's a no-brainer, though. I choose my heart, because that's where Nate lives and I plan to keep him there.

I march to the door but stop and give her one last look. After talking to my mother weeks ago, I know that anger has no place in my heart. I wish Professor Masters realized that being angry only ends up poisoning you, and you can't think clearly.

"Maybe it's time to let go of the anger and concentrate on getting to know your daughter through the one person who knew her very well."

I hear her hiss as I turn and walk out the door. Whatever she decides to do with the photos after this, Nate and I need to be prepared.

I walked out of her office with one goal in mind. I quickly pull up Nate's number on my phone and open a new text and type, "I love you", then press send. My phone buzzes immediately.

"I want you to say it to me face-to-face," Nate says as soon as I pick up the call.

"I have a lot to tell you at dinner. See you in two hours," I tell him, choosing not to tell him about my conversation with Professor Masters. I know him well by now. He'd end up storming into her office. God knows what would happen after that. "I love you."

After we hang up, I cross the quad heading toward my car when my phone starts ringing in my bag. I dig it out and see Nor's name flashing on the screen.

Oh shit. I can't talk to her now. Not after the conversation I just had with Professor Masters.

The phone stops ringing, but then picks up again. I consider letting it go to voicemail but rethink my decision. What if whatever she has to say is urgent?

"Hey, Nor," I greet as I slide into the driver's seat. "What's up, sis?"

"Hey. Shouldn't you be having your cello lesson?" she asks. From her tone of her voice, she sounds distracted.

"My instructor cancelled the lesson. She wasn't feeling well," I lie. "I'm just heading to Studio 22, but I have a few minutes to talk."

"Dad got arrested in Chicago."

I suck in a breath. "What?" I lean back in my seat. Wow. I wasn't expecting that. "Why?"

"Apparently he's being held for homicide."

"Why am I not surprised?" I mutter under my breath. "Was it in the news or something?"

She chuckles. "No. A man who said he was his friend called me."

We stay quiet, my mind running a mile a minute. I hate that man. If he's locked away, then I feel the entire human population would benefit with him behind bars. I search my mind for compassion, but all I find there is anger for what he put us through.

"Did this friend tell you where he's being held?" I ask.

"Yeah," she answers, then she goes on to tell me the details.

I don't have a specific reason as to why I asked her. I hope he's thinking about his life and what he did to the people close to him. My father left almost seven years ago. No one has heard from him or of him until now.

I huff a sigh. This day keeps getting better.

"Anyway, I have a lot going on right now. Are you coming down this weekend?"

"Yes," I agree, still distracted and feeling the anger in me shift to rage. "I have to go. I love you, sis."

"Love you. See you on Saturday."

We hang up, and I throw the phone inside my bag.

Why do I even care about that bastard?

The answer comes to me swiftly: I care because I still crave acceptance from him. I care because deep inside I always hoped he'd realize what he had done to us and beg for forgiveness.

I thought I'd hardened my heart against this kind of pain. I thought I had accepted that those apologies will never come and moved on.

I was wrong. There was only one thing left for me to do.

Stephen Blake was in for a surprise.

CHAPTER THIRTY-SIX

Elon

At exactly 8:45 a.m., I step out of the automatic glass doors at O'Hare International Airport and join the long queue of people waiting for a cab outside the terminal.

Right after work, I drove to Nate's place. He wasn't in when I got there, so I let myself in with the key he gave me months ago. I wasn't sure what the procedures were to visit a new inmate, so I did a search on Google and got the prison's contact details, then called them to check on what was needed to visit Stephen. He hadn't filled in the visitors list yet, since he'd arrived there three days ago. After the warden cleared me as his daughter as per the information in his presentence report, I spent the next thirty minutes searching for last-minute flights on a low budget.

By the time Nate arrived home from visiting Izzy, I'd worked out my itinerary for the following day. I've never done anything spontaneous or reckless like this before, but I was determined to see my father. I needed closure, and I was going to get it any way I could. Somewhere during my twenty-one years on this earth, I'd found my proverbial balls. I was ready to swing them every which way until I found my peace.

11 hours ago. . .

"What's going on?" Nate asks, as he sets two plates on the table.

I open the Chinese takeout boxes and lump food on the plates, then turn to face him. "I love you. It has taken me a while to get here, but we're on the same page now. I'm insanely in love with you."

He grins, sending every part of me tingling with pleasure.

God, he's beautiful.

He cups my neck and pulls me to him in a kiss. His fingers tighten on my hair when my lips part and our lips tangle together.

"I fucking love you, Elon Blake," he murmurs against my lips, and I can feel his smile in his words.

He sits down and pulls me on his lap, lifts my shirt over my back, then kisses the back of my neck. I shiver, squirming on his lap. "I love how you shiver for me, Little Wolf."

"You're pretty addictive," I say, arching my back when his mouth follows a trail down my spine. "W—we need to talk."

"And I need to kiss every inch of you," he growls, sending heat between my legs.

Oh God. He's distracting me, destroying every rational thought.

I jump from his lap and turn around, panting. My eyes dart to his lap, eyeing the bulge in his pants, then I meet his smoldering gaze.

"Professor Masters has photos of you and me."

His brows furrow as he shifts on his seat, adjusting himself with his hand. "What?"

I begin to tell him what went down in Elizabeth's office. By the time I'm done, his eyes are no longer gleaming with heat and lust. Fury leaves his body in waves; he's literally vibrating with it.

"Fuck!" He jumps off the seat and starts to pace, gripping the nape of his neck with his hand. "I knew she wasn't going to stop until she *found something to destroy me. You need to take the deal she gave you."*

My eyes widen. "Are you serious? How can you say that?"

He stops in front of me and cups my cheek in his left hand. "We both knew the risks before this. But she's offering you a way out. Don't worry about me. I'll be—"

"No! God, Nate. I'm not going to take the deal. I knew what I was doing when I gave you my number, when I kissed you first."

"Elon—"

"No. We are in this together, okay?" I take his hand from my cheek and place his palm flat on my chest. "I'm not letting you take the fall."

Nate grunts under his breath, pulling his hand away from me."If she didn't take the photos then that means. . ." His eyes go wide, and I know his thoughts mirror mine.

"Rick?" I ask. "You think he'd follow us around just to take pictures?"

His eyes bore into mine. "He followed us after the fundraising ball because he wanted to see you. He must have figured out who I was."

He said he'd make us pay.

Shit. SHIT.

"That demented fucker," he curses, nostrils flaring. "I should have smashed his face in when I had the chance."

"We know what to expect if Elizabeth reports this to Mrs. Bowman," I say, moving to sit on the couch, our takeout completely forgotten.

He sits next to me and declares with conviction, "I'll talk to Elizabeth."

My man is stubborn, and when he gets like this, there's no way to convince him otherwise. With my thoughts bouncing between my scheduled visit to my father and the looming threat that is Professor Masters, I burrow my head in my boyfriend's chest as he holds me tight.

After I left Nate's place, I drove back to my apartment without telling him about my plans to visit my father. I knew he'd try to stop me or offer to go with me. For me to find the peace I craved, I needed to do this alone.

I packed an overnight bag, then snuck out at five in the morning and drove to the airport without telling Amber. I knew she'd try to talk me out of it, or worse, call my sisters. This was between Stephen and me. It was finally time to close that chapter of my life and allow myself to heal from the past. I have a man who loves me. I don't want to carry all that baggage into this relationship.

I intend to tell Nor and Elise that I visited our father when I fly back to Florida.

10:55 a.m. finds me sitting in front of a man with pale skin and sunken eyes. Eyes similar to mine.

Stephen Blake looks nothing like the man who left his family behind seven years ago. For just a second, his eyes soften, his features gentling as his gaze roams my face. The look is gone as fast as it appeared.

"Hey, Dad," I finally greet.

He sits back in his chair and smiles smugly. "I didn't expect anyone to ever come visit me."

Small talk has never been my strong suit, so I jump right into the issue. "I see you haven't changed."

"Why did you come here?" Stephen asks.

"Closure," I say calmly. He frowns slightly at my words. "You made our life hell. Do you know how much I wanted to have a father who loved me? How much I missed having a father who'd comfort me or someone I could talk to? Every child in school was proud, boasting about what their fathers did. Me, I was busy, trying hard not to cry whenever we were supposed to invite our fathers for Dad's Day at school."

"That bitch you call your mother, it's all her fault. She got pregnant so she could trap me."

"Why did you marry her if she disgusted you so much?" I ask heatedly.

His mouth pulls up into an evil smile. "She had money. And she was pretty."

"So my sisters and I were—"

"Collateral damage."

I stare at him for a long time, blinking back tears.

"You should be thanking me, you ungrateful little shit," he says with a sneer.

"For what?"

"You're alive, aren't you?"

I laugh bitterly, shaking my head. "Yeah. You're right. I should be thanking you for shaping me to be the person I am today. You taught me how to fear my own father. But this—this person sitting here in front of you? This is me. All of me. I rose above my fears and made something of myself. I learned to fight. I learned that life wasn't only made up of shades of black, white and grey, but also color. So much color. I made an effort to learn from my past. I learned to love and trust."

Swiping a hand against my wet cheeks, I take a deep, calming breath. He doesn't deserve my tears or any more words from me.

"We've all left that life in the past. Even Mom is happy without you in her life. Cole and Nor are finally together, despite what you did to them. I met a man who's ten times better than the man you were or ever will be. He loves me."

I rise from my chair and sling my bag over my shoulder and meet his gaze head-on. "So yes, *Father*. Thank you. May you rot in hell."

He laughs. "Cutting your visit short, darling daughter?"

Ignoring his taunting remark, I straighten my shoulders and walk out of the room with newfound perspective and dignity.

That man back there is nothing more than a sperm donor.

I walk into a park and sit on the first bench I come across, then dig my phone from my bag and power it on. Right after visiting Stephen, I couldn't sit still. I've been roaming the streets of Chicago for the past hour. My flight back to Florida is scheduled for 6:25 p.m., which is almost five hours from now.

My phone buzzes nonstop with messages and missed calls. I click on the screen and count a total of ten missed calls from Nate, numerous messages from Amber, Elise and Nor.

I scroll down the list and tap on Nor's name, then hold the phone to my ear. For some reason, I need to hear her voice before anyone else's.

"Elon?" she shrieks, picking up the call on the first ring. "Where have you been? Amber called me when she couldn't find you anywhere."

"Chicago," I whisper, then sniff.

There are a few seconds of silence, then, "WHAT?!"

My head jerks back in shock. I've never heard my sister raise her voice before now.

"Please tell me this is a joke."

"I wanted to see him," I mutter, my throat clogging with tears. I slant my head back and focus on the blue skies. "I just wanted to look in his eyes when I asked him if he ever loved me. Us. I wanted closure."

"Oh, honey," she sobs, and I cry harder. "I'd have gone with you."

I shake my head. "No. I wanted to do this alone, Nor. You've been my guardian angel my entire life. It was time for me to grow up and stop hiding beneath your wings."

She sniffs. "Did you find what you were looking for?"

"Yes. Our father is a psychotic asshole."

She bursts out laughing, which makes me smile, then says, "I'll make sure they put those words on his headstone. So, are you coming home?"

"Yeah. I'll see you tomorrow, okay?"

"I love you, little sis. And Elon," she adds the latter after a pause. "Don't you ever go off the grid like that without letting anyone know where you are. Okay?"

"Okay, Nor. I love you, too."

We hang up, then I realize in my haste to leave Jacksonville, I'd forgotten about my classes at Studio 22. So I call them and give them some bullshit excuse about being sick.

God, I feel like I've become a world class liar these days.

I text Amber and Elise back and give them a very short version of what happened, then let them know that I'll call them later.

Finally, I call Nate, then sit back on the bench and wait. He's the only person who can make this crushing pain go away, who can make me forget everything just by hearing his voice. Right now, I need that.

"Christ. Where the hell have you been, Elon?" Nate asks the second he answers the call, sounding panicked and angry.

"Hey, baby." I take a deep, calming breath. "I'm sorry for leaving without telling you."

"Where are you?"

"Chicago. I got in this morn—"

"Wait, what? *Why*?" He sounds baffled and something else. Suspicious.

"My father was arrested for homicide and got transferred to a prison here in Chicago. I wanted to see him so I—"

"Whoa. When did this happen?" he interrupts my rant.

"A few days ago."

He's quiet for a couple seconds, then asks, "You didn't mention it last night."

"I knew you'd try to stop me or go with me. I couldn't take that chance."

I hear him take a deep breath, as if he's trying to calm himself down. "I wouldn't have tried to stop you. I'd never do that, unless it's something that could hurt you. I'd have gone with you." He sighs. "You shouldn't have to go through this alone, sweetheart," he adds in a gentle voice. "What time is your flight?"

"In about five hours."

"Where are you now?"

I scan my surroundings scattered with people having picnics, children flying kites, the occasional cyclist flying by. "Sitting in a small park."

"Christ. You've been in the park since you left the prison?"

"It's not so bad."

He grunts in disapproval, then says, "Sit tight. I'll call you back in a few minutes, okay?"

"Sure."

True to his word, the phone rings two minutes later.

"Do me a favor, sweetheart. Go to the Waldorf Astoria on Walton Street and ask for Mr. Williams. He's expecting you. I'll text you the exact address."

"What's going on, Nate?"

"I'm coming for you."

Oh no. I know being in this city after what happened to him will bring nothing but bad memories. "You don't need to do that. I'll be home soon, I promise."

"Elon," he prompts in a low, sinful voice. "Listen to me. When I told you I love you, taking care of you was pretty much part of the whole package for me. This is me taking care of you. Head to the Waldorf Astoria. I'm coming to get you. Please text me your flight details so I can call the airline to push back the time, okay?"

Despite my reservations about him flying to Chicago, I smile, enjoying the way he swooped in and took charge. "Okay."

"That's my girl. I love you."

"Love you too."

My phone buzzes with a text from Nate a few minutes later. Standing up from the bench, I follow his instructions to the hotel.

CHAPTER THIRTY-SEVEN

Nate

"Thanks for taking care of my girl."

My long-time friend, Wade Brass, raises a surprised brow. He knows about Camille, and even though I moved back home, we still keep in touch every now and then.

"When did that happen?" he asks, sitting back in his seat inside the hotel lounge at the Waldorf.

"About four months now."

"Well, then." He smiles. "Looks like introductions are in order. How about brunch tomorrow? My Hadley will be there, too. Maybe the girls can get a chance to know each other."

"I'll talk to Elon first." I'm not sure what condition Elon is currently in after visiting her father. The need to see her burns through me. I arrived at the hotel ten minutes ago and found Wade waiting for me. "I should check on her. I'll let you know about the brunch."

He nods as he stands up. "It's good to see you again, man."

"You too, Brass."

Moments later, I'm standing beside the bed, staring at Elon as she snores loudly. She's curled up in a tight ball in the middle of the bed, her hair splayed across the pillow. A white sheet covers her body to the shoulder, but it doesn't hide the soft curves beneath it. She must have cried herself to sleep, given the dried up tear streaks on her cheeks.

Quickly, I strip down to my boxers and join her on the bed, spooning her. She stirs and mumbles something under her breath before her eyes flutter open.

"You're here."

I run my knuckles against her cheeks. "Yes."

"I'm sorry for worrying you."

God, those eyes, so big and scared.

My arm around her waist tightens, and I kiss her hair. When Amber called to tell me she hadn't seen or heard from Elon since the night before when she left my place, I panicked. I must have died a thousand deaths when I tried to call Elon and my calls went directly to her voicemail. The only person I could think of who'd want to cause her harm was her ex-boyfriend.

"You're safe. That's all that matters."

We fall silent for a few seconds before she shudders and mutters, "I hate him so much. Coming to Chicago to visit him was probably one of the stupidest things I've ever done, but I'm glad I did. I won't be holding my breath anymore, waiting for him to come around one day and apologize for being an evil monster."

"Yes. It was a stupid move, especially since no one knew your whereabouts, but it was also very brave of you. You faced the monster that has haunted you your entire life, and won."

She dazzles me with a watery smile, then sniffs. "I'm pretty badass, aren't I?"

I laugh, shoving my head into the crook of her neck, and murmur, "You are, My Queen."

We stay like that, just snuggling and talking. As much as I want to make love to her and make her forget about today, I have a feeling Elon is too distracted tonight.

I jerk awake and peer into the darkness while trying to detect where the familiar ringing is coming from. Careful not to jostle the bed too much, I pull my arm from beneath Elon's shoulder and lift my thigh from between hers. I switch the lamp on my nightstand, drop to my knees on the floor and grab my jeans where I left them last night, then dig my phone out of the pocket. I frown at the unfamiliar number with a Florida area code flashing on the screen.

Who could be calling at 11:30 p.m.?

I'm about to swipe the screen to disconnect the call, but something in my gut stops me. I tap the screen to answer, then press the phone to my ear.

"Rowe," I grunt into the phone, annoyed.

Several seconds of silence pass. I'm about to hang up when a familiar female voice calls out, "Nathaniel?"

"Elizabeth?" I question, shocked to hear her voice. The surprise wears off quickly when I remember what Elon told me. "What do you want?"

"I'm calling out of courtesy and respect for my daughter to warn you. Mrs. Bowman knows about you and Miss Blake."

I look over my shoulder to make sure Elon is still sleeping before striding to the bathroom and locking the door.

"Ah. Let me guess," I say coldly. "You couldn't wait until Monday to show her what you got on us."

"I didn't do it, Nathaniel."

"Bullshit. You've been looking for a way to destroy me. You finally got what you wanted, Elizabeth. Bravo," I grit between my clenched jaw.

She huffs a breath. "I had a chat with Miss Blake in my office yesterday. I had every intention of reporting you two to Mrs. Bowman on Monday, but—" She stops talking abruptly.

Is she fucking kidding me? "Let me guess," I bite out the words. "You decided to call me and give me a heads up?"

I hear her take a deep breath, then exhale. "I changed my mind."

I freeze mid-step. "Really?" I ask sarcastically. What the hell is she playing at?

She clears her throat. "Look. I knew you wouldn't believe me before I called you, but I did it anyway. All I know is that Mrs. Bowman found an envelope stuck on her windshield yesterday as she was leaving work. Whoever it is that has been taking the photos of you and Miss Blake must want to hurt you badly. Anyway, I need to go."

"Why did you call to warn me, Elizabeth?"

She doesn't say anything for several seconds. Then she says, "Miss Blake said some things that made me take a pause and reevaluate my attitude toward you."

My heart beats fast inside my chest, but I don't say anything. I want to hear what she has to say.

" '*Maybe it's time to let go of the anger and concentrate on getting to know your daughter through the one person who knew her very well.*' That's what she said to me."

I breathe out the air trapped in my chest, feeling my love and respect for Elon grow even more.

I don't allow myself to feel hope though. Elizabeth has been the bane of my existence for as long as I can remember. Just because she seemed to have changed her mind doesn't mean I'm going to do the same.

"Thank you for calling, Elizabeth."

I'm about to hang up when she calls my name and says, "For all it's worth, I'm really sorry."

The line goes dead.

I toss my phone on the counter, then splash cold water on my face.

Fuck. *Fuck.*

Shit has hit the fan back in Jacksonville.

I need to come up with a plan to get Elon off the hook.

Restless and unable fall asleep again, I throw my clothes on and leave the room. Outside the hotel, I flag down a cab and give the driver the instructions of where I'm headed.

It's time to put my own demons to rest.

I drop to my knees and tug the weeds that have grown around Camille's headstone, then trace her name with my fingers.

"Hey, Cam. Sorry I haven't been around. Remember the last time I was here and I told you I was thinking of moving back home? I finally did. Chicago reminded me of you. I couldn't stay here anymore. Every day I woke up and went to bed with the same thought in mind: I was alive when you were. . .not here."

My eyes start to burn with tears, but I shake my head, refusing to cry. I was here to slay my demons so I could live my life without looking over my shoulder and asking. . .what if?

"You know you will always be a big part of my life, right?" I wet my lips and fix my gaze on Camille's name on the tombstone. "I met a girl, and she drives me nuts." I chuckle under my breath. "I don't know where this is heading, but all I know is that I met her and my world turned bright again. I don't know why I'm telling you this. I just want you to know, I guess. I still love you, but I also love her."

My shoulders slump forward. "Give me a sign, Cam. Tell me it's okay."

I sit quietly, waiting. From a distance, I hear a car door slam. An owl hoots from one of the many trees surrounding the cemetery.

Then a slight breeze blows across the open space, whistling low and picking up as it whips across the branches. The hair on the back of my neck rises as I jump to my feet and jostle my right arm, causing pain to slice from my arm to my shoulder and down my spine. I clench my teeth until the pain passes, but the wind continues to cut across the trees. Then it's over as fast as it started.

I don't believe in ghosts, but that was some freaky shit.

I look down at the headstone, my lips twitching with a smile. "Still making sure you get in the last word, aren't you?" I lean down and run my fingers on the cold marble. "I have to go, Cam. I'll be seeing you, okay?"

I breathe out, for the first time feeling at peace with my past. I stride toward the cemetery entrance, where the cab driver is waiting to drive me back to the Waldorf, back to my present and my future.

CHAPTER THIRTY-EIGHT

Elon

SUNDAY MORNING STARTS OUT EXCEEDINGLY WELL. I WAKE UP TO the feel of Nate's mouth on my neck as he kisses me, his hands hungrily touching me everywhere. He moves his hips, and I feel his erection poking my back.

Someone seems happy this morning.

I twist my head around to face him and moan as his tongue makes a hot trail toward the sensitive place behind my ear.

"Good morning, Professor," I whisper, twining my fingers into his hair.

"Miss Blake," he murmurs against my skin as he makes his way to the swell of my breasts. He flips me on my back and settles his hips between my legs. I feel the head of his cock teasing my entrance and lift my hips, eager to have him inside me. "How did you sleep?"

"I always sleep well when I'm with you."

"I need you so badly," he says with a groan. "I don't think I can hold off anymore."

I wrap my legs around his hips, digging my heels into his butt cheeks while lifting my hips off the bed. "I'm here. Take whatever you need, baby."

He enters me slowly, his dark, hungry gaze locked on mine the entire time. When he's buried deep inside me, he lets out a long, slow breath through his lips.

"I'm home," he declares, flashing a wide, bright smile down at me, making me melt into him and scattering my thoughts.

He starts to move inside me, kissing me and thrusting into me in slow, torturous strokes that have me moaning and breathless. We don't say any more words, our bodies doing all the talking, responding to each other's touch and kiss and breaths. Nate is usually intense in and out of bed, but I've never seen this side of him. It's like he's finally giving me all of him without holding back.

His thrusts become urgent, propelling me into another reality as he moves in and out of me. My orgasm builds higher. As if he knows I'm almost coming, he pumps twice, his body stiffening above mine just as I go over the edge. I scream his name at the same time he screams mine.

Our eyes are still locked to each other, our pants filling the room, hearts beating to the same rhythm. It's like nothing I've ever experienced before.

He leans down and kisses me softly on my lips, then rolls over and takes me with him. As always, I'm careful not to put my weight on his right shoulder. He pulls me to his chest, throws one long, toned leg over my hips, cocooning me completely into him, then pulls the sheet up to our shoulders.

"Whatever happens on Monday, I want you to know that you are worth everything. I don't regret meeting you. You pulled me back into the light." He breathes in deeply, kissing the shell of my ear. "I want you to know that no matter how this goes, I'm here to stay. I love you, Elon Blake."

I snuggle deeper into him. "I don't know what I did to deserve you, but I will not question it. I love you, Nathaniel Rowe."

Then he tells me what happened last night: the telephone

conversation with Professor Masters. We're supposed to meet Wade and his wife, Hadley, for brunch. But after the news, safe to say my appetite and good mood have left the room. Nate calls Wade to cancel the brunch and promises to call him after he returns to Florida.

We spend the next six hours in the hotel talking. He tells me about visiting Camille last night. He makes love to me twice before we leave for the airport, promising me that everything is going to be okay. I should be worried, but I'm not. I chose him. I knew what I was doing, and I will never regret that decision.

Heart over mind.

Despite knowing what's coming to me on Monday morning, I'm still nervous as all hell. As soon as I walk into class, I'm summoned to Mrs. Bowman's office, only to find Nate waiting outside, as well. Two men I've never seen before—one tall, thin and wearing square glasses and the other one tall with thinning hair—arrive and escort us back to Brown Hall and into separate practice rooms.

The man wearing glasses introduces himself as Mr. John Felix. He's a member of the school board.

Then, the interrogation begins. Photos are tossed on the table, and I'm staring at one of me half-naked with Nate's mouth sucking my nipple in his living room. Whoever took this picture must have had access to the building across from Nate's. My heart beats wildly in my chest. This is so embarrassing, and I feel violated by the photos in front of me.

Then the questions start flying at me.

When did this begin?

Did Professor Rowe trick you into having a relationship with him?

Were you trying to better your grades by sleeping with your professor?

The questions go on and on, mostly trying to blame Nate for misleading a student. But I don't give them a reason to put the blame on him.

We were in this together and what I feel for him right now has surpassed anything I've ever felt, even my passion to play the cello. Whenever I close my eyes, I see him. Loving me. Taking care of me and going to great lengths to make me happy.

Nate is everything I've always wanted.

When I am with him, I feel like I can conquer the world with him by my side.

So I stick to my story, which frustrates the man sitting across from me, throwing questions. He storms out of the room without a glance in my direction.

I'm rudely surprised when Mr. Felix walks back into the room half an hour later and informs me that Professor Rowe has confessed to seducing me.

My stomach falls away, and I want to throw up.

"Where is he?" I ask in a low voice, fighting the tears of frustration burning my eyes.

He nods toward the door just as Nate steps into the room, his face unreadable. He shoots me a cursory glance and then focuses all his attention to the interrogator.

"Mr. Rowe, in your confession, you admitted that you seduced Miss Blake," Mr. Felix states, lifting his brows expectantly.

Nate nods, still avoiding my gaze, his jaw clenched.

"So tell us in your own words, Mr. Rowe." He nods his head in my direction.

"I seduced her. There was nothing going on between us. Just sex."

Mr. Felix scribbles something down in his notebook.

My heart shatters into a million pieces. Why is he doing this?

I'm about to jump up from my seat when Nate's eyes connect with mine. His gaze softens as he mouths, "I love you." I shake my head, ready to speak up, but he sends me a pleading look before focusing on Mr. Felix.

"Don't let my behavior reflect on her." His gaze locks with mine again, and it's cold, so cold I can feel it sink into my bones. I know it's for Mr. Felix's benefit, but he almost convinces me. "She means nothing to me."

Mr. Felix adjusts his glasses and steeples his fingers on the table. "It's obvious you are trying to protect Miss Blake. From these photos, she seems to be quite compliant to your advances." His eyes fall on the images, and I shut my eyes tight. "You knowingly broke the code of ethics. We have no choice but to let you go." Mr. Felix dismisses Nate with a disappointed look and then turns to face me.

His eyebrows furrow as he stares at me. "Rushmore takes this very sternly. From what I've heard, you are very gifted and have a bright future ahead of you. Rushmore has a very strict set of standards and rules, which you knowingly disregarded. Breaking rules has its consequences." He pulls in a deep breath. "You're expelled, Miss Blake."

I open my eyes and meet the unreadable blue ones staring at me.

"Please stop by President Bowman's office on Friday. You're dismissed."

Rising up on unsteady legs, I wipe my clammy palms on my jeans, grab my bag from the floor where I dropped it and leave the room.

Students part in the hallway, whispers following me as I head for the exit.

When I reach outside, I march toward my car, but Elise comes out of nowhere and intercepts me, grabbing me into a hug.

"I'm so sorry. Amber called me, and I got here as fast as I could. I just saw Nate—"

"Where is he?" I question, pulling back while scanning the parking lot.

"He's waiting for you in his car." She points to her right.

I'm about to take off when I hear a familiar voice yelling. I break into a run when I see Rick standing in front of Nate's car, shouting. He raises his arm and slams his fist on Nate's jaw. Nate stumbles back but rebounds quick and livid, swings back his left arm and lands a blow on Rick's gut by the time I skid to a stop in front of him. Rick stumbles back several feet, clutching his stomach, his face screwed in pain. He straightens when he sees me, the look on his face morphing into the definition of evil: wild, crazy eyes and a sneer.

"Stop!" I put myself between Rick and Nate, twisting my upper body to face my boyfriend. My hands immediately brush up and down his body, checking for injuries. "Are you okay?"

His chest rises and falls with quick breaths as he nods. His angry gaze shifts from mine, widening in horror as they focus on something over my shoulder.

"No. No. *Fucking* no. I won't let this happen again," he mutters under his breath, his face pale.

I whirl around and stumble back when I see Rick holding a gun pointed directly at Nate and me.

I gasp, heart beating wildly in my chest. "Don't do this, Rick," I plead with him in a broken whisper, holding my hand up, palm facing him, hoping to placate him. "You're better than this."

He glowers at me, moving his wild eyes on Nate. "I came back for you, baby doll. You are mine. Always mine. Don't you remember how much fun we had together?"

I shudder as one of the many images of what he calls *fun* flashes inside my head: his fingers closing around my throat consumed by jealousy, teaching me a lesson because some guy happened to look at me in passing. Or his verbal abuse, the feel of my skin on my lower back splitting open—

Breathe.

"Yes, I remember," I say, my chin quivering with anger, fear, tears. "Just put the gun away, then we'll talk." A crowd has already gathered around us, and voices rise and fall in fear. A sob tears through the air, but my eyes stay on Rick.

He waves the gun, motioning for Nate to move away, then lowers his arm. Behind me, I feel my boyfriend's hard body tense, his breathing coming out fast. He grasps my elbow tight, as he grits out, "Not going to happen."

Rick cocks his head to the side and grins evilly. "I'm holding the gun here. Move, fucker."

Nate's lips brush my ear. He whispers, "Do you trust me?"

My pulse thuds louder in my ears. "Nate, no—"

"Do you *trust* me, Elon?" he demands desperately, his grip on my elbow tightening.

"With my life," I tell him.

Rick's eyes narrow in suspicion. Then without warning, he points the gun at us. Terror spreads through me, terrified for Nate, for me. Gunshots ring the air at the exact moment the side of my head hits the unforgiving ground and a heavy body covers mine. My vision blurs. Chaos erupts around me. I try to move, but the weight above me holds me down. I pull in a breath, but I can't seem to breathe fast enough. I try to open my mouth, but nothing comes out.

Darkness swirls on the edge of my vision.

"Breathe, sweetheart," a rich baritone that I once compared to evening bonfires, honey and Nutella commands softly and steadily into my ear. "Breathe for me."

Then my world turns black.

CHAPTER THIRTY-NINE

*N*ate

A few seconds before . . .

FUCKING HELL!

This can't be happening again. I won't lose another woman I love at the hands of a madman holding a gun at us.

With my gaze locked on Rick for any sudden movements, I brush my lips to the shell of Elon's ear. "Do you *trust* me, Elon?" I demand again desperately, my grip on her elbow tightening.

"With my life," she says.

Rick's eyes narrow.

His hand tightens around the grip of the gun.

The finger on the trigger moves, and I know Rick has already made his decision.

Even before the loud *bang* cuts through the air, my left arm circles around Elon's waist, spinning us around while shielding her with my body. I twist my torso as our bodies descend to the pavement, attempting to cushion her head with my right shoulder as we hit the ground. Pain bursts through my shoulder and arm. Dots explode behind my eyes. I blink several times to keep my vision clear, then carefully pull my arm from her waist and sit up and do a quick scan.

Blood trickles from the cut on her temple where her head hit the tarmac.

Why the fuck is she so still? So pale? Was I too late saving her?

Images of Camille dying in my arms flash inside my head.

God, no, no. *NO!*

My gaze darts around, taking in the chaos before me. I watch in horror as Rick's finger twitches on the trigger, the look in his eyes determined. Unhinged. Before he has a chance to fire another shot, a heavyset man barrels toward an unsuspecting Rick and slams his shoulder into Rick's chest, knocking him flat on his stomach to the floor and sending the gun flying several feet away. Then, he grabs Rick's flailing arms and twists them behind his back, subduing him.

Screams fill the air. Feet pound on asphalt. Several voices yell, "Call nine-one-one!"

I roll over to my left side, my entire focus on Elon now that Rick is no longer a threat.

"Elon?" I whisper. "Elon! Open your eyes. Look at me." I shout.

Please God, let her be okay. Don't take her away from me. I can't go through this again.

"Oh shit! Oh God!" Elise cries as she drops to her knees next to me. "Is she okay?"

My head jerks up, meeting Elise's tear-filled eyes, her trembling hand covering her mouth.

Sirens fill the air just as Elon groans softly, and her eyes flutter open. She blinks several times, then squints against the sunlight.

"Nate?" she croaks, her eyes moving to my left. "Elise?"

I suck in a relieved breath, and my eyes burn with tears. "Hey, sweetheart," I murmur, smiling down at her. Elise lets out a sob before scrambling closer and taking Elon's hand in hers but doesn't say anything.

"What's going on? " Elon lifts her hand and brushes her fingers across my cheek. "Why are you two crying?"

"Nothing. . . just happy you're okay." The wail of sirens sound close now.

A male voice asks if everything is okay, if we need help, but I can't afford to look away from Elon. She tries to speak again, but I squeeze her hand, pleading with her to save her energy. She moans in pain, her eyes rolling back as she loses consciousness.

Then everything happens fast. Two paramedics rush in our direction and drop at my side. One of them begins to check on Elon while the other shoots questions at me as he checks me over, wanting to know what happened. He's talking about a dislocated shoulder, but my attention is focused on the other paramedic as he finishes up taking Elon's vitals.

"Is she okay?" I ask, shifting closer while clutching my right arm.

He nods. "Everything looks fine, probably suffering from a mild concussion. We need to take her to the hospital just to get her checked." He nods at my shoulder. "You too."

"I'm fine," I grunt, clenching my jaw to ward off the pain. "Take care of her first."

After loading her into the ambulance, I jump in and Elise says she will follow us with her car to the hospital. The last thing I see before the ambulance leaves the parking lot is a policeman escorting Rick into a patrol car, his wrists cuffed behind him.

CHAPTER FORTY

Elon

THE FIRST THING I NOTICE WHEN I OPEN MY EYES IS A WHITE CEILING above me, then the dark sky through the parted curtains at the window.

I wiggle my nose as the distinctive smell of hospital tickles it.

What in the hell am I doing here?

I shut my eyes, trying to remember what happened. They flip back open, and I bolt upright on the bed. I inhale sharply, dropping my head in my hands as pain stabs the right side of my temple, which is covered with a sterile bandage.

Oh my God. I think I'm going to throw up.

How long have I been out? From what I can remember, Nate shielded me with his body when the gun went off.

Nate.

Is he okay? I need to look for him. I need to know he's okay.

I drop my hands and scan the room. My heart skips several beats, then thuds fast as I take in the scene before me.

Cole and Nate locked in a glaring standoff.

Eyes boring holes into each other.

Lips drawn back in a snarl.

Chests rising and falling in exertion.

Oh SHIT.

Nor steps between them and puts her hand on Cole's chest, pushing him back. Then she cups his jaw in her hands and urges him to look at her. When his eyes are focused on her, she says, "Not now, Cole." His nostrils flare, his jaw clenched tight. "We can't do this here, okay?"

Cole shakes his head stubbornly, lifts his hands and signs, "*He ruined her life.*"

Nor throws a glare in Nate's direction, then focuses on her fuming boyfriend, and signs, "*Elon is an adult. She knew the consequences. But right now, we have to look at the bigger picture: no one got hurt.*"

Cole scowls, rubbing the nape of his neck. Then he signs, "*But—*"

She shakes her head, jutting her chin forward, and signs, "*Arguing isn't going to help Elon right now. She has a lot of explaining to do when she wakes up.*"

Ah, crap. I wipe my clammy hands on the sheets and breathe deeply, gathering courage for the conversation to come, then focus on Nate, taking in his handsome features: jaw clenched tightly, face pale and a sheen of sweat on his forehead. His entire body shakes like a junky going through withdrawals, and he seems to favor his right side as he straightens to his full height, still glaring at Cole.

"Nate?" I call out, and his head snaps in my direction, his legs already carrying him to me before my next inhale. Nor lets out a sob as she and Cole rush toward the bed.

He drops into the chair next to my bed and covers my hand with his left hand. Relief floods his face as he leans forward to kiss my forehead.

"Fuck, Little Wolf. You had me worried. How are you feeling?"

"Better. How long was I unconscious?"

"You woke up on and off for almost ten hours." Nate tucks a loose strand of hair behind my ear with his fingers.

I frown, studying him. His usually clear eyes look glassy, and the fingers on his right hand spasm more than normal. "Haven't you taken your meds?"

He shakes his head. "I'm fine."

"No, you're not. Where are they?"

He sighs. "In my bag inside the car still parked at Rushmore."

My eyes widen in horror. "You've gone almost ten hours without them? Couldn't the doctors give you something for the pain?"

He shakes his head, wincing as he stretches his legs. "Let's worry about you, okay? I'll be fine."

"Elon?" Nor calls out my name as she rounds the bed. "God, we were so worried. How are you?"

My eyes move from Nate and meet my sister's green ones filled with tears and concern. A sob bursts through my lips as the events of the last few days hit me hard. Nor quickly hops on the bed and grabs me in a tight hug. I bury my face into the crook of her neck, tears falling down my face.

"Everything's going to be okay," she soothes, her hand running up and down my back.

I pull back and wipe my cheeks while sliding my gaze to Nate, then meet Cole's worried eyes.

"Why didn't you tell us what was going on?" Nor asks, and my attention snaps back to her. "Rick could have hurt you. I don't know what I'd have done if something happened to you—"

"I'm okay. I'm so sorry for not telling you what was going on." I sniff, my hands wrapped around the white bed sheets. "He saved me." I turn to face Nate. "If it weren't for Nate, I can't even. . . "

Nate's fingers wrap around my leg and give me a comforting squeeze. "You're okay. That's all that matters."

Cole digs his fingers through his hair, pulling it back while scowling in Nate's direction.

"Can I talk to my sister alone?" I look at Cole, then Nate.

They both nod.

Cole's eyes flick to mine.

"*Be nice, please,*" I sign. "*I love him.*"

His eyes widen in what I think is surprise at my confession. He eyes Nate before glancing back at me, flexing his clenched fists. "*You are asking too much from me, Elon.*" His words send my heart racing all over again, but when I see his lips twitch, I know things will be okay.

Nate stands up, and I grasp his hand before he turns. "Thank you for saving my life."

Removing his hand from mine, he runs it against my cheek, presses a soft kiss on my lips. He straightens, smiling a tired smile that still manages to weaken my knees. He doesn't need to say anything. His eyes tell me how he's feeling. Then he follows Cole out the door. I pray under my breath those two men don't kill each other in the hallway.

I clear my throat and scoot up on the bed, then tug Nor's hand, silently asking her to sit with me.

I swallow hard, then say, "I didn't come clean about what Rick did to me because I was afraid of what you and Elise would think of me, especially after the way Stephen treated Mom and us. I was weak, and the thought of it made me ashamed because I had turned out to be the woman who let a man treat her like trash."

She opens her mouth to speak, but I put my hand up to stop her. "Please, let me say this while I still have the courage." I inhale a deep breath, then continue. "You have always been a constant for me, Nor. Every time I thought about giving up, I'd just close my eyes and think of you. You never gave up. Always so brave."

I rub my hands along her arms, feeling the small bumps from the scars under my touch.

"The scar on your back. . . did Rick do that to you?" she whispers, lacing her fingers with mine and clutching them tight.

My eyes widen. "You saw that?" She nods, her lips pressed in a tight line. "Yeah. It was stupid of me to believe that he could change."

She drops her head and wipes her cheek with her hand. "What about Nate?" She looks at me, anger and disappointment warring in her face. "He told us what happened. How could you do something so reckless? You've worked hard to get where you are, then you meet a guy and throw it all away. You're the most—wait." She cuts herself off. "He's the professor you talked about months ago? The arrogant ass you couldn't stand?"

I nod, nibbling on my thumbnail.

She studies me with narrowed eyes. "You. . . love him, don't you?"

I straighten my shoulders and meet her gaze head-on. "Yes. I know you're disappointed—"

"Wow." She shakes her head. "*Wow.*"

She hops down from the bed and starts pacing. "I don't even know what to think right now. There's just so much happening at once. I need time to take it all in."

"Nor, please," I plead quietly. She stops and faces me again, scratching the scars on her forearms quickly with her fingernails. She does this whenever she is too nervous or angry. She told me once that the scars start itching.

"I need to think," she mumbles as she storms to the door, swings it open and walks out.

I drop my face into my hands, and I sob. I'm terrified, sad, relieved. I'm just overwhelmed by everything that happened the past twenty-four hours.

About ten minutes later, the sound of soled feet padding on the floor has me lifting my head. I catch a glimpse of sky blue Keds before Nor crawls back on the bed and hugs me tightly.

"I didn't think you'd come back so soon," I mumble into her neck.

"Cole made me come back. Plus, you're my baby sis. How can I leave you when you need me the most?"

I sniff and pull back while wiping my cheeks. "I'm so sorry for disappointing you, Nor. I love him so much. He's everything to me. *Please* don't hate me. I don't know what I'll do if you do."

She sighs. "Who am I to tell you who you should love? Stephen did everything he could to keep Cole and me apart. I don't want that for you, and I don't want to be like him. Besides, we are the Blake girls." She cups my face in her hands and smiles gently at me. "We are fierce. We fight hard, and we love even harder when we find something worth staying around for, because that's what life taught us. That's who we are. I'd never hate you. Disappointed, but never hate."

She rubs her forehead, studying me for a few seconds. "I know how it feels to find someone who takes your breath away with just a look, how it feels to be wanted and loved. Someone who knows your flaws and imperfections but wants you and loves you despite those things, so I get it. You deserve someone who loves you and spoils you."

She bites the corner of her bottom lip and inhales deeply before she continues. "Oh God. I can't believe I'm about to say this, but here it goes. I saw the way he was looking at you. We arrived and found Nate in this room, waiting for you to wake up. He hasn't left your side, even though he seems to be in a lot of pain from his injuries." She chuckles without warning and adds, "Nate didn't even bat an eyelash when Cole threatened to punch him in the face. In fact, he stood his ground. He said he'd only leave when you finally woke up. He refused to take medication for the pain because he was afraid something would happen to you if he did as much as shut his eyes for a second."

Nor crawls back on the bed and pulls me to her. "Our little Elon who never breaks the rules," she teases, fighting a smile. "Tell me about him."

The door opens at that exact moment, and Elise breezes in with a bag in her hands. Upon seeing me awake, she rushes forward and hugs me tight before pulling back.

"Okay, young lady. You seem healthy enough to talk. First tell me what happened in Chicago. Did you see our fucking monster of a father?"

Nor shakes her head. "First, I need to hear about that man out there." She narrows her eyes on Elise. "I'm not even going to pretend you and I are cool. You knew about Nate, but you chose not tell me."

"Don't do this, Nor," Elise whines, then tips her nose up in the air and sniffs. "It wasn't my story to tell. Anyhoo, you should have seen the way Nate handled Rick the Prick. He went all *Khal Drogo* on Rick's ass. It was spectacular."

I bite my lips to stop from laughing when Nor's eyes widen with excitement and shock. Right there, I know everything is going to be okay. It might take a while for my family to warm up to Nate. I cannot wait for them to know all about this wonderful man with his big heart.

CHAPTER FORTY-ONE

Nate

I watch Nor and Cole arguing, signing animatedly. I wish I could understand what they are talking about. If I'm going to survive in this family, I need to learn ASL quick. And I do intend to inject myself into their lives.

Nor stamps her foot and Cole folds his hands across his chest, glaring at her, but his lips twitch as if he's suppressing a smile. Then she spins around on her sneakers and hurries back toward Elon's room, but she stops suddenly and faces me, fighting a scowl. It's eerie how alike the three sisters look: red hair, freckles, pert noses, petite stature, even the way they walk and the stubborn jutting of their jaw when they're angry.

I brace myself, my lungs starving for air as I wait for her to speak. I'll do anything to be in her good graces.

"Would you stop seeing her if I asked you to?" she asks, eyes narrowed. Cole rolls his eyes.

Well, anything except *that*.

"No," I answer.

She nods and says, "Good answer" before whirling around and marching down the hall.

"Sorry about all this," I say, exhaling a breath.

Cole eyes my slumped form with a frown and waves his hand, dismissing my apology, but he doesn't seem as angry as he was hours ago after I came clean about the entire situation. "You look like you could use a coffee. And a shower." He adds with a grin.

It was difficult at first to understand him, but after spending the past six hours with him glaring and spitting words at me, I'm getting better at this.

I could use a dose of Oxy right now, but he's offering an olive branch. I'd be foolish not to accept it, so I nod.

As soon as he leaves, I grit my teeth as pain slices through me. My body feels like it's been tossed around on a hard surface a few times. Every part of me aches, and my right shoulder throbs from the fall when we went down while trying to cushion Elon's head. I clench my fist to stop the shaking ripping through my body. The doctors offered to give me something for the pain, but I declined. I didn't want to risk the medication pulling me under. I had to make sure Elon was okay first.

My phone beeps with an incoming message and I dig it out of my pocket. After reading the email confirming that the doctor has brought the date for the surgery forward, I take off my glasses and shove them inside the pocket of my jacket, along with my phone. Then I lean my head back on the plastic seat and try to block out the noises flooding the waiting room.

I called Dr. Rosenburg after leaving Elon's room and explained about my fall. He sounded worried and suggested rescheduling my surgery. I didn't see the point in waiting since I won't finish teaching the semester at Rushmore. In two days, I will be flying to Chicago for the surgery.

Feet shuffle nearby, and I turn my head to see Cole standing in front of me, offering coffee in a paper cup to me. I cock an eyebrow, eyeing the cup.

"Planning my demise?" I tease. "Is there poison in there?"

He smirks and says, "If I wanted to kill you, I'd have done it already."

I laugh, reaching for the cup.

He sits down across from me and leans forward while holding his coffee with both hands.

I take a sip from my cup, then grimace as bile rises up my throat. Coffee isn't cutting it for me. My body needs its usual fix.

I swallow the liquid in my mouth and set the cup on the table next to me, then take in the man in front of me with features similar to Nick. I can't help admire the loyalty and love these two men have for my girl. They are heroes in my book.

"I love her," I say quietly, firmly. "I'd never hurt her."

"You wouldn't be here if you didn't love her." He gulps down his coffee, swallows and says, "Believe me, I know how hard it is to fall in love with the forbidden fruit."

I remember Elon telling me how her father tried to keep Cole and Nor apart, but I don't tell him that. My shaking fingers rub down my face, and I make an effort to lift my heavy as rock head off the chair. Cole's eyebrows dip as he stares at my hands. He probably thinks I'm a junkie or something, which I am, more or less.

Just then Bennett strides toward us, his eyebrows pinched together, and halts in front of me. He dips his hand inside his pocket and sets a yellow bottle in my hand.

"Dude, you look like shit," he says, as he lowers his heavy bulk on the seat next to mine. "How's our girl doing?"

"Great, actually. Just a concussion. The doctor says she'll be okay." I shake two pills from the bottle and toss them in my mouth, then notice Cole's frown has deepened. "Got shot in the arm a few years ago. Pain's a bitch."

He clears his throat, his gaze moving between me and Bennett.

"Bennett, please be a doll and introduce yourself." I smirk, then close my eyes and pray that the medication kicks in fast. Then I remember my appointment in Chicago, and open them again. I make sure my face is angled toward Cole, then say, "I need you to do me a favor, Cole. I'm flying to Chicago in a day or two. Take care of my girl."

"Leaving the crime scene so soon?" he asks.

What the hell?

The bastard thinks I'd abandon Elon after everything we have gone through?

My eyes fly open, and I glare at him. Bennett snickers beside me, shaking his head.

"I'm scheduled for surgery in a few days," I grit between my teeth, hoping my head won't explode in the process.

Fuck. I shouldn't have gone this long without medication.

"You think she'll let you leave without her?" Cole asks and grins. "If she's wired the same as Nor, you're in for one hell of a surprise. Stubborn is their middle name."

I sigh and shut my eyes again, waiting for my salvation to work its wonders.

CHAPTER FORTY-TWO

Elon

"It's been three hours already since they took Nate in for surgery. Why is it taking so long? Do you think something happened to him?" I wring my hands on my lap.

Elise covers my hands with hers and gives them a comforting squeeze. "I'm sure he's fine. The doctor said the procedure might take hours."

At her words, the knot of nerves in my stomach tightens further. "I know. I just wish someone would tell us what's going on."

"I'm sure they will as soon as they have news for us." She pulls me into her with one arm around my shoulder and kisses my hair.

I rest my head on her shoulder, idly glancing around the busy reception area. "Thank you for being here."

"Like I had a choice," she teases with a laugh. "Nor literally shackled our wrists together when you refused to back down about flying to Chicago to be with your Naughty Professor."

I laugh. "I'm glad she did. I'd be a complete mess if I was alone."

She sighs. "I wish I could stay longer though. I have to go back to work tomorrow. Nate's mom should be here when I leave. You won't be alone for long."

Elise and I arrived in Chicago yesterday afternoon. After dropping our luggage in our allocated room at The Waldorf, courtesy of Nate's friend, Wade, we took a cab to the hospital. Nate informed the nurses on duty that I was his fiancée, as it was much easier for me to stay with him overnight in his room and also spend time with him before they rolled him into the OR for the surgery.

"I have a great idea," Elise announces. "We could go back to the hotel and have them call us when Nate comes out of surgery, or we could grab something to eat at the McDonald's across the street."

I sit up while shaking my head. "I think I'll wait in case, you know. . . "

"Yeah." She stands up. "Happy Meal as usual?"

I snort-laugh. Elise has been teasing me about my obsession with Happy Meals since I was a kid. "Don't forget the toy of the month."

She giggles as she grabs my purse and walks down the hall toward the elevators.

My gaze leaves the darkening sky outside the window and moves to Nate, lying on the bed in front of me. He was cleared by the anesthesiologist three hours ago. Then two nurses brought him into the room about an hour ago. He has been drifting awake on and off since then, demanding groggily for water to drink. The nurse in charge would then place an ice cube on his tongue to combat his thirst.

My eyes keep wandering to his chest every few seconds to check if he's still breathing.

After sending a quick text to Grace, Izzy, Elise and Nor to let them know that he's out of surgery and doing well, I lace my fingers with his and kiss the back of his cool hand, then lean my forehead on top of our connected hands and finally shut my eyes.

CHAPTER FORTY-THREE

Elon

IT HAS BEEN THREE DAYS SINCE NATE'S SURGERY. ELISE FLEW BACK TO Florida two days ago, and Grace is currently on the way to the hospital. As soon as she gets here, I'll head to the Waldorf to shower and change my clothes.

Dr. Rosenburg installed a pump so that Nate could press it whenever the pain became too unbearable. Then last night, Nate requested the doctor get rid of the pump. He wanted to try and train his body to get used to the new pain medication regime, to stop craving it, hoping to eventually break the habit he had acquired over the past three years.

I admire and completely respect his resolution to go cold turkey on this, but seeing the way his body reacts from popping pills hourly to taking the medication every few hours is taking a toll on me. I've never seen anyone go through withdrawals, so I have no idea what to expect, and it terrifies me. Seeing this man I love go through this creates an ache deep inside me.

Just then, Nate stiffens on the bed, his body starts thrashing, which jostles his right arm that is in a sling. I bolt from the seat I've been sitting on the past four hours and cup his cheek, forcing his eyes to focus on mine.

"Hey, baby. I'm here, OK?"

Sweat pours down his face as his wild eyes focus on me. "I ache everywhere," he mutters, his teeth chattering. "I'm so cold."

I kiss his clammy forehead. "I'll call the nurse to give you something for the pain."

"No!" he protests, grasping my hand tight, his breathing fast. "No, don't do that. There's still one more hour to go before my next dose."

"I can't see you like this. You're going to tear your stitches if you don't calm down."

His grip on my hand becomes more desperate. "I want to do this my way. Trust me, I can do this without falling back to the pills to numb the pain."

"Please tell me what to do," I beg him.

He pulls my hand to his lips and kisses my wrist. "You are already doing it by being here."

"Do you think a blow job would help?" I tease him, hoping to take his body off the pain wracking through his body.

He laughs, as his body shivers. "Fuck, yeah. Do you think you could be sneaky and go track down a set of scrubs? It's one of my fantasies, a nurse giving me head." Even in his weakened state, Nate manages to shoot me a wink.

"That can be arranged." I snort while crawling up on the bed and curving my body around his left side and hugging his waist. "Is this OK for you?"

He inhales and exhales a few times before saying, "Yeah. It's perfect." I hear his teeth gnash, and I know he's fighting the pain hard. "Elon? Please don't let the nurse give me another sponge bath. I think she's enjoying juggling around my balls a little too much."

My body shakes with laughter, and I feel the terror from before slowly vanish. "She's just doing her job."

"You think? I swear I heard her sing to my cock after the doctor removed the catheter this morning."

"Oh my God!" I'm laughing so hard now, tears leaking from my eyes. "It's a wonderful cock that deserves to be serenaded."

He chuckles under his breath. "So how about that blow job, Little Wolf?"

"Dear God, Nathaniel," Grace's voice interrupts us, causing me to jerk upright on the bed and scramble off with my cheeks on fire. "There are some things a mother shouldn't hear. At. All." She turns to face me, then pulls me into a hug, then mutters, "How is he?"

"Still in pain," I reply. "But I think he's going to be okay."

"Get some rest," she urges me, while pushing me toward the door.

Nate

As soon as Elon leaves, I bolt upright on the bed just as vomit hits the back of my throat. My hand flails wildly on the side of my bed and clutches the bucket one of the nurses brought in half an hour ago. I shove my head inside and empty my stomach for the fourth time since I woke up. Every part of my body aches and I feel as though I'm on fire. The bed dips as my mother sits next to me and takes the bucket from my hands while rubbing my back.

When I'm done, I lift my head and grab a few tissues from the nightstand while my mother leaves the room with the bucket.

After wiping my mouth, I lay back on the pillows with my eyes closed. The last few days have been hard. The doctor said it might take about a week to almost a month to get the toxins out of my system.

Every waking hour has been a battle. But I won't give in. I intend to win this war. Every time I see the worry in Elon's eyes, I almost cave in and beg the doctor to give me something stronger to relieve the pain and satisfy my craving. Every time I see how proud she is when a day goes by without succumbing to the hunger for pain pills, I feel like I've already won the war.

My mother returns with water in a glass and hands it to me. Then she grabs a wet cloth from the nightstand, and wipes the sweat off my forehead. "I'm so proud of you," she says, smiling down at me.

All I can manage is a faint smile, before shutting my eyes as exhaustion drags me under.

The last thing on my mind before I fall asleep is; I can do this. I've spent the last three years in pain far worse than what I'm currently going through.

I can do this.

CHAPTER FORTY-FOUR

Nate

I SNAP AWAKE SOMETIME IN THE MIDDLE OF THE NIGHT TO THE FEEL of pain stabbing my bicep, but it's not as brutal as it was three weeks ago. Today is officially the eighth week since the surgery.

After I was released from the hospital in Chicago, Dr. Rosenburg referred me to a Dr. James Ashford, who heads the pain management clinic here in Jacksonville. Dr. Ashford had been tapering me off the medication, and so far, everything has worked out great. One thing is for sure: I couldn't have done this without Elon and my family. I know I'm not out of the woods yet. I'm giving this all I can because seeing Elon smile at the end of each day is everything to me. Besides, she's been rewarding my success with blow jobs and mind-blowing sex. I wouldn't trade that for anything.

At my side, Elon snores loudly, and that sound soothes me. With my palm cupping her ass cheek, I stare at the ceiling, mentally counting the lights reflected from the street lamp outside the window of my room. I'll never tire of feeling her soft, warm body wrapped around my hard one. Despite our difference in stature, we fit perfectly, like we were meant to be each other's lock and key.

Her hand, resting a few inches from my crotch, twitches. She moans softly and snuggles closer into me. Images of her fingers wrapping around my cock flash inside my head, and I groan.

I glance at the alarm clock on the nightstand and notice it's already three in the morning, officially my girl's birthday.

Shifting on the bed to sit in a comfortable position without jolting my shoulder, I squeeze her sweet ass until she makes a sound between a moan and sigh. Her eyes flutter open, the pure innocence in them sending my heart racing.

"It's officially July 9th, sweetheart," I whisper, kissing her hair. "Happy birthday, Elon."

"Thank you, lover." She yawns and stretches, her mouth pulling into a smile as her fingers graze my painfully hard cock. "Looks like I'm going to treat myself to a super early birthday present."

She wraps her fingers around me and moves her hand up and down in slow, firm strokes. "How are you feeling? Are you up for some 3 a.m. sex?"

"Fuck yeah," I growl, watching as she sits up and straddles my thighs.

She leans down and licks my neck and starts singing, "Happy birthday to me," while trailing kisses on my collarbone, down my chest. She swirls her tongue around my nipple, then nips it. By the time she finishes singing the song, her mouth hovers above my cock as she looks at me through her lashes.

I grip her hip with my left hand and tug her forward. She scoots up, lifting on her heels and aligning her pussy to my cock. "Always ready for anytime sex with you," I murmur, sliding my hand up to cup her neck and pull her down for a kiss.

She lowers herself on top of me, teasing me as she strokes the head of my cock against her wet heat. My jaw clenches, my heels digging on the bed as my hips thrust up.

"I need inside you, Little Wolf," I grunt, my fingers digging into her skin.

She leans down and kisses my jaw, the corner of my lips, then straightens. "Tsk tsk, Professor Rowe. My birthday, my rules."

"I love it when you call me that." I twist my torso, but the movement jolts my right arm.

Motherfucker.

As if sensing my reaction, she freezes on top of me. "You okay?"

"You know—" I move my shoulder, readjusting the sling. "The second they get this fucking sling off, I'll be all over you—" She slams down, burying me inside her to the hilt.

"*Jesus*, Elon!" I shout, my eyes rolling to the back of my head.

Elon grins sweetly down at me as she starts to move on top of me, scattering my thoughts ten different ways. "Did it work?"

"Yeah. God, I love you." I watch her face as the smile widens and hunger flashes in her eyes. Hunger and so much love for me. "Ride me, sweetheart. Take what you need."

She leans forward and grabs the headboard, circling her hips. "I love you, baby."

Her tits bounce above me, lips parted in pleasure, sweet moans that have my cock hardening more inside her. Heat curls at the base of my spine, licking my skin and my balls draw tight.

"More," she rasps with a little moan. "*Harder.*"

My hips buck off the mattress at her command and she shouts, "*Yes! Yes! Professor!*"

Those words race straight to my dick. Fuck, I'm about to blow my load.

I grip her thigh. "Christ. Your pussy feels so good around my cock, so tight. Come with me, sweetheart," I growl, my eyes locked on hers.

"Nate!" she shouts, her body shaking above mine. I thrust inside her, wanting to savor this feeling but I know I won't be able to hold myself back anymore.

Her name bursts out of my lips in a low grunt as I empty myself deep inside her, pouring my love and everything that I am into her. She slumps forward and drops her head on my left shoulder, then trails kisses along my neck, her soft pants peppering my skin. My arm curls around her shoulder, holding her to me.

God. How did I get so lucky to find someone who's quirky and funny, kind and perfect for me in every sense of that word?

When we finally come down from the high, she slants her head up to me and flashes me a beautiful smile, sending my heart tripping on itself.

"Thank you, Nate," she whispers in a sultry voice that has my cock getting hard again inside her.

"Damn, Little Wolf. I should be thanking you." I tighten my arm around her and kiss her forehead. "Izzy's insisted on having a birthday dinner for you. She wants us to be there by six in the evening."

She burrows her face into my chest. "Dress code?"

I chuckle. "Whatever you want to wear."

"Awesome. I've been saving my Hello Kitty onesie for this occasion."

I laugh, pulling her into my body as my eyes fall shut and peace settles over me.

EPILOGUE

Elon

Four years later

Dreams do come true, even for a girl like me who never thought she deserved a happily ever after.

After being expelled from Rushmore, I continued teaching at Studio 22 while making sure that Nate attended his therapy sessions and doctor's appointments. I wanted to be there for him, to take care of him. Then one year after the surgery, when Nate could perform most duties without assistance, he mentioned that he'd been looking for someone to take me under their wing. At that point, I'm sure my boyfriend was tired of me hovering like a mother hen and forcing him to drink chicken soup that Bennett insisted on bringing over for him.

Nate had called in a favor with a friend of his, a retired professor from Eastman School of Music in New York. We have been working together since then. One year ago I enrolled at the Strauss Music School in Jacksonville, to complete my bachelor's degree in music performance. I will be graduating in May of next year.

After my graduation, Nate and I plan on traveling to Europe for a few months just to take a break from everything. I haven't stopped dreaming of playing in an orchestra in Europe, but for now, I'm just proud to see my man reenter the music world, ready to take it by storm.

Elizabeth finally made peace with Nate. She followed my advice and visited Nate two years ago, wanting to know more about her daughter. At first, Nate was hesitant, given the way Elizabeth had treated him in the past. But after a while, he seemed to warm up to her. Honestly, it was really good for Nate to have someone he could open up to about Camille, someone he could talk about the happy memories they shared that he may not have felt as comfortable sharing with me.

After the incident with Rick, he was arrested and is currently serving a five-year term in prison. Good riddance.

Nate started rehabilitation sessions after Dr. Rosenburg removed his sling. The road that brought him to where he is now wasn't easy, but he was very determined to get his right arm working again. It's been one year since Nate has had to take any form of medication.

There were times when he was very close to relapsing, but he managed to beat the long-term craving by attending regular group therapy sessions, and meeting people who were going through the similar struggles that he could relate to. Nate also underwent counseling, which helped him learn to cope with life without drugs. He focused his energy on exercising his right arm, so he could finally return to playing the cello.

Today is October twenty-fifth, which is Nate's birthday and also the day he returns to the world of music after being away for so many years. One year ago, he received an invitation to play as a guest cellist with the San Francisco Symphony for *Autumn Equinox*, which features pieces by various classical music composers.

From across the hall, I watch the love of my life stride confidently toward me, a sexy grin on his handsome face. My hand curls around the dragon pendant on my necklace he gave me a few years ago, my gaze slowly taking him in. He's wearing black pants and jacket, a white button-down shirt and no tie. He looks debonair with his hair styled back carefully. He stops and leans down, kissing me softly on my lips.

"Damn, you look hot," I murmur against his lips. "Do you think they have closets in this place? I remember you had a thing for them," I say, smiling, and I feel his mouth tug up against mine.

"I think I saw one down the hall—"

"Uncle Nate! Uncle Nate!" Matthew yells, his soled feet slapping against the floor as he runs toward us.

Nate groans under his breath, muttering something about not being able to kiss his girlfriend without being interrupted. He trails kisses along the freckles on the bridge of my nose before turning around to face his nephew with a warm smile.

Matthew flashes me his brightest smile, looks me up and down, then wiggles his nose. "You look like a princess from Kaylie's books."

Fighting a smile, I glance down at the white dress I'm wearing that cinches around my waist, then flows down to my ankles, giving a sneak peek of the silver slippers on my feet. "Is it a good thing or a bad thing?" I ruffle his hair, causing him to jerk back and scowl at me as he tries to brush his fingers through the wayward curls on his head.

"Not bad, I guess," he grumbles while grabbing Nate's hand, as well as mine, and dragging us to where our families sit in the auditorium. "Grandma Grace wants to take a picture of everyone."

Matthew drops our hands and dashes forward and sits between his father and mother. My gaze moves down the row starting with Cole, Nor, Cora, Joce, Bennett, Matthew, Makayla, Izzy, Harper, Grace, Gladys, Alex, Amber, Elise, Nick, my mom, and even Elizabeth, whom Nate invited and she gladly agreed. Everyone came today to support Nate on his return to a dream he thought he had lost, his number one passion: playing the cello. I'm overwhelmed by the love pouring through the ties that bind us.

Blinking back tears, I glance up at Nate and meet his gleaming eyes, and I know he's just as grateful as I am. My heart beats proudly for this man who fought against his addiction and emerged on the other side victorious.

"Happy birthday, baby. You made it. This is an amazing come-back, and I'm so proud of you." I cup his face in my hands, watching tears swim in his eyes. I can't even imagine how he's feeling right now. "You're back, baby," I whisper, wrapping my hands around his waist and pulling him to me. "Are you nervous?"

"No," he answers self-assuredly, raising his chin. "You're here. Everything's perfect."

I tug at the lapels of his coat and cock my head to the side. "Ask me to tell you one sweet truth, Professor Rowe," I tell him in a low voice.

He smirks. "Tell me one sweet truth, Miss Blake."

"You're my whole life, Nathaniel Rowe. I don't want to live in a world without you."

Nate cups the nape of my neck with his right hand, and right there in front of everyone, he presses his lips softly against mine, then nips on my lip, and my mouth parts for him. This kiss is heaven, a sweet prelude to a future that belongs only to us.

He slows the kiss, brushing his nose against mine. "I don't know where our life goes from here, but we will figure it out together. Life has a way of presenting the most wonderful opportunities when we least expect them."

If there is one thing life has taught me, it is that at times we experience pain and loss, we feel hopeless and faithless. But hidden beneath all the negatives, there's laughter, love and hope if you are patient enough.

Before meeting Nate, I wasn't looking for love. Never in a million years could I ever dream I'd find a man like him. But he is so much more than a dream; he is flesh and blood, and he's all mine.

He found me and he loves me. We are both casualties of our pasts; we fought a war called love and we won. Together, we overcame our pasts. It made us stronger and gave us the ability to love deeper.

Where we go from here is something written in the stars. We just have to look for the signs.

Elise yells our names and waves for Nate and me to join them. We try to huddle together as much as we can, then Grace requests a woman sitting in the row in front of us to take our picture.

As the lights dim, indicating that the event is about to start, Nate takes my hand and tugs me to the aisle. He stands in front of me as he tries to get his breathing under control. Then he's dropping on one knee and pulling a little black box from his pocket, sending my already racing heart into overdrive and stealing my breath in the process.

He must see the tears in my eyes, because he lifts his hand and brushes his thumb across my cheek while smiling at me with eyes full of love and happily ever afters.

"Marry me, Elon Blake. I've enjoyed every single moment we've spent together the past four years, but I want more. I want forever. With you."

Everything fades. My world stops spinning as those words wrap around me, transporting me to a place where it's just me and him. Then I'm laughing and kissing him and crying.

"Yes," I whisper the word against his mouth. "Yes, I will marry you."

Our world explodes in cheers and hoots as he slips the ring on my finger.

"I've wanted to ask you to marry me every single second of the day for the past four years. But I'm glad I waited, Elon. We have nothing holding us back now. Our forever begins today."

I lean forward and press a kiss on the side of his mouth as the lights dim darker still.

"Go." I trail my lips to the shell of his ear. "Take the world by storm, baby."

He flashes me an honest-to-God sexy grin as he turns and strides toward the stage. When I turn to take my seat, I find my family watching me, tears and smiles on their faces. After a round of congratulations and impromptu plans about having dinner to celebrate the engagement, I sit down between Nick and my mother. She wraps her arm around me, grinning proudly at me.

Nick bumps my shoulder and I shift my head to the side to face him. He jerks his chin in the general direction of the orchestra, then brings back those beautiful kind eyes to me, and asks, "Are you really truly happy?"

Tears spring in my eyes as I smile at him. "I've never been this happy in my life, Nick. Thank you for standing by Nate and me these past four years. Are you okay?"

He shrugs. "I still feel the need to punch his face every now and then."

We chuckle under out breath, and it feels amazing.

"Seriously, though. I know there's someone out there waiting to rock your world. You deserve the best, Nick."

He rolls his eyes and mutters, "Yeah, yeah. That's what everyone keeps telling me." He looks at the stage. I see his the concerned look on his face fade and peace settles over his features. "He's a great guy."

This time I bump his shoulder and grin up at him. "Are you *finally* giving him an official Nick Holloway stamp of approval? I feel like I should be recording this moment."

"Yeah." He turns and grins at me. "He got my approval the second he confronted me outside that restaurant I used to work at."

"I love you," I whisper, swiping the tears that have fallen on my cheeks.

"Ditto," he whispers back.

Feeling finally at peace, I focus on the stage just as Nate takes his seat in the strings section with the other principal string players and props the Montagnana between his powerful thighs, then winks at me as his right arm poses on top of the strings.

"I love you," I mouth to him, grinning wide while fiddling with the ring around my finger.

The sweet sound of "Autumn" by Antonio Vivaldi fills the air as the Concertmaster starts to play, and soon the entire Orchestra joins in. My gaze is centered on my man as tears fill my eyes. I'm afraid to blink because I don't want to miss a thing.

I grew up believing there was no such thing as happily ever after, but I met a man who blew that theory out of the water. He made me believe that anything is possible.

Amber once told me if I reached for the stars, everything else would fall into place.

I did, and now I'm living my kind of fairy tale with Nate by my side.

PLAYLIST

I'm A Mess—Ed Sheeran

Breathe Easy—Blue

Photograph—Ed Sheeran

Ashes Like Snow—Lily Kershaw

Demons—Imagine Dragons

One Call Away—Charlie Puth

The Sound of Silence—Disturbed

Stay—Hurts

Every Breath You Take—The Police

Fix You—Coldplay

I Walk The Line—Johnny Cash

Belong—Cary Brothers

In My Veins Feat. Erin Mccarley—Andrew Belle

Chasing Cars—Snow Patrol

Running on Sunshine—Jesus Jackson

Gotta Figure This Out—Erin Mccarley

You Got What I Need—Joshua Radin

Terrible Love—Birdy

Kiss Me—Ed Sheeran

Unsteady—X Ambassadors

Come On Get Higher—Matt Nathanson

Just Give Me a Reason—Pink

Kiss Me Slowly—Parachute

Addicted—Saving Abel

Down In Flames—Saving Abel

Fall For You—Leela James

A Thousand Years—Christina Perri

You and Me—Lifehouse

Here Without You—3 Doors Down

Wings—Birdy

Wrecking Ball—Miley Cyrus

All Through The Night—Sleeping At Last

Love On The Brain—Rihanna

Crush—Jennifer Paige

Like I'm Gonna Lose You—Jasmine Thomson

Witchcraft—Frank Sinatra

You Give Me Something—James Morrison

Down—Jason Walker

Fire Meet Gasoline—Sia

Carry On My Wayward Son—Kansas

ABOUT THE AUTHOR

Autumn Grey is a hopeless romantic and an optimist. She writes sexy contemporary romances full of angst and drama, steamy kisses and happy ever afters. And just like her characters, she is quirky, sometimes funny, and definitely flawed. When she's not working as a nurse or chasing her two children around (and a fur baby), she can be found binge-watching Supernatural on Netflix.

CONNECT WITH AUTUMN

Facebook: www.facebook.com/AuthorAutumnGreyAG

Instagram: www.instagram.com/autumngreyauthor

Facebook Group: www.facebook.com/groups/350328071837578

Goodreads:
www.goodreads.com/author/show/7337710.Autumn_Grey

Sign up for her newsletter to receive updates about her upcoming books and exclusive excerpts http://eepurl.com/bZEWzP

ACKNOWLEDGEMENTS

First and foremost, thank you to my two children. Two of my most favorite people in the world.

I want to thank the people who read this story early. My fantastic alpha reader /content editor,, Bex Harper. Thank you for reading this story in its early stages and providing amazing feedback. Keep those chats coming.

To my awesome beta team, Ella Stewart, Maiwenn, Selma Ibrahimpasic, Marian Girling, Sejla Ibrahimpasic, Robyn Crawford, Mg Herrera, Vivian Freeman, Emma Louise, Amy Bosica, Katie Monson, Elaina Lucia, Denae McLennan. Your suggestions and comments made this story better. Thank you for cheering me on and keeping me sane.

To Zuray Yaruz, thank you for taking part in the contest. I am absolutely in love with the quote.

To my editing team, thank you for making this story shine. Vanessa Bridges, your feedback on the content of this story made it better. Tricia Harden, you squeezed me into your schedule at the very last minute. There are no words to express how grateful I am; Virginia Tesi Carey and Bex Harper, thank you for proofreading this story. It was amazing to work with you on this project.

Karen Bill, Elaina, Selma and Sejla. . .thank you for rereading this story and making sure it was ready for the public eye.

To Ella, you inspired me to write this story. Thank you for being you. Keep breaking gravity, my friend.

To the Minxes group on Facebook, my tribe. You guys are on a whole other level of awesomeness. I love you! Thank you for being so incredibly wonderful, encouraging and supportive, You're my happy place.

I'm so thankful for the C.O.P.A. girls and Indie Chicks for your friendship and all the support. You ladies rock!!

Celesha, thank you for putting a smile on my face every time we chat. Also, thank you for the beautiful release day countdown teasers you did for this book. You rock.

Amo Thomson, I love you.

Sasha Brummer, thank you for letting me borrow Wade Brass ;)

Special thanks to R. Scarlett, Jay Mclean and K. Webster for being amazing.

To the bloggers who took a chance on this story, read and reviewed it. There are not enough words to express my gratitude. Thank you.

To Sassy Savvy Fabulous, Kristi. Thank you for everything you've done for me, for this book, and most of all, for being patient with me. Working with you been such an amazing experience.

To Sarah Hansen of Okay Creations, you blew my mind, yet again. I'm in awe of your ability to make extraordinary out of the ordinary. Thank you for the stunning cover.

To Stacey Blake of Champagne Formatting, one of the most patient people I know. Thank you for making this book look so pretty! It's ALWAYS a pleasure to work with you.

To my readers for picking up Breaking Gravity. I hope you enjoyed this story as much as I loved writing it.

I hope I haven't forgotten someone, but if I have, please know that it wasn't intentional. Just know that I love you.

Keep breaking gravity,
xoxo
Autumn

OTHER BOOKS

Made in the USA
Middletown, DE
27 July 2022